In Spite of the Inevitable

Mordena Dawn – Book 1

Morgan Biscup

Author's Note

Welcome, Reader, to my first novel in Vazdimet, a space-faring universe exploring the meanings of technology and interpersonal relationships against a backdrop of magic, war, and perseverance. For as long as I can remember, I've had a need to tell stories. Over time I graduated from short stories submitted in lieu of fourth grade vocabulary assignments, to unfinished science fiction novels drafted during high school religion classes, to fantasy worlds invented for entertaining my kids.

All to arrive here, at this moment, in this universe. Vazdimet.

Of the countless souls you'll meet in your explorations, the one you'll find the most is mine, poured into its many pages of novels and worldbuilding. My hopes and dreams, mistakes and regrets, education and experience, flow through Vazdimet's veins the same way the magical fields flow between its stars.

I'm excited you're here. I hope you enjoy discovering Vazdimet as much as I have.

To our unwritten tomorrows.

The past brought us to today, but we get to choose where our steps lead us next.

1

2291.08.13 EVT

Tightening his grip on the handle, Shane checked his footing and thrust the plunger again. A cold wave of water spilled from the bowl, soaking through his shoes and into his socks. He swore under his breath.

It's no fun, is it? Cleaning up after people's messes. Maybe you should remember that, next time you decide to let someone else take the fall for your choices.

Sighing, he pulled a fresh disposable glove from his pocket, running his thumb briefly across the locket he kept hidden against his chest, beneath his coveralls. It had belonged to his mother, his only possession linking back to his childhood, and now housed the opinionated soul of the only true friend he'd ever had.

Checking carefully to ensure he was otherwise alone, Shane channeled his Necromancy, elevating himself into the higher dimensions beyond the Veil. He reached through the plumbing to retrieve the obstruction, wrapping his gloved hand around the offending material and tugging it with him into the Afterlife.

The toilet gurgled happily, water freely draining once more, as Shane returned to the mortal plane before inspecting the sopping bundle of light green fabric.

"Another uniform shirt," he sighed, frowning at the sopping garment. "Who keeps flushing these things?"

Some people just like to cause trouble for everyone else. But you wouldn't know anyone like that, would you?

The shirt would need a thorough washing, of course, but it seemed no worse for wear despite its unconventional storage location. He checked the label for the size. Keeping Jake clothed was posing a challenge; the growing boy needed a new wardrobe every six months. One less shirt to procure would be a welcome relief for the budget.

He wrapped it in a trash bag and shoved it onto the cart, concealing it under some cleaning supplies. Then, grabbing the mop, he turned his attention to the puddles on the floor.

He was only half finished when the door flew open.

"Bathroom's closed!" he growled, without looking up from his work. "Try the one upstairs."

"Lawrence." The man's voice was unfamiliar, though he seemed to know Shane. "Good. You're needed on the dock. Truck's here."

"I'll be done in five minutes."

"Let me help."

The man was already tugging at the trash, his arms straining to remove the over-full bag from the receptacle.

Shane winced as the bag caught on the edge and began to tear. Surreptitiously casting a Shielding spell to maintain its integrity, he strode over, easily lifting it from its can. "I *said* five minutes."

"Yeah." His erstwhile assistant sheepishly ran his fingers through his short brown hair. "I guess I'd better leave it to the professionals." He wrung his hands, checking his wristwatch as Shane double-bagged the refuse and hauled it outside the door. "Before you came along, I'd never seen the bathrooms half as clean as you keep them."

Shane shrugged, returning to his mop. "Any job worth doing is worth doing well."

You always did put your whole heart into things. Committing war crimes, plunging toilets, murdering your best and only friend...

They spent the next few minutes in awkward quiet, the slick of the water across the floor the only sound.

His visitor was the first to break the silence. "The name's Jeb, by the way. Biology teacher."

"Shane."

Not that this was a secret; his chosen name was embroidered onto his janitorial coveralls in bold, capital letters. But the man seemed to expect an answer.

"I know. Your son's in my class. Brilliant kid."

Jake *was* brilliant, in a way few could ever hope to emulate. Their first meeting, two years prior, had changed Shane's life in more ways than Shane would ever be able to articulate. With the death of the boy's mother, his adoption had been both a matter of necessity and obligation. Not to mention Shane's first step on the path of redemption for his own crimes, both past and present.

"Just doing my best to give Jake the life he deserves," Shane grunted, rinsing off the mop and beginning to set his cart in order.

Too bad he's stuck with you. *Fearless Commodore to skulking janitor. How far the mighty have fallen.*

Shane washed his hands in the sink, drying them on his thick blue coveralls before turning to study the teacher for the first time. The younger human held a bookish innocence, his wiry figure and pale skin a sharp contrast to Shane's dark, muscular frame.

Faced with the necromancer's fierce orange gaze, Jeb shifted his weight, cheeks flushed, and jerked his thumb toward the door behind him. "Uh, loading dock?"

"Lead on."

Shane tucked his cart into the janitorial closet, effortlessly hefting the trash bag over his shoulder. The bag with the shirt remained in the cart; he'd return for it later.

He knew the way to the dock already, having helped unload countless shipments meant for the higher education research labs, but Jeb seemed intent on accompanying him this time. The chance to discuss Jake's education was a welcome opportunity.

"You need something else?"

"Yeah…"

Somehow Jeb looked even *more* nervous.

"To put it simply, Jake has been rather… disruptive lately."

He ran his hand through his hair again, avoiding Shane's gaze. "Don't get me wrong, your son knows his stuff! A little *too* well, honestly. He's not only bored with his lessons, he's stopped following the directions on assignments. He gets the right answers, but we don't know where he's getting them from. We don't understand half the things he writes on his worksheets."

The squelching of Shane's damp footwear echoed with every step through the otherwise abandoned hall as he considered Jeb's words.

"Jake's former school had several teachers from the Space Defense Legion," the necromancer said at last. The same faction he'd sworn vengeance against, after their attack on his original homeworld had killed both his parents, leaving him trapped in oppressive darkness until a rescue team had found him days later. "I've been doing what I can to teach him arcana, but he has a real aptitude for their more mechanical technologies." He paused, grunting slightly as he hefted the trash bag into the disposal unit with practiced ease. "I think because he's learned both so young, he sometimes combines the two."

He risked a glance at Jeb and found the biology teacher nodding his head in understanding. "We thought it might be something like that."

"I'll talk to him," Shane offered. "Ask him to stop using the Legion skills he learned."

"No, no, no!" Jeb looked panicked. "You misunderstand. These are skills we try to teach in later years. Many of them have trouble... And your son's so far beyond even that." He scratched his fingers through his hair. "What I'm trying to say is, we'd like to move him to our gifted classes."

"Oh." Shane stopped walking, his feet sinking deeper into his uncomfortably soaked socks. "I appreciate the offer, but I can't afford special classes. I'm only able to keep Jake here because of the employee tuition discount."

Jeb shook his head, smiling back tentatively. "That's not a problem. There's a small fee for materials, since he'll be doing a lot more hands-on work, but the school's agreed to waive that this year, in his case." The biologist looked up at Shane, holding hope in his brown eyes. "And it would be great for Jake. He's a good kid. I'd hate for his boredom to lead him into trouble."

"Thank you." Shane nodded stiffly before resuming his brisk walk toward the loading dock.

"Wait!" Jeb called out, rushing to catch up. "There's... something else we need to talk about."

Shane kept walking. "I'll fill out whatever paperwork you need after we get this truck unloaded."

"Good. Thank you. But that's not what I meant." Jeb was panting now. "I need to ask. Some of the kids came to us, concerned. Have you been teaching Jake... Necromancy?"

"Necromancy?" Shane froze.

And here it is. You'll never be free from your past. You carry it with you wherever you go. The corruption's too deep in your soul.

Shane slowly turned to look at Jeb. "Yes. He – *we* – lost his mother. To the war." He swallowed past the lump in his throat. "I've been teaching him the Soul Call spell, so he can still talk to her." He shrugged, in an effort to appear nonchalant.

Jeb nodded again. "Was hoping it was something like that." He looked up at Shane, shifting his weight. "It's just... He's been telling his classmates something different. I don't know if he told you, but some of the bigger kids have been singling him out."

"We talked. I've been teaching him some agile sparring techniques. And Shielding magic. If they can't catch him, they can't hurt him."

"That explains the hallway incident the other day," Jeb chuckled politely. "Was wondering how he'd managed that."

His face turned somber. "Many of his teachers, myself included, have been stepping in to protect him, too. But..." He ran his fingers through his hair again. "He's, uh, taken to telling the other kids you'll Shatter their souls if they bother him. And that you're teaching him how to do it."

"Shatter?"

Like father, like son. Grim.

Shane clenched his fists. "No. Just Soul Call. I'll talk to him. About the lying."

Jeb's tone turned apologetic. "I haven't said anything to the Office yet. Was hoping to resolve things with you, first. It's just... I hope you see what a bad spot this puts us in, if parents start to complain. You're the janitor. You have keys to everything. And..." Jeb knotted his hands. "Well, quite frankly, you're rather intimidating."

Shane raised an eyebrow, staring down at the biology teacher. Standard locks had never been much of a deterrent, not with his training, but this was no time to mention that.

"Yes. The man with shoes full of toilet water is always intimidating."

He took a step forward, his socks squishing in protest at the sudden movement.

Jeb broke into laughter, slapping Shane on the back in what seemed an easy, reflexive moment for the amicable instructor. Followed by immediate regret, from the way Jeb cringed notably after.

Shane managed to suppress his natural reaction to recoil from the unexpected contact, instead forcing himself into an attempt at a smile, and watched as Jeb slowly relaxed again.

"Point taken." Shane blinked slowly. "I'll try to be less intimidating. And talk to Jake, about threatening his classmates."

"Many thanks." Jeb nodded quickly. "You work hard. For us and your son. I'd hate to see either of you hurt by rumors."

"Anything else?" Shane raised his brow again, resuming his walk.

Jeb nodded, twisting his hands. "Since you asked... One of today's shipments is for my sister's lab. Was wondering if you could deliver that first? She said it's important."

"Of course. Think I owe you that much."

"It's addressed to Razick. I'll help you find it."

2

Jake stood at attention, jutting his chin in defiance at the barrage of complaints from his Apotheturgy instructor. The headmaster's office felt cramped, filled as it was by her large antique desk and the angry teacher growling beside him.

"Professor Darga. I will *not* allow that language when talking about a student!" Headmaster Corbin admonished, the blue scale-like skin of her face twisting into a frown as her ear fins fluttered with well-contained anger. Jake could see why the old myths claimed dracoling had descended from dragons, even though his former schooling had proven them a close relative to humans.

"He shouldn't even *be* a student," the professor snarled, bristling at the reproach. If he'd been anyone else, the katanoj's luxuriously fluffy fur, accented by thick orange stripes and a smattering of cream across his face and hands, would have appeared cuddly and potentially even adorable. As it was, it only accented the feline's unjustified vitriol.

Jake slowly clenched and unclenched his hands by his sides, fighting his urge to interrupt. *Don't get defensive. Stick to the facts. Be the calm one.* He repeated the mantras in his mind, drilled in over the last two years by the man he called father, and willed himself to relax.

"We're different," his adoptive father had explained. "People are afraid of those who are different. So we have to do better, be better. Or they'll be afraid of us."

"I don't want to be different," he'd protest. "You're the different one. I'm just a normal kid."

The necromancer had always grown quiet at that, his scowl deeper than usual. But he'd always given the same answer. "You're my responsibility now. That means I'll always be here to protect you. It also means that who I am will change people's opinions of you... I'm sorry. We've survived things most people don't want to think about. We know things most people ignore. That makes us different, and scary... and dangerous."

Jake usually took the opportunity to voice more frustrations then, and the necromancer let him, absorbing the verbal abuse as if it would absolve him of some even greater crime. Sometimes Jake wished he could take back the harsh words, and the pain he always saw in his adoptive father's eyes during those conversations. Other times he just wished he could stop adding to it.

"And what do you have to say for yourself, young man?"

Jake tensed at the words, blinking slowly as he extracted himself from his memories to address the present. *All eyes are on you: Make it count. Don't get defensive. Stick to the facts. Be the calm one.* While he felt certain the necromancer would simply relocate them if he got kicked out of school, he doubted his mother would be so forgiving.

He stiffly addressed Headmaster Corbin. "With all due respect, ma'am, I followed the rules of the assignment as written and presented to us in class."

"Lies," Professor Darga sneered, baring his canines. "He made a mockery of the assignment!"

"You've had your turn to speak without interruption," the headmaster admonished, waving her finger in a motion for silence. "I want to hear from him."

She turned back to Jake with an encouraging smile. "Go on, child."

"We had to take a spell we know, and write instructions so someone could dual cast with us," Jake recited from memory. "Our partner couldn't use the spell, but we could use components. No Telepathy."

"There, you see!" The apotheturgist crossed his furred arms triumphantly, claws fully exposed. "He knew the rules and disregarded them!"

Jake shook his head, sliding a small slip of paper across the desk for the headmaster's inspection. "My instructions." He held up a standard tyrellium data crystal. "And my component."

"Start the dual casting link, then direct your Imperium into the crystal to power the spell," the headmaster read. She eyed the crystal curiously before folding her hands in front of her and rotating her ear fins to provide Jake her full attention. "What does it do?"

"It's a Shieldbreaker spell," Jake explained proudly. "I used Runework to weave several Shielding counters into a single spell, then programmed it into the crystal. Shieldbreaking takes a lot of power, so I found a way to temporarily disrupt a single point. It won't last long, but it takes less power, and if someone's actively channeling the Shield, they might not notice."

The headmaster's green eyes sparkled as she accepted the crystal. "This is a complex spell. Why pick this for the assignment?"

Jake shifted his weight. "The assignment said to cast something our partner didn't know. Every spell I picked, Veris said he knew it. So I invented a new one."

"And that's the other thing!" His teacher broke into the conversation again, his long striped tail now waving in sudden, agitated motions that periodically impacted with Jake's leg and the surrounding furniture within the tight office. "This spell is too advanced for a twelve-year-old. He completely avoided the assignment by having his father do the work for him!"

Jake coolly turned his head to address his teacher, impassive green eyes meeting and holding Professor Darga's angrier copper. "My father can't do this. I learned spell fusion at my old school."

"Ah, yes. A Legion education, wasn't it?" the headmaster asked.

Even as he gave a silent nod, Jake smiled inwardly at the glare she directed toward the apotheturgist.

"Well," Headmaster Corbin said, gracefully rising from behind her desk as she addressed the professor. "I fail to see the problem with this young man's assignment. I'm afraid I have to dismiss your complaint."

"And what about my accusation of cheating?"

Jake forced himself to shrug, burying the molten anger deep within. "You can ask my father."

"N-no, that's okay." Jake watched in smug satisfaction as the katanoj backed away at the suggestion. "I-I'm sure it's fine."

Returning his attention back to the headmaster, Jake noted an almost imperceptible amusement at his exchange with his professor. "Can I go now?"

"No," she answered thoughtfully. "I have some things to discuss with you." She directed a glare at his teacher. "Alone."

She waited until the door slammed shut, leaving them alone in the office, before turning her attention back to him. "Talk to me. How are you feeling?"

"Angry," Jake admitted, twisting his hands together in frustration. He was proud he'd managed to keep his voice level during the earlier discussion, but now that the professor was gone it threatened to break. "Veris and his friends always pick on me, and Professor Darga always pairs me with them for group projects. He's trying to make me fail."

He looked at her pleadingly. "You said you could help. I don't want to go back to his class."

She nodded once in agreement, frowning. "I'm sorry you're feeling challenged by those around you, instead of your classes. You should have come to me first, rather than attempting to handle it yourself. I'd have had more options."

Shoulders slumping, Jake nodded. "I'm sorry, ma'am."

"You're quite fortunate Professor Jeb has already been advocating on your behalf. It's not often we find students with your particular talents. We were able to work out an arrangement with the head office, provided your father agrees." She fixed him with a pointed stare. "Of course, you'll also need to stay out of trouble. Do you think you can manage that?"

Shuffling his feet, Jake risked a glance at Headmaster Corbin. "I'll do my best, ma'am," he answered honestly. "I don't *want* to cause trouble. People just don't like that I'm different."

"That's a growth opportunity for everyone," she told him kindly. "It's our differences that make us stronger. Someday they'll realize this." Retrieving a paper from one of her drawers, she passed it to him with a faint smile. "We'd like to transfer you to classes more suited for your talents. Does this sound of interest to you?"

Accepting the paper curiously, Jake read it with care, a smile widening across his face with every paragraph. He was grinning ear to ear by the time he returned the page to her desk. "Yes, please, ma'am!"

"You can keep that," she told him, sliding the paper in his direction. She plucked the Shieldbreaker crystal from her desk when he reached for that too, holding it up to the light. "This, though, I'll need to confiscate. No weapons permitted on school grounds, and by your description, this counts."

Jake felt panic rising, his smile vanishing as his eyes widened. He hadn't meant to break any rules, only pass the class. And she'd *just* warned him of the elevated consequences of any further mistakes. "I'm sorry, ma'am, I didn't mean to–"

"I won't count it against you," she reassured. "*This* time. But maybe run your next few school projects through me, just to be safe."

"Yes, ma'am."

"Good." She slipped the crystal into a drawer, her attention still focused on him. "Since it would be a waste of both your time and mental health to return to your currently scheduled class, and we still need parental approval for your new schedule, I'm granting you the remainder of this period as a free period. Do you have somewhere useful you can go?"

Jake grinned. "I'd like to help Razick. In the labs. Ma'am."

Razick was a friend. Words were rarely necessary around the Antimagic mage, which was fortunate, as she didn't like to talk often. Her stern demeanor frightened his classmates but he'd found it a welcome sense of safety, a shield that also extended to protect him in her presence, much like his adoptive father's own gruff exterior.

"A wise choice," the headmaster acknowledged. "Approved. In fact..." She paused to check something on her data screen. "You can spend your next class with her, too. Her package arrived today. I'm sure she'd be happy for your help."

"Thank you, ma'am!"

His mind charged ahead with possibilities. Razick had been waiting on that shipment for months. Now that it was finally here, Jake wouldn't have to wait any longer either; he'd get to see her next set of experiments in action. Maybe he'd even be able to help in a more formal role, once his adoptive father officially approved his new classes.

As soon as Headmaster Corbin dismissed him, Jake bounded from her office with exuberance. Now that things had finally begun to turn around, the day could only get better.

3

"This is what you wanted help with?"

Shane lifted the thin, lightweight package with two fingers before tossing it to Jeb, who caught it instinctively with a sheepish smile.

"Usually her packages are a lot bigger." Jeb tested its weight, crinkling his nose. "Sorry for wasting your time."

Shane rolled his neck and shoulders, casually stretching his arms before grabbing a handcart overloaded with boxes. "Not a waste. These are for the lab, too. You can join me, if you like. I don't mind the company."

Found another friend to murder later, did you?

"If you don't mind...?" Jeb sounded unsure.

"You can get the doors."

Without waiting for an answer, Shane set off with the cart, leaving Jeb to rush after.

Shane spent the walk listening to Jeb's tales from the biology lab, of student projects gone awry and fantastical genetically altered hybrids which didn't always behave as expected. The necromancer gracefully sidestepped Jeb's occasional attempts to probe about his own past experiences, limiting answers to his and Jake's life upon moving to Baden two years prior.

For his part, Jeb also seemed uninterested in talking about anything outside of teaching, aside from mentioning his distaste for war and commitment to pacifism. Whether he also hid a secret, or had simply built his entire life around the school and the safety of its students, Shane couldn't say.

Not that it mattered. Jeb was welcome to his secrets; Shane had enough of his own to worry about. But he had finally found somewhere to settle and raise his orphaned son, away from the constant wars devouring the universe and the people most likely to uncover his own dark past. He wasn't about to give that up.

Baden was everything Shane had hoped for in a planet, when it came to raising Jake. A thriving, independent jewel just outside the edge of Sparnell Confederation space, Baden was known as a safe haven for many refugees. Two more wouldn't draw attention.

He still cursed his poor monetary choices upon their initial arrival, but with all the time he'd spent on deployment he'd never been the one to handle finances, and asking Jake's advice had merely compounded the error. At least he'd had the foresight to purchase housing before the savings were gone, a cozy single home with a few too many rooms in a rundown but welcoming neighborhood. It was a lengthy commute to the school for most people, but merely a step for a Hyperjumping necromancer and his adopted son.

"Oh, look!" Jeb exclaimed while opening the door to Razick's lab, interrupting Shane's thoughts. "Speaking of your son, here he is."

Shane scowled as he wheeled the handcart into the lab. "Jake. You're supposed to be in class."

Jake grinned at his voice, rushing over to raise a crumpled paper for his inspection.

"Headmaster Corbin said I could take better classes if you say it's okay. Can I? Please?"

"I'll sign the paperwork today," Shane promised, scowling. While it was nice to see the boy's elation at the recognition of his accomplishments, there were more pressing matters to resolve. "What are you doing out of class?"

"I'm helping Razick. Headmaster said I could. Did you bring her package?"

Jeb's face slowly dawned recognition of why they'd traveled to the lab in the first place. "Ooooh. Yes."

The biologist held out the package, a cheerful lilt to his voice. "Razick! Your favorite brother brought you a present!"

The human lab tech emerged from her office, her side-bound ponytail of unruly red hair a stark contrast to her otherwise impeccable appearance. She moved with an overwhelming aura of confidence despite her shorter stature.

When she turned her attention to Shane he felt her melancholic green eyes sizing him up, her fair freckled face a mask he suspected could easily hide a sorrow as deep as his own. A moment later she graced him with a cool nod before delicately retrieving her brother's offering, motioning for Jake to follow.

Shane watched as the boy bounded after her, his face betraying his joy at the invitation to assist in her scientific research.

He turned to his companion. "She doesn't talk much, does she?"

From what Jake had told him, Shane guessed the trauma ran deep.

Jeb looked away. "She's seen things nobody should ever have to see."

Maybe she's met you before, Grim. Look familiar? Or have all your victims started to blend together by now?

Shane shook away the needling voice of his former friend, to instead focus on the teacher beside him. "Think she'd mind if we watched, too?"

Jeb shoved his hands in his pockets, bouncing slightly on his toes. "She didn't kick us out, and she's got your son with her, so I'm sure it'd be fine?"

"Cooooooooool! What *else* can it do?"

Jake's voice cut into their conversation, from deeper within the lab, and Shane turned to follow, Jeb on his heels. Knocking politely on the door he nodded acknowledgement of her brief smile of welcome and strode to take a place behind his son.

"What are you working on?" he asked Jake.

"She's inventing armor!" Jake announced, his attention fixated on Razick's demonstration.

Shane watched as the lab tech clamped a pair of wires from an Electromancy generator onto a thick square of cloth. Formerly pliable, the fabric immediately stiffened at the shock. She offered Jake a sharp rubber-handled scalpel, motioning toward the square. The preteen wasted no time in attempting to cut the material, scraping and jabbing the sharp tool against the fabric, to no avail. Grinning triumphantly, she disconnected the generator and watched as Jake gleefully carved the fabric into strips.

She offered one of the strips to Shane and he accepted, rubbing his fingers across its surface. While several times thicker than normal clothing, the material was still comfortably pliable, although it left a slightly oily texture on his fingertips.

He narrowed his eyes, the demonstration tugging on an old memory. "Tyrellium?" The magic-conducting metal found common use in a variety of technologies. If his assumptions were correct, she'd found a way to convert the energy from Electromancy currents into some form of physical Shielding.

Her smile widened as she nodded, confirming his suspicions.

Shane's attention wandered around the private office, taking in the shelving full of materials and meticulously labeled projects. "What's in the package?"

She motioned him toward a small tank of silver tinted oil tucked onto a shelf, pulling it out to reveal a bundle of dark colored fabric soaking within. Poking it carefully to ensure the oil had been absorbed into each section of the material, she removed it from the vat to dry on a specially constructed rack. As she spread the fabric across the bars, Shane realized it was a long-sleeved undershirt with a matching pair of trousers.

"You're ready for trials, then?" Jeb's words held pride.

She nodded, poking her brother in the chest with a mischievous smile.

"I know, I know. I haven't forgotten my promise. When you're ready, I'll be your test subject."

Shane's curiosity was piqued. "Are you working on anything else like this?"

Razick frowned, studying him again before pulling out a sharply cut suit of rich black fabric. She offered it to Shane, allowing him to feel the thick yet comfortable material before handing him the jacket with a motion mimicking him holding it taut in front of him.

Shrugging, he did as she directed, staggering backward at the unexpected force of an elemental arrow crashing into the suit from a crossbow he hadn't noticed her holding before. The arrow caught briefly in the suit before clattering to the ground. Shane probed the area of its impact, but the fibers remained intact. Letting out an appreciative whistle, he rubbed the side of his neck as he returned the jacket.

She eyed him intently, clearly waiting on his response.

"This is Sparnell technology," he said at last. "Their reinforced fabrics. You've recreated them."

It was a cruder application than that used by the Sparnell Armed Forces, with less mobility, but the implications were clear, nonetheless. The thought of facing SAF battle mages struck fear into the hearts of most citizens of the unaligned Freehold planets. With Razick's invention, Baden's defensive forces might actually stand a chance against the SAF's ground strike teams, when the Sparnell Confederation's leadership inevitably reached to claim the planet.

Nodding solemnly, Razick pointed up.

"You're right," he agreed. "We're on the edge of their space. It's only a matter of time."

The school alarms sounded, as if on cue, followed by the warning lights flashing a repeating pattern of three blinks in quick succession.

"Nobody told me there was an aerial bombardment drill scheduled today," Shane growled, glaring at Jeb.

The biologist's face was grim. "There wasn't."

Shane felt the familiar crackle of a high powered Shield snapping into place, likely Baden's planetary defenses charging to full capacity. He cast his own Shielding spell out of habit and grunted approval as he felt Jake do the same.

"To the vault," he ordered, automatically reverting to his command training. "We'll assess once everyone is safe."

Razick quickly retrieved both sets of experimental armors, and Shane was surprised to see the oiled undersuit had already stopped dripping – but there was no time to wonder about her specialty drying rack.

Shane directed Jake to the hallway before turning to Jeb. "We'll sweep the classrooms on the way. You take the left, we'll do the right."

He paused briefly for Jeb's acknowledging nod before storming down the hallway toward the vault, herding his charges toward safety.

4

Jake quickly picked up his father's rhythm, opening each classroom door while the necromancer checked for occupants before signaling to move to the next room. It was for show, of course, for the benefit of Jeb and Razick. Jake caught the telltale signs as his father's intense orange stare shifted in and out of focus each time he scanned beyond the Veil. The necromancer knew each room was empty before Jake even opened the door.

He'd never seen his father like this before. In their first meeting two years ago he'd witnessed the necromancer's protective rage as he fought off the Sparnell Confederation away team attempting to kill Jake and his mother, but his father had been a barely contained storm of emotion then, each action taken before deciding what came next. Even in the months after, his father had been impulsive and erratic, driven by a desperation to keep Jake safe but with limited advanced planning on how to accomplish that goal. He'd only calmed once they'd finally settled on Baden, developing the routines of daily life they'd continued to follow since.

But today was different. Today, Jake watched as his father acted with the cool efficiency of conditioned reactions, and he wondered how many times in the past decades the necromancer had performed similar drills. Jake imagined he himself likely carried a similar air of familiarity with the task at hand, courtesy of his father's own emergency training.

Clear your mind. Remain calm. Assess, act, reassess. Save the worry for later.

Jake had always protested during those sessions, but feeling his father's tensions at the alarm dissolve as Jake had cast his own Shielding spell had served to reinforce something he'd already begun to suspect.

The drills were always about keeping me safe.

Jake noticed his father's movements begin to stiffen, and reached out to place a hand lightly on his arm. His father returned the gesture by brushing Jake's hand with his fingertips, visibly relaxing.

Comfort given, Jake broke contact. He'd learned the power of his touch early in their relationship, a quick signal to bolster his protective instincts while simultaneously reassuring him of Jake's present safety. Somehow it always helped the Void necromancer concentrate on the present challenge.

"Jake."

Turning at the sound of his name, Jake saw his father pointing to the classroom two doors down. Taking his cue, Jake bolted to the room, slipping inside to begin his search for whoever his adoptive father had felt hiding within. The classroom felt eerie in the dark, lit only by the triple blink pattern of the alarms, the blinds pulled down all the way. He felt around the wall until he located the lights, bathing the room in the bright warmth of the wall lamps.

Need to be quick, he thought to himself as he began to search around the room.

The alarm paused its cadence to repeat the pattern, and in the brief silence he heard a sniffle from the closet. Hiding within, knees curled to his chest with his hands clamped tightly over his ear fins, sat a young dracoling boy no more than eight or nine. He stopped rocking and scrambled backward into the furthest corner of the closet at Jake's approach, amber eyes darting to scan the room from the shadows.

"Hey. It's okay." Jake slowly sank to his knees, holding his palms forward in front of his chest. "I won't hurt you. I'll keep you safe."

The boy shivered in the dark corner of the closet, eyes wide.

This isn't working.

Setting his hands on his knees, Jake studied the boy, noticing him flinch at every sound of the alarm.

It's the noise.

Closing his eyes, he ran through his list of spells. Anemancy would have been the perfect solution, but neither he nor his father had any experience in the magic of air and sound, and while dracoling were born with an innate Anemancy ability, this child was clearly too traumatized to think clearly.

So we can't silence the sound... But maybe I can muffle it? Would Shielding work?

Centering himself, Jake thought of barriers and sound waves, concentrating his intent on his own left ear. With an expenditure of Imperium, the world to his left grew muffled, accented by a faint buzzing of magical power. He shook his head, and the Shield followed.

Not perfect, but it'll do.

He dropped the spell and turned his attention to the boy instead, squinting as he worked to locate the dracoling's ear fins in the dark.

The child emerged a moment later, patting his ear holes as wonder and relief spread across the thick, fractured skin of his face. Jake stood slowly, motioning for the boy to follow him. Only then did he notice his father standing in the doorway, his face unreadable as he watched their interaction with a fierce intensity.

His father knelt at the dracoling's slow approach, hands outstretched and visible, and waited as the dracoling looked up at Jake for reassurance.

Smiling encouragement, Jake nodded his head, sending the young dracoling bounding toward the necromantic janitor. Jake watched as his father scooped up the child with deceptive ease, extending his personal Shield to encompass them both as the boy wrapped his arms around his father's neck.

"Hallway's clear," the necromancer informed him, standing up slowly. "Head to the vault."

Jake walked over to take a place by the Void mage, falling into step beside him.

"You should be proud of yourself," his father growled.

"I've been learning from the best," he answered back, matching his steps with his father's as they returned to the hallway and made their way to the vault.

5

<I THINK HE'S OUR ANSWER.>

Razick scowled at her brother's assertion, her words carrying her displeasure across their telepathic link. <You barely know him. We don't know anything about him. How do you know we can even trust him?>

Jeb opened the door of the next classroom to peer inside for stragglers. <I've got a good feeling about him. You see how protective he is of his son.> He looked pointedly in her direction. <You're friends with Jake. Don't tell me you have doubts about their relationship.>

She watched Shane warily as he and Jake checked the classrooms across the hall. The janitor's steps were purposeful and confident, his bearing carrying with it a comfortable elegance of power. He cut a regal figure, despite the worn janitorial coveralls.

Jake had fallen into step easily beside him, following his father's direction without a word passing between them. Her brother had wondered at the relation between the two despite their physical resemblance, noting how Jake's calm and warm demeanor stood in stark contrast to his father's intensity. But she'd seen the darkness inside Jake, too. He just hid it better.

She remembered her times spent with the boy in the lab, quietly working while he poured out his frustrations. His anger at the loss of his homeworld. His tendency to take it out on his father. The way the janitor's calm acceptance of the blame only served to strengthen Jake's guilt about his own emotions.

<People treat Family differently. Look at us. You're the only person I can talk to, without...>

Scowling, she shook her head, willing herself to rebury the memories. Jeb was her brother and, clueless as he was about a great many things in the darker corners of the universe, the only person she trusted not to use her own words against her. Jake was slowly working his way into that circle, as well, but he had his own family. From the way he spoke about his father, and the trust Jake placed in him despite the mixed emotions about him, she couldn't afford to let down her guard. Family clearly came first.

<Just because he's a vigilant father doesn't mean he'll help us.>

Jeb paused to place his hand on Razick's shoulders, and she turned to meet his gaze. <Raz. Tell me what's bothering you.>

She sighed, leaning against the doorframe. <We know *noth-ing* about him. Is he a Legionnaire? Or Sparnelli? Is he even willing to fight the Confederation? And what would he do if he discovered who I was?>

<Razick. You're worrying about too many things at once.>

<And you're not worrying about enough,> she snapped.

She looked away, her gaze falling on the orderly lines of children further down the hall, most calmly following their teachers and classmates toward the shelter vault. <Okay, tell me this. Why are we checking classrooms right now?>

Jeb shrugged. <Looking for missing kids. Make sure no one's left behind.>

<But why us?>

<Lawrence said–>

She cut him off. <Exactly. Lawrence said. You didn't notice how quickly he jumped into the command role?>

Returning her attention to the Lawrences, Razick grabbed Jeb's shoulder as Shane's orange stare turned their way. She pulled her brother into the classroom. *Can't let him think any-thing's wrong.*

Watching the janitor's reflection in the door's window, she witnessed Jake lightly touch his arm, causing Shane to relax and return his attention toward their own side of the hallway.

Crisis averted.

<That man is used to being obeyed, Jeb. And the way he holds himself. He's ex-military. He served somewhere. And he was no mere Lieutenant.>

<But isn't that a good thing?> Jeb emerged from his sweep of the room, scratching his head, before motioning her to join him with the next. <He's bound to have experience we can use.>

<In my experience? No.> She snorted. <It doesn't bother you that we don't even know which side he was on? Doing what, and for who?> She opened the next classroom, motioning Jeb inside. <The man clearly knows magic. But his son received a full Legion education. That doesn't just happen.>

<Maybe he left Sparnell, found some way to move to Legion space? Fell in love?>

<Then why's he in the Freeholds?> Razick pressed, watching as Shane motioned Jake to a classroom several doors down the hall, Jake following after. <The Legion takes care of their own, from what I've seen. No reason to start over in the *Freeholds* as a refugee. Not like us.>

<Maybe he didn't have a choice?> Jeb emerged from the classroom behind her, shaking his head before moving toward the next. <Maybe they don't like necromancers.>

<If he's a necromancer, why's he working here? There's lots of well paid jobs for that talent.> She laughed quietly, crossing her arms as she observed Shane following Jake into the classroom he'd motioned toward earlier. <Janitorial staff isn't one of them.>

Jeb's laughter joined hers. <He seems to have an aversion to people. I touched him earlier, and he looked like he wanted to kill me for it. Don't think he'd do well as an Afterlife Planner.>

Her brother slipped into the next room, leaving Razick to keep watch on the doorway as the secretive janitor emerged from the room across the hall carrying a small dracoling child in his arms.

<He definitely knows more magic than he lets on,> she reported to Jeb. <He just found someone before even going into the kid's room.>

<Seriously?>

<Void's honor. What magic did he admit to?>

Jeb's telepathic voice was thoughtful. <He mentioned teaching Jake Soul Call and Shielding. And Jake was bragging about Soul Shatter earlier, but Lawrence was evasive when I asked about it.>

Razick's thoughts grew wistful. <Could you imagine if we could Shatter Kydell? I'd been planning to settle for a firm Soulbind, but Shatter...? Would be nice to know he couldn't come back.>

She felt Jeb grab her arm, her brother's fingernails digging into her skin. <Raz, please. Promise me this isn't about revenge.>

<Jeb...>

<Promise me again.>

She sighed, squeezing his hand in hers. <Fine. It's not *just* about revenge. I want to ensure he'll never do to anyone else what he did to me.>

Jeb maintained his grip for several more moments before releasing her. <I'm sorry, it's just... When you escaped, you told me you were done killing. You'd be a pacifist from then on.>

<I *am* a pacifist.>

<Then why are we planning to hunt someone down and kill them?>

She crossed her arms in front of her chest and glared up at him. Of all people, he should already know that answer. <Because it's Admiral Kydell. He doesn't count.>

<Raz... I don't want to lose you to that life again.>

Grabbing his wrists, Razick turned to face him. <You won't. Never again. I'm enjoying science. It's a useful way to employ my skills, better than...> She shuddered, unable to complete the sentence.

<I worry about you, Raz. The things he made you do... The horrors you've seen...>

<Our friend carries the same haunted look I do,> she observed. <Except worse, like someone keeps kicking him in the gut.>

Her thoughts drifted back to her conversations with Jake. <I wonder what he was. If he knows Shatter, maybe he worked assassinations? Except they usually work solo and he's used to command.>

<Battle mage?> Jeb offered, sliding into the next room. <He was familiar with the uniforms.>

<Unlikely.> Razick shook her head. <Necromancy's not the most useful skill on the battlefield. Takes too much concentra-

tion, and they'd need cover for that. Not to mention, you can counter them with Anemancy. Too much dust where they're trying to phase into, and they just... can't.>

She paused to think. <And there's no way a Void necromancer would work janitorial. With that connection of theirs to the stars? They can make a killing in the private sector just Hyperjumping a ship around once every couple days.>

There was a commotion down the hall as a distraught teacher barreled toward them, calling out in desperation. As soon as she spotted Shane and the young dracoling in his arms she made a beeline toward them, her panicked words turning to gratitude.

Razick watched as the janitor carefully transferred the child to his teacher, motioning toward his son in the process. Jake seemed to explain something to her, at which point she extracted a pair of earplugs from her pockets before pressing them into the dracoling's hands and rushing back down the hall with her recovered student.

Jeb interrupted her thoughts. <So you really don't think he'll be a good fit for our needs, then?>

<I didn't say that.>

They'd reached the end of the classrooms now, joining instead the lines of students and staff filing into the shelter vault. <I said I don't know yet. Keep an eye on him, for now. Don't tell him anything.>

She looked over at the father and son duo, flashing Jake a bright smile of reassurance.

"Don't worry," he told her, grinning back. "My father's here. He'll make sure nothing bad happens."

<There's definitely more to Janitor Lawrence Shane than he lets on,> Razick continued, maintaining her quiet smile for Jake. <I just want to be certain it works out in our favor, before we say anything.>

<I'll follow your lead,> Jeb affirmed with a nod. <And see what else I can learn about them in the meantime.>

6

THEY WERE AMONG THE last to arrive. School security ushered them down the stone carved steps into the vault several stories below Baden's surface, already packed with students and staff. Various members of the administration bustled about, sorting students by grade and taking attendance based upon the morning's records.

Shane surveyed the shelter vault with a careful eye. He wasn't experienced with bombardment shelters – he'd been the cause of their use, rather than an occupant – but aside from its present lack of magic Shielding the school's vault covered everything he'd have thought to include if he'd attempted to design one himself. The space was heavily reinforced with stone and metal, its vaulted ceilings built to facilitate Anemancy-enhanced airflow. Judging by the thick seal around the door, the vault would become airtight once closed, the air supply refreshed instead using atmospheric processors reminiscent of those on his former ship, used to scrub carbon dioxide and maintain the oxygen supply.

It was also roomy, as far as underground bunkers went, but his mind still protested against the idea of willingly enclosing himself in rock and metal and dirt. He leaned into his Necromancy, allowing himself a wider connection to the higher dimensions of the Afterlife beyond the Veil in an effort to quell his panic, and felt his claustrophobia recede in gratitude.

It had been a long time since he'd hidden away during an orbital bombardment. The vault was roomier than his parents' chimney, and better protected, but he wasn't looking forward to the reminders. Especially so close to the anniversary of their death.

He remembered back to the parental open house almost two years ago, when he'd first enrolled Jake. The school had provided parents and students with a full tour of the vault, explaining its many safety features. The entire shelter was a maze of rooms and passageways, each with their own basic living spaces, emergency supplies, and fully sealable doorways. If he remembered correctly, there were eight other entrances into the vault spread across the school grounds and local neighborhood, including one leading directly to the primary cafeteria. The majority of the school's food resources were stored within that section, directly adjacent to an underground kitchen. At full occupancy, they'd easily last three months with full access to the facility, or one month if trapped in a single room.

Similar defensive structures lay scattered across the planet, although given the tuition bill Shane paid each year, he suspected Jake's school maintained one of the nicest.

"Really says something when the quality of a school's bombardment shelter is just as important as their education program," he muttered under his breath.

Welcome to the brave new universe. You helped build it. Hope it was worth it.

"This vault's been here since before I was a kid, Feels," Shane replied quietly. "I've certainly contributed, I won't deny that. I know you're angry, and you have every right to take it out on me." He sighed. "But I didn't cause this problem. If anything, *it* caused *me*."

The silence stretched on. Shane used the opportunity to check in both himself and his son, obtaining directions to the designated gathering spot for Jake's class. Razick and Jeb silently followed, seemingly deep in their own thoughts.

I'm sorry... The Anniversary is coming up, isn't it? Feels finally responded.

"Yesterday, by their calendar," Shane muttered.

By the Void, Grim, why didn't you say something?

"What right do I have?" He didn't attempt to hide the self-hatred swirling in his thoughts. "I've committed so many atrocities in their name, by the time I learned to Soul Call they wouldn't even answer me."

Finding a quiet corner of their assigned room, Shane slid to the floor with his back to the wall, watching as the students and other staff hesitantly grouped and regrouped in a liquid effort to find a space of their own and some level of normalcy within the shelter. The steady hum of hesitant conversations merged into a nervous jumble loud enough to allow for private conversation.

Shane debated removing his shoes to wring out his soaked socks, but decided against it. He was no longer standing on his feet. That would have to do for now.

His son settled to the ground beside him, leaning his head on Shane's shoulder.

Everyone has the right to mourn. Especially their parents. It's what keeps us fae. Er, or human, in your case.

"Human." Shane snorted. "You know I'm not human. By all rights, I'm a monster."

He felt Jake's arms wrap around him and squeeze. The boy always seemed to know when Shane needed grounding from his own emotions.

Although in this case, Jake was most certainly eavesdropping. Not for the first time, the necromancer found himself grateful he'd decided not to keep secrets from his adoptive son. Experience had proven the frustration he'd have faced in that futile endeavor.

You... actually believe all my angry rantings, don't you?

Shane felt the regret radiating from his former friend.

"You're the empath. You should know."

He pulled free of his adoptive son's embrace, propping his arms on his knees. Jake responded by returning his head to Shane's shoulder.

I'm... also still angry. And angry empaths are... not a good thing.

Feels paused, likely waiting for a reply, but Shane remained silent.

I've... got a lot to think about, right now. I'll leave you alone for a while.

"Up to you," Shane muttered at last, eyes closed. "It always is."

"Father. We need to talk."

Jake's worried tone, the words slipping into the boy's native language of Loxiran, brought Shane to full attention. He turned to face his son, tracing the boy's frown with his eyes. "What's wrong?"

Jake swallowed, staring at his hands. "I lied today. To Veris."

Shane remembered back to his conversation with Jeb that morning. It felt like a lifetime ago, instead of a mere hour. "Soul Shatter."

His son sat up, nodding. "I'm sorry." His next words came in a rush. "I knew it was a mistake, as soon as I said it. I wish I knew Telepathy so I could warn you right away. I never should have said those things."

Shane exhaled slowly. "When you say or do something, you can never take it back."

The necromancer watched as his son looked away at his words, Jake's hands clasped together so tightly his fingernails left furrows in his skin. He reached out, gently taking hold of each of Jake's hands and pulling lightly until Jake's eyes met his.

"But sometimes mistakes happen. Sometimes things are said that shouldn't be said, but only after it feels like there is nowhere else to go."

Jake nodded mutely, tears swelling in his eyes.

"I've already handled it. Jeb and I talked it out."

"But Veris said he'd get you fired!"

Shane fixed Jake with a stare. "I doubt he'd succeed. But remember when I told you that some problems are grown up problems."

Jake nodded, rubbing his eyes.

"This is one of them. Whatever happens, it's not your fault."

"But if I hadn't–"

Shane cut him off, voice hardening. "Do I lie?"

"No, Sir."

"Did I just tell you it's not your fault?"

"Yes, Sir."

He softened his voice. "So is it your fault?"

Jake sighed. "No, Sir."

"Good."

The two sat in silence, watching as the room monitor finished checking people and inventory off her list and slid the thick doors into their ready position, engineered to remain open enough to allow passage but close enough to closed they'd snap shut if the vault hallway outside either entryway was compromised. Shane noted Jeb and Razick sitting across the room, silent yet animated, casting furtive glances back at him and Jake when they thought he wasn't looking.

Jake broke the silence first. "It's not your fault either, you know."

"What's not my fault?" Shane turned his attention back to his son.

"Everything." Jake motioned around the room. "Sometimes mistakes happen. Sometimes things are done that shouldn't be done, but only after it feels like there is nowhere else to go."

Shane scowled at the use of his own words. "Some things are unforgivable."

"That's not your choice." Jake held Shane's stare with his own. "Everyone gets to choose for themselves. You only get to choose for you. You don't choose for me." He held out his hand. "Give me the locket."

Shane reached beneath his coveralls to clutch at his mother's necklace, the only object of his parents' belongings to survive the attack on his own homeworld, all those years ago. "No."

But Jake wasn't budging. "Now. I need to talk to Feels."

"You just don't want Feels to talk to me."

Jake wrinkled his nose. "Don't make me say it."

"This is my burden to bear."

Who are you calling a burden? They sounded indignant. *Give me to Jake. I could use a good conversation for a change.*

"Give me Feels," Jake repeated angrily. "You exist to keep me safe. I need them so you can do that. Letting them torture you with guilt won't help."

Shane felt himself removing the necklace before his thoughts could formulate a counter to his son's demands. He wrapped his fist around the circular locket, pressing his fingers against the gilded outer casing as he willed himself to argue.

"Keeping them is a threat to my safety," Jake pressed, a faint whine forming under his words. "You're paying attention to them instead of me. You'll fail your mission."

Shane surrendered the locket, an emptiness overtaking him at its absence against his chest. "I hate when you use that against me."

Jake stuck out his tongue, slipping the chain over his head before tucking the locket against his chest. "Now focus."

Sighing, Shane closed his eyes and leaned against the wall, emotionally spent. To anyone but Jake he'd appear to be sleeping.

Instead, he slipped his full consciousness beyond the Veil, bending reality until he could observe the space battle raging above. Anything to distract himself from the reminders of his past, and his son's clear willingness to use his own wounds against him.

He focused his concentration on the Void above, and the spacecraft now maneuvering around the planet. They *were* under attack. If the Confederation had finally grown weary of watching Baden thrive, alone and independent on the edge of their space, he'd need to act quickly to Hyperjump Jake. Start over from the beginning on a new planet.

"Time to find out whether or not we still have a home."

7

Jake's surprising calm despite the present situation was a balm to Feels' own jumbled emotions, and a surprisingly welcome relief from the intensity of the guilt still openly radiating from Grim.

Are you going to tell me I'm too hard on him?

"You already know that." The boy's voice remained soft and even, with undertones of sadness and resignation. "If you won't listen to you, you won't listen to me." He paused. "I'm hard on him, too."

Grim's son had developed a tendency to intentionally trigger his adoptive father's traumas, a coping mechanism for dealing with his own. While Feels was rarely on the receiving end, today he reminded them of how deep his penchant for thoughtful yet brutal honesty could cut.

I listen more than you realize. You're perceptive, for a twelve year old. And a good influence on him.

"Twelve and a *half*."

Feels would have enjoyed watching Jake's indignation, if they weren't stuck as a disembodied soul firmly bound and imprisoned within an antique holographic locket. At least they could still communicate, courtesy of the locket's mechanisms to provide private audio to whoever was touching it, a marvel of vibrational engineering from some of the Legion's finest craftsmen. Because binding spells assigned the selected object as the soul's new body, Feels had full access to the locket's capabilities.

All of which they'd promptly put to use tormenting Grim, in revenge for their murder.

You're still wise beyond your years. You must know that.

Jake's sadness grew, mixing with hints of pride and determination. "I had to grow up fast, after Mom died. It's not easy, trying to hide who I am all the time, and still stay myself."

It must be strange, too. Growing up without a father, and then suddenly there's Grim, granting his full and undivided attention. Feels sent a sense of amusement toward Jake. *Once he gets it in his mind to do something, the man is intense. And he's decided to build his whole life around you now.*

They felt Jake's amusement in return, even before the laughter began. "Intense is one way to say it," the boy managed at last. "Was he always like this?"

Worse.

"No." Jake projected disbelief now.

Oh yes. I told you about the time he stole the experimental mech suit? Wanted to intimidate someone, but it wasn't sized or articulated for him, and he got stuck. Took me five hours to pry him out of that thing, and the whole time he was still *ranting about how next time he'd teach the guy a lesson.*

They basked in Jake's wonder at the thought of his father's early career antics, even despite the sadness that underlay most of the boy's emotions. They hadn't realized how much they needed a break from Grim's guilt, not to mention their own anger.

He used to get into so much trouble, and I always had to dig him out again. Although... Sometimes I wonder if maybe I shouldn't have dug him out. Maybe he'd have been kicked from service. Avoided all the nightmares that followed.

"You feel guilty."

Once again, Jake's calm assessment felt like a kick to the emotional gut.

I put in my time and monopolized his, and then I left. I shouldn't have left Grim alone. Not with the admiral. Feels felt the emotions they'd tried to suppress surging into a jumble of guilt, fear, and sorrow. *Whatever happened to him after, it's my fault for leaving.*

"You know he wasn't ready to leave." Jake's emotions flattened, adopting the analytical stance he relied upon when thinking through a difficult problem. "And you told me you'd lose yourself if you stayed."

I know... But he was my best friend! When you both walked through my door two years ago, asking for help... They paused, struggling to put the feelings into words. *I'd never sensed Grim so broken before.*

"He betrayed everything. And everyone. Just to keep me safe."

Jake's simple statement felt like a knife twisted into their soul.

I should have been there for him. I could have helped. I've been so angry at him for breaking my trust. For killing me and binding me in his locket after everything I did to help you both that day... Their voice trailed off, but they forced themselves to continue. *Still I wonder. Did I betray him first? Leaving him to survive with the admiral alone. How could he trust me to keep his secrets if he couldn't even trust me to have his back when he needed me most?*

"You kept in touch."

Not the same. It's one thing to write letters, but when those letters turned dark... I knew he needed me. I should have helped then, not waited for him to show up and ask. Now that they were finally sharing their feelings, Feels found it hard to stop. *But also... These past few years, I was jealous. Am jealous.*

Jake radiated confusion now. "Of who?"

Feels paused. This was a lot to lay on a kid, but this wasn't just any kid. This was *Grim*'s kid, and Jake had every right to know.

Jealous of you. Grim left the service because of you, turned his life around because of you, built his whole life around you. He killed me in a misguided belief it was necessary to keep you safe. But when I begged him to leave back then, begged him to reconsider what the admiral was telling him, he wouldn't even think about it. Wasn't I enough? Didn't our relationship mean anything?

The anger was back, filling their every thought.

Jake's emotions, by comparison, remained calm and measured. "The locket only works when worn. Does he ever take it off? Even at your worst, angriest moments?"

And just like that, Feels felt their anger deflate. *No.*

"You *do* matter." They felt Jake caress the locket with his fingers, a light touch to sooth a heavy soul. "He knows he was wrong. He knows he betrayed you. And he's showing you he's sorry, the only way he knows how right now."

The touch on the locket hardened as Jake squeezed tightly, his words a mere whisper. "Just like with me, when I pick on him."

The pair existed in silence as Feels did their best to repel the mess of emotions within the confining room in a desperate attempt to make space to work on their own. Tense situations were especially stressful for an empath. Fear, sadness, frustration, and impatience ran throughout the bombardment shelter like an undercurrent, while a tightly wound pocket of panic and paranoia simmered at the far side of the room.

Feels could also sense Jake's resolve, mixed with frustration and concern. Grim's own emotions were the anticipated dark and volatile swirl of guilt and self-hatred, with a new hint of angry vengeance.

Must be Sparnell, judging by your father's emotions, they observed. *Small fleet, probably. Don't feel him worrying. Yet.*

"Good to know we'll survive this, then." Jake's tone was flat, but Feels caught the small wave of relief accompanying the words.

Unless their tactics changed, this is probably an advanced scouting mission. Testing the planetary defenses before a full attack. They hated interrupting Jake's calmed demeanor, but the astute preteen had a right to know. *Baden's at the edge of the Sparnell Confederation's territory. It was inevitable they'd turn their eyes to us. These vault trips will only grow more frequent.*

"Why did you befriend my father?"

Jake's emotions had shifted at the empath's words to hold a mix of resignation and frustration, plus a hint of fear, but also a strong undercurrent of curiosity.

A distraction while we wait? Feels decided they'd be happy to oblige. *Honestly don't know if I can put it into words. Your father was so angry and vengeful, but there was something else underneath. The hurt and pain ran deep, and I found myself convinced that if he'd only be my friend, I could fix it. Not only that. I wanted to fix it.*

Things rarely work out the way we plan, though. Already mentioned I couldn't change his mind about the war. I did change his mind about empaths at least. He's the one who gave me the nickname Feels. Used to mean it as an insult! Have an empath save your butt often enough, though... Well, he eventually realized I was stronger than he'd given me credit for.

"I thought you were a field medic?" Jake was invested in the story now.

Medic. Empath. You'd be surprised how often those two are actually the same thing. Feels beamed with pride. *He managed to have me reassigned as his personal healer. Had to fight for it once, when the admiral tried to separate us, but Void necromancers have a certain level of clout regardless of rank and Grim never took no for an answer. Not when it was about me.*

"So you became friends early, then?"

No. Feels laughed. *In the beginning, I was just... useful. The Sparnelli power struggle is brutal, and having a medic makes you a less opportune target. More likely to survive and all.* Feels remembered the abuse they'd experienced themselves, before they'd managed to catch Grim's attention, and he'd managed to frighten off the competition.

But I made it clear, I wanted his friendship in return. He... didn't agree right away. At first I feared he wasn't interested, but looking back, I don't think he'd made a single friend since he'd lost his own homeworld to planetary bombardment. I think he genuinely didn't know what it meant to have a friend.

But Grim is one of the bravest people I know. He actually asked what I meant by friendship. It hadn't even occurred to me he wouldn't know! Yet there he was, embarrassed but determined to figure it out. And not long after that, I was his personal healer. Untouchable to anyone else.

Feels felt their own sorrow at the memory of those days and what came after. In spite of everything they'd been through together, had Grim still never learned?

They brushed the thoughts aside. Whether he understood it or not, the Void necromancer had gone out of his way time and time again to see that he gave Feels everything he knew they needed. If that didn't prove the effort was genuine, nothing would.

"My father protected you?"

I'm assuming, although he never admitted to it. The bullying stopped the day he rescued me. And after... Even Admiral Kydell left me alone.

"Feels..." Jake's emotions spiked with an overwhelming embarrassment, as if he was braced for rejection. "How did you deal with the bullies until then? Could you teach me?"

I honestly don't know if my methods will help in your case, Feels admitted, *but I'll do what I can. Why don't you tell me what's going on?*

Gratitude washed over them from Jake's direction, as Feels attempted to remember their own experiences at the hands of bullies. They listened closely as Jake began to explain his own personal tribulations, comparing them to their own discoveries in an effort to find suggestions. It felt good to be putting their knowledge toward something positive for a change.

They'd spent enough time fixated on the past, constantly needling Grim about what he'd done to them and their former staff. He *knew* what they thought about him. Hadn't even tried to deny it.

Maybe it was time to find out what Grim thought of everything he'd done. Give him the opportunity to choose whether or not to rebuild their broken trust.

Prove to them that they'd actually been friends, once.

8

JEB TURNED AWAY FROM his conversation with the shelter monitor, casually making his way back toward his sister. <I got us reassigned with Jake's class, so we can keep an eye on Lawrence.>

He hoped it would give her the reassurance she needed, and felt heartened when she gave a faint smile alongside her nod of acknowledgement.

They made their way through the throngs of people, mostly students and staff in this portion of the shelter. Jeb knew they'd have plenty of residents and workers from the local community filling in along the furthest entryways of the vault, most taking up temporary residence within the outer rooms unless they had skills critical to the maintenance of the temporary underground city. Soon the local parents of schoolchildren would also begin trickling to the center to retrieve their kids, although the school was prepared to retain custody of its students for the duration of the bombardment, if necessary.

<Here.> Razick motioned to a spot on the floor, across the room from the Lawrences. <We'll be able to watch without them noticing.>

Jeb grabbed a pair of bedrolls from the room's supply stash before joining his sister. <We'll be here a while. May as well make ourselves comfortable.>

Passing one to Raz, he folded his into a makeshift cushion and set it on the floor. He couldn't help but smile as she propped hers against the wall, still rolled, and leaned against it for lumbar support.

Her eyes never left the janitor and his son, despite the way she moved her head to appear to pan the room. <He's talking to someone.>

<Yeah. Jake's right there.>

<No. Someone else.>

<You sure?>

Jeb turned his attention toward the pair, attempting to observe without being noticed. Shane and his son sat apart from the press of people in the room, those straying too close seeming to back away the moment they recognized him. Jake leaned against Shane's arm, but Raz could be right, he looked more interested in eying Veris and his gang than in speaking with his dad. *Poor kid is probably nervous, stuck down here with his tormentors.*

He turned back to Raz. <I don't see anyone else.>

<His lips are moving, and Jake isn't answering.>

<Ah.> Jeb chuckled. <He talks to himself a lot. I've caught him arguing with his mop when he thinks no one's around.>

The one sided conversations followed a similar pattern to Razick's nighttime mumblings. He debated mentioning this, but decided against it.

<You sure he's not arguing with someone else?> Raz fixed Jeb with a green stare. <Could be communicating with the attack fleet above. Feeding them information about our defenses!>

Jeb sighed, rubbing the bridge of his nose. <Razick...>

She'd been like this since her escape from the Sparnell Armed Forces and subsequent exodus to join him in the Freeholds, always leaping at shadows and insisting on the validity of the most outlandish fears and conspiracy theories.

But he didn't have the luxury of working through this particular fantasy with her today. They had more urgent matters right now, courtesy of the likely planetary bombardment outside. <If he was a spy, why would he be working as a janitor?>

He wondered what horrors Admiral Kydell had forced her to experience. Or inflict upon others.

What happened to you, Raz?

When she'd left for her conscription, she'd been his trusting big sister, with a generous heart. Seeing her now...

Raz wouldn't budge. <To blend in. *Obviously*. People overlook janitors. I'll bet he overhears a lot of private conversations.>

<He probably *does* know everything about which student has a crush on who,> Jeb conceded. <But what sort of military

intelligence could he hope to learn from The Baden City Academy for Gifted Youth?>

<My armor project,> she hissed, clutching the armor to her chest. <Or *me*. He could be telling Kydell where to find me *right now*. That fleet could be here for *me*.> She snarled in Shane's direction. <I'm *not* going back. I'll *die* first.>

Just when he thought the day couldn't get more stressful.

Jeb slowly wrapped his arm around his sister, careful not to startle her. She'd nearly killed him the last time he'd surprised her, her lethal reactions fueled by adrenaline, instinct, and training.

<That would be quite a coincidence. If he was sent to find you, how would he know to take a janitorial job *here*?>

<Divination.>

Her answer was quick and matter-of-fact, and Jeb kicked himself for giving her such an obvious question. It would be even more difficult to convince her otherwise, now.

But he had to try. This was his sister, and he'd promised to help keep her grounded.

<You always told me Kydell would stop at nothing to get you back. So if the fleet's here for you, and Lawrence turned you in... Why did it take so long? He's been here two years.>

Raz turned her attention back to Jeb at that, confusion across her face. <I... don't know.>

Excited at the foothold, Jeb prepared to drive in his point when she suddenly gripped his arm, her face frozen in horror, affixed on the janitor and his son.

<They *are* using a communication device. *Look*.>

Jeb turned his attention back to Shane, just in time to see him transfer some sort of golden medallion to his son, who quickly slipped it beneath his shirt. The biologist watched as Jake's lips began to move, speaking to some unseen entity, while the elder Lawrence settled in for a nap.

Great. Now how was he supposed to talk her down from *this* state?

He ran through his options as he struggled to remove Razick's fingernails from the flesh of his arm.

But what if she was right?

And then Jake laughed, a heartfelt cascade of innocence, and Jeb's doubts dissolved. The boy was a gifted twelve year old student in his biology class, struggling with bullies and teachers and boredom, not some super spy come to conquer the planet. It was a communication device, but not to the attack fleet.

There's nothing strange about calling a friend to pass the time during a lockdown.

He turned to his sister, keeping his telepathic tone logical and even. <Jake's your friend. He would *not* betray you.>

Raz remained still for an eternity, muscles taut and ready, as Jeb watched the internal conflict do battle across her face.

Finally, she relaxed. <You're right.> She leaned back against the wall, still observing the pair across the room. <But they're definitely up to something. You said Lawrence will talk to you. See what you can learn.>

Jeb turned his eye toward Shane and his son, his own thoughts heavy. <He's sleeping right now. He'll get suspicious if I wake him up.> At Razick's frown, he smiled reassuringly. <I'll wait a bit, then strike up a conversation.>

He felt his sister's approval radiate across their telepathic link and calmed slightly. She would let him take the lead for now, then. Good.

In her present state, she was more likely to start a confrontation than a discussion, and without knowing the janitor's background it was impossible to predict the outcome of that fight, especially in a room full of schoolchildren. Instead, she'd wisely delegated the task to him, and granted him some time to pull his thoughts together.

But what in Void's name should I say?

9

Baden's small defensive fleet had the space battle well in hand by the time Shane felt Jake's hand slide into his, the locket between them. He moved to replace it around his own neck, but Jake refused to relinquish his hold.

Grim... We need to talk.

Shane shifted his attention from his window through the Veil, returning the majority of his focus to his immediate surroundings within the shelter vault. "Whatever you need, Feels. Always. You know that." He turned his gaze toward his son. "Jake, too?"

Jake, too. He... keeps me grounded. The empath paused, although whether to gather courage or words, Shane wasn't certain. *Grim... I'm sorry.*

Shane sat up, startled. "For what?"

Realizing the empath wouldn't see the gesture, he focused his emotions on his feelings for his friend. Trust. Respect. Love.

Guilt.

He hung his head, regret in his voice. "You've been nothing but a good friend to me. I broke that. Not you."

The empath held firm. *We* both *broke that. I wasn't there when you needed me.*

Shane scowled, his emotions shifting darker. "I was Oathbound, and your conscription was up. You were better off outside that life. I never faulted you for that."

I shouldn't have monopolized your time. Should have helped you make friends, more than just me. And then, after Loxira...

"Feels..." Shane fought his confusion. "You did *everything* I ever asked. You gave us the information we needed, a place to stay so we wouldn't get caught, and even transferred half my bank funds into a new, safer account. You gave me a new name, a new body, a new life..." He closed his eyes, clenching his fists in an effort to keep his voice calm enough to avoid attracting curious ears in the crowded room. "And in return, I took yours. And Shattered the rest of your team."

The empath was silent for a long moment. *I don't know if I'll ever forgive you for that.*

"Good. You shouldn't." He squeezed his hand tighter around the locket, remembering. He'd betrayed his only friend, Shattering the souls of those they'd hired to help him.

And then murdered his friend, imprisoning them in his locket.

"I was a monster. I *am* a monster. I murdered you, in cold blood, after everything you did for us."

Shane was having trouble keeping his voice low, but a quick scan of the room revealed the only one watching them was Razick.

"I was angry and afraid, and made you pay for that fear. I always make *everyone* else pay for my problems because that's what I am. Selfish. Cruel. A monster."

He felt a warmth within his soul as his jumbled emotions of turmoil began to untangle.

A Psychomorphation spell.

They hadn't used their magic on him since he'd bound them in his mother's locket, choosing instead to torment him using only the tools presented by the locket itself.

Shane wondered if this was to be the next stage in the fae's efforts to punish him for his actions, and decided it didn't matter. If that's what they needed to recover from what he'd done to them, it was only fair he allow it.

But the empath had other ideas.

You weren't selfish. *You didn't do it for yourself.* Feels' voice was quiet, with an anger still simmering beneath, but they'd seemed to set aside the accusations. For now.

"You did it to save me." Jake frowned, leaning his head on Shane's shoulder. "Everything was always for me. And I'm still mean to you."

And I was too angry to see it. Too wrapped up in my own emotions to care about any of yours.

"I'm evil. I destroy things. It's all I know," Shane protested.

Maybe you're right, Feels told him.

Shane felt as if the vault floor had dropped out from under him at the fae's words. He shouldn't be surprised they felt that way. He *wasn't* surprised – not really – and yet somehow having them admit it in the middle of the longest conversation he'd managed with the fae since he'd murdered them gave the words a heavier weight than he'd expected.

But maybe you're wrong. I've been so busy wallowing in my own pain and anger... They paused. *What I'm trying to say is, I'm still angry at you. But that anger hasn't gotten me anywhere.*

"You're trapped in my locket," Shane reminded them. "You haven't been *able* to go anywhere."

Would you let me finish? the Fae snapped. *This is hard enough as it is. I'm trying to tell you I'm going to listen more. I don't want to spend the rest of my life an angry shell haunting someone I used to think was my friend. I'm willing to give you a chance to fix this. To fix us.*

Shane sat in stunned silence as the universe slowed around him. He felt Jake's hand in his, the locket still firmly sandwiched between their grips. He felt Feels' magic in his veins, holding off the worst of his own self-hatred so he could *think*. Closing his eyes, he savored the moment, the weak echo of the emotional warmth he'd once thrived upon, when he was still the empath's friend.

Finally, Shane found his words. "I thought you'd given up on me."

I had, Feels admitted. *But I miss what we used to be. And I don't* like *being angry. Hate is a very uncomfortable emotion.*

Shane found his mind once again in turmoil, not with inde-cision but with fear. To be so close to what he'd longed for...

And so undeserving.

"I'd do anything to repair our relationship, but I don't think I can," he admitted. "I... Nothing is the same anymore. I'm lost without you... And I don't know what to do about it."

I want to have my own life. With the Phoenix Assembly, with the Baden underground, I was helping people like us. Starting over with a new life after escaping the SAF. I was making a difference. I had a purpose... *I want that back.*

"What do you need me to do? Tell me."

That's... not a simple answer. I don't know. *I need to...* Feels' voice faded. *You have company coming. Nervous. Agitated. Worried. We'll talk later.*

"Am I interrupting something?" Jeb's tone held a forced cheerfulness as he scratched his head, looking down at father and son.

Shane looked up calmly. "Jeb. Just passing the time, talking to a dear friend. Would you like to sit down?" He motioned toward the wide aisle of unclaimed floor directly adjacent to him and his son, lips turning upward in a smirk. "My current efforts to appear less intimidating have been quite unsatisfactory, I'm afraid."

Jeb chuckled. "I can see that." He settled to the ground cross-legged in front of Shane before turning to Jake. "How are you holding up?"

He's nervous. Unsure. Something's bothering him.

Feels' report confirmed Shane's suspicions. Whatever brought Jeb over, it wasn't for small talk.

"Okay." Jake's answer was polite and guarded. "Can't wait until we can leave."

"How's your sister holding up?" Shane motioned toward Razick, who immediately narrowed her eyes.

Jeb rubbed his neck. "She's doing great. We both are."

He's definitely agitated. More than before. I wouldn't trust what he tells you right now.

"I missed you." Shane couldn't help himself.

I know. He didn't need to be an empath to catch Feels' smug tone. *I still don't trust you. I still don't* like *you. But I like Jake. So I'll help you, as long as you're not hurting people.*

It was a generous offer. Shane would do his best not to squander it. Not to fracture their trust further.

Jeb shifted his weight. "I'm glad you appreciate my company? I guess? It's only been a few minutes, though."

Narrowing his eyes, Shane stared at Jeb. "Why are you *really* here?"

Now he's afraid. Also... Jake, is Veris heading this way? I feel a lot of negative energy, heading our direction.

Shane turned to look at Jake, watching as his son's eyes locked with those of a snarling blue dracoling almost half again his size. "Is that Veris?"

"Yes, Father." His son's tone was calm and measured. "I think I need to take care of this. Alone." He tightened his fingers around the locket, his attention still locked on Veris. "May I borrow...?"

I promised I'd help, Feels explained. *Don't let anyone else interrupt. We'll be fine.*

"Go. Do what you need to do."

He relinquished his hold on the locket with a sigh. If he wanted to earn Feels' trust, first he needed to prove he trusted the empath. The irony of trusting them with Jake – after *murdering* them, for the boy's safety – wasn't lost on him.

"Remember," he told Jake quietly. "A dracoling's scales are actually thick, cracked skin. Gives them physical resistance, so you can't rely on brute strength. You need smarts."

"I know. Thank you, Father."

Jake tucked the locket safely beneath his shirt as he rose to face the oncoming threat.

Shane narrowed his eyes as Jeb followed suit. "And where do you think *you're* going?" he growled.

"I need to break them up. In case there's a fight," Jeb protested, even as he sank slowly back to the ground like a naughty schoolboy at Shane's stare.

The janitor kept his voice impassive, watching as several other students rose to stand behind the dracoling. He counted one human, two katanoj, and a canid. "Oh, there's going to be a fight."

"And you're not worried? Aren't you going to help Jake?" Jeb's voice rose in pitch, to match his panic. "You know he's on academic probation, right? Headmaster said she'd address it with you, when you signed the paperwork."

Jake's steps were deliberate, slow but unlabored. Shane watched as Veris gave a wicked, toothy grin to his gang, jerking his thumb toward Jake.

"I've already given him everything he needs." Shane watched a few other teachers begin to stand in an effort to intervene. His quick glare sent them back to their seats.

"So you're just going to let him walk out there and start a fight. Outnumbered. Not lift a finger to help. And then hope he doesn't get expelled for it."

"Better than Veris starting it. We're at our most powerful when violence is a choice, not a requirement. Because when it's a choice, we can still choose no."

They'd have to leave the planet anyway, before the Confederation attacked in force. Learning to defend himself was likely the last lesson his son would be learning at this school. He wasn't about to deny Jake the opportunity, especially not in the face of consequences he'd never face, anyway.

Shane's lip twisted up in an attempt at a smile. "You'll see. Watch."

10

Jake focused on his breathing as he walked toward Veris, leaning into the simple meditations his adoptive father had taught him. Intended merely to help center himself for better control of his magic, he'd discovered them useful for almost any stressful situation.

Facing Veris certainly counted as stressful.

Remember, I don't have the same senses as you. I can't see what you see, or hear anything or anyone except you. But I can sense emotions, and I'll let you know anything useful. Where am I?

"Around my neck. In the front." Jake kept his steps calm and confident, maintaining direct eye contact with his persistent tormentor.

Good. Let me know if that changes.

It had been Feels' idea to confront Veris directly. From what the fae had explained, this was an adaptation of their own experiences during the early months of their conscription, when his father had stepped in to save them from their tormentors. His father had barely had to lift his voice, merely standing his ground until the others backed down.

Jake had doubts as to the effectiveness of the plan, but Feels seemed convinced, and it wasn't as if Jake had a better idea.

He attempted to bury the memories of his meeting with Headmaster Corbin. He doubted getting into a fight in the middle of the crowded shelter vault counted as staying out of trouble. Hopefully, if it came to that, Veris would be the only one expelled.

He closed his eyes briefly, whispering one of his father's mantras under his breath.

"Be the calm one."

Opening them again, he resumed his march toward Veris and whatever fate the future had in store.

The blue-skinned dracoling grinned wickedly, running his fingers through his ice blue hair, purple eyes and ear fins both focused on Jake. From what Feels had shared about bullies, if Jake wanted to be left alone he'd need to convince the others he was the biggest threat, and the first step was to show he didn't consider Veris threatening at all.

There's a thick cloud of smugness in front of you. They sent a small caress of pride to brush against Jake's thoughts. *Confidence. Bravado. But there's fear underneath. Use it all to your advantage.*

Drawing his shoulders back, Jake forced his hands to remain unclenched at his sides. He felt his heart rate accelerate and wished he could borrow some of Veris' confidence, just long enough to convince himself he could do that.

Fortunately he didn't have to convince himself today. Just Veris.

"You're such a *loser*, Lawrence. Your Dad won't even stick up for you!" The dracoling crossed his arms and glared, scratching at his blue scaled elbows.

Veris towered over Jake, half again his height and probably at least twice his weight, a healthy mix of fat and muscle which gave most other students pause. The dracoling had been a constant nuisance since Jake's enrollment, but the bullying had grown worse in recent months. Veris laughed now, motioning to the small crowd behind him and making mocking faces in Jake's direction.

"I don't need anyone to fight my battles for me, Veris." Jake let his eyes linger on each member of the dracoling's gang before refocusing on Veris himself. He kept his stance relaxed, with a hint of amusement in his voice. "Unlike you, apparently."

Now he's angry. Feels' tone projected both pride and concern. *Be careful.*

Jake kept his eyes ahead, watching Veris' crew stifle their amusement. They wouldn't be joining the fight any time soon.

"I can take you! I don't need help! They're just watching."

Jake didn't need an empath to catch the defensiveness in the dracoling's voice.

He shrugged. "Then maybe they'll learn something for once." He kept his upper body loose and relaxed, his steps small and controlled, keeping his weight centered on the balls of his feet. So far, everything was going to plan, but he'd be within striking range soon and would need to react quickly when Veris lashed out. "Assuming you can hold out that long?"

No need for insults, Jake, the empath cautioned sharply. *You've already isolated him, so the others won't help if he attacks. Remember: this isn't about winning a fight, it's about preventing them. You're not trying to upset Veris, he'll only want to fight you more! Don't tear apart his character.*

Jake wrinkled his nose. As far as he was concerned, Veris had done enough to ruin his own character. But Feels seemed to know what they were doing, so he flashed a small smile of apology. "Sorry."

Here he comes! Feels warned.

"Oh, you're gonna be sorry alright!"

And with that, the dracoling lunged.

11

JAKE SLIPPED UNDER VERIS' punch, pivoting easily to the side. Veris flailed briefly when his movement found no resistance but recovered quickly, charging toward Jake's new position. Jake waited until Veris was almost on top of him before crouching low, sidestepping to the left and sweeping Veris' feet out from beneath with his right leg. The bully hit the ground in a tumble of limbs and expletives but rolled quickly to his feet, murder in his eyes.

"Stand and face me, Lawrence!" he snarled, charging again.

Once again, Jake danced from his grasp, stepping around the burly bully on highly motivated feet.

Here he comes again, Feels said quietly, the words accompanied by a sharp spike of warning against Jake's thoughts.

Veris hesitated briefly as he approached Jake this time, eyes darting as he searched for any sign of movement. Jake held his ground until the last moment, ducking beneath the dracoling's swing to slide to the side, perfectly lining him up for a punch of his own.

No, Jake, Feels warned, clearly sensing the spike of anger in Jake's emotions. *He's the aggressor. Don't give him an opening to claim it's you.*

Nodding, Jake stepped backward instead, pulling to his full height and positioning his arms in front of him, hands lightly fisted, in preparation for the next attack.

The fight continued for several more moments, Veris repeatedly lunging to attack while Jake calmly slipped and rolled away, Feels helpfully providing advanced warning of each emotional outburst.

He's tired and frustrated, Feels warned as Jake barely dodged a punch, Veris' fist lightly grazing his ear. *And his friends are agitated. I think we need to move to the next phase.*

"You fight like a coward, Lawrence," Veris spat, backing away slightly. "Come back when you're ready to fight like a *real* Freeholder!"

Jake rotated his shoulders, quickly surveying the vault. Veris' gang glared at him with a hunger for violence, slowly inching closer. The rest of the room stared at the fight with emotions ranging from curiosity from some of his classmates to horror from many of the teachers, but nobody showed any sign of interfering, suitably discouraged by his father.

The necromancer sat in the corner where Jake had left him, one hand firmly grasping Jeb's arm, seemingly deep in conversation. Jake knew he was watching every move closely.

He planted his feet firmly on the floor, casting a small Shielding spell to weaken Veris' anticipated momentum, and braced for impact. "Are you sure hitting me would make you feel better?"

"You bet it would!" And with that, Veris swung a right hook, hitting Jake squarely in the jaw.

Jake allowed the momentum of the punch to send him staggering a step to the side, grinning and making an exaggerated show of shaking his head while he refreshed his Shielding. He rubbed his jaw with his hand, the friendly warmth of Feels' healing magic already coursing through his veins.

"I don't think that did very much. Are you sure that helped?"

The dracoling came at him again from the other side, and Jake found himself staggering a full three steps under the force of the blow.

He stood up quickly, flashing a jovial smile as Feels worked their magic. "Good one, Veris! How do you feel, now?"

Veris lunged in response, his next punch catching Jake directly in the stomach. Jake doubled over, winded, grateful he'd maintained his weakened Shielding.

"Better than you," the dracoling chuckled, flexing his fingers and shaking his wrist. "Couldn't dodge that one."

He's happy about something, Feels reported dutifully. *Still agitated. And worried. And... sad?*

"Wasn't trying to," Jake said slowly, straightening to look Veris in the eyes. "We done yet?"

Veris snorted, and ignored the question. "Your dad mustn't like you much. He's just sitting there. Watching."

Narrowing his eyes, Jake clenched his fists at his side, nostrils flaring. His adoptive father had every reason to dislike him. He'd allowed his anger over the bombardment of his planet, death of his mother, and uprooting of his whole life overtake his reasoning on many occasions. The necromancer had taken the brunt of it and continued onward, looking out for Jake's safety and well-being as if it were his only purpose for existence.

Not that his father had much of a choice in the matter, of course. Jake had learned that early, and twisted the compulsion to his benefit on more than one occasion.

But there was something else there, beyond the obligation. His father had been the one true constant in the turmoil as they worked to build a life together. And he genuinely seemed to consider Jake his son.

Jake took a step toward Veris, making no attempt to hide his anger. "You take that back."

Jake! Stop! Do not *cross this line.*

Veris' grin grew wider at Jake's show of emotion. "Hit a nerve?"

"My father will *always* be there for me," Jake growled. "Where's *yours*?"

Jake didn't need Feels' Psychometry to realize he'd struck a deeper blow than intended. The dracoling's face contorted, adopting an almost animalistic hatred as he closed the distance between them, and Jake found himself stepping backward.

"Screw you, Lawrence."

The room gasped in unison as Veris lunged toward Jake once more.

12

Feels' words were accompanied by a spike of emotion pressing against his thoughts, but it was too late. Jake felt a sharp pain in his gut, followed by a blossoming warmth. He grabbed at the object on instinct, spinning out of Veris' range before looking down at the item grasped in his hand, still protruding from his abdomen.

Jake glared back at Veris, incredulously. "A knife? Seriously?"

That was... unexpected, the empath apologized, pausing. *But fixable. Pull it out slowly. This* will *hurt.*

"Not so tough now, are you, Lawrence?" Veris taunted.

Jake faintly noted the pandemonium erupting around him as teachers sprang to their feet, moving toward him and Veris as if in slow motion. The volume in the vault rose notably, as well, but he shut it out, his entire focus on the knife in his hand, still lodged in his gut. He felt Shielding flare around him, wrapping carefully against his own, and relaxed.

His father.

The necromancer's sheer presence pressed insistently against the back of his mind and he accepted the Soul Call, locking eyes with his father's intense stare from across the room.

<<Let me help.>>

The words were clear despite the distance, courtesy of the shortcut through the Afterlife.

"No," Jake commanded sternly. "The Shield is enough. I've got this."

"You've been fighting on school grounds. That makes this *my* jurisdiction, not yours," Professor Darga growled beside him, and Jake winced.

He hadn't realized the katanoj had also been assigned this vault room.

"Don't touch me," Jake ordered.

The Shielding around him flared stronger, forcing his Apotheturgy professor to step backward, still snarling.

"You think you're so clever, Lawrence. Skirting the rules. But you've gone too far this time." The katanoj grinned, gloating. "You'll be expelled this time. Finally."

Jake ignored him, turning his eyes to Veris instead. The dracoling's confidence had fallen away in the aftermath of his attack, especially now as he stood restrained by two teachers Jake only recognized due to occasional sightings in the hall. Trusting his father to ensure no one interrupted, Jake muttered one of his father's mantras under his breath, soft enough only Feels could hear it.

"Never let them see your true weakness. Only the traps you want them to spring."

He locked eyes with Veris, donning a sneer to hide the pain, and tugged slowly on the knife.

True to their word, Feels worked quickly, healing each bit of damage as Jake removed the knife. Each movement sent a sharp slice of pain through his nerves, but he maintained the sneer, his movements slow and deliberate to allow Feels the opportunity they needed for their spellwork. By the time Jake dangled the knife in front of Veris, blood still dripping from the blade, the wound was fully closed.

"I hope this helped whatever you've got going on," he said softly, "because that's the last opportunity you get. These shirts are *expensive*."

Veris gawked at Jake, mouth agape, his stare bouncing between Jake's face and the stained tatters of the uniform shirt at the knife's former point of entry. He attempted to back away, but the teachers held him fast.

He'll listen to you, now, Feels said quietly. *He's not the only one. What you say next decides how this goes. With more than just Veris.*

Inhaling slowly, Jake rubbed the blood from the knife onto his already-ruined uniform shirt before folding the blade and slipping it into his pocket.

"You can't keep a weapon on school property," Professor Darga growled beside him, tail lashing angrily.

"You said I'll be expelled," Jake reminded him. "And the Confederation's attacking. So it doesn't really matter anymore, does it?"

His professor spluttered in frustration, but his words failed him. Jake took the opportunity to stand straighter, projecting his voice as he addressed Veris and, by proxy, the room.

"Listen up. I'm too tired to repeat myself."

If all eyes hadn't been on him before, they were now.

"There's a *war* going on. This isn't the time to fight each other. We need to stick together." He shook his head. "Hiding away in this vault is the closest you've been to a real fight. But I've been out there. I've *seen* it."

He paused to look up for effect, his hands clasped behind his back, before returning his attention to Veris, allowing a sharp edge to his voice. "Yes. I'm not a Freeholder. I'm from the Legion planet of Loxira, and I was there when the Sparnell Armed Forces attacked. I saw my entire village destroyed. My *planet* destroyed. And when the Sparnelli war criminal Admiral Renkash Alenahs led his away team to the surface of the planet to admire what he'd done, they found *me*."

He stepped closer, but rather than attempting to back away, Veris and his friends leaned closer, their attention locked on Jake.

"*Baden* is my home now. You have a *good* planet. I want to stay." He smiled sadly. "I don't want to hurt anyone here, so

I've been holding back. Hiding who I am. What I can do. But make no mistake." He dropped his voice to a mere whisper. "I am here, and Renkash is dead. Remember that, the next time you consider trying my patience."

The stunned silence in the room spoke volumes, although the locket-bound empath rattled off the emotions surrounding them anyway. Even Professor Darga seemed at a loss for what to do, having stepped back to add more space between them, although the set of his jaw warned he wasn't through with Jake yet, merely deciding his best course of action.

Jake silently spun on his heels to return to his father, noting the hints of relief and pride hidden across the necromancer's stoic face.

The room parted to let him pass.

13

Shane watched as the crowd backed away to allow his son passage, the boy's former tormentors now standing with a mix of awe and fear. He himself battled the anger rising inside of him at being forced to watch. Clearly Jake's performance had resolved the bullying situation in some form or another, but now Shane was fighting the urge to rip Veris limb from limb with his bare hands.

Jeb grabbed at the hand gripping his bicep, attempting to pry it loose and free his arm from Shane's grasp. "*Now* can I get involved? *Someone* has to confiscate that knife. You'll be lucky if you keep your job, after…" Jeb's brows furrowed as he grappled with his vocabulary. "*This*."

"I'll handle it," Shane growled, turning his attention to Jeb.

Jeb glared back, briefly, before averting his eyes.

It had been a comfort to note that even in his new body, and without his prior reputation, Shane could still stare those around him into submission. He'd successfully used the skill to prevent Jake's teachers from interfering in his confrontation with Veris, at least until the dracoling had pulled the knife, although he suspected there'd be consequences for that choice later.

Not that he intended to remain to face them. If the Confederation was here to test Baden's defenses, it was best he took Jake elsewhere once the dust settled enough he could do so without attracting too much attention.

Hopefully they'd have enough time to stop by the house first. Sort through whatever was left. Retrieve some dry socks.

"At least let me grab a first aid kit," Jeb offered at last, not quite meeting Shane's eyes.

"Jake's fine," Shane said, his voice turning hard.

But he released the biologist, watching as the biologist scuttled off, until he felt Jake slide to the floor next to him. The boy pressed his locket back into his palm, but didn't let go.

He fixed his son with an orange stare. "And what did you learn?"

Jake smiled sheepishly. "Assumptions are deadly."

"And?" He raised an eyebrow.

Jake sighed. "You can't plan for everything, so stay alert."

"Those are things we've already talked about," Shane admonished, eyes narrowing. "Do you realize how it felt, watching you get hurt like that? Knowing you wouldn't let me help?"

We had it handled.

"And Veris is quite fortunate for that. The next person to try won't survive the attempt. Be sure no one else gains an opportunity to do so."

"Yes, Sir." Jake's response carried the appropriate mix of sincerity and obedience. "I'm sorry."

Shane studied Jake quietly before wrapping his hand around the locket and, upon receiving no resistance from his son, slipped it around his neck and under his shirt. The metal pendant settled comfortably against his chest, and Shane found himself breathing freely once again. Now that he finally had the fae back, he hadn't realized just how much of a void he'd felt in their absence.

"*Never* do that again," he ordered.

Jake's shoulders slouched at the admonishment, his eyes shifting from Shane's to instead study his hands.

"You did well," he added, softening slightly. "Aside from your Shielding. I taught you better than that."

"He surprised me," Jake agreed, risking a glance at his father. "It won't happen again."

"See that it doesn't."

Jake's shoulders slumped further.

I'm the one who failed, Feels said quietly from the locket. *Don't be so hard on him. I misjudged the situation.*

"It's a good thing you've got me," Shane said slowly, reaching to lay a hand on Jake's shoulder. "I've made a lot of mistakes in my day. I'll make sure you don't make the same ones." He sighed. "But you *will* make mistakes."

Jake seemed to consider that for a moment before nodding. He leaned to rest his head on Shane's shoulder but the necromancer shifted, wrapping his arms around the boy and stiffly pulling him into his lap. Jake squirmed briefly at the unexpected affection, but quickly settled into the embrace.

"Father?" He wrapped his arms around Shane's neck, burying his face in Shane's neck. "Thank you. For keeping me safe."

They sat for what felt like an eternity before Jake released his grip, struggling to extract himself. Relaxing his arms, Shane allowed Jake to slide to the seat beside him and rest his head on Shane's shoulder instead.

I'm still angry at you, Feels said. *But you're a good father.*

"Jake is my Purpose," Shane said quietly, surveying the room.

Most of its occupants had shifted their attention toward the throng of teachers and staff huddled around Veris, casting the occasional furtive glance at Jake. Jeb had apparently abandoned his search for the first aid kit, instead talking with several members of Veris' small gang, who appeared animated and excited to answer his questions. And Razick...

The lab tech was still sitting in her corner, her attention riveted on Shane. Catching her eyes, he watched as a triumphant smirk spread across her freckled features, her green eyes challenging him with a stare as intense as his own.

No. He's more than that.

Shane wrapped an arm around Jake, pressing his other hand against the bulge of the locket beneath his shirt. "He's my chance at redemption."

The boy shifted slightly in response, his breath light. Asleep. The adrenaline from earlier must have been too much for him.

You killed your only friend, because of him. You lament the atrocities you've done in your parents' names, but how many have you done in his *name?*

"It's too late for me, Feels," he breathed quietly. "I am who I am. But if I can teach him to be better than me. To be *more* than me..."

You killed me. For him. I did everything you asked and you murdered me and imprisoned me in your locket. Bound me here *so* I can't leave, *ever. You made* certain *of it.*

Shane sighed, pulling Jake closer. "I was afraid Admiral Ky-dell would hunt you down to try and find me. If he couldn't find you, he was less likely to find me." He swallowed, rubbing his thumb around the outer edge of the locket. "But you were my friend. I couldn't bring myself to Shatter you. Keeping you with me seemed the next best thing."

You Shattered my team. They did nothing wrong, except help you.

Swallowing again, he hung his head. "I know."

What more was there to say?

I want my freedom, Grim. I don't want to stay with you because I have to. I want to have the choice. I deserve that.

"You do," Shane agreed, squeezing the locket affectionately.

Please.

"No."

They sat in a heavy silence until Feels finally broke it, their voice carrying a heavy bitterness. *I'm trying to forgive you, but you're making it difficult.*

"Good."

The word was a whisper. He'd never asked for forgiveness, because he'd never deserve it. Not after everything he'd done. Everything he was *still* willing to do, even *knowing* the implications, should the need arise.

Time pressed onward, each minute somehow slower than the next until almost an hour had past, but the fae kept their silence, allowing Shane to wallow in his own emotions uninterrupted. He *wanted* to release his friend, to allow them to slip into the Afterlife, free from himself and everything he represented.

But Admiral Kydell was still out there. Which meant Feels' mere existence was a threat. If the admiral found them, he could find Shane. And if Kydell found Shane...

He shuddered.

Jake stirred from his nap, rubbing his eyes as he sat up. "What time is it? What's the battle like?"

It had been a while since he'd checked. He looked across the room to Razick, her stare still firmly seeking his. "I could look, but that would attract more attention than I'd like right now."

Jake followed his gaze. "Razick?"

Shane nodded. "She's been staring at me since your fight."

"I'll distract her." Jake rose from his seat, poking at the knife hole in his shirt. "Call me when you know."

Shane watched him go, the boy cheerfully waving and shouting across the room at Razick in an effort to pull her attention away from him. Jake had grown up a lot since the fateful day he'd lost his childhood innocence. Shane regretted the loss, particularly his part in it, but one thing was certain.

Jake was going to make his mark on the universe. It was up to Shane to make sure it was a good one.

Razick suitably distracted, Shane centered his magic to ground himself in the moment before sliding his consciousness beyond the Veil.

This is about Jake again, isn't it? Feels asked quietly, their sadness pressing against his own.

"Yes," Shane admitted, his focus currently directed to Baden's primary planetary Shielding.

It was holding, although not for much longer, judging by the power fluctuations. Once it fell, the ground forces would arrive, and it would be up to each city to maintain their own Shielding and defenses.

I miss when it was about us.

"You left."

He hadn't meant for it to sound like an accusation.

You could have come with me, the fae said quietly. *I asked. My Family would have helped.*

Shane shook his head, as if to clear it. "I took the Oath. There's no running from that."

But you did *run. For Jake.*

And he'd paid the price for it. The jagged fissures in his soul served as a constant reminder of the cost of that decision. Of the innocents he'd Shattered on the way, fracturing their souls beyond repair. He'd ended their existence, and any hope of an Afterlife.

"I had no choice."

Was it worth it, Grim? All the destruction you've left in your wake?

He looked to Jake, deeply engrossed in his conversation with Razick.

"Yes."

Void help him, yes. He'd run all over again, cover their tracks as often as he had to, even knowing the cost. Whatever it took, to keep the boy safe. Jake was his Purpose. His reason for existence. And *nothing* would stop him from fulfilling his obligation.

What happened to you, Grim? The empath's sorrow was unmistakable.

"Kydell changed me. Psychomorphation. Twenty three years' worth." He rubbed the back of his neck, casting his attention back beyond the Veil as he reached for the hostile fleet. "I don't have a choice anymore. My mission is clear. Jake is all that matters."

Grim. What did he do to you?

Shane's voice grew quiet. "I don't even know anymore."

14

<YOU WERE RIGHT. HE'S perfect.> Razick grinned, watching the janitor debrief his son from the fight. She'd clearly hit the lottery of potential allies. Between the two of them, Admiral Kydell wouldn't stand a chance.

Jeb's telepathic voice was riddled with concern. <Raz, I don't think you heard me. Lawrence isn't who I thought he was, and we need to stay away from him. Who sends their kid into a situation like that?>

<Someone who knows he can't lose.>

<He saw his own son get stabbed with a knife! And just watched like everything was fine.>

<Everything *was* fine. I don't see if slowing Jake down any.> She observed Shane retrieve the necklace from his son, replacing it around his own neck.

<We're better off without him. He didn't even send backup.>

She shook her head. <But he *did* have backup. Jeb, I know what he was! Lawrence is a TAG! And it looks like at least some of his team came with him when he defected. That pendant isn't for communication, it's a binding talisman!>

She'd met a TAG once, recognized the striped brown canid's cool disdain for those around her as a mark of her role rather than a sign of arrogance. TAGs were battle-hardened necromancers, the leaders and only living members of their assault teams. Called upon in only the most desperate situation, their task was to lead their attendant souls in providing the maximum impact in the shortest time, while surviving as long as possible. They relied on telepathy to serve as the eyes and ears of their soulbound team of deceased battle mages.

The TAG she'd spoken to had been on her seventy-third reincarnation, at least as best as the TAG could remember. If Razick had died in battle she'd have been assigned to the TAG's team, too. One more bodiless soul bound in service to the Sparnelli war machine. The interview had been the beginning of Razick's awakening to the true horrors of her place within the SAF, inspiring her efforts to escape.

Jeb's voice broke her free from her memories. <A TAG? Are you sure?>

<Think about it. He's a loner, but he's also used to command, right? Like, say, leading a Tactical Assault Group?>

<There's lots of command roles. That doesn't mean anything.>

<He admitted to knowing Soul Call and Shielding magic. And he's clearly skilled at defensive martial arts, based on what he's taught Jake.>

All skills needed to excel in the field as a TAG.

Jake brushed her off. <Coincidence. None of those skills are uncommon. The whole *universe* is at war right now! Legion, Confederation, Hydell Order, all at each other's throats for a piece of the Freeholds.> He paused. <And martial arts aren't *that* difficult. I can keep up with you now, in our fighting sessions. And you've had *decades* of training.>

Razick grinned. There was no way she was ever letting him know just how much she held back during those sessions.

<Jeb. You heard what Jake said. After the fight.>

<About how everyone needs to stop fighting their classmates because there's a war going on?> Jeb shook his head, looking up from his interview with one of the onlookers to the fight, a rather animated spotted canid. <And then there's that nonsense about how he killed Admiral Renkash.>

<Admiral Kydell's right hand of vengeance. The timeline fits.>

His eyes widened at her tone. <Raz. What are you saying?>

<Jake says he's Loxiran. Former Legion. Renkash disappeared at Loxira two years ago. Jake enrolled here a month later.>

<Yeah, but you don't seriously believe Jake killed a Sparnelli war hero, do you?> Jeb sounded worried.

<What? Of course not!> She caught Shane's eyes then, holding his orange stare as she grinned in triumph. <His father did.>

<What?>

<He's a TAG, Jeb, I'm telling you! Lawrence and his team killed Renkash. Permanently, or the SAF would have brought him back.>

The janitor broke his eyes away from her, returning to whatever conversation he was holding.

She kept her eyes fixated on him. <And if Lawrence took out Kydell's attack cat, the Black Death himself, he can take on Kydell. I can't believe our good fortune!>

<Raz...> Jeb's tone betrayed his discomfort. <There's no way for you to know that.>

<Jake's coming this way. I'll ask him about the fight. But Jeb... Lawrence just phase shifted. He was in the corner, and then suddenly, for a brief moment, he wasn't.> There was no hiding her excitement now. <It's a less taxing version of the Hyperjump spell. That's how TAGs get into position, they travel close and then phase shift through the Veil for the last step. Jeb! I *know* I'm right!>

Jake was upon her then, his childish smile a stark contrast to his fearsome performance mere moments ago. "Razick!"

His tone carried more force than their usual conversations, and Razick had to smile. *He's trying to distract me from his father. Doesn't know I figured it out already.*

Rather than taking offense, she found it endearing. The boy's loyalty to those he cared about was one of the traits that had earned him her trust, and she knew it extended to more than just her.

<Got to go, Jeb. I'll let you know what I learn.>

Jake slid to the floor by her side, cleverly positioning himself such that she couldn't watch for his father while looking at him.

His voice softened. "Thought I'd let you know I'm okay. In case you were worried."

They sat in a comfortable silence, studying each other, lost in their own thoughts before Razick pointed to the bloody stain on his uniform shirt.

"Yeah," he chuckled, sliding a finger through the hole and wiggling it from the other side. "This shirt's done. Too bad it wasn't one of your experimental ones!" He lifted the shirt's hem and Razick saw only unbroken skin beneath. "I'm still in one piece, though."

She reached out and, when he made no move to stop her, ran her fingers over the skin where his wound should have been. It was smooth to the touch, with no sign of the knife's entry.

"Good Curative Magic," she murmured, the words forming with rusty edges. As she looked up at him, Jake smiled brightly and lowered his shirt. He'd always valued her spoken words, spare as she was with them. He recognized the trust she placed in him, even without understanding the traumas behind her hesitance.

She nodded to his side. "Yours?"

"No." Jake looked away briefly, and Razick recognized his efforts to balance her friendship with his father's secrets. "A friend."

"Of your father's?" she pressed, gently.

"And mine," he added.

She let the silence return, moving her head to observe Veris and his friends, watching out of the corner of her eye as Jake relaxed. Word had clearly gone out about the fight, as the gang was now pleading with the headmaster herself.

Razick raised an eyebrow at Jake.

"Yeah... About that..." Jake scratched his ear. "Just wanted them to leave me alone. Oops."

She laughed silently, and he smiled in return.

"I shouldn't be surprised." His gaze took on a faraway look. "I learned from my father. Of course it turned into more than I wanted."

The silence stretched onward, familiar and comforting with its lack of expectations or demands. After her time in the SAF, not to mention Admiral Kydell's knack of using her own words to find ways to hurt her and isolate her from those she loved, silence had become a welcome friend. She'd always appreciated Jake's acceptance of that silence – of *her* silence – without any demands to fill the void.

But she still had to update her brother. <Jake confirmed someone else healed him. Not him or his father. Jeb, there's not a scratch on him.>

<So you were right.> His brother's voice held defeat. <I'm still not sure we can trust him. Someone that powerful... What is he even *doing* here?>

<Hiding? Like me?> She caught movement and turned ever so slightly, just in time to watch Lawrence briefly blink out of existence before reappearing again. <If he was part of the attack on Baden he'd have done something by now. They'll help us. I just know it.>

She felt Jake squeeze her hand again. "Wish they'd finish out there. I wonder what's going on." He turned to look at his father, half-asleep in the corner across the way. "He was supposed to tell me by now."

She raised an eyebrow. "He knows?"

Jake blushed before leaning closer, conspiratorially. "Promise you won't tell anyone?" He waited for her to nod before continuing. "He's watching the battle. Through the Veil."

And suddenly everything fell into place. He wasn't sleeping. He was *watching*.

She kept her features calm, gathering her words carefully. "You're hiding. From Sparnell."

Jake looked away again, slouching. "Yeah."

She wrapped an arm around him, pulling him close. "Me, too."

They sat in the comfort of the stillness, a haven of peace amidst the turmoil of the shelter vault, hidden from the war torn Void above. Jake leaned into her shoulder, content in the confessions of their shared plight, even though no more words were spoken. Razick watched Lawrence from her seat across the room, carefully thinking through her avenues to broach the topic of Sparnell with the intimidating janitor, when he suddenly sat up and disappeared into the Void…

…only to appear standing directly before her, his arms reaching out for Jake, every movement agitated.

"We have to go."

"What's wrong?" Jake leapt to his feet, clearly worried.

"We have to go. *Now.* It was a diversion. SAF lured all Baden's defenses into the open." He was pacing, his normally impassive face now a conflict of emotions. "There's a whole armada out there now. We don't have much time."

Razick's stomach sank. If Shane's words were true, Baden had no chance at remaining independent. The shelter vault had its own defenses but these were largely nonviolent measures and eventually they, too, would be breached. If the Confederation didn't starve them out first.

Either way… she'd be Admiral Kydell's once more.

<Jeb… I don't think we'll survive this. Lawrence says the Confederation brought a whole armada.> She tried to keep her tone flat, rather than submit to the rising panic. <Whatever happens… Promise me you won't let them take me. Whatever you do, don't let them make me go back. Please.>

<Shit.>

Razick watched as Jake's face hardened.

"I don't want to run anymore."

"Jake," his father protested. "We don't have a choice. I need to keep you safe."

"*You* always said I shouldn't run from my problems," Jake continued, crossing his arms and defiantly jutting out his chin. "I don't want to switch schools."

"After that fight with Veris, you're probably expelled. And your biology professor kindly suggested I'm out of a job after failing to stop you both, so I can't afford to pay for it, either."

"Then we'll convince them to take us back. I finally had a chance at something good here. Please don't make me start all over again."

Shane stopped pacing, looking at his son as if seeing him for the first time. "A whole armada, Jake."

"I want to stay."

To Razick's surprise, after studying his son for a moment, Shane sank to the floor, still seemingly oblivious to her presence. "Okay."

Okay? She marveled. *Is this guy seriously considering taking on an entire armada? By* himself? *Just so his son doesn't have to switch schools?*

She leaned into her link with her brother. <Get over here. We might have a way out after all.>

She watched her brother pull himself away from the throng of teachers and other administrative staff still deciding the aftermath of Veris' fight, then turned her attention back to Shane.

He was in his trance again, hopefully gathering useful intelligence about the invading fleet.

Suddenly he opened his eyes, and Razick found herself unable to interpret his expression. He turned to his son, his words a whisper as he stared, eyes wide.

"It's not just *any* fleet... It's the *Inevitable*."

15

Commander Yiven Alanis pushed against the confines of the tyrellium data crystal currently imprisoning her soul.

Pull yourself together, Alanis. You know how to do this... Don't you?

But every time she thought she remembered the rituals to slip herself past the Veil, just enough to peek at the magical bindings trapping herself within the ship, she found herself floundering.

Get a grip on yourself.

She'd been a Void necromancer for five decades now, and the primary Afterlife Intelligence of the *Inevitable* since her death almost twenty years ago.

You literally carried this entire flagship through the Veil when you Hyperjumped barely a minute ago, she chided herself. *Why are you making this so difficult?*

<Hyperjump complete,> she found herself announcing to the shipboard teleconn, the on-duty Telepath projecting her message across the entire ship.

<Stellar work, as usual, Nav,> Admiral Kydell relayed back, this time on a private telepathic line. <Now conserve your magic. Defensive only.>

Alanis snarled inwardly, attempting to continue her efforts to break free, but Kydell had given an order and she found herself unable to resist.

Damn that wolf. Damn this ship. Damn the whole Confederation.

She'd been so close to freedom. She'd only had two more weeks before her fifty year Soul Oath was set to expire. Just two weeks until the end of her living hell as an Oathbound AI in service to Admiral Kydell. And what had she done?

She'd renewed her Oath, bound herself for a full century this time, merely because the admiral had suggested she do so.

Stupid. Stupid. Stupid. And now I'll never be free.

At one point she'd still been able to resist the canid's influence, even despite his mind altering magic, but sometime after the loss of his precious right-hand katanoj, Vice Admiral Renkash Alenahs, he'd found a way to enhance his powers and tighten his grip.

She was his now, mind and soul, no matter how much of her own considerable power she spent resisting.

If she couldn't use her magic, at least she could watch the battle for the poor planet he'd chosen for annexation into the

Sparnell Confederation this week. Not that she could do anything except join them in mourning their freedom, but at least focusing on the subjugation of someone else would be a distraction from her own.

Baden, she remembered them calling it. *I'm sorry for your loss.*

She stretched her senses, filling her awareness with the whole of the *Inevitable* itself and its many magically augmented sensors and defenses. As much as she hated the SAF, she had to admit she could have done a lot worse than Navigations AI of the *Inevitable*. The ship was the epitome of destructive elegance, a heady mix of technological superiority and engineering design, and before she'd been manipulated into renewing her Oath she'd actually mourned at the thought of allowing someone else to claim her.

Not that it matters now. It's nothing but a fancy prison.

The other bound AI each acknowledged her presence as her awareness approached their respective subsystems, her own bindings the only ones permitted full range of the ship – a necessity for Hyperjumping.

"We jumping again?" Maneuvering asked, the AI preparing her own telekinetic engines to support the action.

"Just stretching, Helm," she found herself reassuring. "But keep an eye on the *Subjugation*. Telemetry says they're drifting a little close."

Better not scratch my paint.

"Roger." Alanis felt the ship adjust its positioning to compensate for her observation. "And thanks."

She moved onward until she could claim awareness of the entire hull and its full arsenal of equipment before centering her mind on the inputs from the ship's countless sensors, compiling their data into an image of the battle. The defenders were heavily outnumbered, their small collection of surviving ships already battered from their battle with Kydell's advanced scouting fleets. When the admiral had received word from the preliminary scouts as to the weakened state of the Baden defense fleet, he'd ordered a second scouting party into the assault. Finding this did not elicit any additional response he'd sent the entire armada, led by the *Inevitable* herself, in to finish the takeover.

Alanis shifted her perceptions, focusing on the lesser monitored sensors. Baden's planetary Shielding was beginning to crumble in places, and didn't even seem to have a necromantic component anymore.

I'll bet Kydell wishes he hadn't sent his personal TAG on that political mission this morning, she smirked.

The frigid canid would have made short work of their remaining Shielding generators.

The *Inevitable*'s own Shielding was holding full and steady, although their Shield mage had opted for ease and convenience over accuracy. The telekinetic engines, including a section of the maintenance tunnel wrapped within the nacelles, had once again been left outside the Shielding, exposed to the chaos of the battle.

It's a wonder nobody's ever taken them out, with how often he leaves them unprotected, Alanis mused. Quite fortunate for the politically connected Shield mage, though.

She switched focus again, this time narrowing in on the necromantic sensor on the ship, intended to assist her during Hyperjumps, or detecting other incoming ships. Kydell wouldn't let her use her own magic, but perhaps she could use the sensor to help her break her own soulbinding. If nothing else, the task would take her mind off things. Including the fact a Void necromancer of her expertise had somehow forgotten how to break from a beginner's binding spell.

Silently reciting her usual litany of curses against her manipulative superior officer, Alanis settled into a personal link with the sensor, adjusting its settings to look beyond the Veil...

And caught a fleeting flash of a familiar soul. *No... It* couldn't *be.*

She stretched the sensor to its capacity, hoping to repeat the sighting, but to not avail.

Mind's playing tricks on me. He was Shattered at Loxira. Same as the rest of the away team.

She remembered Admiral Kydell's desperate efforts to revive each missing soul of the away team in turn, hunting for answers on what had happened to the two most prized members of his Collection. He'd even ordered her into the search but there'd been no sign of any of them in the Afterlife, and the tethers on the Oathbound – the violently bloodthirsty Vice Admiral

Renkash and his dutifully devoted second-in-command, Commodore Lawson Zane – had hung empty.

Good riddance. She turned her attention back to her own Oath tether, and the task of analyzing the bindings tying her firmly to the ship. *I have enough nightmares of my own.*

Some souls were best left Shattered.

16

Shane blinked, not quite believing what he'd seen.

"I know that ship. I know her secrets." He turned to face Jake, faintly registering Razick's eyes boring into him, but far past caring. "If I can take the *Inevitable*…"

"So we can beat the armada?" Jake grinned. "I don't have to go to a new school?"

Shane felt the adrenaline coursing through his veins, his mind running through possible scenarios and plans of attack, just as he'd been trained. "Yes. This is doable. Not easy! But doable. I can do this."

He wasn't sure if he was reassuring Jake or himself. He supposed it didn't matter.

"You'll need help."

Shane jumped as Jeb's voice came from behind, interrupting his thoughts.

"I have help." He caressed the lump of the locket through his coveralls.

With this? Yes. I'll help, however I can, Feels answered, their reply accompanied by a surge of anger, echoed in Shane's own thoughts. *Our former admiral has a lot to answer for.*

"Razick and I would like to help, too." The biologist motioned to his sister.

Shane studied them carefully. "Not much use for a biologist in space. Not a lot of plants to cast Agrokinesis on. Or draw power from, for that matter."

Jeb shrugged. "I'm also good at Telepathy. I know a little field medicine. And an extra pair of hands might come in handy."

"Telepathy?" Shane noted Jake's sudden interest, and remembered an earlier conversation with his son. "Think you could teach Jake?"

"Can't you just... teach him yourself?"

"Not one of my skills," Shane admitted. "Never found the time." He turned to Razick, her face suddenly dark. "And you? What skills do you have?"

He staggered backward under the sudden feeling of oppressive nothingness, his perpetual connection to the Afterlife suddenly interrupted. He reached out with his magic but found no response as only silence echoed back. Without the infinite vastness of the Void beyond the Veil he became intimately aware of the oppressive walls of the vault, buried several stories beneath Baden's surface. He gripped his chest, heart pounding.

We're in an Antimagic field of some kind, Feels informed him calmly, the mechanisms of the locket immune to the effects due to its Space Defense Legion manufacture, and their reliance on more mechanical technologies. *I'm here. I'm with you. You're not trapped.*

He vaguely felt Jake's hands grab at his arm as the boy slipped a shoulder underneath to help steady him, as he grasped at his coveralls to undo the buttons and gain more space to breathe.

The feeling ended abruptly, the infinite Void crashing back into his mind with the welcome exuberance of an old friend returned from a long trip away.

He closed his eyes, centering his breathing and savoring the caress of Feels' calming Psychomorphation, before opening his eyes to snarl back at Razick, jabbing his finger in her direction.

"You keep that Antimagic away from me."

She smiled by way of apology, holding her palms open toward him.

He turned back to Jeb. "I thought you two were pacifists."

"The Confederation is threatening our home. You say you can save it. Razick insists on helping, and I insist on helping her."

Shane studied them both. Certainly not the best mix of skills for a boarding party, but Jake trusted them and Shane was beginning to think he might, too. At least as far as saving Baden was concerned. Razick's Antimagic – a temperamental but useful magic that absorbed anything cast against of equal or lesser power to the Antimagic itself – would be useful in disrupting the ship systems to avoid discovery, and quite possibly to break through the ship's Shields as well, while Jeb's Telepathy would allow them to split up if needed while still remaining in contact.

Not to mention, he'd have better odds of success than if he went alone. Which meant a better chance of keeping Jake safe.

"Fine. You can come."

He'd have preferred someone more useful – memories of Kane Family battle mages, the best in the SAF, came to mind – but he'd have to work with who he had.

He watched as Razick thrust her prototype armor at her brother, followed by a giant glaring contest, before Jeb sighed and allowed her to draw him away to don the outfit. The outer layer had been cut almost like a fancy dinner jacket, complete with buttons crafted to imitate cufflinks. Between Shane's janitorial coveralls and water soaked socks, Jeb's armored former suit, and Razick's labcoat, they'd be quite the sight storming the corridors of an SAF flagship.

He turned to Jake. "Let me talk to Headmaster Corbin, make sure you're looked after while I'm gone. She'll want to talk about your fight with Veris, too. Hopefully she'll withhold her judgment until after the battle."

Jake jutted his chin in defiance. "I'm coming with you."

"War is no place for a child," Shane growled back. He'd been conscripted at sixteen, young enough to completely derail his life. He wouldn't risk the same for his son.

"So you're going to leave me here, alone, on a planet under attack? The last time Sparnell attacked my planet, Mom died."

He crossed his arms, narrowing his eyes as he glared up at the necromancer. "I'm safer with *you*. You *promised* to always protect me."

Shane closed his eyes, flashing back to the aftermath of the attack on Loxira. The flattened cities, the dead littering the streets, the Confederation efforts to ensure no one survived. Utter destruction, at the direct orders of Renkash himself. The handiwork of a Sparnelli war criminal.

Never again.

He attempted to shake the memory from his mind, to fight against the overwhelming urge to bring Jake into the middle of a war zone simply so he could defend the boy personally.

"I'll be distracted. Looking out for you," he attempted, careful not to meet his son's eyes. "I won't perform at my best."

"You'll be *better*," Jake insisted firmly. "Because you can't afford to lose."

Shane's lips twisted into a snarl, attempting to break his thoughts free even as his conditioning narrowed his focus. His purpose was to protect Jake. He needed Jake with him. There was no other way.

Resentment rose like bile in Shane's mouth, but he couldn't fault his adopted son. The boy knew what he wanted, and had learned how to get it. There was nothing wrong with using all the tools one had available to ensure the desired outcome.

The problem was he was so obvious about it. The boy made no pretense of hiding it, which only served to highlight just how easy Shane was to manipulate, when one knew where to press. Each use of Kydell's conditioning to further Jake's goals merely rubbed salt in the wounds of Shane's past service to the psychomorphic canid, and just how much of himself he'd lost in the process.

Sighing, he crouched to meet Jake's eyes, one hand on each of the boy's shoulders as he poured the entirety of his intensity into his stare. "This is war. If I give you an order, you'll follow it. You can ask me why later, when you're safe, but starting right now you do what I say, no hesitation. Understood?"

Jake nodded solemnly as Shane swallowed.

"You're going to see things no child should ever have to see. You'll see me do some things that–"

Jake's face held perfect innocence. "You mean like when you took out that whole Sparnelli away team so they wouldn't kill me like they did Mom?"

Shane felt his fists begin to clench at the reminder, his fingernails digging into Jake's shoulders. "Son..."

"Or the time when we were hiding and someone found us and you–"

"Jake..." The name was a warning.

"Or how about when–"

"Stop." Shane summoned his full years of command into his voice. He noted Jeb's flinch, but his son stood firm, grinning triumphantly as he watched his father.

Shane glared back, but it made no difference.

Still smiling, Jake leaned forward, wrapping his arms around Shane's neck to bury his face in his chest, and suddenly the guilt and anger melted away. This was who Shane was protecting. Everything for Jake. Jake *was* everything.

"I'm sorry I'm such a miserable excuse for a father."

Jake clung tighter, and Shane noted a slight catch to his voice as he spoke. "I'm sorry. Thank you. For looking out for me. For *staying*."

"I promised I'd protect you, but I keep dragging you into these situations..."

"You don't go looking for them." Jake pushed away to look into Shane's eyes. "It follows us. It's who we are. It's what we've already been through. You can't change the past, but..." He paused to wave his arms toward the inhabitants of the room, the loud clatter from before now replaced with hushed whispers and fearful sighs. "That doesn't mean they have to see what we've seen. We can help. *I* can help. Let me help."

Shane reached a tentative finger to wipe a tear from Jake's cheek, marveling at the boy's resilience and resolve. "You've had to grow up too fast. I never wanted this for you. I want you to have a better life than mine."

Jake grabbed Shane's arm, leaning into his palm, the storm in his dark green eyes shifting to resolve. "I do. I have *you*."

Pulling away, Shane rose to his feet, setting his shoulders. "I'm not the only one you have to convince on this. Call your mother. You remember the spell?"

Jake nodded.

"Good. You do that, and I'll..."

His voice trailed off as he looked up, catching the eyes of the angry blue dracoling standing before them.

Veris.

"You have something that belongs to me."

17

Veris swallowed, hoping the janitor and his son couldn't sense the fear behind his outward bravado.

"You have my knife."

He held out his hand, hopeful for a response, but the pair simply stared at him as if expecting him to say more. *Shit.*

When Jake Cartwright Lawrence had enrolled two years ago, he'd seemed an easy target. The quiet kid who always kept to himself. Always did his homework but never the way he was supposed to. His dad was the janitor, for crying out loud. And the human just took it, stoic faced, never lashing back.

How was he to know Jake was actually the toughest kid in the school?

He set his shoulders, turning his attention to Jake's dad. "I never meant to hurt him. Sir."

Why had he added the 'Sir' on the end? The man was the *janitor.*

Jake's dad raised an eyebrow. "We both know that's not true. You stabbed him in the stomach."

Veris winced, the sharp knife of terror running down his spine at the janitor's tone, but managed to recover himself enough to meet the man's eyes. "He insulted Dad! Said he went missing because of me!"

The janitor turned to stare at his son. "Jake, is this true?"

"No!" To his credit, Jake appeared sick at the thought. "He said if you cared about me you'd be helping. So I asked where *his* father was."

"He's been missing for *months*." Veris hadn't intended to talk about his dad, but the topic had been broached and now the words were flowing with no chance to stop them. "On a scouting patrol, for the Baden Defense Force. They keep telling Mom he's not dead, just missing, but..."

He shrugged, helplessly.

"They're probably right," Jake's dad said quietly, although any relief Veris felt at those words disappeared quickly at the janitor's expression. "SAF prefers information. Before they attack."

Veris inhaled sharply. "You mean they..."

He couldn't finish. By the look in the janitor's eyes, he didn't have to.

"I want my knife back," he managed, holding out his hand again, while avoiding their eyes. "It was Dad's. I only brought it to school because it helps me concentrate, to have something of his. To know he's not *gone*, just not... here."

"Veris..."

He risked a glance at Jake, and found the boy avoiding his eyes instead, the knife outstretched in one hand.

"I don't want to take your things. I'm sorry about your dad. But won't you get in trouble if I give it back?"

"They've already expelled me," Veris said with a sad smile, scuffing his foot along the vault floor. "So it doesn't really matter anymore, does it?"

He wrapped his fingers around the weapon, his nerve calming slightly at the familiar shape of the thin, folding knife. "They, uh, decided to expel you, too," he said, quietly. "They were all arguing about who would be the one to tell you. After they told me. I'm sorry."

He watched as Jake and his father exchanged glances.

"You'll fix it," Jake told his father firmly. "You always do."

The janitor turned toward Veris, opening his mouth as if to speak, when suddenly he paused, his attention locking onto the knife with an expression Veris couldn't place. Looking up sharply, Shane fixed Veris with a focused glare. "Where did you get this?"

"I already told you. It was Dad's. My grandfather gave it to him."

Jake's dad seized the hilt, and after a brief internal struggle Veris allowed him to take it.

"Son, remember when I told you that behind the Veil there's a whole second universe, for those who decide to ascend rather than returning to the mortal planes?"

Veris furrowed his brows, attempting to follow this unexpected conversation, and figure out what it had to do with his knife.

"A long time ago, people used to find ways to bring back metals and work them into our own, to make a blade that can cut not just the body but the very soul of a person." He slid the safety latch downward and extended the knife, studying it. The thin, double edged blade glistened menacingly in the lamps of the vault. "I'd always thought it was a legend."

"Sir?" Veris questions. "It's... it's just a penknife."

"That's what it looks like on this plane," Jake's dad growled angrily. "But if you'd stabbed Jake in the wrong spot..."

Veris jumped back as the familiar silver of the blade suddenly developed veins of deep blues and purples, an otherworldly aura now radiating from the metal. He blinked and the vision dissolved, replaced again by an ordinary silver.

"You're fortunate you missed his soul, or nothing would have saved yours." Jake's father re-folded the knife, re-engaging the safety latch before handing it to Jake. "I'm keeping this. It's not safe with you."

Veris swallowed. He didn't even *want* to consider the implications behind that threat. "And it's safer with you?"

Jake's father smiled cruelly. "No. And that's exactly why I need it."

The whole room shook then, dust and dirt falling from the ceiling above. "Family Disown them. The Shields are failing. I need to finish planning. Jake, Call your mother."

And with that, the man was gone, disappearing from view before reappearing beside Professor Jeb and one of the lab technicians, engaging them in conversation.

Veris looked at Jake awkwardly. "So, uh... Can I have my knife back?"

The boy shifted his weight, his attention shifting between the knife and Veris. "My father told me to keep it."

"It's not yours."

"No, but..." Jake glanced at his dad as if to check the man was still busy, before turning back to Veris. "We're going to save Baden."

Narrowing his eyes, Veris leaned into his natural Anemancy, attempting to pick up words from Jake's dad's conversation, but no matter how he shifted his ear fins or focused the air around them, he came up blank.

He turned back to Jake. "You're bluffing."

Jake shrugged, sliding the knife back into his pocket. "I don't want to switch schools. I told him to fix it. And he's taking me with him."

Veris' eyes widened. Jake was being serious. "What can I do?"

"Morale is half the battle," Jake answered right away, closing his eyes as if reciting something from memory. He opened them again, staring at Veris. "Right now people need to know everything will be okay. And the best way to show it will be okay is to act like it will be okay, and help people keep their usual schedules."

"So... You want me to act like this is normal?" Veris asked incredulously.

"Yeah. Sing. Play. Do normal kid stuff. And help the grownups when they need it." Jake blinked slowly. "When Mom died, my father made sure I didn't just stop doing things, even though I wanted to. We had to hide from the Sparnell Confederation, so I couldn't do everything I used to, but he still made sure I ate, and he played with me and we sang songs..."

Jake's face grew thoughtful, and Veris forced himself to suppress a laugh at the thought of the stern-faced janitor playing games.

"I was angry at him for making me do those things," Jake continued quietly. "I didn't want to do them. But it helped."

Veris nodded. "We can do that. Protect people from getting lost in the worrying."

Jake nodded. "Exactly."

"Protect their hope. I can do that!" Veris grinned proudly, then looked away, swallowing nervously. Speaking of hope... "You think you'll find Dad?"

"I don't know," Jake answered honestly. "Maybe?"

"Keep the knife," Veris said firmly. "I'd rather have Dad. You send him home, okay? Please?"

"If we find him," Jake promised. "I need to Call Mom, first. Let her know where we're going."

Another thought crossed Veris' mind, and he wrung his hands, watching Jake carefully. "Do you think you could teach me that spell? I know your dad says he's probably alive, but just in case..."

"The dead don't always answer." Veris felt Jake grab his hands and squeeze. "But you can help me Call Mom, and I'll show you how to do it."

18

Jeb frowned. <I look ridiculous.>

Razick grinned back. <You look great. I knew it would fit you.>

<Raz...> He tugged at the imitation cufflinks. <We're trying to hijack a ship, not sneak into a fancy dinner party.>

Not that I'm well equipped for either of those scenarios.

His sister surveyed him again, tugging and adjusting the fit of the reinforced fabrics. <I had intended the prototype as civilian protection. Wasn't going to suggest it to the Baden Defense Force until after I knew it worked. Figured I'd make it look nice in the meantime.>

<If you were trying to make it blend in, you did a poor job of it.>

<Maybe I just like the look of my brother in a good suit!> She laughed, and Jeb couldn't help but smile in return. It had been a long time since he'd genuinely seen her laugh.

And yet... <Why am I the one wearing this thing? You're the battle mage.>

<Because I'm the battle mage.> Raz made one last adjustment and stepped back, admiring her handiwork. <I fight better when I know my little brother's safe.>

Jeb mulled on that, turning to watch as Shane held a heart to heart with his son. He wondered at how it felt, leaving a family member behind, not knowing if he'd survive to return.

<Raz... Why didn't you tell him? Why won't you let *me* tell him?>

She moved to stand beside him, her eyes also fixed on the Lawrences. <You're the one who keeps reminding me we don't know who he is. I thought you didn't trust him, after that fight?>

<Minutes ago you were convinced he's a TAG.>

<That was before he mentioned he didn't know Telepathy.> She sighed. <TAGs need Telepathy, or their Tactical Assault Group is blind. So he couldn't be one.>

Jeb observed Veris shuffle closer to Shane and his son, shoulders set for confrontation. He wondered if the school had decided on the repercussions for earlier, or if the status of the battle above had forced everything on hold.

He turned to his sister. <Why don't you just ask him yourself?>

<Why haven't you?> She crossed her arms in front of her chest. <*You're* the one he talks to.>

<I guess...> Jeb scratched his head. <Maybe I've been afraid of the answer. What if I don't like it?>

<At this point, we've committed. You ask. If he answers, then I'll tell him.>

They stood in silence, watching as the conversation with Veris grew heated. Jeb broke the quiet first. <I'm beginning to think that man isn't afraid of anything.>

<You didn't see it?> Razick's voice was soft in his mind. <When I cast the Antimagic field?>

<He's a powerful mage. Clearly has some spell or another working all the time, he noticed yours right away.> Jeb scratched his chin thoughtfully. <Nothing strange about that, though.>

<That was fear, Jeb.> Her voice was quiet. <I recognized the panic in his eyes. It's the same I see in mine most mornings. After the dreams.>

Jeb reached out to grab her hand. She'd been having nightmares every night since her escape from the SAF. This was the closest she'd ever come to talking about them, and whenever he'd brought it up she'd refused to even acknowledge the conversation much less accept his offer to share her burden via his Telepathy.

But I can let her know she's not alone. That I'm here for her. And maybe that's enough.

<He's seen things, Jeb,> she continued. <He has more ghosts than *I* do.>

<We *did* establish he's a necromancer. So that's a given.>

Jeb's observation brought a smile back to Razick's face, warming his own heart in the process. She pushed him away playfully and he responded in kind, same as when they were kids. Unlike their childhood, though, this time she was faster, reflexes honed by her time and training.

His playful punch missed its mark, instead striking nothing but the air where she once stood.

<Hey, no fair!> He waved his arms in the air, grinning. <Stand still so I can catch you!>

She laughed, the warm, genuine laugh he hadn't heard since before her conscription, and for those brief moments Jeb didn't care that they were stuck inside a shelter vault while the Confederation rained raw military power down upon their planet. His carefree sister was back. And if she could come back, even for a moment, she was still in there somewhere, trapped inside the war-hardened exterior.

The room shook then, battered by a blast from the battle outside, and the moment was gone.

<The Shields!> Razick's eyes widened as she turned to Jeb. <We're losing time.>

"We need to be quick and efficient." Shane appeared beside them, face grim. "I can get us up there, into the *Inevitable*. Once we break through her Shields we'll make our way straight to the AI server."

"Not the bridge?" Jeb asked, confused.

"No." Shane shook his head, dark hair cascading across his eyes at the sudden movement. "The AI are the souls of the ship

– literally. We have them, we have the ship, and once we have the *Inevitable* we can turn her against the rest of the fleet. Hopefully do enough damage that Baden can pick off the pieces."

<His logic is sound.> Razick's telepathic voice carried a heavy measure of respect. <Still a massive undertaking. No guarantee of success.>

Jeb nodded. <We have to try.> His sister needed this, whatever happened. And he'd promised himself to stand by her, wherever those needs led them.

"Once we're on the ship, I'll have to conserve my Imperium," Shane continued. Jeb noticed his confidence falter briefly, but the necromancer recovered. "I'll have to fight the ship's AI, past the Veil. She'll be tired from the Hyperjump here, but I can't rely on that. Which means it's up to you to get us there safely, to conserve my magic reserves." He raised an eyebrow. "Are you two up for that?"

<You going to tell him or should I?> Jeb eyed his sister.

<Ask him first,> came the reply.

<Raz...> Jeb sighed. <You owe me.>

He steeled his resolve. "Lawrence... Who are you, exactly?"

The janitor grew quiet, turning toward the small crowd scattered about their room of the shelter vault. "We all have our secrets. You haven't been upfront with me, either. But all that matters right now is keeping Baden safe." He turned back to them, his gaze questioning. "You leave me my secrets, and I'll leave you yours. Can you get me safely to the AI server room or not?"

Jeb watched Raz nod. <We'll get him there, Jeb. But if he won't tell us who he is, we won't tell him what I was.>

Shane caught Razick's nod as well. "Good. Once the AI are dealt with…" He wrung his hands, turning to Jeb. "I need to ask you a favor."

Jeb furrowed his brows. "What kind of favor?"

"Nothing against your morals. Don't worry about that." Shane gave a sad smile. "But if something happens to me… I need you to keep Jake safe."

<What isn't he saying?> Raz narrowed her eyes, but the necromancer continued, unprompted.

"Once I defeat the AI, I'll have to take her place. The ship needs someone in that role. I'll do everything I can from that point to help you clear the SAF and turn the *Inevitable*'s firepower onto the rest of the armada, but I'll have to do it from inside the ship's systems."

Jeb furrowed his brows. "What do you mean?"

"I mean I'll bind my soul into the ship." Shane scowled. "I mean I'll be dead."

"But why?" Jeb pushed. "And why you?"

"I'm the only one who can do it. The *Inevitable* needs a Void necromancer as the primary AI, or the whole ship is useless. And I don't get the impression either of you fit that description."

<Void necromancer?> Raz raised her telepathic voice in alarm, her attention darting between Shane and Jeb. <They just Hyperjump ships around. They're *not* trained for combat.>

<Maybe this one is? He was ready to take on the armada solo, before we volunteered,> Jeb reminded.

And he has no idea what Raz can do.

<Must be more to it,> Raz agreed, cautiously. <The ones I knew were lazy and selfish. Promoted too high, and *spoiled*, just because they can steal magic from the stars or some such nonsense. Don't even have to learn it. They're *born* that way.>

<He's a lot of things,> Jeb said slowly. <But he doesn't seem lazy. Or selfish.>

As if to accent Jeb's point, Shane's voice grew soft. "Besides... The *Inevitable* was built for me. Optimized for me. When I died, that ship was my intended Afterlife. If we want to succeed at this..."

He met Jeb's gaze again, and for a moment the biologist could see the regret and darkness hidden within the necromancer's mind.

"It has to be me."

19

JEB LOOKED LIKE HE wanted to say more, but Shane shook his head. Jake was on his way back, and while Shane had made a vow to never lie to the boy, this was a truth he wasn't yet ready to share.

"What did she say?"

"It's okay, as long as I stay with you and..." Jake tapped his chest in their silent signal to indicate Feels.

Shane nodded understanding before turning to face the rest of his ragtag team. "Alright. Looks like we're ready."

He grasped Jake's hand, pulling the boy toward him, and Jake responded by clinging to his side and grinning upward expectantly.

Releasing his grip, Shane turned to the others, arms outstretched. "We'll have to hold hands and group close. Use less Imperium that way."

"Wait." Jeb turned to Jake. "He is *not* coming with us."

"He is." Shane caught Jeb's eyes with his own. "His mother and I agree on this. He's safer with me. We don't have time to argue."

As if to underscore his words, the vault shook again, sending more dust and dirt cascading down from the rafters above. Shane watched as Jeb and Razick turned to look at each other before Razick shrugged her shoulders and moved beside him.

And with that, Jeb smiled nervously, joining them as directed to grasp hands and bunch together into an awkward press of limbs and unspoken secrets. Shane felt fear begin to lick his consciousness, rebelling at the close proximity of Jeb and Razick, but pushed it back and opened himself fully to the unlimited expanse of the Void. He felt his mind calm, soothed and rocked by the rolling waves of power, before turning his attention to meditate upon the press of people surrounding him until he was certain he held them all in his mind.

He slipped beyond the Veil and into the higher dimensions of the Afterlife, shifting reality around them and bending the space between his boarding party and their destination, until the distance between them no longer held meaning. Now aligned with their intended target, he gently returned them to the land of the living.

Their exit point was a cramped alcove in the maintenance tunnel adjacent to the *Inevitable*'s telekinetic engines. It was a tight squeeze, and if not for the fact they'd huddled together before the transfer, they may not have been able to fit.

Shane surveyed their immediate surroundings before pointing to the passageway ahead. "The ship's Shielding actually starts right here. Lazy Shield mage never extends it."

This had been a frequent topic of contention in his time on the *Inevitable*, but today Shane was grateful it had never been resolved.

He turned to Razick. "We'll need to get through here before we can access the rest. Perhaps you could use your Antimagic to make an opening? Just be careful. We don't want to alert the Shield mage we're here, so you'll have to–"

Razick shook her head, pointing behind him, and Shane spun, prepared to meet the oncoming threat.

Instead he saw Jake, the boy's hands pressed lightly against the invisible Shielding, an intense concentration on his face.

"Jake, what are you–"

"My school project," he grunted. "Help?"

Jeb was faster, stepping forward to lay a hand on Jake's shoulder. "I'm here."

The two worked together, largely in silence. After several minutes they'd successfully altered the Shielding enough to allow passage, rerouting the physical protections of the Shield to bypass a small section of the corridor.

"That kid never ceases to surprise me," Shane muttered to himself. "He's going to change the universe someday."

You taught him well, Feels answered slowly. *He's a smart kid, and you've always supported* him.

Shane flinched at the accusation in the last word. "Feels..."

"Are you coming or what?" Jake asked, now standing on the other side of the Shield. "You always said it's bad to linger."

"How'd you do that?" the necromancer asked, following Razick through the gap before turning to watch Jeb and Jake quickly and carefully allow it to close behind them.

"Would have been faster, with my crystal," Jake grumbled, shoving his hands in his pockets. "But the headmaster took it."

"You'll have to teach me, sometime," Shane said by way of answer, squeezing past Razick to take the vanguard.

He paused, listening, before turning as best he could in the tight space to address Jake, who'd adopted a position directly behind him.

"We'll have to be quiet from this point on. Can't afford to fight our way to the AI, so we'll need to avoid discovery as long as we can. Follow my lead, and tread quietly."

"Now that we're inside the Shields, can't we just Hyperjump there?"

Shane smiled at Jake's astute question as they made their way single file through the passageway. The tunnel was tight but well maintained, a credit to the meticulous standards of the Confederation war machine.

"Those touched by the Veil always recognize their own. If the *Inevitable*'s AI is still who I think it is, she'd find us as soon as I tried, now that we're inside her Shielding." It was risky enough Shane still kept a part of his mind open to the Void, but he'd be no use to anyone if he had a panic attack due to the tight walkway, so the gamble was necessary. "She's also quite skilled at blocking jumps, so there's a good chance it wouldn't even work."

He watched Jake's expression blossom understanding before turning to the others, holding his finger to his lips in a call for silence. His companions nodded understanding, Razick promptly dropping into a stealthy crouch reminiscent of some kind of field training. Shane filed the discovery away to ruminate on later.

They continued stealthily onward until Shane spotted the end of the tunnel itself. Here was where the path would grow difficult. Ahead lay their shortcut to the primary Afterlife Intelligence server, an entrance to the Portal Transit System central to all Sparnelli capital ships, while the open doorway to their right represented the first real hurdle to remain undetected. Catching murmurs of conversation from around the corner, Shane motioned for Jake to hold his position, resisting the urge to use his Necromancy to peek around the corner.

But Feels had him covered. *I'd say... three people? Ahead and to your right. Happy, tired, bored, amused. No sign they've noticed you yet.*

Shane rubbed his thumb over the locket in gratitude before inching forward, rotating to peer carefully into the engine maintenance workshop. The left hand wall was covered with lockers labeled with crew names and subsystems, depending upon whether they held personal belongings or specialized equipment. A cream-furred katanoj Sub-Officer, denoted by the thick single silver stripe on the shoulders of her brown uniform shirt, was busily bouncing a rune assembly absent-mindedly in her clawed hand, her attention on someone else beyond Shane's line of sight. He could make out three distinct voices now, deep in discussion about a friendly game of chance played the night before, and mainly focused on teasing guesses at how many times each had cheated to tip the dice in their favor. These were telekinetic mages, trained for ship maintenance but still potentially lethal in a fight. Shane and his team could not afford mistakes.

The seconds ticked onward until Shane was certain the maintenance crew was deep within their discussion. Readying himself, he lightly sprinted across the doorway to reach the safety of the other side.

He spun lightly to observe the other two inhabitants of the room, still unaware of his presence. A blue-scaled dracoling bearing the rank of Senior Sub-Officer stood busily greasing one of the large wrenches used to replace engine runes, her attention drawn by the initial maintenance worker. Shane's experience labeled her the commanding officer of Maneuvering's branch of the Maintenance Department, reporting directly to both the Maneuvering and Maintenance AIs.

A vibrant purple fae, back to the door, wings folded neatly against their back, busied himself actively carving Runework replacements at a cluttered workbench running the full length of the aft bulkhead. Shane guessed him to be another enlisted of some level, merely based upon his knowledge of the usual staffing choices in ship maintenance. Unlike the larger bipedal species, fae stood mere inches tall and rarely wore clothing, much less uniforms. The SAF assigned them hats – name and rank embroidered on the dainty headpieces, as if anyone but an Advanced Scout would be able to read the tiny lettering – but most refused to wear them, claiming they required all six hands for their work and couldn't afford to waste any on holding a hat in position. From what Shane could see from the doorway, this fae also subscribed to those beliefs.

A pair of maintenance pods hung strategically on the far end of the workshop, open and waiting.

He motioned the all clear to Jake who began to make his way across the opening when suddenly the juggled rune assembly clattered to the floor, rolling to a stop in the doorway. The SAF crewmembers' teasing jokes about their coworker forgetting how Telekinesis worked slammed to an abrupt halt as all eyes in the room locked on Jake, frozen in the hatchway.

You've been spotted.

True to her SAF training, the team's senior officer launched her wrench at Jake, its momentum boosted to lethal heights by her own Telekinesis. Shane reacted on pure instinct, phasing beyond the Veil and bending the mortal plane to shift the wrench's trajectory with one hand, grasping the non-commissioned officer's heart in the other. The wrench slammed into the bulkhead behind them before clattering to the ground, sending a shuddering boom throughout the rest of the ship.

Immediate crisis averted, Shane stepped into the doorway, still holding the Senior Sub-Officer's heart as she clutched her chest and collapsed to the ground.

He raised his brow. "Anyone else?"

The room's remaining occupants wasted no time accelerating themselves towards one of the maintenance pods, triggering a silent alarm as they launched into the Void. The main lights dimmed quickly, replaced with the slow-blinking red of the alert, as Razick pushed past her brother to lunge into the room.

Shane held her back with his arm. "Unless you know Telekinesis yourself, there's no point trying to stop them. We'll have the rest of the ship chasing after us soon enough."

They felt more frightened than anything, Feels observed. *Felt a lot of fear from you, too, for a moment. You okay?*

Razick stared at Shane as if she was about to say something, but shook her head and stalked back to her brother instead. Sliding to the floor, Shane wrapped his free arm around Jake as the boy leaned into the hug, shaking.

Jeb glared in Shane's direction, his eyes fixated on the heart still clutched in Shane's hand. "What the hell was that? What kind of person *are* you?"

Shane shrugged, his focus still on Jake. "I'm a problem solver. We had a problem." He raised his hand, the heart resting on his palm. "I solved it."

"But was that really necessary?" Jeb's face was pale in the slow blinking of the alert lighting.

"You're the pacifist," Shane pointed out. "Not me."

"But in front of your son?" Jeb floundered, looking toward Razick as if for agreement, but she shrugged.

"He's seen worse."

Having regained his composure, Jake pushed free of the hug, blinking slowly at his father. "I had my Shielding up. I'll be okay."

By his tone, Jake wasn't certain himself of the truth of those words, but the ruse was clearly important to him.

Shane rose, nodding faintly in acknowledgement to the unspoken request, and returned his attention to the room. Walking to the fallen enlisted officer, his features softened as he crouched once more, reverently placing her heart on her chest and crossing her arms over the still warm organ.

Rising, he motioned them back to the doorway. "They know we're here. Our timeline just got a lot shorter. We can't afford to linger."

Jake smiled slightly at that, slipping his fingers between Shane's. Shane squeezed back in reassurance, his thoughts racing. The *Inevitable*'s Navigations AI had likely spotted them by now, and he'd need every advantage if he wanted to survive her attention.

"Jake? I need to borrow your knife."

20

ALANIS MUTTERED HER FRUSTRATIONS, her attention consumed by repeated failures to break any of her bindings. She *recognized* the firm binding spell, *understood* what she needed to do to break free, and yet despite everything she attempted she couldn't slip from Kydell's conditioning. She'd spent almost five decades under his direct influence, the remaining duration of her Oath transferred to the canid admiral at his request after her original superior, Admiral Margold, was found guilty of treason.

She'd never trusted the charge, particularly since all the evidence traced back to then-Commodore Kydell himself. Not to mention the way Margold had disappeared abruptly and under suspicious circumstances. Margold's successor, Commodore Trujix, had been implicated as well, his entire Family labeled Dishonored for daring to profess his innocence.

This had left Kydell in position to neatly claim the newly-vacated vice admiralty, and as much of Margold's fleet as Fleet Command would allow. Including Alanis.

And now he was a full admiral and she was stuck, trapped in his service for eternity, if the strength of the Psychomorphic canid's grip on her mind was any indication.

Kydell will pay, she promised herself. *For me, and for Margold. I'll make sure of it.*

She widened the focus of the sensor, hoping to learn something new about her predicament. Her attention was instead drawn to a sudden burst of necromantic power to the rear of the ship, just before the engines.

You feel familiar...

She adjusted the sensor again, refocusing for a better look.

"Commander?" Maneuvering's tentative question pulled her from her focus. "My engineers have taken to a maintenance pod and set off the emergency alert, but I'm showing no damage to my engines. Did the admiral give an order for something?"

Coincidence? It was possible, but unlikely. "Not that I'm aware. I'll look into it."

"Should we alert Admiral Kydell? He'd want to know."

Alanis smiled inwardly. "Too bad nobody's going to tell him. And Helm? Cancel that alert."

He's conditioned me to follow his orders to the letter. Too bad he didn't consider this scenario.

The Maneuvering AI gave a chuckle. "Aye, aye, Commander. You're a real piece of work, you know that?"

"Yup." Her tone held defiance. "You have a problem with that?"

"Of course not. We're *your* team, not *his*. *You* look out for us." There was a pause. "I've erased the sighting from the records, and filed the alert as a false alarm. Let me know what else you need."

"Where'd they launch from?"

Just because she wasn't going to tell Kydell didn't mean she wouldn't check it out herself. Especially since it might mean *he* was back.

"Rear maintenance workshop. The one near the shield gap."

"Got it." Definitely not a coincidence. "I'll check it out. If you don't hear from me in ten minutes, *then* tell the admiral. Blame the record changes on me."

<<Yes, Ma'am.>>

Alanis finished adjusting the necromantic sensor, directing it to the workshop to confirm her suspicions. There he stood, her old rival himself, still channeling the Void in the back of his mind, same as always.

Now what are you doing here…? She mused, pausing her study of the Void necromancer to survey his four companions. Three of them also bore the fingerprints of the Void: the boy a budding relationship with the Veil, the woman the mark of Kydell's personal TAG, the fae a firmly bound Afterlife Intelligence themselves. *The Void always calls to its own.*

The fifth member of the team reeked of life and nature, his aura out of place in the expanse of the Void between the stars.

Now what are you doing on my ship? It wasn't a question of how they'd managed to board. He knew about the Shield gap by the engines. He knew this ship and her quirks. He knew *her*, or at least, who she'd been prior to Kydell's meddling, better than anyone.

But he was supposed to be dead. Not just dead, *nonexistent*, his soul Shattered and destroyed. He'd sworn the Oath to Sparnell and Kydell, just as she had, but after Loxira that tether had been found tattered and broken. Nobody – *nobody* – broke the Oath. To be Oathbound was to remain bound until the terms had been met.

And to be an Oathbound of Kydell, Alanis had learned, meant those terms would never be met.

So how'd you *manage it?* She tried to refine her necromantic sensor to look closer, but the Runework had limited its range to the *Inevitable* and its surroundings only, barring its interior from inspection for security reasons. She was part of the ship, a living entity bound within the craft's main server room, destined now to serve as the primary AI until her destruction. Whereas he... was not.

I need my own magic for this.

Kydell had cut her off from the Afterlife with his last order, telling her to conserve her Imperium for defense only, but surely this would count. The Void necromancer was a threat to her ship, after all, and therefore a threat to her.

Abandoning the sensor, Alanis pulled her consciousness from the ship itself centering her awareness onto her crystal alone...

And easily slipped behind the Veil.

Relief flooded her soul at the return of the planes beyond the Veil, their power lapping at her mind like a lover's caress. She might be bound as the *Inevitable*'s primary AI, but she was also a necromancer, which meant the Void was always home. Kydell didn't seem to understand this, despite her pleading and repeated efforts to explain.

Or perhaps he just doesn't care. Stupid, arrogant, controlling *wolf.*

Whole again, she quickly located her target, his own necromantic aura as imposing as it was familiar. Pulling herself closer she inspected his soul, confirming the absence of the Oath tether, and noting the jagged gashes and fractures cutting deep within.

She couldn't help but look closer. With his constant connection to the Void he had to recognize her presence, but aside from maintaining his Shielding on both sides of the Veil he made no effort to stop her from satisfying her curiosity.

What happened to you at Loxira?

She had to admit, he'd always been a tough bastard, but surviving something like Shatter was unthinkable.

How did you do it?

She had to know. He still made no move to attack her, so perhaps he'd be willing to talk first. She'd satisfy her curiosity, and then she'd find a way to Hyperjump him off her ship and into the Void outside. Intelligence gathering *was* part of defending. She could justify the spell to Kydell's conditioning.

Focusing her intent, Alanis concentrated on her memories of the necromancer on the other side of the Veil, sending a Soul Call to scratch at the back of his mind.

To her surprise, he answered.

21

Shane felt the Navigations AI's attention hone in on him, and shook his head. "Too late. We'll have to make our stand here."

One of your companions needs your attention. Fear. Stress. Panic.

Scanning the room, Shane settled on Jeb.

"I thought you said we'd have to get to the AI?" the biologist demanded.

"She came to me." He bolstered the necromantic aspects of his Shielding spell, tracking the dead fae through the Afterlife. "If we had reached her crystal I could have used that to my advantage, but I'll have to make do. Hopefully I have enough to pull this off, or our adventure ends here."

Selecting an empty section of the floor against the back wall – ensuring a comfortable distance from the dead Senior Sub-Officer – he crossed his legs and turned to Jake. "I'll need your

Shielding. Think you can cast your Shieldbreaker at the same time?"

"But I thought you said you could do this?" Jeb resumed pacing, his steps harried and uneven. "*First*, you rip out someone's heart with your bare hands. And *now* you're telling me you don't even know if you can do the *one* thing you need to do?"

"It depends how tired she is." He looked up at Jeb. It was important for him to understand the risks, but also the facts. "She's a powerful Void necromancer, older and stronger and more practiced than I am. And clever. This won't be an easy fight. But she also just Hyperjumped this entire carrier and everyone in it, and she's still recovering."

I don't think you're helping the situation, Feels warned. *If anything, you just made it worse.*

Scowling, Shane muttered under his breath. "Would've worked for Jake."

And Jeb's not Jake, is he?

Razick grabbed her brother's shoulder, spinning him around to face her as she wrapped him in a hug. Jeb struggled momentarily, but physically relaxed at her persistence.

Seeing Razick had the situation well in hand, Shane returned his attention to Jake and Feels, blinking in the sudden light as the ship resumed normal operation status.

"While they're distracted... I'm going to need your help with this. Jake, I want you to cast an Apotheturgy spell to link up with Feels. When they send the signal, cast your Shielding on all three of us. Necromancy was her only offensive magic, so she'll probably rely on Shatter, which means you can't leave any crack in our Shields. Okay?"

He'd be trusting their entire defense to his son, Shane's own attention and magic consumed wholly on the offensive. It was a huge responsibility to lay on the boy's shoulders, but history had shown he was up for the task.

"I'll keep us safe," Jake promised, frowning. "But I don't have my Shieldbreaker crystal. I've never cast both at the same time. And if I'm Shielding you in the Afterlife..."

Shane nodded acknowledgement. The loss of the Shieldbreaker was unfortunate, but not unexpected. "Your Shielding will be enough. Feels?"

Don't hurt her, Grim. She's a good person in a bad situation.

"I don't want to. But if I have to choose between her and an entire planet..."

His voice faded. She'd always held his respect, despite her undisguised scorn for him and his beliefs. That was a lifetime ago, and he'd been the one in the wrong, yet now that he finally understood they still remained adversaries. "Hopefully it won't come to that."

He felt Feels pause, then send a quick burst of approval. *You're right, of course. What do you need from me?*

He felt the Navigations AI circle closer. It was only a matter of time before she did more than just look. He'd have to be quick.

"Watch her emotions. Warn me if she's about to attack. I'm going to try to talk her down, first."

He had no doubt she was the one who'd canceled the alert, which meant either she wanted to Shatter him herself, or he had a chance.

Thank you.

The words were accompanied by a caress of gratitude, and Shane rubbed the locket in return. Maybe he and the fae could work through their differences after all, once this was all over.

He turned his attention to Jeb and Razick, the biologist still wrapped in his sister's arms, a faint smile now written across his face.

"Jeb. Razick. You feel confident you can hold the door? Someone canceled the alert, but we might still get company."

Razick fixed him with a cool smile. "Consider it done." She began peeling the workbenches away from their floor fixtures, fashioning them into a defensive wall just inside the doorway. Jeb watched her work for several moments before jumping in to help.

Shane blinked. "You can talk?"

His amazement earned a fit of giggles from Jake. "That means she trusts you."

He felt a familiar scratching at the Void in the back of his mind. *Soul Call. Commander Yiven Alanis.*

"Hopefully I continue to live up to her expectations." He carefully returned Jake's smile, to put the boy at ease. "Right now I'll settle for continuing to live. You both ready? She wants to talk. Don't join yet. On my signal."

He waited for their confirmation, then accepted the Call, Alanis' voice passing through the Veil from the Afterlife.

<<And what brings you to my ship, Grim? Have you finally decided to reap my soul?>>

Her voice was as melodic as he remembered, and twice as deadly. She was the only other person who'd dared call him Grim to his face, and he discovered to his surprise that he'd missed it.

"*My* ship," he corrected, wrapping his fingers around Jake's knife and preparing to slip behind the Veil. "And that depends on you."

<<Do your companions know they have a war hero in their midst?>>

Her tone was mocking and derisive, her words an echo of his own from their conversations years ago.

"War criminal," he corrected, using her own typical response to the claim. She'd been right. He knew that, now.

She pulled back for a moment, but recovered quickly. <<That depends on who's winning, doesn't it?>> His own words again, in the same mocking tone.

He broke script. "Nobody's winning, Yiven. Everyone's too busy trying not to lose. You were right. I finally understand."

<<How magnanimous of you, Commodore.>> Alanis' voice projected scorn. <<Although I believe congratulations are in order. For the promotion.>>

"That's not who I am anymore." Shane's voice was soft.

<<Let me be the judge of that,>> the AI snapped, her tone harsh. <<Want to prove it? Drop your Shield. Then come here so I can look at you.>>

Shane did as he was told, slipping easily through the Veil and into the fourth dimension. The engine room shifted and twisted in his vision, his eyes attempting to reconcile what they expected to see with the strange *wrongness* the higher dimensions projected on mortal sight.

Meeting her gaze, he dropped his Shield. If he wanted to recruit her to his cause he'd need to earn her trust. Showing she already had his was important.

She was at her strongest in the Afterlife due to her presently deceased state, allowing her full access to her necromantic abilities, with no effort to maintain her presence within the Void. Shane had hoped to fight her on more even terms, as the Imperium costs of his own efforts to remain behind the Veil were a notable drain on his reserves, but he'd been unable to gain access to the server room. He'd have to manage the disadvantage.

Alanis projected herself as an ice blue fae, her delicate wings and diminutive stature a sharp contrast to the lethal threat she posed to both him and his plans. Courtesy of the higher dimensions, she appeared slightly hazy and out of focus as his eyes attempted to adjust.

Shane had never quite mastered the art of reading the insectoid features of fae facial expressions, but hers clearly radiated disapproval and distrust. She sized him up critically, her eyes coming to rest on the stains left by the engineering officer's heart.

"Nice to see you're no longer hiding the blood on your hands."

He twisted his hands nervously, suddenly reminded of the aftermath of his prior encounter. This was *not* how he'd hoped this conversation would go.

Other discomforts flooded his mind soon after. His frustrations at bringing Jake into an active war zone. His reliance on Jeb and Razick, two pacifists he barely even knew. His damp socks.

"Oh, yeah, that'll help. Really work it in." Her laugh was harsh and full of judgment. "You may be wearing a different face, Grim, but changing your stripes on the outside doesn't change who you are on the inside. Get off my ship."

"I don't want to fight you," Shane said quietly.

"Of course you don't!" Her face contorted into something mildly representing a sneer. "You already know how that ends. Spoilers! Not well for you. Crawl back under whatever rock you came from. Live this imaginary 'new life' of yours. Leave the universe to the people who care."

"That *rock* is called Baden," Shane answered quietly. "And I'm here to defend it. I'd prefer your help."

He heard Feels' cry of warning, and felt Jake's Shielding snap into place with a sudden resolute force.

And immediately after, Shane found himself reeling from the full force of her attack.

22

Jeb was in over his head and he knew it.

Raz had always been independent and outspoken growing up, and even on her sixteenth birthday when her ten year conscription came due she'd regaled him with an assortment of her opinions on the matter. He barely recognized the silent and sullen Razick who'd returned to him afterward.

He watched her now, deftly pulling the workbenches from the wall and converting them into an effective defensive barrier, and wondered at just how much she left unsaid. She wasn't weak, never had been, and he ground his teeth at the realization he'd been underestimating the very things that had changed her into the distrustful woman she was today.

When she found him after her escape from Kydell she'd been jumpy and anxious, a far cry from the clear headed protector she'd always been. He'd done his best to step into the role and do for her all the things she used to do for him, but he *missed* who she used to be, his confident older sister, his shelter from the storms of life.

Today he was finally seeing a glimpse of the things she wouldn't talk about. Today he was learning she was still the same competent and protective older sister she'd always been, not the broken fragile child he'd imagined when she'd reappeared on his doorstep.

And the truth was, as much as he'd promised to protect her, today he realized just how empty a promise that had been.

Raz pulled him from his introspection. <Grab that small table and bring it over here.> She pointed to a gap in her makeshift wall, blocking the corridor just outside the doorway. <I'll weld it on.>

Jeb moved to follow her instructions, letting her puzzle out the logistics herself. This was her world, not his. He wondered why he'd insisted on coming in the first place, but he'd promised to look out for her and watch her back and he was going to do his best. Even if she insisted he wear a ridiculous armored dress suit to do it.

He swallowed, hoping he didn't become a liability.

Table positioned as directed, he held it in place as Razick poured her magic into the metallic surface, melting them together. He watched the Lawrences as she worked, both sitting cross legged with their backs to the far wall and their eyes closed. *Like father, like son.* Shane disappeared as Jeb watched, and he wondered how the janitor was faring in his attempts to defeat the formidable AI.

Such a calm looking battle. But what did he know? He tugged at the sleeves of his suit. *Nothing, as it turns out.*

Welding complete, Razick pulled him back into the room, tugging the locker doors off their hinges to search inside. She retrieved a large reflective roll of thin metallic sheeting, and waved it at him. <Help me spread this out front.>

Eager to avoid his own thoughts, he grabbed the end she offered him, slowly unrolling it across the front of the makeshift wall.

<This isn't very thick,> he observed. <Aren't the workbenches enough?>

<This will reflect laser pistols.> Her tone was patient and instructive. <And the tables are thick enough to withstand most projectiles, at least for a while. They'll need a battle mage if they want to make it past.>

A battle mage like you.

It all made sense now. The regular nightmares, the constant furtive glances at strangers, the casual scanning of their surroundings no matter where they went, and her insistence on mastering Antimagic. Razick's protective nature hadn't disappeared, but the threats she watched for had grown bigger.

She wasn't worried about an unkind word or a missed promotion. She was too busy counting shadows and mapping escape plans to guarantee some evil force wasn't going to steal away any more of the people she loved.

He tried to smile as she surveyed their handiwork, her proud stature betraying her own thoughts, but the moment was short lived. <Get back inside. They're fighting now. We have to prepare.>

The order reverberated in his mind and he scrambled to obey, taking a position just inside the hatch. <I thought they were already fighting?> His eyes widened as he looked to her for answers, her own form crouched behind their constructed barrier as she peered through the single hole she'd kept for that express purpose.

<No. Probably just sizing each other up. But someone just cast a full power Shielding spell. Can't you feel it? At the back of your neck?>

Jeb closed his eyes, his breath slowing as he strained his perceptions, but he felt nothing. He told her as much.

<Must be my training. The crackle of Shield energy lets you know when there might be a threat nearby.> She turned from her vantage point, narrowing her eyes as she watched him. <I'll hold the corridor. You keep an eye on the rest of our squad. Let me know if there's a problem.>

She waited until he nodded, before adding, <Dog the door behind you.>

<Lock you out?> His eyes widened in alarm. <I'm not letting you stay out there alone!>

<Let me do my job, Jeb.> She'd already turned away from him, her attention focused once more on the corridor ahead. <Close the door, or I'll do it. And if I do it, I'm welding it shut.>

He'd learned long ago not to argue with that voice, as much as he wanted to.

<Raz?>

She looked up with a glare, her face softening as she noted he'd already begun to rotate the door into place.

<Stay safe, okay?>

Her face twisted into a feral grin, and Jeb found himself stepping backward on instinct.

<You're the pacifist, Jeb. Don't worry about me. Worry about *them*.>

Jeb pushed the door the rest of the way closed, manually spinning the wheel to lock it into position rather than attempting to bother with the electronic controls. He found the wrench the engine crew had thrown at Jake earlier and wedged it into the wheel, forcing the memory of Lawrence holding the katanoj's heart from his thoughts as he barricaded himself inside – and his sister outside.

Raz was right. Despite his Family of origin, he wasn't a battle mage. Kydell had Claimed him in the hope he'd be just as effective as his sister, a living example of the Kane Family reputation, but the truth of the matter was he hadn't had enough of the skills to justify the time it would have taken to build up the *stomach* for it. They'd pushed him into field medicine for a bit, but that required a steadier hand than he'd managed in the heat of battle, so he'd instead been reassigned to Hydroponics.

Which had suited him just fine, then. But now? Now he was a liability, plain and simple.

Exhaling in frustration, he turned to watch Jake, strain and concentration now written across the boy's face as he stared blankly ahead, eyes darting occasionally as if watching something Jeb couldn't see.

He shook his head. *Even the kid's more useful than me.*

Not that Raz would ever tell him that. Even when he'd been officially discharged from the SAF, tasked to serve the remainder of his conscription at a small military research facility investigating possible improvements for the hydroponics systems found in most capital ships across the fleet. The transfer was a mark of shame within the Sparnell Confederation, not to mention a barrier to employment once his conscription ended, but not once in her letters had Razick treated him as anything less.

Instead she'd praised him for his projects, encouraging him to study Agrokinesis to further his work, and reminding him of the importance of Hydroponics in generating the Nature Magic fields required for Curative Magic to function in the otherwise barren Void. She'd pushed him to take pride in his own achievements and their importance, rather than lamenting that they didn't match the achievements of others.

The way she'd written about her feelings on the war, Jeb assumed she was eager to settle down into civilian life. He'd begun researching his options to start a private hydroponics lab with her once they both completed their conscription, his Agrokinesis augmented by her talents in Elemental Magic.

She'd seemed excited at the prospect, so when she wrote that she was re-enlisting for a twenty year tour instead, he'd been hurt and surprised.

But that had been Kydell, too, hadn't it?

Jeb swallowed, pressing his hand against the door before forcing himself to turn away.

There was no sense dwelling on the past. Razick had a chance for the closure she so desperately needed, and he'd do everything in his power to give it to her. Even if that meant leaving her on the other side of the bulkhead door. Alone.

He turned instead to the lockers she'd demolished, picking through their former contents in search of a weapon. He tried to ignore the pit that opened in his stomach at the thought of using it, both given his own thoughts on violence, and what that would mean about his sister's success at the door.

They'd brought a necromancer, after all. After he finished up his fight with the AI he could make sure everyone's souls were where they needed to be.

All Jeb had to do was make sure nobody got inside the room to stop him.

ALANIS FELT HER RISING panic as Kydell's programming kicked in with Grim's words.

No! No! No!

But it was too late, her surprise Shatter hitting the invading necromancer squarely in the chest, sending him reeling backward and away through the Void. With the already tattered state of his soul, there was no way he could have survived.

Damn that wolf and his mind control!

She couldn't even have a conversation anymore without setting off one of the canid's haphazardly-set triggers. She'd had so many questions she'd wanted to ask, so many things she needed to know. But not only had Kydell's conditioning kept her from mentioning the Oath at all, now she'd just killed the only Oathbound who'd ever managed to break one.

And yet suddenly and unexpectedly he was back, pinning her in place with a binding spell. There'd be no finishing that conversation now. She'd started the fight against her will, but now she had to finish it, or he would. She'd served under Grim long enough to know how *that* went.

Twisting the Void around them both, she extended the extradimensional distance between them while casting a spell to undo her constraints and dart away.

Too slow.

She felt a burning sensation as he nicked the edge of her soul, twisting her awareness to see...

Is that a knife *in his hand?*

She bolstered her defenses, dodging his next spell as she repaired her Shielding from the intrusion. Tapping into the *Inevitable*'s processing power to accelerate her own thinking speeds, she pondered on the knife, and her next moves.

He's conserving spell power. It's costing him a lot just to stay behind the Veil.

The answer was obvious. *I need to drain his Shield.*

She loosed a spell volley of her own, peppering his position with offensive necromantic power, but this time he was prepared, contorting himself so they glanced off his Shielding.

Before she could marvel at the feat he was upon her again. She bent the Void in her favor, dancing away to position herself behind him for a counterattack. Those spells failed, too, dissipating against his impenetrable Shielding in a fury of sparks.

"Yiven..."

His tone was more plea than command as he called her name, but she ignored it anyway. She didn't want to die, didn't want to join the many souls Grim had erased at a whim throughout his career. He'd needed little provocation then, and she'd cast the first spell.

She gathered her magic for another Shatter, letting loose the full hostility of her spellwork upon him while dancing through the higher dimensions as if her very existence depended on it.

In her experience with Grim, it did.

"Hold still," he commanded, another binding spell flying from his fingers to brush past where she'd been mere moments before.

"No," she countered, gathering her full strength for the next spell.

By all accounts, Grim was a powerful Void necromancer with an impressive combat record, but he wasn't fae. He could borrow magic from the stars, just like her, but he didn't have the headstart she'd had, with her naturally larger Imperium reserves. He'd learned exercises to strengthen his powers, of course, but so had she. And unlike him, she'd remained in the Afterlife when she died, allowing her to keep much of her power rather than starting over in a new body, like he'd clearly chosen.

I don't need to win. I just need to outlast him.

"How about *you* hold still?" she taunted, augmenting her Shatter spell with a draw from the Void before driving it home.

To her surprise, he paused, tilting his head to watch as her high-powered spell fractured against his Shielding in a fury of power.

How in Void's name...?

She cursed. He wasn't alone. In her unfamiliarity with direct conflict, she'd canceled the alert, leaving him and his companions free to support him without distraction. Of course he had more resources than her.

He didn't even have to cast his own Shielding.

She turned her eye to the mortal plane, the lower dimension currently out of focus, the very nature of the Afterlife's higher dimensions further interfering with the standard nearsightedness of the fae. The distraction could easily turn deadly, but she had to look, had to see, had to know what she was facing.

Grim let her, the necromancer shifting to take up position beside her instead as she strained to watch his companions dig into their preparations to defend him.

"You won't win," he said softly. "But you can end this now."

Alanis' stomach turned at the pity in his voice, a wave of intense despair washing over her as his words sank in.

I'm outnumbered. I'm not going to survive this.

But she had to try.

"You're right," she told him, careful to keep her tone even. "I *can* end this."

She hit him with another Shatter, the spell once more cascading across his Shielding as she darted away. She followed it quickly with a necromantic interference spell, limiting his ability to follow her easily.

"Yiven!"

He looked almost hurt, the frown lines deepening across his face as he tightened his grip on his knife as he attempted to chase after.

Pushing away the doubt in her mind, she cast another volley of spells in his direction, darting and weaving through the Afterlife with an ease only a skilled, dead necromancer could achieve. It was a dangerous game, burning so much magic so quickly, especially when coupled with the interference spellwork, but if the only advantage she had was the breadth of her repertoire, by the Void she was going to use it.

"I don't want to hurt you!" he growled, nonetheless countering her magic with some binding spells of his own.

"I can break free of those!" she cried, more to keep her mind off his own attempts at distraction. It wasn't like he didn't know that already.

But why he'd picked *that* spell was too enticing a question to ignore for long.

She dodged another volley of binding spells, countering with a Shatter of her own and an instinctive check of her Shielding as she pondered the question. Shatter was expensive to cast but he clearly had the resources, even accounting for the extra draw on his own reserves from the channel elevating him beyond the Veil. It wasn't like he had to channel his own Shielding.

Yet instead of Shatter, another binding spell barely missed her as she chewed on the questions in her mind. What had brought him here in the first place? Would he have even sought her out if she hadn't found him first?

And why in the Void had he–

Her loss of focus cost her dearly, as her adversary took full advantage of the lull in her attention. Alanis screamed in agony from the burning slash, Grim's knife finding her earlier injury and using the opening as leverage to cut deeper into her soul.

"Why?" she cried, her mind reeling as she darted away, pouring her magic into the waning Shield.

"It must be done."

The sorrow in his voice did nothing to quell the rage within her mind. She lashed out, this time aiming for the boy, but the relentless necromancer moved to take the blasts instead.

"No."

She needed a new plan. She was tired, alone, and wouldn't last long by herself. But who could she rely on?

Her challenger renewed his offensive, another quick array of binding spells which she neatly dodged before retaliating with her own concentrated Shatter. It once again set him reeling but did little to weaken the boy's Shielding spell.

The Shielding spell.

While Grim had elevated himself to the Afterlife, his Shielding mage was still on the mortal plane, relying on a simple Necromancy spell to reach through the Veil. And while most of the *Inevitable*'s battle mages had joined the assault on the planet below as soon as Baden's primary Shielding had fractured, Kydell always kept a small but loyal contingent available to repel boarders and prevent mutiny.

Battle mages which would be responding to Maneuvering's alert, as soon as Alanis missed her ten minute check in.

Dodging another of Grim's spells – she'd been too distracted to note what he'd chosen to cast this time, just that he'd cast it – she prepared a simple binding spell of her own. It wasn't much, just the usual low-Imperium spellwork often cast on Sparnelli prisoners of war to prevent their souls from escaping through death by binding them into their bodies. But it was cheap, and offensive enough to hopefully appear she was still trying to fight back, rather than merely maintaining her own Shielding while biding her time to wait for backup.

"I can undo that, you know," he said, clearly puzzled, but he used the energy to dodge it anyway.

"Doesn't matter," she answered honestly, briefly phasing into an even higher dimension to avoid his knife.

"I don't *want* to fight you."

"Then you shouldn't have come here."

"Yiven..."

Whatever he'd intended to say was replaced by a snarl, his attention drawn instead to the current scene in the engine room. Whatever he saw had startled his Shielding mage, as well, and she cursed herself for not casting Shatter instead as her useless binding spell bypassed his former defenses and took hold.

He seemed disinclined to shake it off, instead refocusing his attention on her with a newfound resolve – and his own Shielding.

The next several moments were spent in a flurry of phases and dodges as she spun away from his own binding attempts, nonetheless risking a quick look herself to the mortal plane.

And smiling. Maneuvering had done as she asked. Kydell's mages had arrived.

She was no longer alone.

24

RAZICK GRINNED. IT WAS a near-feral, toothy thing, and for once she was grateful her brother wasn't there to see it.

She'd meant what she'd told him, about looking for a life outside the one she'd been forced into as a battle mage for Admiral Kydell. Something that allowed her to create instead of destroy. Something that left the universe in better shape than it was before she'd come along and put her fingerprints on things.

Ridding the universe of Kydell's most loyal battle mages would suffice, for now.

She could hear the soft quiet of their whispers and the clink of their rifles with carefully controlled puffs of Anemancy, manipulating the very air of the spacecraft to carry the soundwaves to her ears. They could counter, twist the air around themselves as a shield of secrecy, but they never would. In their hubris, they'd mistaken her for a last ditch effort of the Baden Defense

Force, and she would not grant them the satisfaction of discovering their mistake.

Not until it was too late.

"Over here," their leader whispered.

Vernell.

She pictured the tall, black katanoj in her mind. Wondered if he still kept the brown scruff of mane down the back of his neck trimmed even with the rest of his fur. Or if his tail still gave away his feints by its incessant beating when he grew excited.

"Can't be many of them," his communications officer whispered back.

Razick remembered her, too. A disgrace by her Family's standards, what Cunningham lacked in her Family's expected Telepathic prowess she made up for in the exercise room. She was a muscled bully of a dracoling, her blonde hair most often imprisoned in tight, twisted braids that caught in the cracks of her thick, red skin.

There were twelve, all told, by the irregularity of the vibrations to their footsteps, and the hesitating cadence of their voices. Three she didn't recognize, their pitch revealing them as newer members of Kydell's team, and a lack of footsteps and riot rifles marking two as likely fae. But the rest?

She knew the rest. She'd *trained* the rest, not by choice, but by command. And soon, she'd teach them one final lesson.

She hadn't taught them all she knew.

"Helm said they're just around the corner," one of the younger newcomers reported, their voice just a little too high-pitched.

Fear.

Razick, too, was familiar with the sentiment. Even now, she felt it, flowing through her veins and hammering in her ears and pushing against her chest. She was good, but twelve was a lot, and her brother was on the other side of the bulkhead, counting on her to keep him safe. Was she good *enough*?

Only one way to find out.

"Stop right there," she growled, attempting to mimic Lawrence's gruff tone, with a touch of Anemancy to add further distortion.

Ordinarily, she'd make full use of the element of surprise, attacking first before anyone saw her coming. But today wasn't ordinary. As much as she needed to *win*, she also needed to *stall*. Her forces were split, the necromancer in her charge caught in his own battle with the ship's Nav. She needed to keep the pressure off him so he could hopefully return the favor. Which meant conserving her resources, by hopefully drawing Kydell's mages into a discussion first.

"And who in the Void are you, to give commands?" Vernell laughed, the mockery of someone assured in their superiority.

Razick had to admit, in this case he was probably right, although his advantage wasn't as great as he assumed.

Or maybe he had *some* idea. He hadn't turned the corner yet. She doubted that was by accident.

"Not a command," she called back, pitching her voice high this time. Slowing her words, she settled on a tone somewhere in the middle, further altered with her magic. "Just a suggestion."

Vernell snorted, his amusement echoed by the whispers of those under his command. "Doesn't matter how many of you there are. You'll find no success here. Baden is ours."

"Not yet, Vernell," Razick told him, injecting more cheer into her own voice than she felt. "But you're welcome to fight us for it."

"Kane!"

She wished she could have seen the look on his face – not to mention his subordinates' – at that realization.

"That's not her," Cunningham whispered. "Can't be. Just a trick."

Razick lowered her voice again. "You're welcome to come here and find out!"

"Not necessary," Vernell purred, venom dripping from his voice. "Come back where you belong, Sub-Officer. We can put this whole mess behind us. No one will think less of you."

"Shouldn't we tell the admiral she's here?" one of the newer voices asked, hesitantly.

"No. She's one of ours, which means we bring her ourselves. She deserves nothing less." His voice took on a bitter edge. "Besides. We tell him, he'll recall the Selkirk, and *she'll* get all the glory."

Razick couldn't suppress a shiver at the name of Kydell's TAG. Although by the sound of it, she was away on another mission, which significantly improved their chances of success today. He could call her back at any time, but he'd have to know he needed her first. And at least for now, those aware of their presence seemed to think they could handle themselves without Kydell's involvement.

Thank the Void.

"I'm retired!" Razick quipped, hoping he didn't notice the warble to her voice.

"Taking up a hobby of piracy, then?" Vernell laughed. "Suppose I should be grateful. Your disappearance got me a promotion. Might even get your old *job*. Our admiral appreciates my contributions... But we'd do even better together."

She could hear the others drawing into position, setting their rifles aside in favor of their magic. Sparnelli riot rifles were the best in the universe for suppressing poorly-armed rebellion, but against a skilled battle mage such as herself they'd be forced to rely on the highest power setting to hold any chance against her Shielding.

And Kydell never took kindly to holes in his ship.

Checking her Shielding, she focused her attention through the small gap in her barricade. "You can keep the job," she spat. "He doesn't appreciate *you*, just your *obedience*. You have a lot to learn, Vernell."

"Not as much as *you're* about to learn."

They flew into the hallway in a flurry of sparks and rage, but Razick was ready. She pushed them back with a well-timed Shielding burst, sending Vernell scrabbling to maintain his footing. Cunningham wasn't so lucky, slamming backward into the mages behind her, sending many of them toppling beneath her into a single, indignant pile.

"Cheap tricks are beneath you, Kane," Vernell snarled, planting his feet firmly in the corridor.

A wave of Electromancy cascaded over Razick's outer Shielding, carefully set outside the barrier currently hiding her from view. It was a small matter to redirect the currents, one of the skills she *had* shared with Vernell.

Which meant he had other motives.

Her hunch was confirmed as he summoned a fireball to his fingertips with a smile. "You're fighting solo today."

She hit him with her Telekinesis before he could throw it, locking his arms to his sides before sending him careening into his subordinates just when they'd rediscovered their balance.

"We have more magic than you," Vernell purred, seemingly nonplussed as she tossed him about the corridor like a ragdoll.

But why would he be? They'd practiced this, too, so he wouldn't panic if caught by one of the Order Militants. As long as he kept his Shielding up, her Telekinesis couldn't actually hurt him.

The mages behind him had already recovered. While the majority – including Vernell – had only trained in Elemental Magic, she could already feel at least two of their telekinetics tugging at her hold over their superior.

"Don't suppose you've developed vertigo in the last few years?" she asked hopefully.

Vernell laughed. "No. Don't suppose you're ready to surrender yet?"

"No."

She released him with a telekinetic push, sending him tumbling once more toward the mages in his command. Her smile faded as they adjusted quickly to the loss of resistance, halting his flight before setting him down gently in the corridor instead.

"Shame. You were my favorite Instructor, you know. Would have loved to bring you back willingly," He shrugged, the somber expression on his face betrayed by the excited jerking of his tail. "So now, we dance."

At his cue, the passageway erupted in a firestorm of sound and fury.

ALANIS DIDN'T HAVE TO play nice anymore.

It was a freeing sensation, not worrying about conserving her magic or upsetting Grim enough to unleash his wrath or that of their admiral. She was still trapped in service to the manipulative wolf, but as far as Grim was concerned? Her backup had arrived and she was free to do as she pleased – as she *needed* – to ensure her own safety and that of her team.

And right now, what she *needed* was to Shatter that arrogant affront to the Void.

She dodged his next collection of binding spells, unleashing another Soul Shatter in his direction as she folded the higher planes of the Afterlife around herself to emerge behind him.

He didn't even attempt to dodge it, merely rotating to cast again toward her new position as her spell impacted with his Shielding in a flurry of angry black sparks. She folded the planes again, neatly avoiding his attack as she danced away across dimensions.

They'd both dropped any pretense at finesse, flinging their full intentions directly at the other's Shielding with an earnest desperation. Grim had limited his spellwork, seeming to rely on the cheaper, repetitive Soulbind. While ordinarily Alanis would consider it a mundane spell to counter, the blue-green glint of Grim's blade recalled the devastation she'd face if caught today.

For her part, she'd settled on casting Shatter, over and over and over again until she got lucky. She still cursed herself for wasting her first opportunity by casting the mostly-harmless Soulbind spell earlier. She had no intention of repeating the mistake.

But it was she who faltered first, her moments of introspection allowing him to phase away from where he'd been quietly countering her attacks to instead land behind her for a quick jab of his knife, the moment startling *her* into dropping her Shielding at just the wrong moment.

She hissed in pain as she folded the Afterlife to add more distance between them, forcing herself not to check the damage as she poured more power into her Shields. This was a luxury she didn't have, not until she'd Shattered the soul of the relentless necromancer now phasing around her, fracturing his intentions for her and her ship in the process.

"We don't have to fight," Grim said quietly, nonetheless hurling more binding spells in her direction.

She didn't answer, pushing down the pain of the wound he'd inflicted to aim another Soul Shatter his direction. He'd been more agreeable than usual, even including their present duel in the equation, which meant he wanted something. The *Inevitable*, if their prior interactions were any indication. She'd been his flagship before, when he'd been a revenge-thirsty Commodore and her the primary Afterlife Intelligence tasked with Hyperjumping the deadly carrier across the stars.

But she wasn't *his* ship anymore. He'd lost that privilege when he'd disappeared without a trace two years ago in the aftermath of their bombardment of Loxira, and she'd been reassigned to Admiral Kydell directly.

When he'd left her to face the full brunt of the admiral's Psychomorphation, twisting her emotions and her impulses until she could do little but obey the wolf's every command.

If she'd hated him before, she hated him even more, now.

Some crimes were unforgivable.

She miscalculated her next dodge, or perhaps he had merely learned to anticipate her movements. She gasped in pain as a binding spell caught her and held her fast, several others quickly layering over it, each pulling in different directions at the already tender fractures he'd cut into her soul.

She was tired, so tired, and even with help waiting on the other side of the Veil, it was clear there was no way she was winning this fight. He had her now, and he could rebind her faster than she could shake herself loose.

"I surrender." She closed her eyes and dropped her Shield. "Tell me what you want from me, Grim. Just... Please don't hurt me anymore."

"It's going to hurt. I'm sorry." His tone was surprisingly soft and apologetic. "But if you hold still, this will all be over soon."

It wasn't going to be much of an Afterlife anyway, she consoled herself, opening her eyes to face her fate. At least this was on her terms, and Grim's, rather than Kydell's.

"Then make it quick."

Alanis watched as he carefully lowered the knife to her soul, its blade shimmering in an otherworldly blue and purple. She found herself mesmerized by the beauty of its shifting patterns.

And then it was cutting into her again, slicing through her core with a burning indifference to her pain. She heard her own screams, piercing and distant as if they were emanating from someone else, their volume muted by the vast expanse of the Void.

Just as soon as it began it was over, his binding spells slipping away and leaving her feeling violated and...

Different. Something definitely felt off, more than just the throbbing from her wounds.

"Grim... What did you *do?*"

She attempted to review the damage, but Kydell's orders blocked her casting. *Magic. Defense. Think. I... I need to know what shape I'm in, so I can defend myself properly...?*

Justification given and accepted by the wolf's conditioning, she cast her eye inward, surveying Grim's handiwork.

He'd cut two deep incisions with a careful hand, centered on each of the branches of the tether that had marked her as Oathbound. She poked at the wounds, finding no trace of the ties which formerly bound her to SAF Headquarters and the Oathstone locked deep within its Vault.

"You're free now." His tone stated fact, with no sign of expectations. "I need to save my son."

And without waiting for an answer, he slipped through the Veil, and back to the mortal plane.

26

Shane exhaled, finally taking a moment to shake loose Alanis' binding spell as he quickly surveyed his surroundings. Jake nodded faintly as he rose from the deck to meet him, his motions stiff despite his clear relief at Shane's return. The boy's eyes darted to Jeb, the biologist crouched just inside the hatch, an oversized telekinetic wrench gripped in both hands, his muscles tensed as if to swing it the moment anyone attempted to push their way through the rough barricade of worktables and equipment lockers he'd stacked within.

A cacophony of sound echoed through the bulkhead from the corridor beyond, clearly announcing the team of battle mages come to put an end to their desperate venture.

No one was beating against the door – not *yet* – but by the sound they'd overwhelmed Razick's Antimagic. It was only a matter of time.

<<Why didn't you tell me?>> Alanis' accusations reverberated across the Veil, demanding his attention. <<I wouldn't have fought you.>>

It appeared she wished to continue their fight, just with words instead of actions.

"We both know that's not true," he said quietly.

Jeb jumped at the sound, raising his wrench as if to strike before recognition flashed across his eyes. "You need to help her. There's *twelve* of them out there."

<<True.>>

There was a grumpy acceptance to Alanis' voice now, and Shane felt some of the tension drain from his shoulders. They still had a fight ahead of them, but at least Alanis had decided she'd no longer participate.

"Lawrence, Raz *needs* you," Jeb protested, waving the wrench toward the door before hefting it onto his shoulder. "You said you could do this, so do it."

The fact the lab tech had held them off this long was impressive in its own right, but Jeb was right, they couldn't afford delays.

Slowing his breathing, Shane focused on his present surroundings. Jake's comforting warmth at his side. The scent of grease and sweat filling the workroom. The sensations at the back of his neck at the Imperium storm of magic demonstrations in the corridor beyond. The faint sound of his own breathing, nearly drowned out by the noises beyond.

Sufficiently grounded, he reached beyond the Veil and through the spaces between them to grasp Razick with his magic, pulling her to safety within the barricaded room.

"What in *Void's name* are you doing, Lawrence!"

He winced at the clear anger in her voice, reinforcing his Shielding on instinct. "Saving you. Jeb said–"

A sudden invisible impact with his chest forced an abrupt end to that sentence, and he found himself doubled over in pain, despite the Shield. Gasping in an attempt to catch his breath, Shane looked up in time to catch Razick's deadly glare toward her brother before the noise from outside pulled all their attention away.

The mages had quieted, shortly after he'd rescued her from the fury outside, but they'd returned with a vengeance, now beating directly at the door.

Razick's glare turned toward Shane as she motioned angrily toward the door behind her with large, exaggerated movements.

"She had a barricade," Jeb translated. "You let them tear it apart."

Shane blinked at her. "A barricade?"

<<Always getting in everyone else's way,>> Alanis laughed from beyond the Veil, but her former bitterness had fled. <<Kydell's got a tight hold on me, Grim. He's even stronger than when you left. But if you can help me get free...>>

"We need to get to the server room," he told her, frowning.

Razick waved her arms toward the hatch again, where the wheel lock now rattled from unblocked outside attacks, threatening to break itself free of the wrench someone had jammed in to stop it from turning. Apparently they were no longer on speaking terms, short-lived as it had been.

<<Make me a promise. Give me my mind back. Undo what that flea-bitten wolf did to me, and I'll join you.>>

Shane exhaled slowly. It would be a small matter to promise her anything she wanted in exchange for her loyalty, but the truth of the matter was, he didn't know if he could keep it. And after everything she'd been through, the dead fae deserved more than empty promises.

"I can't," he told her. "He's been at this a long time. I don't know if we have the skills we'd need to undo it."

Razick glared daggers at him as the wrench in the door began to bend from the strain. Jeb tugged at her arm but she shook him off.

"We have to do *something*," Jake said, his fingernails digging into Shane's arm.

"When this is over, I'll do all I can to help," Shane promised, pulling Jake with him as he moved closer to Jeb and Razick. "You don't even have to help us. You never deserved any of this."

He grabbed Razick's arm, but she jerked it free. Shaking his head, he grabbed Jeb's arm instead, holding out his hand for hers as Jake wrapped his arms tighter around his waist. Recognition dawned in Razick's eyes as she grasped his hand in hers, although the glare never left her face.

He flinched at the contact – aside from Jake, he rarely felt comfortable even with the touches he initiated directly – but forced himself to keep his focus, slipping behind the Veil to emerge in the server room.

The emergency doors slammed shut upon their arrival, the room lit in harsh, blinking red once again.

"State your business," an angry voice declared.

"Stand down, Maint," Alanis ordered, "and cancel that alert. They're with me."

"Ma'am," the AI protested. "Helm told me what happened."

"We've come to an agreement," Alanis insisted, activating her hologram to survey the new arrivals in the server room. "Cancel that alert."

"Yes, Ma'am."

"So… we're *not* fighting anymore?" Jeb asked hesitantly, lowering his wrench slightly.

"No," Shane and Alanis informed him at the same moment, exchanging glances.

Alanis tilted her head to study him. "Are you *really* taking on the whole fleet, Grim?"

He nodded, lightly tousling Jake's hair as the boy slowly released him to instead study the careful arrangement of tyrellium crystals and circuitry comprising the *Inevitable*'s main server. "Made a promise to the kid."

Her wings fluttered at the mention of Jake, and she turned to watch him, her voice thoughtful. "I can't do much to help," she admitted after a moment, returning to meet his gaze again. "But I can solve your battle mage problem. If you tell me everything."

"Our time is limited," he reminded her. "Your fleet's attacking my planet."

"I still don't know I can trust you," she pointed out. "You've hurt me before. You've hurt me *today*."

He set his jaw. "Fine."

"Good." Alanis turned her attention to Jeb, pointing to the wall speaker that had carried the Maintenance AI's voice mere moments before. "First things first. See that speaker over there?"

"Yes?" The confusion was clear in Jeb's voice.

"Smash it."

"You want me to...?"

"With that wrench of yours? Yes." Her wings fluttered in frustration. "We don't have much time."

"Do it," Shane growled, immediately recognizing the AI's plans.

Jeb eyed between the two of them. "Okay..."

Swallowing, he took aim, checking his range from the other delicate equipment in the room before landing a full-strength hit against the metal grating. It bent inward with little protest, the delicate electronics behind it following shortly after.

"Thank you." She grinned at him. "Now. You may want to hold on to something."

27

ADMIRAL KYDELL SCOWLED, RUBBING the fur along the top of his snout, all eyes on the bridge upon him and the imposing figure he cut in the gold-trimmed pristine white and deep brown of his dress uniform.

And today had been going so *well.*

"What do you mean you can't aim it?"

The human battle mage before him flinched at every word, pale skin now drained of all semblance of color, but held his ground. "The new experimental weapons, sir. They amplify the spells I send through them, exactly as we were told." He squeezed his eyes shut, the next statement cascading from his mouth in a torrent of disowned words. "But there's no way to direct it where to go so it just hits *everything* in front of us please don't hurt me I'm doing my best I swear." He cracked one eye to watch Kydell, his fear palpable even without the use of Psychometry. "Sir."

Kydell felt his hackles rise as he eyed the sniveling mage, some newly conscripted child barely finished basic training. The fleet admiral herself had assigned him to the *Inevitable*, and – even worse! – had dictated that he was to replace the *Inevitable*'s highly-experienced Weapons AI. The admiral could only wonder whom he had annoyed this time, to warrant such a punishment. He'd spent decades conditioning that AI until he'd become the epitome of deadly efficiency and unquestioning obedience, two things this sorry excuse for a battle mage could never hope to emulate.

"How did you get assigned to my ship?"

The question came out as a growl, causing the young mage to jump backward with a yelp. Partially recovering, he turned to Kydell, wringing his hands. "My father, he..."

Kydell turned out the rest of the words, wrinkling his nose at the scent of terror now filling the recycled air of the bridge. A political appointment, then. He sighed, shaking his head.

Just my luck.

The incompetent fool had only been on his crew for two weeks and already it was a wonder he hadn't yet been *accidentally* pushed out an airlock. One thing was certain, he would *not* be joining Kydell's Collection.

The admiral turned from the monotony of the mage's words to instead survey the remaining bridge crew, all three pairs of eyes suddenly darting away from his renewed attention.

He glared at the back of Shielding's head. This sorry excuse for a mage was the reason Kydell no longer bothered with political appointments. Lazy, overconfident, and underperforming, no amount of Psychomorphation had been able to fix *that* mess.

What a waste of my best efforts.

He'd even tried giving the slacker to Renkash to chew on, but the fearsome katanoj had similarly failed to breach the indifferent incompetence. Kydell was counting down the years for the end of *that* conscription.

The other two had been much more promising. Their quiet compliance and complete lack of ambition had been the perfect canvas on which to paint his masterpiece. Now the pride of his Collection, they readily assumed whatever positions he chose to assign them with unquestioning obedience and loyalty. Currently he'd named them Captain and Morale Officer for the *Inevitable*, and at present they were intent on the task of coordinating the ship's response to the battle – including the small party of boarders Shielding had allowed onto the ship – despite their apparent lack of functional weaponry.

Sensing the return of silence to his bridge, Kydell bestowed his attention back to the Weapons mage. "Did you at least read the manual?"

The human's fear was palpable now, filling the room as it embedding itself in the young mage's heart. "M-m-manual, sir?"

Kydell circled the air with his fingers, filling his words with the entirety of his impatience. "The instructions you were given? On how to operate the experimental weaponry? The very expensive experimental weaponry that it is your job to learn and operate?"

"Ooooooh, thaaaat manual." The mage grimaced, rubbing the back of his neck with his palm. "Uhhhh... No."

The admiral was on him in an instant, lifting the worthless officer by the scruff of his uniform shirt and holding the young mage's eyes level with his own. "If you're lucky, I'll see you exiled to the botany labs for this incompetence. If you're *lucky*."

He growled, baring his canines as he tugged expertly at the human's terror with his magic, unraveling the last of the Weapons mage's attempt to regain his composure. A flood of memories rewarded his efforts, a collection of the officer's greatest fears and deepest hurts, ripe for manipulation should Kydell choose to reprogram his emotional responses after all.

He had to admit, the thought was tempting. A waste of his talents, certainly, but a good release for his frustrations. Not to mention, a safer outlet than risking the conditioning of his Collection by imposing alterations before he'd brought his own emotions back under control.

The emergency lights flashed again, accompanied by the sound of the anti-mutiny door locks clicking into place. The alert was canceled as soon as it began, flooding the bridge once more in stark white lighting.

Kydell dropped the mage to the floor with contempt, adding a kick to the quivering pile of limbs for good measure. "Get out of my sight. Fortunately for *you*, I have a new crisis to resolve."

Turning his back on his worthless Weapons Officer, he made his way toward the *Inevitable*'s Captain. "*Now* what?"

Before they could answer, reality shifted around him, leaving him alone on the bridge. He sighed, rubbing his nose.

And now Commander Yiven has found a way to slip my control again. Just what I needed today.

He'd never understood what the *Inevitable*'s former Commodore had seen in her. She was certainly a powerful talent, but her incessant insubordination was a constant thorn in his footpads. The necromancer had rarely been wrong in his assessments, and so Kydell had altered her to renew her Oath in the hope he could eventually adjust her into a more compliant subordinate, but he was beginning to recognize the futility of that goal.

"Comms, get me Nav."

The Communications AI's telepathic reply was immediate. <She's not answering, sir.>

Kydell twisted his lips into a snarl. He hadn't told her to accept all his telecomms when he'd given his last set of orders. *She must have decided that rule no longer applied.*

"Then connect me with the speaker in the server room. I'll *make* her answer."

<Currently nonfunctional, sir.>

"And when did that happen?" He felt his snarl grow larger.

<Recent, sir. Must have overloaded something, in the battle. Maintenance logged it.>

"Fine." Kydell massaged his temples. "Get me Maneuvering, then. And link in Telemetry."

<Sir?> Both AI questioned in unison.

"Where the hell are we?"

<Baden, sir.> Telemetry answered first, her tone annoyingly chipper. <We've jumped to the rear of the battle. Far outer orbit.>

"And why would we waste a Hyperjump on *that*?" Kydell felt his patience wearing even thinner than usual.

<Nav said something about a boarding party,> Maneuvering said thoughtfully. <Maybe she was trying to get rid of them?>

The *Inevitable* shuddered, rocked by a direct hit that had somehow managed to avoid the forward lines of their formation.

Immediately after, Kydell recognized the familiar sensation of a high powered Shielding spell. "It would appear they're still on board," he observed wryly.

<Maybe they portaled back? Since our Shields were down?> Telemetry offered.

Kydell had a sneaking suspicion she'd kept them on board to begin with. He began to pace, hands clasped behind his back as he evaluated his options. "Why wasn't I informed immediately about the boarding party?"

<You ordered me not to disturb you, unless it was an emergency.> Maneuvering's tone remained flat. <Navigations said she had it handled.>

"*Navigations* was ordered to conserve her magic so we could jump home." Kydell injected venom into every word. "*Meanwhile*, I had an entire crew who could have handled it, had they known. Now *she* has no magic, my crew is *gone*, and the boarding party is *still here*. Tell me, Helm, what part of that sounds 'handled' to you?"

There was a brief pause. <A misjudgment on my part, sir. Won't happen again.>

"No. It won't." Kydell's voice grew dangerously quiet. "After we take care of Baden, you and I are going to spend some time together. Clearly, I have been neglectful in your training. I will rectify my oversight."

<Of course, sir.>

Kydell dropped the link, suppressing the growl threatening to escape the back of his throat. *Why must I do* everything *around here myself?*

"Comms. Get me Maintenance."

<Maint, go.>

"There are intruders on my ship, and I suspect your mages are no longer on board to stop them. I want you to track them and tell me where they are at all times."

<I'm afraid I can't do that, sir. The internal sensors are down. The whole array.>

Kydell gripped the nearest console, his claws digging into the metal. "Let me guess. They overloaded during our battle today?"

<No, sir.> Maintenance sounded surprised. <Early last week. I've ordered the parts, but they're out of stock.>

"Why am I always surrounded by incompetence?"

<I can't presume to answer that, sir. Is there something else I can help you with?>

The admiral growled deep in the back of his throat, canines fully bared. "Communications, get me the *Reckoning*. Connect me to their Navigations AI."

<Yes, sir.>

Kydell scratched his claws slowly across the useless new weapons console. His present situation was coming into focus, and he didn't like what he saw. There was only one way to deal properly with a ship full of mutinous AI.

Time to recall my TAG.

28

Jake traced the air over several of the delicate lines of circuitry visible within the server room, the majority hidden within an assortment of carefully positioned access hatches. While his old school back on Loxira had taught the many uses of tyrellium crystals and Runework circuitry, and he'd been able to apply the basic principles in practice both then and on Baden, the Confederation attack had ended his opportunities for a formal hands-on education in the more advanced principles. It was fascinating to see them in use now, although he noted at least one location where the Legion's more practical approach would improve the efficiency of the Confederation's more haphazard reliance on large Imperium reserves.

He felt the ship shudder under a sudden barrage from the battle outside, and reflexively extended his Shielding to encompass the entire ship, his focus still on the circuits. After the near escape from the engine room, he realized he held a surprising lack of fear, even despite the present dangers he *knew* they faced.

His father was here. His father would fix everything, whatever it took. Just like always.

"So *this* is the young man who allowed you to defeat me. He even Shields the engines." Alanis' face was unreadable, but Jake heard the telltale rustle of fabric as his father straightened with pride. "You always did surround yourself with competence."

His father's voice was soft. "There's a reason I put up with you even back then, you know. You really *were* insufferable."

"So were you..." She paused to read the name on his father's coveralls. "Shane." She turned to Jake. "And who might you be, child?"

"Jake, Ma'am." He reluctantly pulled his attention from the circuits to bob his head politely. "My father speaks highly of you. It's nice to finally meet you."

"Father...?" She swung her head to stare at his father before returning her attention to Jake. "You never struck me as the sort to have a kid."

His father rubbed his neck. "Was a surprise to me, too. Jake... changed my life. Made me realize..."

Jake swallowed, remembering the first day he met his father. The Sparnell Armed Forces had been bombarding Loxira for days, first to break through the planetary Shielding, then to raze their cities. He'd spent most of the attack hiding in the reinforced bombardment room in the center of their house, but when Scudder escaped after a particularly close barrage, he'd foolishly chased after his pet. His Mom had run after him, using her own body to shield him from the shrapnel as a strike demolished their house.

The fae was still talking, her voice now teasing. "She must have been some woman, to cut through that cold exterior of yours."

"Caroline is... something special." His father rubbed the back of his neck, looking away. "I've no doubt she'll take me to task if I ever fall short. I'm haunted by enough demons from my past, I don't need any more. Especially not hers!"

Jake subconsciously noted Jeb and Razick leaning closer to hear more of the conversation, but he was still reliving the past. The planetary attack had ended shortly after the house explosion, but it had been too late to save his mother.

If only I'd waited a few more minutes, she wouldn't have died.

Or she still may have, his father had helped him realize, eventually. The SAF away team had materialized directly in front of him minutes later, advancing on them with murderous intent. She'd thrown herself in harm's way once more, pleading for his life...

And the man he now called "Father" had answered.

"I promised Jake we'd save Baden," his father was now protesting. "We have to go."

Alanis shrugged with two pairs of arms, pointing to the door. "You're here until I'm satisfied I can trust you. Tell me about Jake."

"He's a good kid," his father said slowly, nonetheless unable to keep the pride from leaking into his voice. "I'll never deserve him, or the trust he has in me, but he's exactly what I needed."

But you've earned that trust, Father.

Jake moved to stand by his father, wrapping his arms around the necromancer who had betrayed everything he thought he stood for to save the boy he'd never met. The man who had never stopped putting Jake first, no matter the personal cost. The man who was clearly uncomfortable with affection, but nonetheless constantly proved his own commitment to Jake with large actions, even when he had trouble with the smaller ones.

"What happened that day, Grim? What happened on Loxira? We all thought you were dead."

Jake knew this was the question everyone wanted to know. Razick in particular was watching his father with laser focus.

His father stiffened. "I..." He faltered, but only for a moment. "I killed them all, Yiven. Shattered. Every last one. Caroline was dying. They were going to kill Jake. I... I couldn't let that happen." He buried his face in his hands. "I still see them at night. I trained with half of them. I..."

"You saved me."

Jake squeezed his father tighter, nuzzling the rough fabric of the man's coveralls with his cheek. He remembered the stranger in the uniform of the enemy who'd broken ranks to wreak sudden and terrible destruction upon the others. His Mom's sobs of relief when the stranger had answered her pleas. The necromancer's growing frustrations when he couldn't save her, too, and all the energy he spent trying. The months spent hiding in that bunker deep beneath the ground, until finally meeting with Feels on Baden.

Feels had even merged their genetics, folding Jake's into his adoptive father's to grow the necromancer a new, less-recognizable body. They'd masqueraded as biological father and son but the necromancer had stepped readily into the role, to the point Jake had no doubts his adoptive father genuinely considered them a family.

Even despite how many times Jake had manipulated his father's protectiveness for his own benefit.

He pulled away, pressing both hands against his father's chest as he looked up, his practiced eye catching his father's attempts to hold back tears.

"You *always* save me."

Alanis' voice was soft. "Where's Caroline now?"

"The Legion believes we were only meant to live this life once," Jake answered for his father, earning a look of gratitude. "My father offered to resurrect her, but she said no. So he taught me Soul Call instead."

"A *Legion* woman?" She stared at him incredulously for a moment, but then her words shifted into kindness. "You've changed, Grim. And not just on the outside."

His father exhaled. "Some people don't deserve second chances." He glanced at Jake. "But when you get one anyway, that carries the obligation to do the best you can with it, no matter how broken you are. How irredeemable. How much of a monster." His father closed his eyes, and Jake could hear the regret in his voice. "So here I am, trying my best to undo my worst. I've been living in the shadow of Renkash for too long. Decided it's time to change that. For Jake."

"This second chance of yours. It suits you." Alanis paused. "So does fatherhood. I'm happy for you."

She shook her head, talking as much to herself as to his father. "A *Legion* girl. Never saw *that* one coming."

29

"Now that you've satisfied your curiosity at my expense, we need to focus. The *Inevitable* is ours, but the rest of the fleet is still out there." Shane shifted his weight, sighing in relief when Alanis accepted his change in topic. He looked down at his son. "Think you can keep up the Shielding?"

Jake made a face. "Of course."

Shane nodded, turning to Alanis. "I'm prepared to take over as Navigations."

The fae bristled. "You'll do no such thing. You *left*. This is *my* ship now."

"It was built for *me*," he reminded her.

"And it's been *mine* for two decades," she shot back, pointing several legs in his direction. "The other AI don't trust you, but they're loyal to *me*. You *need* me." She jutted her chin in defiance.

He shook his head. "You've got to be low on magic by now."

She held his stare for a moment before sighing. "Used the last of it on our jump," she agreed.

Jeb wrinkled his nose. "Lawrence said you were powerful."

"She's a Void necromancer. Like me," Shane agreed. "That means we can cast unbelievably powerful spells, even borrowing strength from the stars themselves. But we're not built for endurance."

"Have to be careful we don't borrow more than we can pay back," Alanis added. "I'd be dead by now, if I wasn't already."

"But you *are* dead." Jeb tugged at his hair, brows furrowing. "So nothing else can hurt you."

"I wish that were true!" Alanis crossed all three pairs of arms, her holographic projection fluttering at eye level. "There are things worse than death. Cosmic burnout is one of them."

Shane felt himself shudder at the reminder. While most mages only ever had to worry about spending too much in the short term, disabling their ability to metabolize more Imperium, Void mages required a detailed understanding of not only how much Imperium they'd cast, but also how quickly they'd refresh their own stores. Miscalculation led to death first, then burnout after. To be Voidburnt meant to lose access to all magic, forever.

The SAF regularly poured research funding into the condition in an effort to find a cure. Thus far, they'd remained unsuccessful. From Shane's understanding of the effects, there would never *be* a cure.

"You said she's stronger than you. How's *your* magic?" Jeb's sudden panicked question pulled Shane from his thoughts as the biologist stepped closer to stare at him accusingly.

Checking his reserves reflexively, Shane fixed Jeb with a pointed stare. "Sufficient."

The truth was, he'd spent more of his reserves than he'd hoped on the battle with Alanis. But the ship was theirs now, and she'd already cleared the other passengers. From this point on, he shouldn't need much.

"I Hyperjumped a ship twice today. He only jumped you," she reminded Jeb. "Wouldn't have managed that second jump, but I *know* this ship, and I left the crew behind."

"You left the..." Jeb visibly shuddered. "You left them in the *Void*?"

Shane shrugged. "They'll be fine. We have drills for this, and the uniforms have protections. Doesn't often happen on purpose, though."

"I seem to recall otherwise," Alanis laughed, with a pointed look at Shane. "Your codes were still in the system. Had Maintenance shift you to the captain's clearance." Her wings ruffled behind her in amusement as she motioned toward the hatch. "Admiral Kydell might discover some technical difficulties with his own codes, trying to navigate the anti-mutiny protocols Maint dialed in earlier. But he's got us all wrapped around his will, so only a matter of time before that changes."

Shane felt the blood drain from his face. "*Kydell* is here?" He thought she'd jumped the ship empty. Who else was on board?

Razick lunged forward, snarling, despite her brother's attempts to hold her back. "Then he *dies* on this ship. *Today.*"

Shane didn't have time to process the lab tech's reaction as Alanis' explanation tumbled out in a rush. To avoid being swept away in the flood, he had to concentrate on her words. Words that struck against his own memories, and the guilt that accompanied his role in what came after.

"I told you, he's stronger than he used to be. And he's done... things. I can't do *anything* to hurt him. I can wish for it, dream about it, fantasize about it all I like, but when the time comes for action? All I can do is protect him." Her hologram shuddered. "It's part of why I drained my magic, so I can't use it anymore. The other AI have been covering for me, to keep him away from me, but eventually he'll get through. But this way, I can't hurt you."

He remembered all those years ago, his own personality slowly altered and strangled beneath the white wolf's claws. The overwhelming efforts to bury his past and begin a new, peaceful life with Jake as he worked to break free from the conditioning. The relentless drive to self-improvement, so he could provide Jake with a better childhood than his own. All his progress, now under threat of crashing down around him because Admiral Kydell had found him.

Shane closed his eyes.

When he opened them again, he wasn't Janitor Shane, protective father and quiet war refugee, he was Commodore Lawrence, the assertive and ruthless military tactician. He'd tried to put this part of his life behind him, but he'd need all his skills if they were to survive and save Baden.

"Jake, you stay here with Alanis. Just keep the *Inevitable* Shielded, that's your only job."

"I want to stay with *you*," Jake protested. "I can be your Shielding mage again! I'll be *safer* with you."

Shane held up a finger, easily brushing off the reactions his conditioning usually caused at that particular assertion. "Not this time. Before I agreed to let you come, you promised to follow my orders no matter what. *This* is one of them. If we lose the *Inevitable*, we lose everything. And *you* can keep her for us. As Shielding mage for the *Inevitable*."

He shook his head as Jake attempted to protest again. "You'll be safer here, with Alanis. I made a promise to you *and* your mother."

Jake jutted his chin, crossing his arms in defiance. "You *killed* my mother."

Shane's face hardened as he fought against the knives of guilt summoned by the boy's statement. "My choices led to her death, yes. I won't allow the same to happen to you. You stay here."

"I'll show you how to use the ship's Runework, to strengthen your Shield," Alanis promised, with a quick glance of apology at Shane. "Maybe you can think up some improvements?"

Shane noted the way Jake perked up at the thought, despite the scowl still written across his face. "I guess."

Shane took a moment to center himself before addressing Alanis. "What other AI systems can we rely on?"

"We have most of them. You've filled Shielding, so just Weapons to fill."

"What happened to Jarkin?"

"Fleet Admiral Valcore," Alanis informed him. "Politics. Don't know what he stepped in this time, just that it was big." She turned her attention to Razick. "You wouldn't happen to know a battle mage we could plug in, would you?"

Shane shook his head. "Just Telepathy, Agrokinesis, and Antimagic. Plus my Necromancy. But I have someone in mind already, for Weapons AI."

Grim, no... He felt a strong sense of panic accompanying Feels' words. *I put that life behind me. Unlike you, it seems.*

Shane scowled. "I'm not built for peace. I'm a weapon. I don't know how to be anything else."

He watched Razick lean forward, clearly accustomed to necromancers and their periodic one-sided conversations. Jeb, meanwhile, was staring wide eyed, attention darting between Shane and the nonchalance of the others in the room, frantically searching his companions' faces for an explanation.

You could try. Don't ask me to do this.

"I *did* try. You saw how that turned out." He began pacing. "But this mission... I can be their shield, and their sword, so nobody else has to grow up a monster like me." Shane focused his thoughts on the fear and helplessness he'd felt after his parents' deaths, and the hatred and vengeance for the Legion that had followed.

I won't kill all these people. Feels' words were accompanied by resolve and stubbornness.

Shane stopped pacing. "Then convince them to surrender, so they stop killing innocent people. I'm *not* the aggressor here." He sighed, his voice betraying a quiet resignation. "Not this time."

There was a long pause before Feels voice returned, accompanied by remorse and resignation. *Okay. But only to save Baden. And you have to promise to let me free, after. I refuse to remain your prisoner.*

Shane meditated on appreciation and understanding, trusting the imprisoned empath to discern his meaning as he carefully removed his mother's locket and offered it to Alanis. "I have someone. Where should I bind them?"

"What offensive magic do they know?" she asked, pointing two legs to the locket. "That's not your old medic, is it?"

"They've agreed to help."

"Doesn't matter!" Alanis crossed her legs. "The *Inevitable* doesn't have standard weapons anymore. They were replaced by some new experimental prototype, just last week. Amplifies whatever spell you send through, but there are no presets. You have to know the spell." She let loose a sarcastic laugh. "Oh! And our battle mage couldn't even figure out how to aim it! It just... hits everyone."

Alanis exhaled. "And, call me crazy, but healing everyone seems counter to our goals right now."

Shane felt his stomach wrap in knots at how quickly his tentative plan was beginning to unravel. "So... We can't aim with the weapons, and they only amplify the spells you cast through them. So we'll need to send an offensive spell through them."

The repetition was for Feels' benefit.

Grim... The empath's voice was a mere whisper. *No. That's a line I'll* never *cross. You can't ask this of me. Not for my freedom. Not even to save a planet. I made a promise to* never *use my Psychomorphation to cause harm, no matter the reason, and I will* not *break that. I will* not *become Kydell.*

SHANE FOCUSED HIS THOUGHTS on apology. The fact Feels *believed* Shane would ask that of them showed just how badly he'd fractured the trust of his former friend.

"Alanis, you coordinate the AI from here. Have Comms notify us if anything changes." His voice turned grim. "And if it looks like we won't win our battle with Kydell, or the fleet, you get Jake out of here. He knows Apotheturgy, he'll loan you his magic for the jump. Just get him somewhere safe."

The fae nodded. "You have my word. But what about Kydell's conditioning?"

"That's why Feels will run Weapons." He ran his fingers lightly over the locket. "They're also an empath, and can Shield you. We can't lose the *Inevitable*, or Baden is lost."

"What are you going to do?" Alanis scoffed. "Get them to surrender, using the power of love?"

Shane gave a sad smile. "Something like that."

Grim, you can't make me do this! Anger had joined their fear as they beat against the confines of the binding spell in the locket.

"I'd never ask that of you, dear friend. You knew that, once. I'm sorry I betrayed your trust so much that you forgot." He turned to Alanis. "You're better versed in Necromancy than me. Is there a binding spell we can use, that would allow them to come and go as they please?"

"Yes," she answered slowly. "But my magic–"

"We'll use mine," he interrupted quickly, offering her an apotheturgic link to draw freely from his own reserves. "Cast it twice, please. Once on Weapons' AI crystal... and once on the locket."

He'd never imprison them again. After today, he'd either be free of Kydell, or trapped once more in the wolf's service. Either way, he owed Feels their freedom.

He rubbed the locket again, tenderly, as Alanis set to work with her magic. "I remember how you used to tell me what it was like to be a natural born empath. How people's strong emotions would often amplify your own experience of those emotions, if they matched something you felt. And how you learned to do the inverse, cheering people up by projecting your own happiness at them."

I... didn't realize you listened to my rambling. A short flash of surprise accompanied the words. *I hardly think that will help here, though. They're temporary. And I can only project the emotion at the strength I feel it.*

"I *always* listened," Shane answered quietly. "Could you do the same with someone else's emotions? Store mine in one of the crystals? Cast that through the weapons?"

Maybe... Feels sounded thoughtful. *Yes. Yes, I could make that work. What did you have in mind?*

"Guilt." He swallowed. "Use your Psychomorphation on me. Pull up every last piece of my guilt. Use it to hit the fleet."

"You're going to *guilt* the fleet into surrendering?" Alanis was beside herself with laughter.

Grim... I didn't do that to you when I hated you with every last ounce of my soul. I refuse to do it now. Do you know how debilitating that would be? If I bunch it all together like that and force you to feel it all at once... I won't be able to split it up again. I can't do that to you. I won't.

"I'm asking you to." He swallowed, his chest constricting at the thought of the emotional ordeal to come. "I *know* it won't be pleasant. But I trust you. To put me back together again. To make it manageable."

Shane turned to watch Jake, the boy looking up at him with a mixture of concern and affection. "My guilt saved me from myself. Maybe you can use it to save someone else, too. Please."

Moments passed. Shane held his breath. And then...

Okay.

Without warning, Shane felt the weight of all his past mistakes. The countless deaths he'd caused, the people he'd Shattered himself, the lives he'd ruined for reasons as simple as a perceived slight. He sank to the floor, grabbing at his chest as the weight of all the worlds and lives and existences he'd destroyed slammed into him at once to rip his breath away. He found himself reviewing every past decision, longing for the chance to relive his entire life, or erase it completely.

And still the memories of his past vengeance pressed their accusations against his heart, crowding out his thoughts with their demands. Each face somehow both familiar with long-harbored memory and faded through the passages and ravages of time and obsession. Each soul he'd Shattered personally with his own magic, their lives and Afterlives wiped from all existence outside the memories of those who knew them once.

He knew them all. Remembered them all. Not a day went by when he didn't think about them.

And rising above them all was Shane's greatest betrayal, face twisted into a desperate, tearful plea as he reached toward his own destruction in fruitless supplication to avoid the fate Shane had laid upon him.

Shane felt himself break under the weight of it, his emotions shattering like the souls of his victims, but the guilt of his deeds wasn't done with him yet.

The tally of his victims continued to grow, cities and planets and entire star systems ravaged in the name of Admiral Kydell, the Confederation, and Shane's ever growing rage. Fleets pulverized for daring to defend themselves. Civilizations toppled and subjugated under Confederation boots, solely in the name of glory. Innocents maimed and murdered by the SAF, deemed too weak and insignificant to retain their former freedoms.

All on his orders. All to continue feeding the Sparnelli war machine. All in a fruitless attempt to sooth the jagged edges of the death of his own parents under the single-minded ships of the Space Defense Legion, two more innocent victims to those like him spreading hateful vengeance across the stars.

All *his* fault.

We can't change the past. Only ourselves.

His mother's voice broke through the self-loathing, her warm and loving words another ghost from the past, an excerpt from the holographic recording tucked away inside her locket. Shane hadn't been permitted to listen to the messages since he'd murdered Feels – the Soulbind had given the fae full control of the locket's capabilities, and they'd been understandably determined to bar him access, aside from a rather unpleasant incident involving the image of his father – but he clung to it now, allowing the familiar mantra to guide him through what happened next.

Yes, he was responsible for his own choices, decisions he should have made differently, but his past mistakes weren't his alone. His idyllic childhood had been a far cry from the standard provided to the average Sparnelli citizen, their lives built around the ideals of patriotism and Family glory. He'd learned that quickly, first at the orphanage after his parents' deaths, then in his extended years of military service for the Sparnell Armed Forces beginning with his mandatory ten-year conscription at the tender age of sixteen.

Even more importantly, he'd been confronted with the severity of his mistakes that fateful day on Loxira. The day he'd finally been permitted to enact his vengeance on the SDL for their role in the bombardment of his own homeworld of Yarva, only to find the mirror to himself in the eyes of his enemy as his landing party had discovered Jake holding his dying mother in his arms.

That day, the full weight of his actions had crashed down around him, giving home to the guilt that until then he'd managed to hide beneath pretenses of justice.

And every day since, he'd attempted to turn his life around. To live for the future, and the boy he'd promised to raise as his own son, rather than continuing to perpetuate and further inflict the pains of the past.

He'd made many mistakes since then, too. He'd allowed Admiral Kydell to hone him into a single-minded weapon of necromancy and vengeance, and the results still showed in his reactions and problem-solving methods. But it had taken decades to become the war criminal he'd been and it would require just as many years of effort to find himself amidst the wreckage.

He was trying. Raising Jake, protecting Baden, safeguarding what bits of the future he could against those that would snuff them out for their own benefit.

Maybe he'd never find redemption. He certainly didn't deserve it. But maybe that didn't matter. He still had a role to play, to ensure a better future for Jake than his own.

He felt a weight lifting from his shoulders, a bright light of hope now burning in his chest and expanding to warm his entire body. His past wouldn't control him. He'd allowed himself to be manipulated to serve the purposes of another, his pain twisted and amplified to hone him into a vengeful shadow of who he could have been.

But it had also given him the tools he'd need to protect Jake.

He felt the guilt twist and shift within his soul, releasing its hold on his emotional state and instead weaving itself into his protectiveness for Jake, and his newfound determination to guard the universe from those like his former self.

Yes, his actions and choices had still been his own. Manipulated or not, all these things were his doing and it was up to him to undo them, in whatever way he could.

The guilt solidified into its new form, a driving force to propel him forward rather than a weight to hold him back. His past had forged him into a monster, but starting now, he would be the one to hold the other monsters at bay.

His penance to the universe.

So. The bad news is retirement is permanently off the table. You wouldn't be able to live with yourself. Unfortunately. But I think you'll be happy with this? Let me know if you need me to make any adjustments.

The empath sent him a flash of insecurity, mixed with pride.

I've... never done anything quite this scale before. Changes this big take a lot of time and patience, but... You didn't fight me. I couldn't have done it, without that trust.

Shane stood slowly from the spot where he'd fallen, calmly wiping away the damp from his eyes before turning his attention to the others with an intensity that caused each to take a step backward.

Jake tilted his head, meeting his father's stare before running to wrap him in a hug. Shane returned the gesture, crouching to Jake's level to squeeze him back, and for the first time since he could remember Shane felt pure joy, untainted by regrets of the past.

Alanis stared, wide eyed and open mouthed. "I take it back. This might actually work."

"I'm glad *someone* feels that way." Jeb was focused on Shane, wide-eyed, his arms wrapped around a rather angry looking Razick. "What in the Void was *that*?"

"Guilt," Shane said simply, rubbing gently at the locket beneath his coveralls. "And our key to saving the planet. We can't linger. We have to go."

"I just watched you have a breakdown on the floor. I don't think you're in any state to go *anywhere*."

"It doesn't matter," Razick said, the softness of her words nonetheless failing to hide her rage. "Kydell's here. And so are we. Either we do what we came to do, or he wins. And he'll take Baden with him."

"We'll find him again," Jeb began, but Razick cut him off.

"Has to be here. Has to be now." She turned her attention to Shane. "Regardless how we feel about each other. This is the team we have. There's no time to find a new one."

Shane tugged a scrap of paper from his janitorial coveralls, scrawling down his old access code and holding it out to the siblings. "Meet me in Hydroponics. We'll lure Kydell there. Use this to bypass the securities."

He waited until Jeb reluctantly retrieved the paper before addressing Alanis. "What's it look like out there?"

"Telemetry says the fleet is keeping their distance for now," she reported. "We're no threat without weapons, anyway. Kydell must have told them to ignore us."

"How'd he get the message out?" Jeb asked after a moment. "He's no telepath."

Shane narrowed his eyes. Jeb knew a lot about Kydell, for someone claiming to be a Freeholder. And Razick's combat training felt suspiciously familiar.

"Comms said the admiral made him contact the *Reckoning*. Direct to their Void necromancer. All he said was to wait one minute, then call him back."

"So they know we have the ship, but Kydell ordered them away, anyway. It'll have to do." He punched in his code to override the door, waving the siblings toward the corridor. "I'll join you in a bit."

"What are you going to do?" Jeb asked, narrowing his eyes at Shane as his sister pushed past him into the hallway.

"Need another favor from Feels," Shane said quietly, rubbing at the locket. "Then a quick trip to raid Laundry."

"Laundry?"

Shane raised one of the legs of his overalls, fixing Jeb with a stare as if the answer should be obvious. "My socks are still wet."

Feels attempted to process their own feelings from their emotional surgery on Grim. The task had been a difficult one, not just in finding places to safely hang the guilt he'd been using to mentally flay himself but also in the act of collecting it all in the first place. Feeling their friend – they couldn't consider him any less than that, not after the realization of how much of the guilt he carried was over what he'd done to them and their technicians – dissolve into despair and self-hatred, knowing they had been the cause, had been the most difficult thing they'd ever experienced. Or *done*.

But Grim had known exactly what he was asking, and who he was asking it from. He always did, that calculating mind of his, always several steps ahead, only failing when it ran up against another of Kydell's carelessly applied roadblocks. And Feels had to admit that his logic was sound. From their memories of their time in the SAF, amplified guilt would go a long way toward bringing much of the fleet to its knees, saving a great many lives on both sides in the process. They should probably already be using the weaponized guilt against the fleet, but Grim had mentioned needing them to help finalize his plans and maybe he'd need them to adjust the results of their emotional surgery.

And as much as they told themselves they were still angry at him, that they could never forgive him for what he'd done to their team, that Baden was home and her people deserved protecting...

Grim's needs came first.

The necromancer seemed calmer and more focused now. Feels inhaled his emotions, wrapping themselves in his feelings of hope and determination, even on the eve of his fight against one of the most dangerous admirals in the Confederation's fleets. The guilt was there, underlying everything, but now it served only to strengthen his resolve.

Still, Feels would be haunted by Grim's emotions at his weakest moment, and the knowing that they had caused it. They'd heard wild tales of surgeons in the Space Defense Legion who actually cut into their patients to reach the parts they were fixing, adding more wounds as a step of the healing process. Feels wondered if this was how those healers felt, knowing they were adding more pain before administering the cure. How could they live with themselves after, even knowing the pain was necessary?

They would need to learn.

"Feels..." It was Grim again, his emotions shifting to fear and apology. "I need another favor."

What do you need me to adjust? What doesn't feel right? They must have made a mistake with the spell. So they would fix it. Whatever Grim needed, whatever he wanted to become, they would help him get there.

But Grim had other intentions. "There's nothing wrong with your spell, dear friend. I wish you'd done it years ago, although I suppose I wasn't ready yet."

Feels stretched their senses and realized they were now alone, the emotions of others now far away in other parts of the ship. The empath's rising concerns were briefly derailed by a burst of joy radiating along their Insight into Grim, quickly fading back into apprehension and doubt.

Their necromancer must have changed his socks. He'd always hated feeling wet; Feels had always found that endearing.

Grim quieted, his words sincere. "This favor is... a personal request."

They felt their thoughts quicken. Grim never made purely personal requests, everything had always been to further his current plans.

I'm here for you. I'm sorry I wasn't before. What else do you need from me?

They felt Grim's gratitude wash over them with a warm familiarity. "You've never had a selfish bone in your body, Feels. I don't know what I did to deserve your friendship. Or... your forgiveness?"

I don't have a body, Grim. Just your locket. Feels radiated amusement, and was pleased to note Grim's emotional response did not contain the usual guilt. Their emotional surgery was holding. *Even when I did, I had an exoskeleton, not bones. So that's not the achievement you think it is.*

"I'll get you a mortal body. When this is all over," Grim promised.

I...

Feels paused. Now that the option was before them, they realized they didn't want it anymore.

I'd rather stay with you.

They felt Grim's surprise, and sent a wave of amusement of their own, hoping it didn't carry any of their underlying confusion at the discovery.

I've seen the trouble you cause by yourself. Can't leave you alone for a second, they added, although whether the justification was intended for Grim or themselves, they weren't sure.

"That... Makes this easier to ask."

They felt Grim rub the locket, his grip tight, his emotions shifting to a roiling cloud of worry and nervousness.

"I'm afraid. Of what Kydell can do. Of what he's *already* done. I can't go back. I can't allow him to use me to hurt anyone else, ever again."

But that was him, not you, Feels protested. *He changed you with his magic. Made you into the monster you're running from.*

"You of *all* people know that's not how it works." Grim's remorse carried through every word. "Psychomorphation can only make changes to what's already there. It needs a foothold, something to work with. Kydell may have been the reason for a lot of it... But at least *some* of it was me. My anger and fear over my parents' death. My hatred of the Legion for causing it. My quest for revenge, to take from them more than they'd taken from me."

But two decades... That would change anybody.

They wrapped him in their forgiveness. It was easier than it would have been, mere hours before.

His friend's emotions turned to shame in response. "Feels... In the beginning? I *asked* him to do it." He shifted back to determination, mixed with stubbornness. "That was the past. I'm not the same person anymore. But it's important to me that you understand. *I can't go back.*"

I'll do everything I can, Feels promised. *What do you need from me?*

"I want to take the Oath. To *you*."

Time stood still, the seconds slowed as Feels attempted to process Grim's statement. The request was unexpected, although far from unwelcome. Ever since the early days, when Grim had approached them and earnestly asked what they meant by friendship, Feels had wondered what it would be like to have more. To *mean* more to the fierce orange-eyed fury that was Grim. Sometimes they'd caught flashes of the possibility, gone so quickly Feels wondered if the feelings were imagined.

That was why his betrayal on Baden had hurt so much. Finally free of the SAF, Grim had immediately looked to them for help, turned to them in his hour of need… and then murdered them and Shattered their people in an effort to defend someone else.

Not that they blamed Jake – or even Grim, now that they understood his thought process at the time – but that moment of hope in the future followed by the cold reality of Grim's infernal logic…

The realization had been devastating.

Feels tried to keep their tone calm, and hoped they'd successfully suppressed their sudden desire from transmitting through their words. *Where I come from, that's a marriage proposal.*

The reaction was immediate, unmistakable, and exactly what Feels had feared.

"Shit, Feels. I didn't mean to make you uncomfortable."

Feels felt their own embarrassment, amplified by their friend's. So, this was just a business transaction then. These weren't the circumstances they'd wished for when dreaming of this moment, but of course their answer would be yes. With Grim, the answer was always yes, in the end.

They buried their disappointment.

I just wanted to check we were both agreeing to the same thing. You already cut your way out of an Oath once. Why are you so eager to take another one?

"An Oath to you is different." Grim's emotions radiated trust. Safety. Belonging. "If Kydell manages to control me again, you'll be able to use the Oath tether to find me. If I run out of magic while fighting him, or if I die, my soul will return to you.

He won't be able to take me. I *refuse* to spend the rest of my existence as Kydell's *puppet*."

He paused, and they felt a flash of sorrow and regret. "My soul is fractured, Feels. I didn't have the benefit of time or skill when I broke that Oath. I had to use *Shatter*..."

The empath caught a glimpse of their friend's loneliness and despair from the days after Loxira and his resultant desertion, their own soul filling with sadness at what he must have done to survive before turning to them.

"I need an Oath to reinforce the cracks. To *survive*. And if I'm going to live up to this drive you've given me? To change the universe? I... I'll need you to hold me back. To help me be better than I am."

As always, his logic was sound. And with no trace of reciprocating their own feelings at the thought.

Why me? they asked softly.

"You're the only person I can trust with this." His words were quiet. Solemn. "The only one strong enough. I can't ask Jake to carry this burden. And I know you won't use it to hurt me."

Trust was a start. They could work with trust. He'd recently regained theirs, after all, and now look where they were. Pining after the necromancer, same as they'd done since the beginning.

Won't you be able to break it yourself whenever you want? Since you'd be the one casting it?

A flash of pride radiated toward them. "If you cast a spell on me at the same time, I'll use Apotheturgy to weave the Oath into it. Count your spell as primary, which would make my Oath yours to keep or break as you see fit. I'll have no control over it after casting."

Grim sent them thoughts of concern. "There's a risk to you, though. If Kydell catches me, he could have one of his necromancers trace the tether back to you. And if he wants me as his Oathbound again, he'd happily Shatter you to break it."

Let him try *to separate us again.*

Their answer was fierce and angry, and received a flash of love and amusement from their friend in return.

I accept your proposal.

Grim sent a caress of gratitude, and nothing else, so Feels continued.

I'll absolve the Oath as soon as Kydell is dealt with.

"No." Grim's voice was soft but resolute. "If you're going to hold me accountable, then you'll need leverage. You *know* I don't listen when I think I'm right. The universe is a better place when we're on the same side."

And what will keep me on your *side?*

"You always have been."

The conviction, admiration, and appreciation in Grim's words despite their two-year disagreement would have taken Feels' breath away, if the empathic fae still breathed. Perhaps they had a chance with him after all, although that was a conversation best left until after the psychomorphic admiral was dealt with.

Following Grim's direction, Feels slid loose from the locket's bindings into the Afterlife and began to cast a Psychic Shielding spell. This variation was a supercharged version of the basic Shielding taught to most natural empaths, a tool to defend their emotions from both accidental and intentional tampering. With any luck, it would also help Grim deflect at least some of the effects of Kydell's own magic during their confrontation.

The necromancer for his part kept busy muttering vows and carefully weaving strands of the Oath through their Shielding spell and into his own soul. Feels wondered at exactly what he was promising, but Grim had presided over enough Oath ceremonies for Kydell, they trusted he knew what he was doing.

As an afterthought, they wove a strand of Empathic Insight around the Oath and tether itself, allowing them a direct channel to Grim's emotional state. If they were to hold the responsibility of helping moderate his actions, then they would give themselves the tools needed to do it properly.

Grim caught the spell through their link and flashed approval.

Finally, it was done. The empath felt a sense of calm confidence running along their link to the necromancer, his mind now at peace for the confrontation ahead. The subtle gossamer black of Grim's necromantic Oath, the tether running straight from Feels to Grim before splitting into a complicated web twisting its way around and into every available surface of the necromancer's soul, stood in stark contrast to the blue-green shimmer of Feels' own spells, winding around the tether and encircling Grim's soul in perpetual color.

Grim smiled beside them. "That's what I call good spell-work."

Surveying the results of their joint handiwork, their light encapsulating his darkness, his darkness eternally linking his soul to theirs, Feels couldn't help but agree.

RAZICK FOLLOWED HER BROTHER down the hall, her heart still pounding at the realization of exactly what kind of soul the necromancer kept bound to his person. <I don't know what to do, Jeb.>

<We have a chance, a real chance, of taking out Kydell. You can be free again!> The biologist had finally stopped tugging at his armored dress suit, ushering her down the corridor with eager steps, the large wrench still propped on his shoulder. <You should *tell him*. He's gotten us this far. Let him include the rest of your skills in his plan. At *least* tell him you're a Kane battle mage.>

She knew he was right. Logic dictated she tell him of her extensive special forces training, and the offensive magic she'd sworn would never be used to harm anyone else until the day she could take her revenge on Admiral Kydell.

But she couldn't.

Memories of her subjugation at the hands of the admiral's Psychomorphation came flooding back. <What if he wants to use his bound mage on me? Alter my mind?>

<Like they did to Lawrence?> Jeb frowned. <What *did* they do to him?>

<If I had to guess? Rewrote his emotions. Probably turned his guilt into something else, when they were done with it.>

<That's great!> Jeb's face brightened at the thought, a sharp contrast to her own anxiety at the prospect. <You've spent too much time living in fear. And maybe they can undo whatever Kydell did. You heard. They're a healer *and* an empath. They *must* know how to help.>

Razick watched as her brother punched Lawrence's code into the keypad of the locked hatch in front of them, waiting until it slid open with a reluctant hiss. <They use the same magic as Kydell, Jeb. Nobody's messing with my head *ever* again. I don't care *who* they are.> She crossed her arms, fixing her brother with a piercing glare. <*Never* again.>

Jeb sighed, shoulders dropping as he stepped through the hatch. <At least consider it? You saw what they did for Lawrence.>

<And how do we even know he's still himself?>

Hearing the janitor's side of his argument with the mage before they'd apparently agreed to his request, she already knew this fear was unfounded.

But fear didn't care. *Never again. Never again. Never again. Never again.* The words repeated in her mind like a mantra.

<Raz... Just think about it?> Her brother had resumed tugging on the cuffs of his suit, his former elation now replaced by trepidation. <It's got to be better than whatever Kydell did to you.> He stopped in his tracks, brows furrowing as he looked up at her. <How do you know this fear isn't *him* talking?>

Panic gripped tighter at her heart, either confirming his suspicions or merely that she shared the same fears. She opened her mouth, attempted to refute him, or agree, but no words came out.

She brushed past him down the corridor instead, toward the next closed hatchway. <Kydell dies today, and then it won't matter anymore. I'll be *free*.>

Jeb didn't answer, merely picking up his pace to follow behind.

<AI said she'd have her team delay Kydell as long as they could,> Razick added after a moment, waiting at the hatch for Jeb to punch in the code again. <Just have to tell Comms when we're ready.>

The hatch slid open with an angry hiss and Razick continued onward, without waiting for Jeb to catch up.

<You know you should tell him,> Jeb repeated softly across their link.

She shifted her weight, eying him uncomfortably as she waited at the portal transit node. <I know,> she admitted finally. <I just... I can't.>

He watched her, not even attempting to hide his concern. <Would you like *me* to tell him?>

<What if he won't let me help?>

<Raz...> He gripped her arm, brown eyes wide as his fingers bored into her elbow. <Of course he'll let you help. You're a *battle* mage. You're–>

<Better at this than him,> she finished, with a sad smile. <Jumping me from my defensive position. Claiming he was helping me.>

Jeb winced, tugging his hair as he turned away. <That was my fault.>

<*You* told him to jump me away?>

<I *expected* him to go out there, too,> her brother admitted. <But I didn't *say* that.>

<Which is why *I* have to take out Kydell,> Razick said quietly across their link, squeezing Jeb's shoulder in reassurance. <Lawrence thinks he knows combat, but he was an officer. I doubt he's ever been in a real fight.>

<Same could be said for Kydell,> Jeb reminded her. <Always sent others to fight for him.>

<Others like me. Twisting our minds to better suit him.> Clenching her teeth, Razick found herself squeezing Jeb's shoulder tighter than she'd intended.

To his credit, he merely smiled down at her, his fingers brushing reassuringly against her white knuckles. <We should still tell him. He needs all the facts. If *you* won't...>

<Let's... Let's get to Hydroponics,> she managed, releasing him. <Maybe we can sort it out there.>

And perhaps the familiar mechanics of prepping for their next battle would calm her mind. Hopefully she could find something of use against his laser pistols. Her Shielding could manage, and Lawrence would be fine if he had half the skill she'd seen from Jake, but she didn't have much faith in Jeb's. Not with someone actively shooting at him.

Especially if she hadn't managed to shake enough of Kydell's influence, and that someone was *her*.

Her brother hesitated, before nodding and inputting Lawrence's code in a quick flurry of beeps. Razick wondered if he'd memorized it by now. Or whether the string of digits held any significance to whoever the orange-eyed janitor had been, back when he'd served on this ship.

The panel lit up with a list of locations, and Razick scrolled through them to find the hydroponics bay. He'd been granted full access to the ship, which meant a lot of scrolling.

<Let me,> Jeb offered, pushing her hand away to tap in a few more buttons.

Hydroponics jumped to the top of the list, the portal opening in front of them with a *snap-hiss* of light blue energy before resolving into the corridor outside their destination.

<How did you...?>

He shrugged, stepping through. <Hydroponics has the same portal code across the fleet.>

She rolled her eyes at her own ignorance before following. Jeb had been a Confederation botanist, after all. If anyone knew how to find Hydroponics quickly, it'd be him.

He was waiting for her at the door, eyes glistening. <Always wanted to see how the *Inevitable* did her hydroponics. She's the flagship, after all. She'd have the best of everything.>

<I'm sure you'll tell me all about it,> Razick laughed, grateful for the distraction as the double doors hissed open before them. <After you.>

Jeb's smile faded as he stepped through the door, face paling. "No! No! No!"

<What is it?> Razick's pulse quickened as she sank into a ready stance.

"This is all *wrong!*"

Jeb didn't seem to hear her, wandering instead to inspect rows of metallic tables housing countless plants in various stages of growth. "They should be using a *vertical* setup, to make the most use of this space. And the growth substrate is a *terrible* choice. It's cheap for a *reason*. Roots need space to *breathe*..."

"Finally! Someone who knows what they're talking about!" An unfamiliar voice radiated from the wall speakers, joy apparent at the sound of a kindred spirit. "I keep *telling* them that, but *nooooo*. Nobody wants to listen to *me!*"

<And who in Void's name is *that*?> Razick asked, sweeping the room for any further surprises.

"Hydroponics?" Jeb asked tentatively.

"The one, the only! On this ship, anyway," the voice answered, voice bubbling. "You must be our boarding party. Nav told me to expect you. Should I let her know you're here?"

<No,> Razick reminded Jeb. <Waiting for Lawrence.> And she'd need to acclimate herself to their chosen battlefield.

"You got it!" the AI answered cheerfully as Jeb relayed the message, before striking up a lively conversation about the pros and cons of various nutrient balances.

<Any thoughts?> Razick asked, inspecting the rows of shelving housing an assortment of hydroponics supplies: large crates of seeds and substrate materials, testing kits, various bits of plumbing in a wide array of shapes and sizes, and other odds and ends.

<We need to redo this entire lab,> Jeb informed her. <It's all wrong.>

<Don't think it'll survive our battle today.> She shook her head. <So you'll have a blank slate. We need to focus.>

Jeb nodded, resuming his conversation with the AI as Razick returned her own attention to the shelves. She pulled two packs of sharp metallic stakes the length of her hands off the shelf, the opposite end flat and rectangular, likely intended to hold plant labels. She tested their weight, determining their balance sufficient for Telekinesis, and slipped them into one of the deep pockets of her lab coat.

Turning her attention upward, she eyed one of the many lighting fixtures hanging from the ceiling, a small box about a third of her height and half her width, the sides perfectly angled outward to reflect the light on the plants below. Channeling her Telekinesis, she tugged at the fixture until it came free, drifting gently to her hands. A quick rap against the metal confirmed its sturdiness, while a quick twist of her magic pulled the lighting fixture free to leave merely the shield behind.

She hefted it in her arms, weaving the former support cables into a passable handle, and grunting at her handiwork. She'd need two more just like it, but then they'd each have a suitable reflector shield against Kydell's usual laser pistols.

"Are these ionized mist fixtures? Just like I recommended for growing Ballanick?"

Razick looked up from her work to watch her brother, head tipped back as he stared at the sprinkler system across the ceiling of most of the room.

"That's the *one* improvement they let me make." Pride radiated from the AI. "Set them up exactly as recommended in *On the Cultivation of Ballanick in Recirculating Air Environments.*" Her voice shifted to a conspiratorial whisper. "One of my favorite reads."

Jeb rubbed his chin. "Seeing them in action here, I would have made a few alterations to the recommendations in my white paper..."

"*Your* paper...? No... That means..." The AI's tone jumped up an octave. "You're Kane Jeb? *The* Kane Jeb? I'm a *huuuuuuuge* fan of your work. I can't believe you're actually *here!*"

<Jeb.> Razick waved her arm at the unaltered lighting fixtures she'd pulled from the ceiling, before pointing to the one she'd crafted into a shield. <I'm glad you made a friend, but I could use your help.>

<Sorry.> Jeb's cheeks flushed with the admonishment. "I'm sorry, Hydro. I need to prep for the fight with Kydell now. Maybe we can talk more after?"

"I'll still be here! Just let me know if I can do anything to help!" She squealed. "*Kane Jeb* came to fix my lab! *And* teach the admiral a lesson for *ignoring* me! Just *wait* until the others hear about this!"

Razick found herself smiling despite herself as she split her attention between her shield and Jeb's. At least the Hydroponics AI had faith in their success.

She wished she shared the dead woman's optimism. This was one fight she couldn't afford to lose.

Alanis' warnings about Kydell's mysterious increase in magical abilities still rang in Shane's ears as he slipped through the Veil to emerge in the corridor outside Hydroponics. The Navigations AI had been under Kydell's control for so long it was certainly possible this was merely a manifestation of her extended exposure, but she'd never been one for idle warnings.

If she said there was trouble, she was usually right.

He flexed his toes within his boots, eying the large door in front of him. His feet still felt waterlogged from the hours marinating in his toilet-soaked socks, but the sensation of dry cloth under his feet had already greatly enhanced his mood.

Being back in uniform, however...

Shane tugged at the stiff leather shoulder pads. He'd changed into the shirt and trousers of the Sparnell Special Forces uniform to take advantage of the built-in protections, a second set clutched against his chest which he hoped would fit Razick.

While not as robust as Jeb's suit, and offering no protections against Kydell's Psychomorphation – since he'd been unable to determine where they kept the armored helmets – at least the high impact dissipation and mild magic deflection capabilities would limit the wolf's options. The adjustable camouflage coloration was currently set to the standard Sparnell browns, colors Shane had consciously avoided since his desertion.

But at least it wasn't the same cut as the service uniform he once wore on a daily basis. He hoped Razick wouldn't object to him bringing her a set, especially since he suspected it was the same exact uniform she'd managed to escape. She'd tried to hide her past from him but the SSF training had been easy to spot, once he'd started looking.

Especially her frustration when he thought he'd been rescuing her, and instead had destroyed her defensive position. *That* had been a familiar look. He'd seen it often enough when he'd interrupted his Fleet Captain's—

He shook his head, as if he could shake the memory from his mind. Another soul Shattered, lost to his single-minded path of destruction. He had enough on his mind today. No sense digging up the souls of the past. *Especially* not the ones who couldn't haunt him themselves.

He rubbed his fingers against the locket, devoid of his loyal empath but still lovingly tucked safely beneath the Confederation uniform. Feels must have sensed his loneliness, as they sent a quick burst of reassurance, the spell vibrating along the

Oath tether before embedding itself into his own tangle of inner turmoil.

The emotional gift was stronger than usual, slipping easily past Feels' Shield encircling his soul.

Did my Oath amplify that?

Voids, he hoped so. The empath's magic had always been a source of comfort, and even the trauma of his emotional surgery earlier had been bearable due to the knowledge that Feels was behind it. As much as Shane recoiled from the physical touch of everyone but Jake, he found he craved Feels' empathic caresses.

Now that the fae had forgiven him for their murder he wondered how he'd survived so long without their touch on his emotions. He smiled in anticipation of the eternity of Feels' spellwork ahead of him, courtesy of the Emotional Insight spell they'd wrapped around his Oath, and the empathic fae's generosity in responding.

Chest lighter, he pushed his way into the hydroponics bay, his attention drawn past the endless rows of plant-laden tables to the wall of thick-plated windows revealing the battle outside. Feels must have turned the weaponized guilt on the fleet, as the *Inevitable* appeared to have caught their attention. A scattering of sparks danced across his view, an Electromancy spell deflecting off Jake's Shielding.

The boy had taken to magic faster than Shane had, at least from what the necromancer could still remember of those hazy early days of his career in the Sparnell Armed Forces. He remembered having to work hard for every spell in his repertoire, a trait his son didn't seem to share.

Not that Jake didn't put in effort. He poured his whole soul into things, with an enviable focus his mother continued to encourage, even from beyond the Veil. He just didn't seem to *need* to, when it came to magic or Runework or any of the other multitude of skills that happened to strike his fancy. He did it for *fun*.

The majority of the fleet wasn't visible from this angle, but Baden's own Shielding sparkled below in a rainbowed patchwork of angry flickers of raw, magical energy. By his practiced eye he confirmed the primary automated Shielding had already failed, the planet now reliant upon scatterings of mage teams actively channeling their own Shielding spellwork.

The method was effective, but also tiring. From this point on, the battle would be a challenge in endurance as both sides tested who could outlast and outmaneuver the other.

Shane could only hope his small but determined boarding party could effectively turn the tide before that question was answered.

"Nice of you to join us," Jeb said from his perch on the edge of one of the hydroponics trays. The biologist was busy attempting to imitate his sister's movements with a large lighting fixture, clearly altered to form a makeshift shield against Kydell's favored laser pistols.

"Now would be a good time for the Telepathy," Shane informed him, retrieving the third homemade shield from where it rested against the wall. He looked up at Razick. "You make this?"

She narrowed her eyes at him, her attention locked on the fabric pressed against his chest, before nodding.

"They'll be very useful. Thank you." He offered her the shirt and trousers. "Thought you'd want at least the *option* of the uniform. Not as good as what you made for your brother, but it's something."

She wrinkled her nose at the clothing before meeting his eyes. "No, thank you."

Shane tugged at the sleeve of his own uniform before setting the rejected garment on one of the many hydroponics tables, watching as the water soaked quickly into the fabric.

He felt a scratch against the back of his thoughts and accepted the link. <Jeb?>

<And Razick,> the lab technician confirmed. <When were you going to tell me you had a Psychomorphic Mage?>

Sighing, he turned away to stare at the battle outside as he dug into the pocket of his pilfered uniform. <Wasn't sure they'd help. They've been angry at me, last two years.> He met her eyes. <With good reason. I have a habit of mucking things up. Worse than I did with your barricade, in their case.>

She glanced briefly at her brother, before tilting her head at Shane. <I'm a battle mage.>

<I know,> he told her, offering a pair of nutrient bars. <Sparnell Special Forces, right? I tried to raid the armory on the way over, in case there was something there you could use, but even

Yiven couldn't get me access to that one. Sorry. I did grab you these. To replenish your magic.>

He'd already forced one down himself, the tasteless brick still heavy in his stomach.

A slow grin blossomed across her face as she accepted, tossing one to Jeb before ripping open the package of the other with her teeth and devouring its contents with a surprising indifference to the flavor. <That was thoughtful.> Her eyes widened, briefly, and she dug into her pockets, pulling out a small handful of what looked like planting spikes. <This useful to you?>

<Special Forces and their weapons.> He accepted the offering, feeling the weight of them before slipping them into one of the many pockets of his borrowed SSF uniform. <Thanks. Anything else you need? Don't think the AI can hold Kydell back much longer.>

"Hydro?" Jeb asked tentatively. "Anything else we should know?"

"I'm here if you need me!" the disembodied voice of the *Inevitable*'s AI announced, as cheerful as always. "Setup's two years old. We've been neglected since the admiral took over. Downgraded, even. *You* know how it is. We were state of the art under the Commodore, though. He *always* signed my requisition requests."

Shane remembered her. Another of his regrets, although in her case, for something he'd failed to do, rather than the willful harm he'd enacted against so many others.

Perhaps he'd have a chance to apologize, when all this was over.

But there were more important matters to attend to, for now. <Remember: Kydell's Psychomorphation works by altering your responses based on your feelings.> The physical preparations were as good as they could make them. As their time rapidly dwindled, Shane gave a quick rundown of the mental defenses they could use as well, such as they were. Slowing down or weakening the mind-altering magic could give them critical seconds in this fight. <The stronger the feeling, the stronger the effects of the spell. So dull your emotions as much as you can, or try to feel the opposite to suppress his tampering completely.>

Jeb reached for his sister, squeezing her arm. Whether he was offering her reassurance or asking for it himself, Shane wasn't sure.

<Shields up. Psychic Shields especially.> Shane bolstered his own Shielding as he sent the reminder, gripping one of the plant spikes in his right hand as he held the laser shield against his chest.

Razick nodded her acknowledgement, her eyes locked on the doorway as she gripped her makeshift laser shield. <We should work out a battle plan. Ambush him when he gets here.>

Shane briefly closed his eyes and exhaled. He should have thought of that. He was losing his touch.

Opening them again, he locked eyes with the form of Admiral Kydell, standing in the open doorway, and suddenly the oversight didn't matter anymore.

The golden-eyed wolf stepped into the room, teeth bared in a calculated smile. His white fur matched the white of his dress uniform, the jacket wrinkled from daily wear, his vast collection of ribbons and medals proudly displayed. Shane recognized several he himself had earned for the canid, his stomach churning at the reminder.

Kydell was exactly as Shane had remembered, a towering pillar of narcissistic confidence and mind-altering manipulation, and yet somehow he also appeared younger than before.

Alanis was right. Something definitely felt different about the admiral. More dangerous. More *feral*.

The wolf eyed each of them in turn, sneering. "Three against one? You flatter yourselves." His tone turned sickly sweet, and Shane felt the familiar pull on his mind. "But you're not here to fight me today, are you? No, my child. You have returned home. Where you belong. With me."

Shane felt the fear clawing at his mind. He couldn't go back. He *wouldn't* go back.

His heart pounded in his chest. Feels had given him a new body. How did Kydell even recognize who he *was*?

A soothing caress of assurance pierced his soul through the Oath.

Feels.

His breathing calmed.

"I'm glad you brought your friends with you," Kydell continued. "We'll put them to good use. *All* can serve the greatness of the Confederation, in their own way. By their lives..." He turned a feral grin toward Jeb. "Or by their deaths."

<Don't listen to him!>

Jeb's telepathic voice was firm, with an authority Shane hadn't heard him use before. <He's trying to manipulate your emotions!>

Shane still felt the guilt like a kick in the gut, pulling his mind toward Kydell. He never should have brought Jeb. The man was clearly out of his element, and now he was going to die for Shane's mistake.

Everyone always died for his mistakes.

But he couldn't change the past. Only himself. And starting today he'd do everything in his power to protect the universe from Kydell and those fueling wars of death and destruction for their own personal gain.

Today was the first day that mattered.

Shane squared his shoulders, his guilt lending him strength, metamorphosing into resolve in response to Feels' reconditioning. As his thoughts focused on protecting Jake and ridding the universe of Kydell's influence, he felt something fracture and fall away in his mind. The admiral's words no longer held sway on his thoughts, and he found himself able to think clearly in Kydell's presence for the first time since the manipulative wolf had Claimed him on his conscription.

Kydell must have tied his conditioning into his guilt. It made sense. His anger over the death of his parents had been his driving force within the SAF, but Kydell would have seen through the façade to glimpse the survivor's guilt below. Feels' alterations had put the two in conflict.

Shane carefully probed at Kydell's Shielding with his Necromancy, but found no weaknesses. He recalled the times he and the admiral had met for friendly sparring matches, noting that the wolf's Shielding today was noticeably stronger.

Jake's Shieldbreaker would have been nice, but the spell itself had been too complicated to learn, and too complex to Rune on short notice. He'd have to have the boy make another copy later, whenever they got out of this.

For now, he'd need to distract Kydell instead. Confuse and overtax his Shielding enough to find an opening.

Shane hefted one of the spikes in his hand, feeling its balance and sharpened tip. Kydell was speaking again, the biologist adding his own telepathic counterarguments. Shane only half-listened as he focused his aim. He launched the spike, readying a second as he watched the first sail easily through the air on a direct path toward Kydell's head.

"Nya left you. That useless brother of yours won't save you. The only one who will always be there for you? Is me."

<I'm right here. I'll never abandon you.>

The spike froze in midair the same moment he recognized the true target of Kydell's words.

Razick flinched but held her ground as the admiral placed a hand on her shoulder, baring his teeth in triumph.

"Welcome home, Sub-Officer Kane."

The planting spike reversed course, accelerating toward Shane.

Well, shit.

FEELS HAD DECIDED THEY were *not* a fan of warships. The *Inevitable*'s AI were nice enough, and genuine in their welcomes, but the empath had never quite fit in with the cold militaristic mentality shared by the others. Their cultivated calm detachment from the direct consequences of their actions, the layers of separation from all but each other, proved an impossible feat for an empath who required full Psychic Shielding simply to prevent mistaking the feelings of others for their own.

"We doing this or what?" Alanis' emotions betrayed impatience and a hunger for retribution, coupled with an undercurrent of exhilaration.

They couldn't blame her for that last one. Grim had freed her from her Oath, and the taste of freedom after decades of imprisonment was still intoxicating. They shared a similar emotion, courtesy of her adjustments on their bindings in Grim's locket to allow them to come and go as they pleased.

"This won't be as easy as it sounds." Feels settled into the Weapons-designated binding crystal, centering their thoughts on their own trepidation at the task ahead. "You're not an empath, so you won't have to worry. But I need to anchor my emotions first or I'll get lost in everyone else's."

Alanis grew thoughtful. "Considering what I saw that Guilt do to Grim, I'm guessing that would be bad."

"In your entire fleet? The only one with the skills needed to pull me back out of *that* would be Admiral Kydell." Feels let out an emotional shudder at the thought. "And that's assuming he's feeling generous."

Alanis' emotions shifted quickly to apology and determination. "Point made. Take all the time you need. What can I do to help?"

"Right now, the inability to aim won't be a problem. But eventually? It's probably important." Feels shared their sense of conviction, to underlie their words. "Is there a manual for the new weapons? Maybe Jake can find a solution."

"It's on the bridge." Alanis' emotions flattened as she thought, and Feels wondered if this was a habit learned over her decades under Kydell. "I could jump it in if I had Imperium. I'll ask the kid for a link."

Jake's answer was immediate, his typical calm unbothered by their present situation. <<I've been listening. I'll do it.>>

"Forgot you knew Soul Call." The Navigations AI let out a soft laugh before her emotions shifted to concern. "But are you sure? The Shielding is important. Conserve your magic. I don't want to overburden you."

<<The Runework makes it easier,>> the boy reminded her, referencing the Shielding Runes arrayed around the ship to help direct and augment its Shielding mage. <<And I do the same endurance exercises you do.>>

"I very much doubt that. I'm a fae. And I've been at this many times longer than you've been alive, kid. I'll bet you use a beginner's set, maybe?"

Alanis' rising emotions were making it difficult for Feels to focus solely on their own. They decided to set her straight, soothing feelings so they could concentrate on the task at hand. "You'd lose that bet. You forget. That's Grim's kid. He knows the TAG's Shielding tricks, too."

"Well." The empath noted Alanis' shift to respect and curiosity. "Let's get that book then, shall we?"

As the gifted preteen and the Navigations AI switched their attention and conversation back to logistics, Feels resumed the critical process of blocking out all feelings but their own. The assorted emotions drifting in from Kydell's armada remained distant and cold, but that would change quickly once the weaponized Guilt was unleashed.

Even more than usual, remaining emotionally anchored would be critical today.

Assorted smaller pockets of stronger emotions – fear, determination, anger, courage, exhaustion, hatred, love – told them Baden still had some ships in the fight, although the defenders were dangerously outnumbered. These ships held the possibility of greater problems, as their potential reactions to the Guilt remained unknown, and unless Jake managed to locate some useful direction in the manuals there'd be no way to avoid hitting them, too.

Feels focused their concentration solely on themselves, endeavoring to block out the errant emotions bombarding them from all directions. It had always been a difficult task during their time in the SAF, and their current lack of practice in high stress environments wasn't making it any easier. Back when they'd served as Grim's medic they'd often grounded their emotions in the necromancer's instead, as choosing to follow one individual's emotions was always easier than attempting to focus on their own.

Grim's standard seething fury had been an experience itself, but the necromancer had asked what he could do to make life easier for the medic. As a result, Feels had taught him a spell to temporarily mask his emotions, and he'd dutifully cast it whenever the empath requested to use him as their emotional anchor.

Happiness radiated along their Insight spell to Grim, mixed with hints of anticipation, reluctance, and discomfort.

The empath stopped their meditation, realization dawning. *Grim*. There'd be no need for complicated spells, they could simply anchor themselves to their friend once again, a feat made even easier courtesy of the Oath's Insight. They wouldn't be able to tune him out anyway, and he might even need their help defending against Kydell.

Decision made and spell adjustment cast, Feels threw themselves at the Weapons systems, performing some last minute calibrations to allow the use of the weaponized Guilt Jake had cleverly programmed into the ships circuits.

Taking one final scan of the system, they were hit with a sudden spike of nervousness from Grim, then amusement paired with an analytical calm. They completed the checks with ease despite the interruption.

Yes. This will work.

They settled deeper into the tyrellium crystal currently housing their soul, reaching back to the other AI. "Everyone ready? We'll likely have their full attention once I start."

"Helm, aye." The telekinetic Maneuvering AI projected a cool confidence.

"Nav, aye." Alanis was wrapped in barely contained excitement.

"Telem, aye."

Feels felt the knock of a telepathic link request, their acceptance rewarded with a spatial layout of the battle with relation to the *Inevitable*.

<<Shielding, aye.>> Jake carried his usual confidence, and by the subtle pattern to his shifting emotions, Feels recognized he was reciting one of his father's many mantras.

As the final ship systems checked in, Feels readied their spell, braced themselves for the impending emotional onslaught, and fired.

35

RAZICK WINCED AT KYDELL'S smirk, the wolf baring his canines in pleasure as Lawrence phased to the Afterlife to avoid the plant stake he'd thrown mere moments before.

"You've brought me a necromancer. How lovely! He'll make a fine addition to my Collection."

<Kane. Razick. *Fight* him.> Shane's voice betrayed a hard edge she hadn't heard him use before. <Figure out what emotion he used. Find a way to feel the opposite.>

<Fear. Abandonment.> She knew this answer, but the knowing didn't help. Her panic clawed its way deeper, visions of her father entwining with the wolf beside her. <I can't go back. Don't let him take me!>

<I'll never abandon you, Raz.> Jeb's words were soft and soothing, and for a moment she felt the wolf's grip on her mind abate.

But Kydell's next words tightened it further. "Test your brother's devotion, Kane. A duel. To the death. Give him all you've got. See how long it takes him to turn on you." His words held an air of casual disinterest as he kept his eyes on Shane, slowly drawing his ever-present laser pistol. "Leave the necromancer to me."

<Raz. You don't have to do this.> The fact Jeb somehow kept his tone calm as she turned to him with murderous intent only served to feed her desperation.

<I do.> Her vision blurred. She dropped her Shielding and her shield, briefly closing her eyes against the tears. <Jeb. *Kill* me. Before I kill you. It's the only way.>

<Never.> His smile was calm, his steps certain as they circled. <I promised to protect you, and I'm not going anywhere. We'll figure this out. *Together*.>

Razick continued her pleading, her brother calmly refuting each claim of helplessness, her steps locked with his as they squared off within the hydroponics bay.

She heard Kydell's voice behind her, rife with self-assurance as he taunted the janitor, her focus remaining on her brother and her desperate efforts not to harm him.

But Kydell's orders won out in the end, eliciting a gasp from Jeb as lightning shot from her fingers to engulf him, joined quickly by several of the planting spikes Shane had repurposed, propelled toward his chest at telekinetically-enhanced speed. Her breath caught in her throat as Jeb froze, his suit hardening just as she'd designed it to, holding him in place with the electromagnetic currents generated by her magic. The wrench he'd brought from the engine room clattered to the floor, his grip slipping from the surprise of her attack as the stakes she'd thrown impacted with his chest, a direct hit... and bounced off to join the wrench on the floor, unable to pierce the suit's protections.

A moment later she found herself helplessly entangled in some sort of flowering plant. Jeb had maneuvered her with her back to the hydroponic garden, using her distraction and their environment against her.

He was *paying attention to my lessons.*

She beamed her pride at him, even as she watched the vines grow thicker before flowering and fruiting. Her fears eased, just a little. Just enough to unwind some of Kydell's conditioning. <Nice work.>

<You're fighting him!> Jeb's pride echoed her own. <I knew you could!>

<For now.> She squared her shoulders, already feeling her conditioning urging her to break the vines and resume the offensive.

<A distraction would be nice.> Shane's voice was strained.

Razick thought for a moment, her memory mapping the layout of the room with well-trained precision. <Got it. Close your eyes. You, too, Jeb.>

She turned her attention to the shelves of hydroponics supplies behind her, using her Telekinesis to pull the seeds and substrate materials from their bins and suspend them in the air. Soon the room was filled with rocks and dust, obstructing vision.

"What the... Razick!" There was anger in Kydell's voice. "Stop. Clean this up! Focus on your brother. *Fight* him."

She dutifully did as she was told, sending the mix of materials back to their bins. With a high speed detour to pelt Kydell on the way. <Sorry, Lawrence. One time deal. Hope it helped.>

Kydell's conditioning took hold again, new orders overriding the old to force her attention solely onto her brother. She burnt the plants encircling her with carefully controlled Pyromancy before launching another Electromancy burst at Jeb. His suit's underlayer went rigid once more at the electrical contact, and Razick made a note to solve the problem of joints before completing her next model.

<Raz...> Jeb had opened his arms, palms out, his face lined with concern. <You don't have to fight me. You can fight Kydell instead.>

<I *am*.> She channeled her Pyromancy into a small ball of fire, forcing her breathing to still in an effort to push down the panic threatening her thoughts. <I'm stalling for time. Doing everything I can to avoid hurting you.>

He dodged to the side as the fire exploded in the spot where he'd stood only moments before. <Doesn't feel like it to me!>

<You *did* promise to test the suit.> She wrinkled her nose as she forced a smile, summoning another ball of flames. She might have to fight Jeb, but the admiral had been even less specific this

time than last. He was her brother. If she could turn this into a sibling rivalry fight instead... <Look sharp!>

This time the fire made an impact, licking at his sleeves with a lazy but persistent flame. <Not what I had in mind when I volunteered!> He shook his arm in panic, which only served to fan the flames.

<Fire resistance could use some work.>

Summoning a ball of water from the hydroponics table behind her, Razick used her Hydromancy to guide it through the air until it hovered over Jeb's head. She briefly wondered what her mother would have done, had their childhood spats involved magic, and found herself smiling as she released her present spell to douse Jeb in the water.

Her brother spluttered, shaking excess water from his arms as he glared at her angrily. <What was *that* for?>

<You were on fire. I put it out.> But her smile faded as she realized she'd summoned more flames to her hand without meaning to, Jeb's anger feeding into her own emotions to grant Kydell's orders a stronger hold.

She felt the fear settle deeper, curling uncomfortably in her gut. Her attempts at resistance were only as strong as Jeb's willingness to play along, and right now he seemed more intent on undermining them completely.

<I'm going to win if you don't take this seriously,> she told him as she launched the fireball. She hoped he still had that competitive streak he'd had when they were kids.

Jeb grabbed at his makeshift light shield, successfully blocking the heat from the flames but not the force of the blow. <Thought you said you weren't trying to kill me!> He stumbled backward, the plants behind him suddenly growing in size to soften the impact against his back.

<How about you make it easier not to?> she shot back. <The longer we treat this like sparring lessons, the more I can fight off the fear you'll abandon me. No fear, no conditioning.>

She'd hurt so many innocent people, trapped within the nightmare of service to Kydell. Someday she'd hopefully forgive herself. Allow herself to acknowledge herself among the victims that haunted her dreams at night.

Unless Jeb ended up among them.

She felt plants growing to encircle her legs, but kicked them aside, aiming another bolt of Electromancy at Jeb. <This level of resistance is all I've got in me right now. Let's hope our necromancer is having better luck.>

LEAVE THE NECROMANCER TO ME.

Shane's blood had run cold as his former admiral turned the entirety of his attention against him, although thus far Kydell had remained oblivious to his former identity. This clearly weighed heavily on Kydell's mind, as the wolf had paused his own assault to tilt his head, watching the necromancer intently.

Shane took the opportunity to back away in an effort to retake his breath. Practice sparring with Jake had helped him retain at least some of his former knowledge, but none of his former endurance, and the earlier fight with Alanis hadn't helped. His foot slipped in the fine layer of dirt coating the floor, remnants of Razick's earlier whirlwind attack, his elbow throbbing as it connected with the fixtures on the hydroponic table behind him.

"We don't have to fight, you know," the wolf said conversationally. "I'm always seeking talented individuals to mentor.

With my vast resources, I could help you reach your peak potential. Show the universe what glories you can accomplish."

Shane held his silence, tightening his grip on Razick's makeshift reflective shield as the psychomorphic admiral coolly waved the pistol in his direction. He felt Kydell probing at his mind but Feels' Shielding held firm, automatically replenishing its strength from Shane's own magic reserves.

Just like the Oath, Shane marveled. They'd merged into the same spell, since they'd been cast together.

He focused his thoughts on gratitude, knowing the empath would feel them through their Insight spell. Courtesy of Feels, Kydell would never again alter his mind.

Confident in the safety of his own thoughts, Shane tuned out the sounds of Jeb and Razick's battle on the other end of the bay and opened himself fully to the Void, reaching to Baden's star to strengthen his spellwork. The raw magic of the universe flooded his veins, with its dark promises of unlimited power.

He snapped his own limits in place, a familiar spell born of reflex and intensive practice, locking his eyes onto the manipulative white wolf. Focusing his thoughts on the Afterlife, he crafted a condensed pulse of pure necromantic energy in an effort to mimic the effects of Jake's Shieldbreaker spell, followed by the more familiar casting of a firm soulbind, and launched both at his former admiral. He felt Kydell's Shielding fracture under the sudden assault of star-powered Necromancy, observing the admiral's golden eyes widening in surprise before settling into amusement as Shane's spell dissipated harmlessly.

Nobody can recover their Shielding that quickly.

Shane eyed the admiral with renewed fear and felt the familiar pull of Kydell's conditioning on his mind until Feels dissipated the emotion with a condensed burst of courage.

Guilt wasn't the only emotion Kydell had used to program him.

Making a note to talk to the empath about rerouting his fears next, Shane turned his full attention back to the admiral. He lamented the Imperium spent fighting Alanis, and the depleted state of his reserves. He'd need to find a way through the wolf's defenses, and quickly.

The Navigations AI hadn't exaggerated. Kydell *was* much stronger than he'd been two years prior, when Shane had managed to shake the admiral's influence just enough to rescue Jake and flee, leaving a trail of Shattered lives behind him.

But how?

"I can tell you've already had training." The wolf cocked his head, eyes focused, and Shane knew from experience the admiral was casting to read his emotions. "Let me help you succeed. Someone of your talents – with your raw power – surely deserves the best life has to offer. I can assure you, my resources are superior to whoever sent you after me."

He spread his arms wide, left palm open toward Shane, the laser pistol clutched in his right hand now pointed at the ground. "What is it you seek? Power? Fame? Wealth? Tell me. I can make it happen."

Shane kept his emotions flat, burying them deep with an old spell Feels had taught him. No Shielding would protect against the reading of active feelings, and even without the use of Psychomorphation, Kydell knew well how to weaponize the emotions of others.

Best not to feel, not to give him more ammunition than absolutely necessary.

Shane was evaluating his options, preparing another burst of power to attack Kydell's Shielding, but the wolf acted first, aiming his pistol. Shane pulled his makeshift shield into position to deflect the anticipated blast, checking his own energy Shielding spell, eyes focused on Kydell.

<Lawrence!> Razick's voice broke his concentration, the Kane battle mage clearly still struggling against Kydell's control. <You better find some way to incapacitate Kydell. Preferably *before* he realizes he didn't order me to *kill* my brother.>

Kydell noted Shane's momentary lapse in attention, surprising him by instead lunging to the left, sharpened claws at the ready. Shane phased through the attack, darting forward and spinning around to face the wolf again, but not before the admiral managed a deep slash against his right cheek.

"I hope you're considering my offer. Everyone makes mistakes. Join me, and I won't hold this one against you." Kydell's voice remained conversational, with no signs of strain. "It's the only way you'll survive this."

Shane poked the inside of his cheek with his tongue and tasted blood and air.

That'll leave a mark.

Mentally berating himself for dropping his physical Shielding at the distraction, he slid three of the planting stakes between the fingers of his right hand, flat ends gripped against his palm.

Not claws, but they'll have to do.

One of the lighting fixtures flew from the direction of the Kanes before crashing into the back of Kydell's right shoulder, and Shane felt the wolf's Shielding falter. He used the opportunity to cast Shatter, launching himself on a straight path toward the admiral's soul at the same time. The canid had clearly anticipated more Necromancy, the spell scattering across fresh Shielding, but Shane grinned as he felt the thin stakes sink satisfyingly through fabric, fur, and flesh.

Shane pulled his fist away, two plant stakes still gripped in his fist.

"Do you know how much paperwork it takes to get *replacements* for these?" The admiral tugged at his dress uniform, pacing angrily as blood dripped through his pins and ribbons, one of Shane's stakes still firmly embedded in his chest. Shane couldn't remember ever seeing the admiral in the standard working uniform most wore outside of formal SAF ceremonies. Kydell had always defaulted to the white dress jacket and its corresponding chest of ribbons, most of them earned off the backs of those he'd manipulated beneath his control.

Shane noted with satisfaction that somehow he'd managed to slip his makeshift weapons between the array of medals adorning Kydell's left breast.

By their location, he'd punctured the wolf's heart once and left lung twice, yet aside from a faint panting the admiral looked no worse for wear.

Shane broke his silence. "What *are* you?" The words tore at his clawed cheek.

"So. You *do* talk." Kydell sneered, plucking the third stake from his chest and carelessly tossing it to the ground, his attention wholly focused on Shane. "Tell me who you are, and maybe I'll answer."

Shane noted Kydell's efforts to read his emotions again. He buried them, shrugging instead. "I'm just the janitor."

Technically, he wasn't even that anymore. But Jake wanted him to fix things and so he'd do his best, provided he survived Kydell.

"As if someone with your skills would waste them plunging toilets." The admiral scoffed, revealing his teeth. "But no matter. You'll tell me soon enough. Once you're mine."

Shane winced as he rubbed his cheek onto the shoulder of his pilfered shirt to clear some of the blood. "You sound rather confident of that." He ignored the pain from speaking, his efforts instead focused on replacing the missing plant stake in his fist, bringing his total back to three.

"Alive or dead, they always talk in the end." Kydell's smile turned feral. "And, unfortunately for you, I've decided that dead will be sufficient in your case."

The admiral's assault was sudden, brutal, and reassuringly familiar. Shane easily avoided the barrage of laser fire, deflecting the opening volley with the lighting fixture shield before phasing briefly into the Afterlife to avoid the second, less concentrated burst. He used the phase to bridge the distance between them once more, closing the gap to force Kydell to abandon his pistol and engage hand to claw.

Shane had always bested the admiral at close range combat, although today was a risk, since he was unaccustomed to fighting in his present body. He made a note to talk to Razick about changing that.

He still couldn't believe he'd managed to find a *Kane*. If he could only find a way to break *her* conditioning...

Kydell bared his canines at Shane's sudden proximity. "Brave."

He deftly holstered his pistol before swiping at Shane, the whole fluid maneuver a well-practiced motion. The necromancer ducked and spun underneath his former admiral's claws, pivoting behind him before jabbing at him with the planting stakes.

The admiral's Shielding repelled the blow, and Kydell used the opportunity to swipe back at Shane with his tail as he spun to face him. The thick club of fur connected with Shane's thighs and sent him staggering several steps backward but he recovered quickly, dodging then phasing through a quick double punch of the wolf's clawed strikes before once again connecting his own counterattack with Kydell's Shielding.

Shane allowed the fight to continue for several more minutes, Kydell attacking with claws and occasionally teeth or tail,

Shane dodging or phasing through each before counterattacking, Kydell allowing his Shielding alone to defend. Once Shane grew confident in Kydell's adherence to the pattern he gathered his Necromancy for another concentrated burst, augmenting it with power borrowed from Baden's star and weaving Shatter into the very nature of the spell. He waited until the admiral began to attack again, launching his spellwork as Kydell reached the halfpoint of his swing.

It fizzled on Kydell's Shielding, his golden eyes betraying amusement. "That didn't work the *first* time. Did you really think I wouldn't have learned to better counter it the second time?"

Shane felt his stomach sink. Kydell shouldn't have been able to defend against that. The wolf's present magical strength was orders of magnitude greater than it had been during training when they'd last fought, more than two years ago.

Practice, certainly, would always strengthen a mage over time, but this was something more. Shane prepared to dodge again, but Kydell seemed content to allow him the moments to puzzle out the riddle, golden eyes watching intently.

And then Shane caught it, the small Imperium drain in his own reserves. It held the profile of an apotheturgic link, but he hadn't accepted any energy sharing spell.

There was only one possible explanation. The seemingly endless magical reserves. The supernatural healing. The small drain on his own magic.

"Vampire."

"Very good." Kydell gave a mock bow, baring his teeth and keeping his eyes on Shane even as he dipped at the waist. "And now, you finally begin to understand your dilemma."

"When?"

"Does it matter?" Kydell shrugged. "I decided I needed to strengthen my own skills. No more relying on the loyalty of others. Never know when they'll disappear."

So after Loxira, then. Renkash's away team had included several of Kydell's favorite acquisitions to his conditioned Collection, not just Renkash himself. The loss of so many at once would have been quite a blow, particularly the loss of a cosmically attuned Void mage.

Not everyone could borrow from the stars. Kydell himself lacked the ability, a flaw which Shane suspected had always rankled the admiral. Vampirism was therefore a logical next step, the virus granting a sustaining endurance for magic casters, but at the expense of completely blocking any cosmic attunement in the afflicted.

"Last chance to join me." Kydell tilted his head, once again tapping in to read Shane's emotions. "I'll even grant you the gift of vampirism. If you like."

"No."

Kydell scowled. "I grow tired of your insolence." He bared his teeth, voice rising in volume and annoyance. "Razick, finish off the necromancer. Leave just enough intact we can force him back later. I'll handle your brother myself."

37

Jeb froze at the words, spoken so casually from the snout of his sister's nightmare. He and Raz had found their own rhythm for their duel – Jeb learning in the process just how much she'd been holding back during their training sessions – but now he'd be facing the biggest threat in the room. Alone.

He watched, eyes wide, as Kydell stalked purposely toward him, and noted for the first time the fresh blood marking Lawrence's right cheek and dripping to his shoulder, staining the light tan camouflage of his jacket with trails of red and black. Kydell's own wounds appeared minor in comparison, the blossoms of red scattered across his dress jacket small and concentrated.

If the necromancer hadn't been able to hurt Kydell, what hope was there for a mere biologist?

<He's a vampire now.> Lawrence didn't even attempt to hide his frustration. Or his fear. <Couldn't break his Shielding. Take every advantage you can.>

"*You* are remarkably intact." Kydell's lips rose into a snarl. "Your sister is clearly overdue for reconditioning. You have my gratitude for her safe return to my Collection."

The guilt hit him like one of Razick's fireballs. What had he done, allowing her to talk him into this foolish endeavor? He'd promised to protect her. Instead he'd lured her into a trap.

He felt the guilt wash over him, and looked up to see Kydell grinning, head cocked.

No.

That was Kydell in his head, attempting to override his emotions. Jeb brushed the feelings away, tightly gripping his makeshift laser shield in front of his chest.

Kydell scowled. "No Shielding, Kane!"

She's still fighting him!

Raz must have helped snap him out of it with a Shielding spell of her own, thwarting the psychomorphic admiral's efforts to alter his mind. He heard Shane's words of encouragement over their telepathic link.

If she can fight him, so can I.

His resolve arrived just in time for the volley of laser bolts Kydell let loose in his direction. Catching them neatly on his shield, he relaxed slightly at the ease of reflecting them back to the admiral.

His confidence was short-lived as the volley of laser fire increased in both spread and frequency. The shield wasn't large enough – and Jeb wasn't fast enough – to catch them all, leaving them scattering across both shield and Shielding until one snuck through. He felt the blast graze his ear, both cutting and cauterizing as it burnt its way through skin and cartilage.

A cry escaped his lips and Kydell smiled, the expression dripping with venomous confidence.

Panting, Jeb pried his fingers from the table he'd grabbed in his pain, just in time to dodge another volley from the imposing white wolf now slowly stalking toward him with all the satisfaction of a cat tracking a wounded bird.

Lawrence said to take every advantage.

He already had an advantage over his sister, in that he'd been classed as a waste of the admiral's time once he'd proven himself unable to master even the basics of battle mage training. As essential as Hydroponics remained for Curative Magic to heal those requiring medical attention while in the largely lifeless expanse of the Void, biologists were rarely recognized as important by *anyone*.

It had hurt, at the time. But he'd survived, and Admiral Kydell's disinterest had left his mind intact.

Another several bolts made their way through his Shielding, one burning a path along the side of his neck, and he cursed inwardly.

So what could counter a laser pistol?

Ducking behind one of the hydroponics tables, he bought a few seconds to weigh his options without the threat of further burns.

His eyes caught the wrench he'd dropped in his fight against his sister. Potentially useful, if he could get close.

He wracked his brain for memories from his weapons training, before he'd been written off as a lost cause.

The ship shuddered as a spray of bolts erupted from the admiral's pistol, knocking him off balance and allowing enough laser shots to scatter across his Shielding and break his spell. A pair of bolts struck him in the wrist of his suit as he attempted to regain his balance and he tightened his grip, briefly, on his makeshift shield.

It went clattering to the ground a moment after as the pain shooting up his arm forced his grip free. He followed after, retrieving the shield in his other hand as he darted behind another table.

He kept his focus on Kydell, forcing down concerns as to the state of his wrist, or the *Inevitable*. Whether or not the AI succeeded in their mission, it wouldn't matter if the admiral won because Jeb wasn't paying enough attention.

The higher the power, the slower the rate of fire.

Kydell's current rate of fire implied a lower power setting, higher than the stun options on the SAF's famed riot rifles – his burns were proof of that – but not by much.

Concentrated beams of light and heat...

"You can't hide forever," Kydell growled, baring his teeth as he rounded the edge of the table. "Or you could give up now. Save us both the effort."

Water. Yes!

Jeb rolled to a new hiding spot, leaving the next volley to pepper an overgrown collection of miniature fruit trees as a plan formed in his mind. "Hydro! Activate the sprinkler system."

"You got it, sir!" The room filled with the chipper voice of the Hydroponics AI, followed immediately after by a fine mist of water.

"Sprinklers *off*," Kydell ordered. "Need I remind you who gives your orders? Useless AI."

"Yup! Totally useless!" she agreed brightly.

The sprinklers' water pressure mysteriously increased.

Kydell scowled and fired another scattering of pistol shots, the beams now highly visible as they refracted across the droplets. This volley overwhelmed Jeb's Shielding before impacting directly with the suit, the rain-weakened bolts dissipating through the fabric.

He rubbed his shoulder, skin stinging where he'd received the highest concentration of laser shots, but aside from a faint numbing sensation he felt no other damage. This time, Razick's suit had fully absorbed the bolts, the conductive tyrellium-weave she'd included throughout the suit spreading the damage over a large enough area to keep it manageable.

<I *just* found dry socks,> Lawrence growled.

The threat of imminent death now resolved into slightly less imminent death, Jeb tuned out the banter of the battle to focus his concentration on the plants near Kydell. The admiral had turned his attention from Jeb to adjust the settings on his laser pistol, likely trading speed for power to counteract the effects of the rain and Razick's suit.

Jeb used this distraction to his advantage, commanding the vines to wrap around Kydell and bind him tightly to the edge of the table, darting closer to his discarded wrench in the process.

The canid raised his claws, slicing through the vines with ease as he raised his adjusted pistol for another shot. "Cute." His scowl deepened a moment later, engulfed by a wall of flame and fire from Jeb's sister. "Razick. Check your aim."

Jeb suppressed as smile at Razick's sarcastic <Yes, sir!> over their telepathic link, another idea forming in his mind.

<Lawrence? Do vampires have any weaknesses?>

<Sure.> The janitor's tone was surprisingly conversational, given their present predicament. <Vitamin D toxicity. Good luck with that one. Iron deficiency. Painful way to die, but not practical. Prolonged exposure to Antimagic. We'd have to keep the field constant for several days. And heat. Tough with your sprinklers. But the best option we've got right now.>

Jeb nodded understanding as another wave of flames washed over Kydell. <Like Razick's Pyromancy?>

<Yeah. Any heat source.>

Kydell was stalking toward him now, a menacing figure of sharp teeth and damp fur, but it didn't matter. Swallowing his fear, Jeb squared his shoulders and narrowed his eyes. He knew what he had to do.

"Hydro. Activate hull breach protocols."

Both doors slid shut with a hermetically sealed hiss.

"Cutting off your own escape route?" Kydell growled. "Not very smart. Not that you'd get very far, of course."

He lunged at Jeb with his claws but the biologist was prepared, ducking behind a suddenly overgrown table of fruiting bushes.

Jeb heard the wolf growl something in frustration but kept his focus on his current plan. He found the wrench, gripping it gingerly with his injured hand. "Hydro, new climate profile. I'm thinking... Tropical 16D? But leave the sprinklers on."

"Oooooooh, you like it *steamy*," the AI crooned happily, sliding several pairs of heated blower fans from their recesses in the ceiling.

Jeb's sweat began to mix with the fine spray of water as the humidity in the bay spiked.

Kydell's eyes widened before he caught himself, narrowing them at Jeb instead. "Belay that order. This is still my ship!"

"And *you* told me I wasn't *important* to *your* ship," the Hydroponics AI shot back, gaining speed and volume with every word. "But look at me now! Sure would be nice if you'd installed that emergency safety I've been begging for, wouldn't it? But that's not important until it's important. Isn't that how it goes? Bet you wish you'd spent the time to condition *me* instead of telling me how *useless* I am, huh?"

"You *are* useless." Kydell's lips twisted into a terrifying smirk. "But I'll schedule you for a session after I've dealt with our boarders."

Her words came out even faster at that pronouncement. "I don't *want* you to condition me! I just wanted to feel important! I wanted you to listen to me and recognize my contributions to the well-being of this ship!"

Jeb wiped the sweat from his brow onto the arm of his already soaked shirt. Things were turning from uncomfortable to unbearable quickly, but whatever he felt, Kydell had it worse. He watched the wolf stagger forward, struggling to undo the buttons on his dress jacket, and allowed himself a smile.

"Bad day to wear a fur coat, am I right?"

"This doesn't change anything," Kydell growled in return, panting as he slowly stalked toward Jeb. He slipped in the water pooling on the floor between drains but quickly caught himself on a table, his laser pistol clattering to the floor in the process. "Except now, you're going to suffer before I kill you."

Watching the admiral attempt to retain his composure, Jeb backed away, heart pounding from adrenaline. He'd managed to hold his own, and even put the dangerous wolf at a disadvantage, but from what he'd understood from Raz it wouldn't last long.

The wolf was a master at adaptation, twisting situations – and people – to suit his own needs. Already, Kydell was stalking toward him, teeth and claws bared.

Jeb tested his grip on the wrench again, wincing as a bolt of pain shot up from the thumb of his injured hand. Whatever Lawrence and Raz intended to do, they'd better do it soon.

38

JAKE CLOSED HIS EYES, massaging his temples as the fleets outside battered against his Shielding spell. Telemetry's map of the battle remained in his head and he wished he could block that out, too, but the AI would ask questions if their Shielding mage suddenly withdrew from the battle readout. And so he remained, cross-legged in the corner with his back braced against the wall and his Shielding braced as best he could against each projected attack.

Kydell's fleet had reacted immediately to Feels' initial barrage. For a handful of the larger ships, this meant an immediate halt to their prior activities. One of the battleships closest to the *Inevitable*, previously occupied with firing on the planet below, halted its efforts in mid-barrage to sit indecisively in orbit. Two others had turned on their neighbors, the quad of ships now exchanging fire with each other as if resolving an ancient grudge. The fighters and other small craft closest to the *Inevitable* –

Telemetry's readout noted these were too small to utilize a full Shielding suite – had ceased their assaults, likely disoriented by the unexpected wave of Guilt washing over them.

Subsequent attacks from the *Inevitable*'s emotional assault had added to the count of disoriented ships. Accounting for those, plus the ships Baden's Defense Force had managed to incapacitate or otherwise destroy, still left almost forty capital ships of varying sizes and classifications.

Most of them now focused on the *Inevitable*, surrounding the oversized flagship with relentless sparks of Electromancy, punctuated by some sort of laser fire and waves of torpedo-like projectiles whose explosive impacts set Jake's teeth on edge.

He'd thought withstanding Veris' punches in the shelter vault had been an impressive feat. He'd been wrong.

Jake cycled through his father's mantras, seeking one to soothe his nerves given their current situation. Despite the necromancer's best efforts, Jake couldn't help but feel his father had failed to adequately prepare him for their present situation, but perhaps he could find something useful anyway.

Reputation matters. Make it a good one.

He had. And that reputation as a solid Shielding mage had led him to this situation in the first place.

Well, that and his insistence at accompanying his father. Not to mention the SAF's decision to attack Baden at all.

It's okay to admit you don't have all the answers, but it's never okay to give up. Figure out how to learn what you need.

What he needed to know was that his father was okay. That the Void necromancer was going to save the day, just like he always did, just like he'd always done. That he'd negotiate to get Jake back into school and things would continue onward exactly like they had before.

<<Have you learned how to aim yet?>> Alanis asked suddenly, interrupting Jake's thoughts.

He sat upright, opening his eyes to stare once more at the book full of empty gibberish sitting in his lap. "No." He gritted his teeth at a particularly painful attempt to overwhelm his Shielding. "I... don't think the person who wrote this thought anyone would read it."

He released his grip on the book, panting, and realized he'd ripped several of the pages. "This is hard. I need to focus."

<<Helm?>>

<<Evasive actions, aye,>> the Maneuvering AI confirmed the unspoken order, immediately matching words with movement as she increased power to the Telekinetic engines.

<<We're a team,>> Alanis said quietly. <<If you need something, ask.>>

Learn, apologize, and try again.

"It's hard to repel everything," Jake admitted. "I'm sorry."

Back at school, and under the protective presence of his father, it had been easy to believe he was invincible. That he could do anything. Even when facing Veris and the other bullies he'd consoled himself with the fact that he *could* do more, he was simply choosing not to.

His Shielding magic had been no different, particularly given his father's quiet endorsement of his skills. He'd begun to convince himself that practice no longer mattered. He already knew everything he needed to know.

Here in the *Inevitable*, facing down the entirety of a Confederation armada, he'd realized the fallacy of that belief. Too many possibilities fought for his attention – the Shielding, the weapons manual, his Shieldbreaker spell – and while each would help, he only had the capabilities to support one of them. His father had tasked him with Shielding, so that's what he'd do.

But it didn't stop the feeling that he should be doing more.

<<Then don't block it all,>> Maintenance told him. <<Some parts of the ship are more important than others. Experienced Shielding mages know how to adapt during battle. What to defend against. What to protect. I can help you pick.>> The AI laughed. <<Not much use to anyone else. I can track the damage, but I've no team to coordinate repairs with.>>

Jake felt himself relax at the AI's apparent calm. Focusing on his studies had always helped him work through his own emotions. Perhaps learning from Maintenance now would help. "Please."

Telemetry's rendering of the *Inevitable* shimmered slightly, lighting up in an array of colors with captions and extensive maintenance style notes.

<<Don't let them hit the red stuff,>> Maintenance explained. <<Ship'll be a mess, but we'll keep the essentials running. Since it's just us AI.>>

Jake nodded, although the Maintenance AI probably couldn't see him. "Where's Hydroponics? Is that red?"

<<It is now,>> the AI amended, as the colors shifted slightly. <<And now the Bridge isn't. Since there's no one home today.>>

If you don't know the answer, find where to find it.

That one was his mother's mantras, something she'd drilled into him since before he could remember. She'd be proud of him today. She'd also be in his ear constantly about proving himself the best Shielding mage the AI had ever seen, but there was a reason he'd asked her to stay on Baden when they jumped to the fleet. Sometimes it was just easier to concentrate without her constant encouragement.

Another collection of missiles aimed their warheads at the *Inevitable*, and Jake listened with awe as Maintenance took charge, ordering Helm to maneuver so they'd aim at a less vital location along the lower hull.

<<Let those through,>> she told Jake. <<Conserve your Imperium.>>

He nodded again, shifting the physical components of his Shielding to allow the torpedoes to strike the hull. "What's that part?"

<<Crew quarters.>>

Jake blinked. "But isn't the crew important?"

<<Not if you can just resurrect the useful ones,>> Alanis said bitterly. <<We're all expendable.>>

<<And no one's home,>> Maintenance repeated.

If she'd intended to say anything else, her words were cut off by the *Inevitable*'s heavy shudder as the weapons struck true, knocking dust from the ceiling supports as the ship groaned from the effort of remaining intact.

<<That'll be expensive to fix,>> Alanis grumbled.

<<Everything important is holding,>> Maintenance said firmly. <<For now,>> she added, quieter.

Jake furrowed his brows, setting aside the manual to focus his full attention on Shielding, and the crashing waves of power now dancing across it as the remaining ships of Kydell's fleet attempted to press their advantage.

A lot more than there should have been, if he'd extrapolated their earlier success rates correctly.

<<Weapons, talk to me,>> Alanis ordered. <<We need to end this.>>

<<They're Shielding against us,>> Feels admitted. <<They figured it out, and now I can't get through. They can probably feel some of it – Psychic Shielding isn't perfect – but not enough for it to work anymore.>>

If your plan isn't working, learn why and adapt.

His father's words echoed in Jake's thoughts as Alanis cursed first her former fleet, then Feels for withholding the information.

<<Anything *else* you're not telling us?>>

<<…They're also reacting whenever I send emotions to Grim,>> the empathic fae added after a moment. <<I can't isolate my spells. They all send through the weapons.>>

<<Selkirk Shatter me,>> Alanis cursed. <<She probably will, at this rate.>>

Morale is half the battle.

His father had told him that once, after convincing a tough crowd of Baden's criminal element to give them a wide berth using intimidation alone. He'd seemed sad when he'd said the words, as if he was reliving a memory rather than imparting another important mantra, but Jake had memorized it anyway.

He hadn't quite understood the meaning, until now.

Gritting his teeth, Jake dug his fingers into his palms as his Shielding repelled another wave of the Confederation's explosive missiles, this set aimed toward one of the sections the Maintenance AI had marked in red. She'd been too wrapped up in the brewing argument to direct Maneuvering, and Jake wasn't familiar enough with the lingo or ship battles in general to know what to do except reinforce against it as best he could. But he couldn't take much more. And if someone didn't do something quickly, it wouldn't matter how his father was faring against Kydell.

It was up to him to protect the ship. He had to make them focus.

"Stop!"

He stood as he spoke, pressing his back against the wall for support, his breathing heavy from the strain of maintaining the Shielding.

The bickering ceased instantly, the ship's AI likely focused on him as they awaited his next words.

Be the calm one. All eyes are on you: Make it count.

"We have to work together," he told them, remembering Razick's words earlier. "This is the team we have. There's no time to find a new one. Either we do what we came to do, or Kydell wins."

The silence stretched on several seconds longer before Telemetry broke it. "I don't see any way we *can* do this. It's over, kid. We tried, we failed, and now we face the consequences."

"Shieldbreaker," Jake ordered through gritted teeth, hands fisted at his sides. Kydell's fleet had seen their opportunity, and they weren't wasting it. Attacks against intact Shielding might not harm the mage powering the spell, but that didn't mean he couldn't feel the pain of every assault against it. "It's expensive. But it works."

<<Emotions aren't physical,>> Telemetry said slowly. <<*No one* knows how to break Psychic Shielding. Not even Kydell.>>

"I do," Jake elaborated, with a grimace at a particularly draining barrage against the Shields. "School project."

<<I taught him everything I know,>> Feels agreed, hope rising in their voice. <<If anyone could figure it out...>>

<<Maint, reinforce Shield,>> Alanis ordered. <<Full Apotheturgy, give him all you've got. Shield, teach Telem the spell. Telem, here's your chance for that offensive role you've begged for. Only cast it on the important targets.>>

<<Telem, Aye.>>

Jake felt the press of an apotheturgic request and accepted, his breathing slightly easier as the Maintenance AI's magic swelled to bolster his own. He felt it wrap around his spell before squeezing gently, prying the physical Shielding away from the rest of Jake's Shield layers.

<<I've got you, Shield,>> she reassured. <<Don't have your reserves, but I'll manage 'til you're done with Telem.>>

<<Good,>> Alanis growled. <<Any other secrets I need to know?>>

<<I'm the one who organized the snake in Admiral Kydell's sock drawer last week,>> Communications offered, joining their conversation with a forced attempt at levity. <<Convinced Logistics it was a training exercise.>>

Jake exhaled, allowing himself to sink to the floor as he offered Telemetry a link to his and Maintenance's magic. They had a path forward now. They could do this.

<<On a more serious note,>> the Communications AI added quietly, <<the admiral's winning.>>

Jake swallowed. Or maybe not.

39

Feels attempted to bury their shame as Jake began to walk Telemetry through his Shieldbreaker spell. Grim had been relying on them to lead the attack on the fleet and they'd failed, instead drawing the other AI into an argument that would have likely cost them the *Inevitable* if Jake hadn't intervened to salvage the situation.

They'd been jealous of Grim's obsessive devotion to the boy and his safety ever since they'd realized their necromancer's every decision revolved around Jake's continued existence. And yet Jake never let him down, whereas the one time he'd decided to trust them to accomplish something in his absence...

"Shieldbreaker online," Telemetry reported. "Updating targeting... now."

The AI's telepathic battle map updated moments later, each of the remaining ships now prominently displaying information on the state of their Shielding.

Feels tuned out the subsequent chatter of the other AI, co-ordinating with Jake for the transfer of Shielding duties. They had an armada to assault, and they would *not* disappoint Grim.

Or Jake.

As they prepared the next barrage of the weaponized Guilt, another of Kydell's battleships broke apart under a heavy onslaught of concentrated fire from the battered remains of the Baden Defense Force. Without Grim's intervention the BDF would have been thoroughly overwhelmed by now, but with the majority of Kydell's functional fleet now targeting the *Inevitable*, whoever was leading the planet's defense had rallied their forces to take full advantage of the unexpected reprieve.

Feels' next volley of Guilt pulled two more ships from the fray, both smaller destroyers. The ships hung calmly in space for several moments before accelerating away from active combat, settling in an outer orbit beside each other as if to regroup.

Grim's fear spiked as Feels tracked their next targets, and Feels automatically sent a wave of reassurance and courage in return. The ships Telemetry's Shieldbreaker had pierced rallied at the spell, one even repairing their Shielding, but it couldn't be helped. Their necromancer needed them, and he took priority. Always had, always would.

The BDF, meanwhile, had turned their attention to another of the larger battleships still intent on bombarding the planet. Baden's Shielding had already fractured before they'd even left the shelter vault, replaced instead by the more localized Shields maintained by the various municipal governments scattered across the planet. This particular ship had found a section without Shielding at all, directing their armaments to demolish whatever they could target on the ground.

"Target that ship," Feels snapped, not even bothering to hide the anger welling up inside their thoughts.

"On it," Telemetry responded immediately, their battle map updating to report the truth of his words immediately after.

Feels loosed another shot from the Guilt cannons, pouring their anger into the weapon as well for good measure.

If anything, the ship intensified its attack on the planet.

"I *said* target that ship," Feels demanded, preparing their spell again.

"I did," Telemetry protested. "Not everyone *feels* guilt. You know how we're taught."

"Kydell loyalists," Alanis confirmed. "Leave that one to Baden."

Feels chafed at that, but didn't push it. They'd already come close to fracturing their team once. They weren't about to risk it again.

"Then we'll target their screens," they directed. "Take out any ships defending them."

"That leaves Shielding as our only defense." Alanis's words were punctuated by the structural protests of another barrage of torpedoes impacting against the hull. Kydell's fleet was rapidly closing the distance. "We need to cull their numbers. Take out those attacking us."

<<No,>> Jake protested, his words strained but firm. <<We're here to help Baden. Not ourselves.>

"Can't take many more hits like that," Maintenance warned.

<<Then I'll go back to blocking them.>>

Grateful for Jake's understanding, Feels focused their attention on the battle with renewed intent, firing their weaponized Guilt immediately upon the appearance of another of Telemetry's Shield breach notifications. They'd never wanted to become a Weapons AI – they'd been raised to save lives, not end them – but the focus on saving the planet below softened the blow. They were here to help. They *were* saving lives.

Grim's emotions continued to radiate along their Insight spell, revealing the necromancer's thoughts at his own fight with his former admiral. Their reconditioning of his own guilt seemed to be holding fast, the emotion quickly shifting into determination and resolve each time it appeared. He seemed to be managing his other emotions effectively, only requiring occasional assistance from Feels to break free from his fears.

Their spells subsequently emboldened the attacking fleet, but surprisingly less than before. The Psychic Shielding they'd added to their ships would have helped, but there was something more there. Telemetry had been reporting other ships leaving combat, despite their apparently intact Shielding, as if their crews had stopped to consider their actions without further outside prompting.

<<Helm?>> Jake's voice was strained, although he was clearly trying to hide it. <<This is getting... very hard.>>

The ship shuddered again, as if to emphasize his point. This time the movement was accompanied by the sound of screeching metal.

"Hull breach contained," Maintenance reported. "For now."

"We'd swap Shielding mages now, if we had an Auxiliary," Communications observed. "Can I help?"

"We need to target the ships targeting us," Alanis growled. "Telem."

"Aye, sir."

They'd pushed Jake too far. Their plan had allowed Baden's ships to eliminate most of the ships targeting the planet, but at the expense of allowing the *Inevitable* to suffer through the attention of the rest of the fleet uncontested.

But the fleet was a threat they could no longer afford to ignore.

Arming the Guilt once more, they paused as a seething hatred seeped into Feels' mind from their Oath's Insight to Grim. They felt hints of his love as he attempted to fight it, but the hatred settled deep.

Feels hesitated. Grim needed them. And yet once those doors were opened, it would be difficult to close them again.

Grim's needs won out. As always.

Feels sent a caress of love, tentative at first, but growing in strength and intensity until there was nothing left to try to hold it back, decades of pining for Grim pouring out in a single overwhelming cascade across the Insight spell wrapped around Grim's Oath, and through the *Inevitable*'s spell-enhancing weapons to bombard the enemy armada intent on their destruction.

It felt like ages before the empath was able to end the spell and bottle up their unrequited dreams. Their beloved necromancer sent a quick flash of gratitude in return, his emotions returning to focus on his present task.

Whatever you need, Grim, Feels thought to themselves. *More than you'll ever know.*

They attempted to refocus their thoughts, preparing to fire another burst of Guilt at Telemetry's latest targets, but the emotions required to trigger the spell again remained frustratingly out of reach.

"Uhhh… I've got a call here from the *Relentless*." Communications' voice embodied pure confusion. "They, uh, said they want to talk to the person who can *love* enough to get through their Shielding. Any idea what they're talking about?"

"Love?" Feels felt Alanis' confusion join with Communications'. "Weapons, I thought we were using guilt?"

"Figured I'd mix it up a bit. See what happened. It was *your* idea." There was no way Feels would allow anyone to learn the truth. Not about this. Not about Grim. "What do they want?"

There was a pause. "They refuse to talk to anyone but you, sir. Switching to Telepathy."

A faint insistence brushed against the back of Feels' mind, and they accepted.

<This is Commodore Javon, Captain of the *Relentless*. Who am I addressing?>

Feels kept their tone even, scrambling for a suitably impressive title. Grim would hate it, but they needed something convincing.

<I am but a humble emissary of the Grand Navarch Shane Lawrence, Captain of the *Inevitable*, Guardian of Baden.>

<*Bastard* of Baden's more like it, if he can take the admiral's ship from right under his nose.> Javon laughed nervously. <Since we can't reach the admiral, I have authority to speak for the fleet. Do you speak for this Grand Navarch?>

<I do.>

There was a pause. <What are your intentions?>

<We have no quarrel with you.> Feels did their best impression of Grim, adding a push of confidence and intimidation to their words and hoping they carried the needed sense of authority. <Our mission is to defend Baden and end the career of Admiral Kydell. You are welcome to help, hinder, or stay out of our way. Just know this: whatever your choice, we will remember.>

<I've already ordered my ships to stand down as I discuss with the others.>

Feels was relaying a summary of the conversation to Alanis, mentally preparing for the Commodore's response, when they felt a condensed burst of love from Grim. Vivid, alive, and deeply personal. Feels couldn't help but hope it was for them.

The empath projected confusion with a touch of love back at their necromancer... only to be greeted by strong feelings of surprise, followed immediately by a burst of anger.

Oh.

They were still stinging from Grim's rejection when the Commodore returned. <We accept your proposal.>

Quickly burying their hurt, Feels wracked their brain. Proposal? The only one they wanted to propose to was Grim, and he'd made his thoughts on the matter perfectly clear mere seconds ago.

<The *Inevitable* and *Relentless* fleets will join forces with you. Defend Baden against those still loyal to Admiral Kydell. On one condition.> The Commodore's tone turned vengeful. <Promise us that conniving canid will never again see the light of day.>

Already reeling from Grim's rejection, Feels found themselves at a complete loss for words. They buried those emotions deep, too, instead projecting an outward calm.

Grim's presence at the end of their Insight spell began to fade, sending the empath into an absolute panic at the thought of what might be happening to their necromancer. Was Kydell attempting to claim the Oath for himself? Had Grim decided they no longer wished to tie themselves to Feels?

Or, worst of all, was Grim *dying*?

Grim's emotions disappeared from their Insight completely.

"Comms. Add *Captain* Yiven Alanis to the call."

They choked on the words. Their necromancer needed them, but they were stuck here playing politics.

And then Grim was back, overwhelming Feels with his pain and resignation, coupled with the empath's own desperation to solve it.

<Yes, sir?> Alanis made certain to show suitable deference upon joining the link.

Feels found themselves relying on every last bit of self-control they possessed to maintain their front of authority. Grim needed them. The worst was happening.

<Commodore Javon has pledged her allegiance to our cause today. Coordinate with her on what needs to happen.> Their voice caught as Grim's emotions faded. <The Grand Navarch has called for my attention. Commodore, the Captain will tell you what we want from you.>

Leaving the negotiations to Alanis was likely not the best choice, especially considering she was still compromised by Kydell's conditioning, but she had more experience with fleet affairs than Jake – and her words would carry more weight.

<Yes, sir,> the two answered in unison as Feels quickly dropped the telepathic link, then their bindings to the *Inevitable*'s weapons, intent only on Grim.

Grim needed them. That was the only thing that ever mattered.

SHANE BRACED HIMSELF FOR another attack, checking his Imperium – and his Shielding – as he slowly backed away from Razick's reluctant advance. He'd been forced to discard his makeshift shield. Against Razick's magic, it had been nothing but a liability, a conductive channel for her Electromancy.

Not that there weren't enough of those already present. Especially with the water from the sprinkler system now overwhelming the floor drains.

Razick's labored footsteps betrayed her efforts to fight Kydell's orders, but the admiral had commanded and she'd had little choice but to obey.

Her next wave of flames came thick and fast. At the last possible moment, Shane phased briefly through the Veil into the Afterlife to avoid them, emerging quickly once they passed to conserve his magic as best he could. He felt the heat where the Pyromancy had passed, even warmer than the elevated ambient temperature in the enclosed room, the water from the hydro-ponics bay's sprinklers now filling the air with an oppressively humid steam.

Kydell growled deep in his throat from behind Shane, a seething and familiar fury overtaking the canid's voice. "Cut the games, Razick. Stop fighting me, and finish off the necro-mancer."

<There goes that plan,> Razick said quietly, expertly maneu-vering herself between Shane and Kydell. <Should have killed me when you had the chance.>

<I don't want to hurt you, Razick.> He was fighting for survival, but he wouldn't hurt her.

Couldn't, really. She was the better mage, and they both knew it.

A cascade of Electromancy danced across his Shielding, run-ning to ground in the water pooling around their feet.

<You have to. My Shielding's still down. *Kill me,*> she plead-ed. <Bind my soul somewhere I can't hurt you. You and Jeb take out Kydell. Resurrect me after. It's your only chance.>

<No. Jake would never forgive me.>

A familiar face rose in his memories, features twisted by pain and fear and misplaced trust and a single, desperate plea – *Shat-ter me!*

He'd had no choice.

He had no excuse.

Lost in the overwhelming memory, he failed to dodge Raz-ick's next attack. The sudden burst of Electromancy traveled along the metal of the large hydroponics table between them, jumping to the fine mist of water before tearing through Shane's Shielding with unrelenting fury. The magic caught him on his right side as the spell failed, knocking the breath from his lungs and – mercifully – the memory from his mind.

<You're making this harder on yourself,> Razick warned.

The water level rose, pulling at his ankles to slow his movements as a ball of fire formed between Razick's fingers.

<Seems to be how this works,> Shane agreed, hastily refreshing his Shielding. <Still trying to figure it out. Doing the right thing. Instead of the necessary one.>

<A mistake.>

<Perhaps. We'll see if I survive.>

He lunged to the side, using his weight to pull free of the Hydromancy pressing against his calves. Razick's fireballs sailed past harmlessly overhead, her own aim interrupted by another impact against the ship.

He hoped Jake was okay.

<Kydell *ordered* me to kill you,> Razick reminded him sadly. <I *can't* disobey.>

Shane felt his hatred for the admiral resurface, and once again felt the familiar tug to return his allegiance to Kydell. The wolf had stolen so much, twisting the hopes and fears and futures of everyone in his path to suit his own needs.

He tried to pull himself away, focusing his thoughts on his love for Jake, but that only served to remind him of those he'd already Shattered in pursuit of that goal. Of how eliminating

Kydell had now become a necessity for providing his son with the bright future he deserved.

The hate clawed deeper, warring with his protectiveness over Jake.

And then he felt it, tentative at first but growing stronger: a steady stream of love from his stalwart empath, strong enough to take his breath away.

He felt his guilt-turned-resolve rekindling at the unexpected *longing* it ignited in his heart. After what he'd done, he'd ruined any chance of genuinely earning their love. And he didn't have time to play pretend now.

Drawing the gifted emotion into his heart, he returned his thoughts to his son instead, using Feels' love as a template to draw out the love he and Jake shared and the hope he held for the future. The hate pressing against his soul fell away, allowing him to return full focus to his fight with Razick. His fight for survival.

<He ordered me to kill you,> she repeated quietly. <That means one of us is going to die.>

The water level rose again, this time pulling at Shane's hands and knees where he knelt on the floor, catching his breath.

<I'm a necromancer. I'm used to death.>

<And how do you think *I'll* feel? Knowing I killed you? And then probably Jeb, after? *Kill me.*>

Setting his jaw, Shane allowed the power of Baden's star to mix with his own, pouring the borrowed magic into his Shielding. He didn't have the skills for this fight, or the Imperium.

And if they continued much longer, if he kept borrowing power from the Void, he'd not only risk death but the burnout that often followed. People weren't built to *channel* that kind of power, especially not for extended durations, and borrowed power always came at a price. With interest.

Razick's request made sense. It *was* the most logical choice. And it would keep Jake the safest, eliminating one threat so he could focus on ending Kydell. Already he could feel his conditioning pulling at him, directing him to accept her offer. For Jake. Always for Jake.

But he'd killed too many friends already, Shattered too many innocent souls, their pleas haunting his dreams each night and stealing the sleep from his thoughts. He wasn't about to add another. Not even by request. *Especially* not by request.

Jake mattered. Jake's *safety* mattered. But he wasn't the only one.

And with that realization, Shane felt Kydell's conditioning shift inside him once again, his once narrowed focus expanding to include the Kane battle mage and her brother. They were family, too. He had to protect them, at all costs.

<You should have told me you were a battle mage. A *Kane* battle mage,> he told her, phasing into the Afterlife to pull free of the water holding him down. He emerged several inches off the floor, grabbing one of the hydroponics tables to keep from slipping as he fell into the water again.

Not the most preferred landing, but the best he could do, unless he wanted more than his socks filled with water. Phasing into the middle of something tended to mean they both occupied the same space, with disastrous and painful results.

<I did. Eventually,> Razick answered defensively, hitting him with a wall of Anemancy that knocked his breath away *and* sent him slamming into the table behind him. <And *you* said we could keep our secrets.>

Shane forced himself to dodge as fire followed air, consuming the plants that had once been behind him. He was panting now, water and sweat soaking into his skin in all the ways he hated, the humidity so oppressive he may as well have been drowning. Any more and his reactions would grow too sluggish to withstand her assault, even if he had the magic to do so.

<I know,> he managed, once he'd regained his bearings. <But I was Kydell's, too. I know what it's like. I could have helped.>

<How could I know that?> she asked, Electromancy arcing from her fingers once more to pry for weaknesses in his Shielding. <You have secrets, too. And you don't seem the sort to share them.>

He checked his magic again. There was a truth to her words, deeper than she knew. And with the state of his Imperium, he'd likely be taking them to his grave shortly.

<Fight him. Not me.>

<We've already established I can't,> she said bitterly. <His hold's too deep. I hate that wolf. So much.>

<Then try love,> he told her, barely dodging as she sent another wave of fire at him. <Focus on your feelings for your

brother. How he's always there for you. How he supports you, no matter what.>

As Shane spoke, he couldn't help but think of his own stalwart friend. The fae who always had his back, and forgave him for everything, whether he deserved it or not.

He rarely deserved it.

Feels projected confusion, and Shane quickly buried his thoughts of love with the others, deep within. They'd made their own feelings clear enough long ago when he'd asked what kind of friendship they wanted from him, and again when he'd offered the Soul Oath. After everything that had happened between them, the last thing they needed was to feel obligated to deal with his emotional baggage.

Instead, he began to focus his thoughts on reassurance, but was interrupted by a flood of Razick's Hydromancy. The water hit with surprising force, forcing his back into another table.

He cried in pain from the impact.

<Pay attention,> Razick scolded. <I'm doing my best here.>

<At fighting Kydell? Or fighting me?> Shane shot back, snarling.

<We *both* need to fight Kydell.> Razick narrowed her eyes. <I know I'm a distraction, but we have to figure this out. Put yourself between us again.>

Exhaling, Shane mentally berated himself for falling into the wolf's trap. He'd been so focused on Razick, he'd allowed himself to subconsciously write off the admiral as Jeb's problem to solve.

Jeb.

He needed the biologist's knowledge again.

<Jeb. Is there anything flammable in here?>

<Not much,> the younger Kane admitted. The answer came quickly, although his voice was strained. <Maybe some fertilizer. Hydro said they reverted to older practices. When I was first assigned Agrokinesis, some of the stuff we used could get pretty nasty.> Jeb's voice turned pleading. <Whatever you're doing, do it quick. I don't have much longer.>

Shane made his way toward the storage shelving, carefully reinforcing his Shielding with the limitless power of the Void. He had to carefully ration his power now, but if these shelves had what he needed...

"Sub-Officer Kane, you have twisted my orders for the last time," Kydell growled loudly. "Stop hitting me with collateral damage. Kill that damn necromancer, as fast as possible. Don't hold back, use *all* your magic."

Shane's Shielding failed immediately, the mortal plane squeezing in on him as he lost his connection to the higher planes of the Afterlife, and the telepathic link to Jeb and Razick. His eyes widened, chest heaving as his Necromancy-induced claustrophobia took hold without the limitless expanse of the Void inside his thoughts.

Antimagic.

The room erupted around him in a ferocious storm of magical power as the entire contents of the hydroponics bay tore from their shelves and fixtures, swirling around him in a telekinetic tornado before battering against his skin and stolen uniform with a haphazard cruelty.

He squeezed his eyes shut, unable to do much else against the onslaught without his magic.

Slumping to the floor, he barely had time to breathe in relief as Razick dismissed her Antimagic. He quickly summoned his Shielding, struggling to stand, but the battle mage wasn't done yet.

An Electromancy bolt crackled, lightning following a course from the tables to the water on the floor, then to the spray from the sprinklers, and finally Shane's own soaked uniform. Strengthened by the sheer volume of water available for conductivity, and no longer restrained by Razick – how much *had* she been holding back – Shane felt the strike completely overwhelm both his Shield and his casting ability, the power of the blast knocking the air out of his lungs and temporarily disrupting his connection to the magical fields of the universe itself.

The spell's current took on a life of its own, crawling under his skin like a million tiny creatures biting and scratching for a way out. And then they found it, in the form of his locket, searing the metal of both pendant and necklace into his neck and chest.

He cried out in pain, panting as he lay on his back in the water, his muscles still spasming despite the departure of the current.

He felt Jeb's Telepathy scratch against the back of his thoughts, and accepted.

<What happened?> the biologist demanded.

<You can stop attacking now,> Shane managed at last, the sprinkler directly above him shifting in and out of focus as he stared up, unblinking.

<I'm trying,> Razick apologized. <I... He told me to use everything. Said I had to kill you.>

<You just did.> Shane felt his heart beating in his chest, a trapped animal desperate to claw its way free. Closing his eyes, he focused all his energy on his next breath. <I'm not coming back from this one.>

He opened them again in time to watch Razick round the corner, wild red curls framing wide green eyes. <You *can't* die. What about Kydell? What about Jeb?> She stood over him, hands on her hips. <You said we could do this!>

<You're a necromancer! I thought death didn't matter!> Jeb argued. The biologist's voice in his head felt miles away.

<My resources are finite. Once I'm dead...>

Shane paused, gathering his words.

<I'll use all I have to finally break the last of his Shielding and Shatter him. Should have done that from the beginning. Left my body in the server room and gone after him from inside the Void.>

He felt a brief surge of anger and frustration, but it quickly slipped from his grasp. Breathing was a distant memory.

<Damn vampires and their endless magic. Look out for Jake for me? Tell him... I did my best. Tell him... Call me. If he can forgive me.>

<But can't you just bring yourself back?>

<I'm spent. Channeling the stars now... Borrow too much... Lose it all...>

He had to concentrate on each word now. The room was growing terrifyingly small.

<Taking more than I can repay.>

The Void beckoned from beyond the Veil.

41

TALK ME INTO A mutiny, then leave me alone to coordinate it all, Alanis grumbled to herself. They'd had a great thing going, disabling the fleet and wreaking havoc, when suddenly Weapons had abandoned their post with no explanation and now *she* was stuck playing diplomacy with yet another of Kydell's Commodores. *I really need to stop getting sucked into these things.*

<I've relayed your orders to the fleet, Captain.>

Commodore Javon's words carried more emotions than the aloof communications Alanis was accustomed to receiving from her. Committing treason had that effect on a person, she supposed.

<Good.> Now perhaps she could return her attention to her own ship, and working with Maintenance to survey the full extent of damage. <All further transmissions will be relayed through *Inevitable*'s Communications alone. I still have Kydell's conditioning, so may become compromised.>

She prepared to end the transmission.

<Alanis...>

Javon had *never* called her by her first name. It was a breach of formality. An implication of a friendship they didn't share.

Alanis didn't keep the ice from her voice as she answered. <Something else you need, Commodore?>

<How did *you* get involved in all this?>

On any other day, Alanis would have considered this an accusation, but today there was something else in the Commodore's voice. A need, as if the knowledge itself would decide their fates.

She supposed, in a way, it would.

<I saw my chance, and I took it. Same as the rest of you.>

<No, I mean...> Javon paused. <You've always been meticulous. Never one to move unless under orders you couldn't refuse, or you were certain of success. So... What makes you certain this will work? How did this Grand Navarch win your loyalty?>

How much do I tell her?

Alanis thought fast. She could tell her it was Grim. That he'd promised to help her. Even now, his word still carried weight.

But his medic had introduced him as Shane Lawrence. He clearly wished to keep his past a secret, and if she told Javon, the whole fleet would know within seconds.

No. She wouldn't betray his trust.

<I'd trade helmets with him,> she said instead. <He broke my Oath.>

That, too, would carry weight.

<That's impossible.>

<Yet here I am. Free.> She sent a flash of her memories from the moment the Oath was dissolved. <When he came to take possession of the ship, I tried to Shatter him. He could have easily Shattered me in return, but he freed me instead.>

<And your weapons officer?> By her tone this question also held importance. <When we felt all that love... It overwhelmed the *Shields* for Void's sake...>

<They were *supposed* to be using guilt.>

Javon let a chuckle slip into her words. <Believe me. We got plenty of that, too.> Her voice turned serious. <But when we were hit with that last wave... And then learned they were after the admiral himself... Please tell me your weapons officer is a psychomorphic mage.>

Alanis jumped to the defensive. <They didn't use it on you.>

<But... could they?> The Commodore's voice rose in pitch, pleading, and Alanis suddenly realized *exactly* why they'd earned the armada's new allegiance. <We... We want our minds back, Alanis. Admiral Kydell has taken so much from so many of us. We don't want him to keep it.> Her voice turned hopeful. <And if your mage can send love as strong as we felt... Well. If we're going to trust someone to alter our minds? I'd prefer someone who can not only love like that, but feel confident enough in that love to send it to complete strangers. Strangers who had been trying to kill them, no less.>

Alanis smiled to herself. Grim's medic would definitely be hearing about this, as would everyone else. Fair payback for abandoning their post.

<They can help. They promised to help me, whether I helped them or not.> She stopped, debating just how much to share, but it was critical that Javon understood Alanis had witnessed the process herself if she was to guarantee their allegiance. <I've seen them recondition someone. He asked them to, in preparation for facing our admiral. It was fast, and it wasn't pretty, but it worked.>

When the Commodore spoke next, her words carried the conviction of someone who had just committed the most important decision of her life. <You lick your wounds. We'll clear up the last of this mess. And you tell this Grand Navarch of yours, if he'll do this for us, we'll owe him a debt we could never hope to repay. Although I, for one, will do my best to try.>

<I'll relay your message. *Inevitable* out.>

Alanis terminated the link.

<<Feels! I figured it out!>>

Jake's triumphant cry interrupted her jumbled speculations. *Not even the dead are allowed to think around here.*

"Figured out what?"

<<How to aim. I'm sorry. I should have figured it out sooner.>>

"It's okay." Without someone on Weapons, there wasn't much the *Inevitable* could do to help, anyway. She may as well console the kid. "Sometimes it takes a few times reading things for the information to sink in. And less people shooting at you."

<<Reading?>> Jake laughed. <<I don't often read Sparnelli, but the manual was useless. No, we just have to put the filter on the spell itself. Like I did with my Shieldbreaker. For school. I'll need help to set it up, but–>>

<<No.>>

Alanis reactivated her hologram, projecting herself into the server room. "Weapons left. Said Grim needed them."

Jake's smile turned sour. "When." The word was a demand, more than a question.

"Ten minutes ago, maybe?"

She shrugged two pairs of arms, and saw traces of Grim echo back in his glare.

"You should have told me."

"Why?" She crossed all three pairs of arms. "Doesn't change anything. You promised him you'd stay here with me. The *Inevitable* needs her Shielding mage."

"And my father needs *me*." He made his way to the door. "Without him, our plan also fails. I can Shield the ship from anywhere inside."

"I promised your father I'd look out for you," she protested. "Hyperjump you away if you were no longer safe here. He'd *Shatter* me if he broke that promise."

Jake paused in the doorway, his back to her. "Then I'll keep our Apotheturgy active."

"Show me your knife," she ordered. If he was going to leave, at least she'd make him easy to find.

Slipping free from the *Inevitable* to enter the Afterlife, she found the knife, as intoxicatingly beautiful as she remembered. Borrowing from Jake's magic, she cast a binding spell, creating a binding point for her soul on the knife.

Spell complete, she slipped back into her crystal in the server room. She searched for the boy to provide further directions to the hydroponics bay, but he was already gone.

There is zero *discipline on this ship.*

She sighed. "Telemetry?"

"Yes, Nav?"

"I'm handing you control of Weapons, also. See if you can run a Shieldbreaker through our guns. Help our new allies."

Technically they'd been allies before her own mutiny, too, but it was nice to have them on her side again. She didn't know this Commodore well – Javon led the *Relentless* armada, Kydell's ground-assault-heavy fleet – but her reputation was solid. Most of the *Inevitable* armada – the orbital-bombardment-focused fleet where Alanis served – would willingly follow her lead.

"Yes, sir. Thank you, sir."

At least *someone* on her team was still having a good day. Although...

"Just make sure you don't forget your primary responsibility. Last thing we need is someone ramming the ship."

"Oh. Um. Yes."

Like a kid with a new toy, she sighed to herself. *He forgot. At least it shouldn't matter at this point.*

"Helm!" Telemetry's voice held sheer panic. "Up! Up! *Reckoning* is on collision!"

Alanis shifted her attention to the ship's systems, cursing herself for allowing the politics to distract her from the welfare of the ship. While the ship's AI could handle basic operations for short durations and off-shifts, there was a reason she usually relied on a crew of two thousand. Everyone's attention was stretched thin today, but they couldn't afford mistakes.

She watched through Telemetry's overlay as the *Inevitable* sought to push away from their rapidly encroaching neighbor, *Reckoning*'s nose crumbling at the impact with their Shielding. She could feel Jake straining against the impact, pouring his magic into his spellwork until size and momentum overwhelmed him and the *Inevitable*'s Shielding Runework – much of it missing by this point, courtesy of the earlier missile hits.

But he'd bought them time. The *Reckoning* sailed underneath, scraping against the *Inevitable*'s lower hull in what felt like slow motion before Helm added enough distance to safely correct their flight path.

Alanis felt the familiar power surge of the *Inevitable*'s Shielding re-engaging moments later.

Some kid. Shielding mage indeed.

Crisis averted, she turned her attention to preventing a repeat performance.

"Telem! You're off Weapons until you get your primary responsibilities under control. Comms! Get *Relentless* and *Reckoning* on the link. I want to know what the *hell* that was. Maint, damage report!"

Still seething with frustration at her own complacency, Alanis was pulled from her crystal and forced to manifest in the server room before the Maintenance AI could respond. A self-satisfied growl that greeted her arrival.

"Hello, Alanis. It's been a while." Fleet Captain Selkirk eyed her appraisingly. "I see our admiral's been too lenient on you. I'll have to fix that."

Alanis shuddered as the TAG bared her canines, but held her silence.

"Oh, not just yet, little one. You've been very naughty, but you're not going anywhere. There are others more important to reclaim first." She narrowed her eyes. "Our Admiral would prefer we take our time with you. Tell me where he is."

"Hydroponics." Alanis found herself unable to resist answering.

"Good girl." Selkirk's voice remained nauseatingly sweet. "And who is with him?"

"Sub-Officer Kane, her brother Jeb, and..."

She screwed her eyes shut, fighting against the conditioning demanding she answer.

"The Kanes?" The canid's face brightened at their names. "Razick's loss was a tragedy. One I am eager to correct. Who else?"

Miraculously, Alanis managed to hold her tongue, although it took everything she had.

It also didn't matter, in the end.

"Now *there's* a soul I thought I'd never feel again," Selkirk purred. "And he's brought his medic, too. Come now, Alanis. You know you can't hide these secrets from a necromancer."

"It's Grim," the fae confirmed at last, unable to justify fighting any longer. "He survived."

"I must say, Alanis, you certainly know how to make friends." The TAG growled with pleasure. "My compliments to your Shielding mage. I was beginning to worry I'd never get through."

Alanis struggled to break the canid's control, but Kydell had rooted her conditioning deep within her insecurities and she found them doubly impossible to shake now.

"As a reward," Selkirk continued, "I'll let you stay bound here while you think about your fate. You certainly can't go anywhere. And I find our sessions so much more rewarding when you've already had time to try and clever your way out of them, don't you? I'd like to savor this last one."

The oppressive hopelessness of Alanis' situation pressed down on her mind. *I was so close to freedom.*

"Oh. And one last thing?"

Alanis felt the Void begin to wrap around the brown striped canid. "Don't tell them I'm coming for them. Don't let those mutinous AI of yours tell anyone, either." She gave a menacing grin. "I have one final lesson for your precious Grim. And surprise parties are much more fun."

With that, the TAG was gone, reality bending around her to carry her to the hydroponics bay and destroy Alanis' last chance for freedom from the Sparnelli war machine.

What do I do? What do I do?

Alanis clawed at her mind, desperate to break free from Kydell's mental rewiring, but to no avail.

I need to warn Grim.

No, the order had specifically stated not to tell them.

Communications can–

No, the infernal canid had cut off that option, too, and as Weapons AI, Feels also fell in that same category.

She dropped her bindings to the ship, rushing to Hydroponics. She could already see the TAG's magic at work, souls rushing from the Afterlife to take their place within the binding buttons specially arranged on her uniform, the team haplessly bound to her commands for an eternity of servitude. The process appeared slower than usual, but it didn't matter. TAGs were formidable at any state of readiness. Time would only make her deadlier.

So what now?

Alanis forced herself to slow her thoughts, focusing on each occupant of the *Inevitable* and running them through the TAG's exact orders. Who could she...

Jake.

Alanis hoped he was up to the task. As talented as he had shown himself to be, her continued existence, the fleet's chances of breaking free from Kydell's influence, and Baden's chances of autonomy now rested entirely in Jake's hands.

The fate of billions, resting on the shoulders of a twelve-year-old kid.

42

Dying won't absolve you of your obligations, Grim.

He felt Feels' words, more than heard them, and struggled to assign them meaning. Was he hallucinating?

I forgave you for murdering me, but I'm not letting you forget it. So no heroic sacrifices today. You've a lot to make up to me, still!

Shane felt a warmth in what he assumed to be his chest, spreading outward. His breath returned, labored and heavy, his heart resuming a jagged rhythm, every moment still a struggle.

But alive.

Time for me to save your butt. Again.

<Feels...> Shane struggled against the heaviness within his mind as the empath's magic slowly mended his insides. <Jeb. Add Feels. Telepathy.>

<No,> Jeb said, his voice strained but firm. <Razick doesn't want another psychomorphic mage inside her head. For *any* reason.>

<Jeb. Do it.> Razick's telepathic voice was rife with fear, and Shane felt a pressure squeezing what felt like his hand. <As soon as Kydell realizes I killed Lawrence, he'll make me kill you, too.>

Shane's heart resumed a regular rhythm, faint and slow, but reliable. With the return of his pulse, so too came the pain, sharp and insistent and everywhere. He threw his head back, grinding his teeth to keep his silence. Whatever he did, he couldn't afford to alert Kydell to his current plight.

Jeb and Razick's survival depended on it.

Don't move. This was an order, the words edged with a harshness Feels rarely employed, and Shane felt a burst of urgency from the empath. *Let me work.*

<Feels... No... Stop... Need you...>

He struggled against the fae's magic. He had to make them understand.

I need you, too. Stop fighting me.

<Razick needs...>

Shane's breathing eased as the empathic medic continued their work. *She can wait. I'm healing you first.*

<I need you to use your magic on me. Psychomorphation.> Razick's words carried a nervous edge, and Shane felt the pressure on his hand increase. <Undo Kydell's hold on my mind. So I can fight him.>

Feels paused their efforts. *Grim, is this true?*

<Yes.> He focused his thoughts on love and gratitude, and attempted to ignore his pain. <Kydell is priority. And we need Razick whole.>

Promise me you'll stay here and rest until I return. Just lay here and breathe. Another order. *No heroics. Promise me.*

<I'll never leave you,> Shane promised.

As reward, he felt the soothing numbness spread through his veins, pushing away his pain and every other discomfort. The hard tile floor pressing into his back, the fine mist still falling from the ceiling, the water soaking uncomfortably into his clothes and every available surface, the oppressive heat and humidity, none of it mattered. Nothing mattered but his next breath, and the presence of his empath radiating once more from his chest where the locket had seared into his skin.

<Okay, Razick. Here's how this is going to work...>

Shane dropped from the telepathic link, focusing his thoughts instead on each successive breath, just as he'd promised.

In.

Out.

In.

Out.

Snarls and shouts echoed in his ears, their volume rising easily above the steady patter of the water raining down.

In.

Out.

He felt the floor shudder repeatedly beneath him, and fought the urge to grab on to something.

In.

Out.

The room filled with the protests of metal bending and twisting, and Shane felt a flood of even more water within the already drenched hydroponics bay. He kept his body still, his mind focused on his task.

In.

Out.

In.

Out.

A welcome and cooling breeze caressed Shane's face, and he realized the sprinklers had ceased their relentless spray. He found breathing easier as the temperature dropped, the humidity falling with it.

In.

Out.

And then he had Feels' full attention, the empathic medic resuming their purposeful efforts to mend his wounds.

What have you done to yourself? The words held rebuke, but Shane felt the shadow of a tease. *I put a lot of effort into making you this body. You need to take better care of my gifts.*

Shane fought the urge to smile. "In my defense, Razick did most of it." His words were quiet, his lungs just barely healed. "And I distinctly remember paying you."

With my *inheritance.* Feels' words carried a mock defensiveness. *You faked your death, remember? They sent me all your money.*

The friends worked in silence, Shane continuing to focus his efforts solely on breathing while Feels deftly repaired his most urgent injuries. The necromancer felt himself slowly returning from the brink of death, the Void's efforts to claim his soul as a permanent resident easing with each welcome, soothing spell.

It was Feels who finally broke the silence. *I'm sorry, by the way. About earlier. I hope you're not still angry with me.*

Shane wracked his memories in confusion. "Why would I be angry at you?"

Not long before you got hurt, I sent you a question, and you got angry.

"Oh." He remembered that moment. His reassurance to the empath had been interrupted by Razick's Hydromancy. "That wasn't at you. Razick got me *wet*."

Feels didn't answer, but Shane caught a wave of relief with a hint of amusement mixed into their next healing spell. He *did* smile then, his pain numbed enough he forgot about the rip in his cheek.

The rebuke was immediate. *I said don't move.*

"Sorry." His voice was a whisper. "And thank you."

You really ripped yourself to pieces today. The empath radiated amusement... and fatigue. *I haven't seen you this bad since the time you stole that electroglider. This is probably worse.*

"Borrowed," Shane corrected. "And *that* wasn't my fault, either."

You're nothing without me, you know.

"You're just figuring this out now? I used to think you were smarter than me."

And I *used to think you'd never notice.*

"I always noticed," Shane admitted. "Thanks for 'saving my butt.'"

It's a nice butt. The empath's emotions burned with mischief. *Made it that way on purpose.*

Shane's uncontainable snort quickly devolved into a coughing fit. He slowly turned his head to the side to spit out the viscous fluid rapidly filling his mouth with each forced exhale.

Blood.

"I think you missed a spot."

Everyone's a critic.

Feels' tone contained sarcasm but Shane caught the concern rolling underneath. Time for a change of topic.

"How'd the space battle go?"

There's a few holdouts, but the fleet can handle them. I left Alanis in charge. Their tone turned sheepish. *Told her she was captain now. Hope you don't mind.*

"Fleet?" Shane attempted to sit up, his muscles quickly giving out. "Baden's defenses are taking orders from *us* now?"

Stop squirming and hold still, or I'll remove the analgesia spell and let you feel everything again. Feels' words were accompanied by a burst of annoyance, followed by a prickling warmth within his chest as the medic repaired something Shane had probably just torn open.

Crisis averted, they resumed the conversation. *No, my fleet. If you're good, I might even share.*

Shane felt a moment of panic. "Feels, you didn't..."

The fae projected mock insult. *Of course not! I'm not Kydell.*

There was a friendly caress of magic within Shane's skull, the medic likely checking for internal bleeding. Apparently satisfied with the results, they continued.

Turns out, we're not the only ones he's angered. When they learned we were after the admiral, they volunteered to help.

Shane exhaled. "I'm sorry. Was worried you'd spent too much time with me."

No such thing.

Shane wasn't sure if the sudden warmth in his chest was from Feels' spell or their words.

It didn't matter. He realized he could happily stay in this moment forever, content in the care of his friend, even despite the searing pain he knew lay lurking beneath the empath's spell-work.

They were here. He needed help, and they came for him.

They forgave him.

43

WE NEED RAZICK WHOLE.

Razick hadn't felt whole in a long time. Not since…

She didn't even remember.

The janitor's psychomorphic mage sounded kind, at least. A point in their favor.

<I'm going to cast an Emotional Insight spell on you, so I can track your feelings, and the thoughts attached to them. Don't try to fight it. I need to know exactly where you're at, if we're going to do this.>

<Okay.>

Standing slowly, Razick prepared herself for the incoming spells. She hated the thought of surrendering her mind to another's control, but Lawrence trusted this Feels and anyone had to be better than Kydell.

Eying the room, she noted Jeb had angled the admiral with his back to them, her brother's Agrokinesis proving a useful frustration on the wolf's attentions, although not much else. She felt a swell of pride, and moments later a caress of reassurance against her mind.

<Done.> Feels paused. <You're thinking of your brother, right? You *should* be proud. Not many can stand up to Kydell. Much less successfully.>

<Could use some help, though?>

Jeb's voice betrayed exhaustion, his face flush from the heat, and possibly embarrassment.

<Cast your spells. Let's get this over with.>

Razick realized her voice came out harsher than she'd intended, but the mage didn't seem to notice.

Or maybe they didn't care. She'd gathered enough from Lawrence's side of their interactions to suspect their friendship was even more complicated than hers with Jeb.

<Already did.> She felt a surge of confidence delivered with Feels' answer. <You do what needs doing, and I'll help secure your emotions until you don't need me anymore. They'll be in direct conflict with what you're actually feeling, though. You'll need to focus on the emotions when I send them, or it won't work.>

<Wait... that's it? You're not going to take control of my mind or something?>

<Any day now!> Jeb pleaded, blocking a swipe of Kydell's claws with his oversized wrench.

<I'm not Kydell.> The mage's voice was bitter. <Psychomor-phation is meant to heal, not to harm. Now *go!* If you start to fall, I'll catch you.>

Closing her eyes, Razick focused her Imperium into thoughts of flames and broiled wolf, launching a living wall of fire at the canid while simultaneously drawing water from the room to shield her brother.

"Hey! Kydell! Your turn!"

She tightened the fire around him, still feeding the flames, grinning wildly as they kissed and clung to his fur.

"Welcome back, Razick. You've finally finished off the necro-mancer." Kydell's voice carried a surprising calm as he turned his back to Jeb, expanding his Shielding to block her Pyromancy. "Good girl. Now kill your brother."

"Not today."

True to their word, Feels filled her emotions with thoughts of comfort, confidence, and love to block Kydell's pull on her mind. She greedily accepted them, fanning her Pyromancy and sending the flames dancing around his Shielding.

<Jeb, step aside.>

With a slight twist of her finger she pried the hydroponics tables from their floor fixtures, the room shuddering from the irresistible power of her magic.

Her brother nodded silent understanding and made his way toward the corner.

"My dear Sub-Officer Kane." Kydell bared his teeth, slowly stalking toward her. "We've been through this before. Many times. You already know how this ends. Why make it harder for everyone?" He spread his arms, palms toward her, head cocked to the side. "I'm the only one who's *always* been there for you. Your family, your squad, your Nya... All gone."

Razick felt her emotions spill into fear and loss as the admiral's grin turned feral, his words still suave and alluring. He was lying. She *knew* he was lying. Why was she...

Her wall of fire faltered as he pulled on her allegiance, but the psychomorphic mage in her mind filled her thoughts with resolve, trust, and courage, allowing her to reclaim herself.

Kydell continued, emboldened by the brief disruption of her spell. "And soon your brother will join them. It's only fair I let you do it yourself. A reward, for your loyalty." He spread his arms wider, claws at the ready. "It'll be more painful for you both if you leave him for me."

She dropped her elemental spells, switching instead to channel her Telekinesis. Kydell's eyes widened, his attention drawn to the hydroponics tables now suspended in the air behind her, plants and water sloshing over the edges as she flung them through the air with the invisible might of the gravity-based magic.

He spun away in an effort to run from her fury, but Razick was faster, pinning him in place before pelting him with the full complement of her rage. The admiral's Shielding fractured at the onslaught, the tables and their water slamming him to the floor in a pile of bloody fur and broken bones, neatly pinned beneath the twisted metal.

And through it all she felt Feels' light touch in her mind, gently tweaking her emotions until neither Kydell nor her own bitter lust for revenge could distract her.

She glared down at the canid, but her anger was gone, replaced instead by a sense of confident accomplishment and a burning need for answers. "You've only *begun* to understand pain."

"You haven't won yet."

Kydell's faint words of resistance betrayed his intentions. As Razick watched, his wounds began to mend, one of the benefits of the haemovampira virus coursing through his veins. But vampirism needed magic to operate, so this, too, was a problem she could fix.

His eyes widened as he felt the crush of her Antimagic field, unable to overwhelm its magic negation in his weakened state. This was *her* magic, carefully selected and mastered after her desertion. He'd had no part in it, which made its use in her victory all the sweeter.

"How? When?" he spluttered.

"I am more than what you made me," she spat, venom dripping from her every word. "Now tell me about Nya."

Kydell regained his composure, grinning with victory despite his present predicament. "So. You really *have* forgotten. Interesting."

Razick faintly registered Jeb requesting the Hydroponics AI open the doors and adjust the environmental settings, with an added request dictated by Feels to do so slowly to avoid sending the necromancer deeper into shock, but none of that seemed to matter.

Jeb's telepathic congratulations at defeating Kydell rang hollow in the back of her mind.

"Tell me about Nya!"

Razick didn't know why this was suddenly so important – the name felt familiar, like a whisper from a dream – and at this moment it seemed her life hung on the admiral's response.

"I'll grant you the answers you seek," the wolf offered smoothly, his breathing labored. "You know what you have to do."

She found herself genuinely considering it, her mind rebelled at the thought and yet strangely drawn to his promise. She waited desperately for Feels' spellwork to pull her back from the edge, but nothing happened. Kydell's grin loomed in her mind.

"I think I'll have you take the Oath this time." His tone turned conversational, and confident in his victory. "You really are quite talented. I have no intention of allowing you to hide away from my influence again."

Salvation came from Jeb, at the end of the telekinetic wrench he'd brought from the engine room. The wolf yelped in surprise before succumbing to the blow.

<You killed him.> Razick didn't know why she was so angry. That's what she wanted, wasn't it? That's why she'd insisted they join the janitor in his assault in the first place.

So why did she feel so empty?

<No, I didn't.> He pointed his wrench at the admiral's chest, rising and falling in a steady rhythm. <But he can't stay awake. I promised I'd keep you safe from him, and he almost got you back.>

She ran her fingers through her hair, her thick red curls helplessly tangled from the battle. Her emotions felt raw and strangely foreign, and for a moment she panicked that Kydell or the necromancer's Psychomorphic mage had somehow altered her further during the battle.

But no. It was over. Kydell had lost and they had won and why didn't it feel that way?

She clenched her fists, drawing on her anger in an effort to stave back the despair threatening to spill into her thoughts. <But now I'll *never* know about Nya.>

<What about her?> Jeb carefully eyed the wolf, clutching his bludgeoning wrench tightly. With a wince, he tentatively wrapped his free hand around her wrist. <It's just us in the link now. What do you want to know? Maybe you wrote it in your letters.>

<Who *is* she?> Razick pulled free of her brother's light grasp, brushing away the sting of tears tracing down her cheeks as she began to pace. <I keep trying to figure it out, but every time I think I remember something it slips through my fingers.>

Like water, she wanted to add, but not even water could do that anymore. Not with her Hydromancy. She was strong and capable and even still the damned wolf kept his cursed control over her.

She turned to watch Jeb and saw a flash of pity and anger cross his face before settling into sorrow. He stepped closer, reaching toward her. <Raz... Nya was your fiancée.>

She grabbed at Jeb's hand, squeezing until she was certain she'd crushed each of his fingers. She didn't care, barely registering his quiet whimper. <My... What?>

<Fiancée.> He didn't even attempt to pull away from her bone-breaking grip, instead meeting her gaze. <You were together for... seven years? Wanted to settle down. Get married, once your conscription ended. You couldn't wait. Wrote about her all the time.>

Her knees betrayed her and she sank to the floor, her fall arrested by her brother's steady hand. She faintly noted the loud bang as his wrench hit the deck. <What... What happened to her?>

<I don't know.> His words came faster. <You stopped answering my letters for a while, and then suddenly you broke the silence to say you'd re-enlisted. You... never wrote about her, after that. I assumed you'd had a falling out and didn't want to talk about it.>

She buried her face in her hands. "Nooooooo!"

Grabbing Jeb's discarded wrench, she rose to stalk toward the unconscious Kydell, her mind full of murderous intent. <Even when I think I'm free he *still* finds a way to steal my future from me!>

"Ah. Kane Razick. There you are!"

Her newfound fury froze solid at the voice from the door, and Razick raised her gaze to find the cool green eyes of a striped brown canid. Her crisp brown and khaki uniform bore an excess of golden buttons across her chest, accented with a single golden triple-claw pin at the collar, the mark of those personally Claimed by Admiral Kydell.

Their visitor calmly stepped through the doorway, expertly assessing the scene within the hydroponics bay. The canid's eyes grew distracted, betraying her present effort to Call and Bind her attending team of souls to her side.

Razick's heart sank as she took a quick inventory of her magic. *Kydell's TAG.* They hadn't won, after all.

Fleet Captain Selkirk Larissa graced Razick with a smile, but there was no kindness in the welcome. "Nav said I'd find you here. Am I interrupting something?"

44

Jake balled his fists in frustration, eying the locked bulkhead door in front of him. His father's teachings once again echoed in his mind. *The Order of Success: Learn. Plan. Act.*

He should have at least asked Alanis for the codes to the ship. Or found a way to see what was happening there. Or... anything, really, instead of storming out on a personal mission he'd already doomed to failure.

He prepared to return to the server room and apologize to Alanis, when he felt an insistent pressure against the *Inevitable*'s Shielding. Gritting his teeth to bite back a scream of pain, Jake braced himself against the wall, pouring everything he had into the spell.

But he couldn't stop it. He fell to his knees as his Shielding fractured under the continued pressure, leaving him gasping as a sickening screech slowly rang through the ship.

He quickly re-engaged the Shielding, reinforcing it as best he could. *I had* one *job to do, and I failed at* that, *too.*

He slowly picked himself up off the deck, brushing at the knees of his school uniform before turning back to the server room. *Alanis was right. I should have just stayed with her.*

Stewing in his frustration, he felt the Void pushing against the back of his mind, and let it enter. "Mom?"

<<Sorry, kid, it's just me.>> Alanis' Call held a sense of urgency which overrode the apology in her voice. <<How's your Shielding? How's your Imperium?>>

"I'm sorry I failed." His shoulders slumped, the knot in his stomach tightening. Whatever happened, it must have been bad. "I don't know what happened. They're back up now. I hope we didn't lose anything important."

<<No, I didn't mean...>> Her tone turned flustered, and it seemed to take forever before she gathered her thoughts. <<Jake, we were rammed by another *ship*. Telemetry screwed up, not you. Your Shielding bought us enough time to *save* the ship. But someone got through when it went down, someone who can destroy everything we've worked for today, and you're the *only* one who can stop her. So I need to know. How's your Shielding? How's your Imperium?>>

Jake paused to check, running the exercises his father had taught him. He wasn't a Void mage like his father, and therefore lacked the ability to borrow power from the stars, but the necromancer had insisted Jake learn his personal limits anyway, despite his protests.

Perhaps his father *had* prepared him for combat on a space-craft, after all.

"If nobody else rams us, I'll be okay for another... half hour? Maybe?" He frowned. "Would have been an hour, I think, but I used a lot of Imperium trying to stop the ship ramming us."

<<Another... *Damn.* You *are* Grim's kid.>> Alanis' voice turned dark. <<But I need you to do the most difficult thing you've ever done. We need to kill a TAG. She's still binding her team, so this is the most vulnerable she'll ever be. We don't have much time.>>

The Order of Success: Learn. Plan. Act. He wasn't going to make the same mistake twice.

"What's a tag?"

<<Stands for Tactical Assault Group, eight to twenty souls, usually battle mages with medic support, plus a Tactical Lead. Lead's always a necromancer, also called the TAG. Hyperjumps in, Binds the team, they cause hell until their TAG dies. Resurrect, repeat.>> Alanis paused. <<Your father and his friends are in no shape to face her.>>

"You should have told me."

The words were thick with accusation, and she sighed. <<Was worried you'd run off. Just like you did. We needed our Shielding mage.>>

"I need my *father*. I need him to be okay. I need..." His voice cracked.

<<And he needs you,>> Alanis said sternly. <<Focused. Alert. We don't have the luxury of infighting, remember? What happened to working together?>>

He opened his mouth to argue, to tell her this was different because it was about his father...

And closed it again. She was right. His father was in trouble, and arguing with Alanis wouldn't change that. But it could make it worse.

"Weaknesses?"

More lessons would help.

<<The TAG herself. She's their link to the mortal plane. Without her Telepathy to share what she sees, the rest of her team is blind.>> Alanis' words came faster. <<I'll jump you behind her while she's still binding her team. Hopefully she'll think we're just one more of her souls. But you'll only get one surprise attack.>>

"So make it count." Jake nodded, squaring his shoulders. "But can't you just Shatter her?"

<<I'm still Kydell's. Conditioned to do whatever she says.>> Alanis' Call turned to anguish. <<I feel so useless. I can't fight. Has to be you. Has to be now.>>

"Then I'll use my knife." He pulled it from his pocket, gripping the handle as he mouthed a brief thanks to Veris. He wondered briefly how the older dracoling was faring, back home in the vault. But his father needed him; he didn't have time to worry about Veris, too. "Can you guide the blade to her soul?"

<<You'll have to get through her Shielding first.>>

"I will." He already held the early components of a necromantic Shieldbreaker in his mind.

It's okay to admit you don't have all the answers, but it's never okay to give up.

"I'm ready."

He felt the Void twist around them, bending reality to place him directly behind the fierce brown striped canid, her very posture oozing confident power. Time seemed to slow as he grasped his knife in his fist, aligning it with Alanis' guidance before leaping to thrust it upward into the TAG's back, casting his Shieldbreaker at the same moment.

The TAG tensed the moment his blade pierced flesh. Jake tightened his grip to counter her attempts to spin and face him. Twisting the hilt, he pushed it upward to shift the blade down and guarantee the most damage against his target. He felt something give as she fell to the floor, slowly sliding off his knife to crumple into a heap at his feet.

<<You did it.>> Alanis' voice held awe. <<She's... gone.>>

He slowly knelt beside her, wiping the knife blade on her shirt before carefully folding it and returning it to his pocket. The TAG's wide green eyes looked up at him from where she fell with a dull, empty gaze, her chest still heaving in short, uneven gasps as her blood began to pool on the floor.

"Jake..."

Strong hands gripped him to pull him to his feet, thick red hair crowding his face, and only then did time resume its steady march forward. He stood mute as Razick clung to him, her tears tracing pathways down his cheeks, his mind only dimly aware that he, too, was crying.

Jake pulled away from her then, wiping his eyes on the back of his fist and looking up into another pair of green eyes, these full of friendship and tinged with concern. Razick's hair was a tangled mess of curls, plants, and dirt, her once-pristine lab coat now spattered with random patches of blood.

"Jake, are you okay?"

He shook free from her grasp, forcing a smile before taking in the rest of the room. He felt nothing. Empty.

Jeb stood awkwardly to the side, his attention split between Jake and the large white wolf poking out from beneath a twisted pile of bright silver metal. He brandished a giant wrench in both hands, although only one held it with any kind of force, judging by the white of his knuckles. Plants and stones and small puddles lay scattered throughout the room, signs of battle damage readily apparent.

And at the far side of the hydroponics bay lay his father, perfectly still on his back in a pool of blood and water.

"Dad!"

Jake felt the word tear out of his lungs at the sight, his stomach crashing into his throat as he sprinted to his father's side. He only noticed the faint rise and fall of breath as he grabbed his father's hand in his own, burying his face in the necromancer's chest.

His father tensed at the contact, coughing, and Jake watched as more blood joined the puddle.

"Jake..." His dad locked eyes with him as Jake sat up. The necromancer's voice was barely a whisper, his squeeze of Jake's hand feeble, but his eyes held the same intensity as the first day they'd met. "What's wrong?"

"Dad, are you...?"

He couldn't speak the words. But he didn't have to. The love in his father's eyes said everything.

Dad.

He'd always tried to hold the necromancer at arm's length. Punishment for the death of his mother? Protection from the guilt of his constant manipulations of his father's need to protect him? He wasn't certain.

But the thought of *losing* him...

"It's just... a flesh wound." His father smiled slightly, his expression turning quickly to a wince as his cheek opened to reveal four angry red gashes. "Lots of them... But I've been... worse. Always... getting into trouble. Feels could tell you... all sorts of stories." He squeezed Jake's hand again, his grip stronger than before. "What's wrong?"

Jake found he could no longer hold back the floodgates, the realization of what he'd just done cascading to consume every thought in his mind. "I... I just killed someone, Dad. Shattered. With my knife."

He carefully returned his head to his father's chest, listening to the soft but steady beat of the necromancer's heart as the seconds ticked past.

Finally his dad spoke, his words slow but clear. "When you say or do something, you can never take it back." His father's free hand slowly crawled its way across Jake's face to tangle fingers in his hair. "Sometimes mistakes happen, and things are done that shouldn't be done, but only after it feels like there is nowhere else to go. But sometimes..." The necromancer paused, breathing, before continuing. "Sometimes those things aren't mistakes. Sometimes they're necessary." His grip tightened on Jake's hand. "Sometimes the things that shouldn't be done are the things that *have* to be done, because not doing them would be worse. Do you... Do you understand?"

"If you have to pull the trigger, you've already lost," Jake recited. "Violence works best as an option, not a necessity."

"Yes. Exactly." Even the pain couldn't hide the pride in the necromancer's voice. "We don't want to have to do these things. But sometimes they're the best option we have."

"What do you tell yourself? To feel better after?" Jake barely recognized his own voice, the words falling from his lips of their own accord.

"There are no mantras for this, son. There never should be." Jake heard the memories in his dad's words. "Choices like this should *never* be easy, no matter how necessary."

Jake balled his fists, sitting up suddenly to punch the floor next to his father. "They're easy for *you!*" He felt the necromancer's drying blood staining his fingers.

His dad winced at the sudden movement, but kept his orange eyes locked on Jake's. "And that's why you're a better person than I could ever hope to become. It's *meant* to be hard."

Jake reached for the necromancer's chest. "Dad. I need Feels. Ask them to–"

"No shortcuts, son. You need to feel this." His father squeezed his hand again. "The healing can come later. This memory is important." Orange eyes closed, his voice fading. "Because the next time you're faced with a choice like this, you want to be certain it's still for the right reasons."

"I never want to make another choice like this." Jake's tears fell faster.

"I'll do everything within my power to make sure you never have to." By the tone in his father's voice, Jake knew this was a promise. "Unfortunately, right now we need to deal with Kydell, if we want to hold our present victory."

"He's unconscious for now," Razick said from somewhere behind Jake. "Jeb's going to keep him that way."

His father swallowed. "Good. I need to regain more of my strength. Feels is... rather low on Imperium at the moment."

"I can help with that!" a cheerful voice sang forth from the room's speakers. "You kinda trashed all my plants, so it's not like I need my magic for anything else."

"Thank you, Hydro." His dad coughed again. "Could I perhaps rely upon your reserves to help me deal with Kydell, as well?"

"Are you kidding me?" Hydroponics practically squealed with delight. "That would be the second most amazing thing that ever happened to me."

"What's the first?" Jake couldn't help himself. Her joy was infectious.

"I met *Kane Jeb!*"

"You saved my life, actually," Jeb announced from across the room.

"There'll be no living with her now," Razick snorted.

"I need something to bind her in," his dad continued softly. "So I can bring her with us."

"Jeb!" Razick called. "Toss me your watch!"

She laughed as he began to protest. "You'll thank me later!"

A silver wristwatch flew through the air several seconds later, Razick deftly catching it with her Telekinesis before carefully placing it in Shane's free hand. "Alanis?" the necromancer muttered, closing his eyes.

<<I'll teach you this one, so you stop asking me,>> she grumbled from beyond the Veil. <<Done.>>

"Put it... on my wrist."

Jake waved Razick away, kneeling by his father to affix the timepiece. "What else do you need me to do?"

"Ask Alanis... Hyperjump new clothes. *Dry* clothes."

<<You and your damn wardrobe changes.>> But there was relief in the AI's voice as a small pile of fresh uniforms materialized by Jake's side. <<Also, someone has to talk to that fleet on

your behalf. I'm still compromised, and they want to hear more from this Grand Navarch Shane Lawrence.>>

"Grand Navarch...? That's a bit pretentious, don't you think?"

<<Blame your medic,>> Alanis snickered. <<Not me.>>

"Feels..." His dad paused. "No, we are *absolutely* talking about that. As soon as I sort this out."

Jake found his father's eyes on him again.

"I need... Jeb and Razick with me. To watch Kydell. You... Take the *Inevitable*, and the fleet, until I get back. Trust the AI. They know their jobs." The necromancer paused, closing his eyes to catch his breath. "They just need you for the rest."

"Yes, Sir." If his father said he could do it, he'd figure it out.

"Alanis? Carry him back to the server room. Or the bridge. If we still have one."

<<Yes, Sir.>>

Jake felt the Void's caress as Alanis began to shift him into the Afterlife for the jump.

"And Feels? I need to be able to stand." He could still hear his dad as the room began to fade. "Yes, I know, but it'll have to wait. I have to take care of Kydell."

45

COMMODORE JAVON STARED AT the young human child perched in the captain's chair of the *Inevitable*, the giant fixture dwarfing his adolescent frame. Any other day, the proud katanoj would have laughed at the thought of some kid sitting in Admiral Kydell's seat, but not today. Today she'd committed treason on the promise of help from a band of space pirates who apparently thought it amusing to hand her off to some juvenile delinquent.

She gritted her teeth in an effort to hide her displeasure, straightening the collar of her service uniform. If this was a test, she had every intention of passing. "I asked to speak to the Grand Navarch."

"He's busy." The boy shrugged casually as he brushed unruly strands of brown hair out of his face, his dark green eyes studying her with an intensity unusual for a child his age. "With Kydell."

She scowled, baring her canines, and felt her tail begin to twitch with agitation. "I was told the admiral had been neutralized."

The kid smiled, leaning back into Kydell's chair. "He was unconscious when I saw him. And there was lots of blood."

"But he's still alive."

"Of course." He smiled wider. "For now."

Javon watched as the child began to poke at the console built into the armrest.

"Do these things do anything?"

She felt a growl forming in her throat. "Are you enjoying the Admiral's chair?"

"No." He shook his head, still poking at the console. "I don't like it. It's lumpy. And it doesn't spin. All the good chairs spin."

She summoned her decades of authority into her words. "I demand to see Admiral Kydell. *Now.*"

Javon had seen grown men cower in fear at her voice but the kid didn't even blink, eyes still studying the panel of buttons. "Bad idea. Can't risk him controlling you again." And then suddenly his eyes were locked on hers, and Javon was hit with the uncomfortable realization that *she* was the one under scrutiny. "You don't *want* him controlling you, right?"

"Of course not!" She pulled her head back, her eyes repeatedly scanning him from head to toe. "I'm just trying to decide..." Her voice trailed off.

"What to do next?" The boy slid from the admiral's chair, casually walking toward her. "You could join us. Keep people safe. If you want."

The Commodore eyed him warily, noticing for the first time the red lined puncture, to all appearances the entry point of a knife, marring the front of his light green dress shirt. As he drew closer she noted the spatter of blood on his face and hands, previously camouflaged against his darker skin. Dried blood caked the knees of his pressed black pants.

She exhaled with a start. *He's more than he appears.*

"Why would we join you?"

She kept her tone cautious, her whiskers splayed to match. *Let's see what he has to say.*

She'd received offers before, typically in the form of bribe attempts from planets under assault, but never from a child.

Instead of promises, he merely shrugged. "Where else can you *go*? Can't go home. Confederation doesn't like treason very much. Can't go somewhere else. Most don't consider Psychomorphation a valid defense for war crimes." He cocked his head to the side, hands clasped loosely behind his back. "But you're welcome here. With us."

Javon's lungs deflated. This was not the conversation she'd expected. "And why would I take advice from some ten year old child?"

"I'm twelve and a half." He rolled his eyes. "Because I'm right. And you know it."

She smiled at the admission of his age. So the boy was willing to divulge personal information. Time to find out how much she could learn from him. "I don't even know how to address you."

"Oh!" He brightened, straightening. "I'm Jake."

"Captain Jake?"

He *giggled*. "Nah. Just Jake. Dad's the one with the fancy title."

"And who's your dad?" Now she was getting somewhere.

Jake eyed her cautiously before answering. "The Grand Navarch."

She raised a brow. *This* was unexpected. "And he left you alone with me? How does he know you're safe?"

"I *hope* I'm safe with you." Jake's voice grew quiet, and the Commodore caught the telltale electrical spike of a Shielding spell. "I don't want to kill anyone else today."

"I'm sorry, I didn't mean to imply…" She shook her head, trying to make sense of his words. "I'm just surprised, is all. Why did he bring you?"

"Because I asked him to." Jake turned his back to her, although Javon had the distinct impression this did *not* mean he'd relaxed his guard. "Safer with him, than on Baden."

Commodore Javon remembered the few landing parties she'd joined after planetary conquests, and felt her stomach twist into her throat. The SAF was nothing if not thorough. While she and her officers had always held their own ground forces to higher standards, the truth was the SAF had no such requirements, and many enjoyed taking advantage of this fact. Admiral Kydell's former Commodore, her predecessor, had been particularly notorious for that.

If this Grand Navarch was anything like what she'd been led to believe, he'd have an easier time defending the boy than Baden's planetary forces. Even so, the choice to bring a child along with a boarding party was unusual. Unless...

"Where's your mother?" she asked kindly, sinking to her haunches. "Does she know you're here?"

"Dead." He shrugged. "But she said I could come."

So this Grand Navarch was a necromancer, or had ready access to one. She doubted he'd asked Alanis to Call the boy's mother in the middle of combat.

"She's okay with you assaulting a Confederation armada?"

Jake spun back to face her. "I wasn't supposed to do any of the fighting. Just the Shielding," he confided, and suddenly Javon found herself buried in information. "But Telemetry got distracted, and a TAG got in when that ship rammed us, and someone had to take care of her while everyone else was busy with Kydell." He blinked at his own wall of words. "I can show you the TAG if you want?"

Commodore Javon slowly rose to her feet as she tried to parse which information to pursue first.

The threat, she decided. "You have a TAG on board? Kydell's TAG? Brown wolf lady?"

If Selkirk is here...

"Yeah." Jake shoved his hands in his pockets, avoiding Javon's gaze.

"Is she fully guarded? If you look away for a single second she'll just kill herself, then come back as–"

"She's already dead," the kid interrupted quietly, looking at the deck. "I killed her."

Javon tensed. "Then she's already loose again. I'll call my ship, we'll–"

"No." Jake's eyes briefly met hers. "Gone. Shattered." He turned away again, and Javon realized he still carried the weight of his kill on his shoulders. "She died before her body did."

By the Void, who is this kid?

"Captain Yiven? Is this true?" The Commodore searched the bridge, awaiting a response, but the AI remained silent.

Jake finally looked up from the floor. "You can answer that, Captain. It's okay."

"Yes. It's true." The fae's voice projected from the armrest console. "I was there. Helped him aim the knife. She's gone."

"And the Kid did it?"

"With his own bare hands." She paused. "And a Void knife."

Javon bit her lip, spine straightening in newfound respect. This was... unexpected. The risk of Fleet Captain Selkirk returning to claim vengeance against her defecting fleet had been a major security concern, particularly among her officers before they'd formally switched allegiance. To learn this threat had already been eliminated by the twelve-year-old in front of her...

Twelve and a half, she mentally corrected, smiling.

Perhaps this meeting with Jake was intended as a compliment, not an insult. Or an opportunity to learn.

She redirected her attention to Jake. "Since you're the Shielding expert here, was that your Psychic Shieldbreaker spell, too?"

"Yeah!" He perked up at the change of subject. "My school project."

"Your teacher must have been impressed." Javon certainly was. Her Family was known for Shielding, but they'd never bothered much with emotional ones, or their counters.

Perhaps they'd come to regret that.

"No." Jake shoved his hands deeper in his pockets, rolling on the balls of his feet. "He tried to flunk me. But the headmaster expelled me, so it doesn't matter now. Not unless Dad fixes that, too."

"It's their loss." The Commodore tilted her head. "How does it work?"

"The Psychic Shieldbreaker was just one part of the project," he told her, standing straighter. "Dad taught me all the Shieldbreakers he knew, and then I learned more about the Shielding he didn't know how to break until I could make a Shieldbreaker for those, too. Then I programmed them into a crystal, to make one giant spell." When she didn't interrupt, he continued in a rush of words. "You know how Necromancy lets you manipulate the spiritual vibration of things? And if you find a complimentary resonance, they interact? That's how Soul Call works, and spells like that. But each *spell* has its own *magical* resonance, too, and if you match up the frequencies just right, you can make them stronger! You can use it to make really strong Shielding spells, by weaving all the layers together, and the Shieldbreaker does the same thing except it *disrupts* those frequencies to make them break apart. It takes a lot of Imperium for a Shieldbreaker, though, and even more when you're casting *all* of them, so I needed to target it over a small, focused area or else you'd need a Void mage to cast it each time which is *a lot* to ask for a spell like that, but..."

Javon laughed when he paused for breath. "I have no idea what you're talking about Kid, but it sounds like smart people stuff." She scratched her chin. "It makes sense, though." It certainly didn't contradict her own vast knowledge of Shielding spellwork.

"It's just Legion stuff." Jake shrugged. "Mixed with what Dad taught me. But my teachers don't always like it. Like Professor Darga."

"Legion? You mean the Space Defense Legion?"

Could the Grand Navarch be a former Legionnaire? It would certainly explain a lot. His familiarity with SAF combat maneuvers, his vendetta against Kydell, and even the fact he'd found a way to break a Soul Oath. She'd always heard the SDL had an impressive grasp on the more mundane technologies, far greater than societies like the Confederation which relied so heavily on magic. "Where are you from, Kid? Before Baden."

"Loxira."

"You were away when Admiral Renkash's attack happened, then?"

By all official reports, nobody had escaped the planet alive. Including Renkash's away team.

"No." Jake shook his head, his eyes suddenly carrying a lifetime of sorrow. "They killed Mom, and tried to kill me. So Dad Shattered them."

"By *himself*?"

Who are *these people?*

Jake shrugged. "I guess."

"And now he's part of Baden's planetary defense?" The Commodore felt a sinking suspicion in the pit of her stomach. "Or is he on a crusade against the SAF? Do I need to worry about my people?"

"No. Of course not!" Jake laughed, a surprisingly innocent sound from someone who'd just admitted to Shattering a TAG. "He likes you, or we wouldn't be talking. He wanted to leave Baden when you attacked, but I reminded him he told me I shouldn't run from my problems. So we stayed."

The Grand Navarch's son shrugged, as if this were the most obvious answer in the universe. Javon suspected that to him, it was.

This meeting is a sign of trust, she realized with a start. *They've decided I'm an ally, not a threat.*

She swallowed, retracting her claws to ensure their assessment remained that way, imagining the Kid's father would topple whole governments for lesser threats. "You said you're doing Shielding for the *Inevitable*? So when the *Reckoning* tried to ram you..."

"That *hurt*." Jake massaged his temples at the reminder. "What happened, anyway?"

The Commodore began to pace, frowning. *May as well give the Kid a status report.*

"Many are still loyal to Kydell. Some even by choice." Her fists clenched. "My officers are weeding out those we can find, locking them in the brig for now. Especially the ground forces who disobeyed my initial stand down order. But we'll need help from your psychomorphic mage if we hope to find everyone."

She'd left her command staff to clean up that mess in her absence.

The Kid nodded, brows furrowed. "They can do that. They'll need an apotheturgic link, though. We're all low on magic. And Dad promised Alanis we'd help her first."

"It'll take time to sort through everyone," Javon agreed. "We recognize this."

Alanis' voice rose from the console again. "We'll need to sort out who wants to join us, who wants to leave, and who we should give to Baden."

"I'm not giving my people to Baden." Her claws extended as she snarled. No matter *how* much she might be drawn to the promises of this mysterious and powerful Grand Navarch, this point was non-negotiable.

"If they're loyal to Kydell, they're not yours, they're *his*." Jake climbed back up into the captain's chair, kicking his feet. "Baden wants *someone* to hold responsible. Dad won't let them have Kydell, so that means the next person in charge: *you*. If you want to join us, we need to give them someone else who matters. Or... we give them *a lot* of someones. Everyone loyal to Kydell. That gets them off your ships, too, so they don't hurt you later."

The Kid's right.

There was logic to his words. And yet...

"What makes you think I'll join you?"

"You already did." Jake shrugged.

"And how did you come to *that* conclusion?" she snorted, crossing her arms as she leaned back against the weapons console.

This'll be rich.

The Grand Navarch's son leaned his elbows on the armrest, propping his chin in his hands. "You're still here. And you stopped asking questions about us. Now we're planning what happens next. Means you made up your mind."

Javon started to protest, but bit her lip when she realized she had no argument. *Damn. He's good.*

"You got me, Kid. Looks like we're in." She stood up, shaking her head in amusement. "Let me get back to the *Relentless*, convince the others. In the meantime, if there's anything we can do..."

"Actually..." Jake turned thoughtful. "There *is* something you can do for me."

46

"No, no, like this." Veris adjusted the young katanoj's grip on the ball, showing her the optimal locations for her fingers. He carefully positioned her hand and arm, mimicking the correct throwing posture. "And then you throw."

Her aim fell short, the ball catching on her claws as she let go, bouncing twice before rolling to the feet of her intended recipient.

Veris cheered anyway, eliciting an excited squeal from the katanoj as she lunged in for a hug. Her parents nodded a silent thanks in his direction before returning to an animated discussion that seemed to involve some sort of charades.

Ever since the fight with Jake that morning, he'd been hard at work trying to spread some sense of cheer and normalcy throughout the shelter vault, drawing in anyone who was willing to join him. The adults had been confused at first, but once they'd verified his intentions they'd adapted to help him find ways and places where he could do the most good. The mood within the vault had subsequently shifted to take on an air of socialization and community, just as Jake had predicted, even despite the periodic reminders of the battle outside.

Although those reminders had slowed, as the battle had progressed. Veris had to admit he wasn't certain when he'd heard the last evidence of bombardment, which had also likely improved morale.

He'd attempted to enlist his former gang in his new plan, but they'd kicked him out instead. Called him weak, and simple-minded.

He watched the young katanoj, now playing catch with her brother, and smiled. He wasn't weak. He was the most powerful person in the vault. He'd changed the whole mood of the place, just like he'd done at school. But this time, he'd been surprised to see how much faster compassion and kindness took effect, rather than his former fallback of violence and anger.

More importantly, this time he wasn't just venting his fears at his dad's disappearance. This time, he knew his dad would be proud of him, and his mom would worry less about him, and that made all the difference.

He'd told his mom about his expulsion, when they'd finally reunited. He could tell she was disappointed, both with him and the disruption to his education, but she hadn't said anything about it. Merely told him they'd figure something out together, once his dad and Aunt Fang came home.

The unspoken *if* had sat heavily between them, neither wishing to voice it.

He shook his head, pulling his thoughts away from the past. Whatever happened, he still had his mom. She was right. They'd sort it out together.

And if Jake and his father succeeded in taking on the SAF, maybe they could help, too.

The faint tickle of a telepathic call brushed against the back of his mind and he accepted automatically, suddenly tense. Not many organizations relied on Telepathy as their primary communication, most choosing to instead send calls and messages via tablet. Organizations such as the Baden Defense Force, however, often relied on Telepathy due to its unhackable security. Which meant...

<Dad? Did you find him?>

<Veris Asik?> the unfamiliar voice asked. <This is Communications, from the Liberated Flagship *Inevitable*.>

He blinked, slowly making his way to the wall before sliding down to sit on the floor. <That's me. What is this about?>

<Please hold while I connect you.>

Jake joined the link a moment later, accompanied by someone else Veris didn't recognize.

<How are you, Veris?>

<I should ask you the same thing,> Veris told him. <I thought you were fighting the attacking fleet.>

<Not anymore,> Jake said, a sense of urgency in his voice. <Communications is going to change this link so you can share

memories with us. I need a memory of your father. Recent. Can you do that?>

<Yes.> Permitting the more invasive link, Veris focused his thoughts on breakfast with his dad, the morning before his disappearance. <Are you going to look for him?>

<They're going to try. Is this enough, Commodore?>

The stranger answered, her voice gravelly and confident. <I'll disseminate this to the fleet. If we've seen him, we'll find him. Javon out.>

<Who was *that*?>

<Commodore Javon. Formerly of Sparnell.> Jake's voice was a lot calmer than it should have been.

<And she's taking orders from *you*?>

<For now.> Jake's tone was unreadable. <How are you managing?>

<Your idea worked! Everyone is happier now.> He exhaled, shaking his head, although he knew Jake couldn't see him. <I'm sorry I stabbed you earlier. I'd undo it, if I could.>

<My father says we can't change our past. Only ourselves,> Jake said slowly. <Hopefully you'll be able to leave the vaults soon. The fighting is over, but Baden doesn't believe us when we tell them that.>

<What happened? Did you blow up all their ships? Get them to surrender?>

<Commodore Javon switched her allegiance to Dad. Most of the fleet came with her.> Frustration filled Jake's voice. <Com-

munications says the Baden Defense Force wants to talk again. I have to go.>

Veris found himself alone in his head once again, thoughts racing. *I need to tell Mom.*

He scanned the room until he spotted her, now talking wearily with the parents of the katanoj child he'd been helping earlier, and made his way over. "Mom! I just talked to Jake!"

"That's the boy you told me about earlier?" she asked, the hint of a frown threatening the edges of her lips.

"This is good news, Mom, I promise," he told her, grinning. "He said the battle's over, and we won. And now they're looking for Dad!"

As if on cue, reality twisted in the center of the room, reforming to reveal a young human woman, crouching as she tended to a sleeping canid and dracoling in Baden Defense Force uniforms. She checked their vitals as the rest of the room froze in shock, before turning to face Veris and his mother, now rushing to greet her. She wore the standard brown service uniform of the Sparnell Armed Forces, her light brown shirt and matching hat displaying the triple red rings of the medical corps alongside the usual insignia of the SAF.

"Asik?" Her speech was heavy with a thick Sparnick accent, although her words were spoken in careful Galactic Common. "Caught together, so keep together. Put sleep... Coma? For jump. Stable, but need healer." She handed his mom an important looking paper, its words in a language he didn't recognize. "Medical history. Need translate. Sorry."

His mom fell to her knees between the stretchers, tears spilling from her eyes as she buried her face in his dad's chest. "Rabert. Rabert. You're home. You're safe. You're *alive*."

The Sparnelli medic began tracing a portal to return, but Veris had to ask. Had to know. "They were your prisoners. Why are you giving them up now?"

The medic shrugged. "Orders. From the Kid." And with a salute, she disappeared, the portal pulling closed behind her.

Veris stared moments longer, his gaze drifting between his dad and his dad's wingman, Aunt Fang. Their chests rose and fell in the calm rhythm of induced sleep, his dad's breath slowly shifting its pattern to match the cadence of his mom's sobs.

Swallowing hard, he knelt to bury his face in his father's chest, next to his mother, before tugging the paperwork from his mother's hands and forcing himself to stand again.

"You stay with Dad. I'll... I'll go find them a medic."

47

ADMIRAL KYDELL AWOKE WITH a groan, squinting in the darkness. He attempted to move his arm and rub his head, the throbbing clearly indicating some sort of impact, only to discover the limb was immovable, and tightly bound in place. He attempted to shift his weight to no avail, the torn cloth straps pulling at his fur and the remains of his dress uniform, holding him fast to the uneven metal frame of his chair.

He turned his head, recognizing with relief that he was at least free to look around his dimly lit surroundings. The room somehow felt both cramped and cavernous, the feeble light illuminating little beyond his immediate surroundings and yet still sending nightmarish shadows into the darkness. While the space was well-furnished for a cave, a thick layer of dust coated every visible surface, revealing the hideaway to be long-abandoned by whoever had once called it home.

Flexing his claws, he dug their razor sharp tips against the chair to test his ability to cut through, only to discover that someone had clipped and dulled them.

Now it's personal.

He still had other options, of course, but it was a matter of principle. He was Admiral Kydell of SAF Fleet Command. Nobody made decisions for him. *Especially* not about his own hygiene.

Reaching instead to his magic, he stretched his empathic abilities and discovered he was not alone. Straining his eyes against the dark he could barely make out the figure of a human, their emotions strong yet somehow still indiscernible.

"Who's there?" he snarled into the darkness.

His question was immediately rewarded as a second dim lamp appeared at the individual's feet, revealing the necromancer from his earlier fight aboard the *Inevitable*. The man's face remained a statue of confident intensity, complimented by a pair of fierce orange eyes Kydell felt boring into his very soul. His captor's shoulder length black hair perfectly framed his menacing smirk, the standard browns of his impeccable SAF service uniform complimenting the deep ochre tone of his skin.

"Kane said she killed you," Kydell growled, baring his canines.

The necromancer raised an eyebrow but otherwise gave no reaction, remaining stoic and impassive in his observations.

"Good help is so hard to find these days." Kydell sighed, struggling to find a purchase within the necromancer's emotions. All he needed was a small opening, and he could make the necromancer his own. "As I'm sure you've discovered yourself, once she turned on you."

The eyebrow lowered again, emotions still unreadable.

"But no matter. These things happen to the best of us."

Finding no ready path into his captor's mind, the admiral cast one of his emergency spells, activating a hidden chamber within one of his molars. He tipped his head back in an imitation of amusement, emptying the tooth's contents with his tongue before swallowing.

"You must think you've won."

Kydell could already feel the poison coursing through his veins. In less than a minute he'd be dead, a homeless soul wandering the Afterlife, on a direct path to his loyal TAG and a subsequent binding within a resurrection clone, comfortably surrounded by his loyal subordinates.

And Void help the necromancer and whoever sent him, once his people tracked them down.

"Very well. Since I'm your prisoner now, who are you? Who sent you to kill me?"

The necromancer stared, silent and imposing.

"Not much of a talker, are you?" Kydell felt his lids grow heavy. It wouldn't be much longer now.

The necromancer held his silence, immovable and unshakable.

"No matter. I never forget a face. It's only a matter of time before I learn who you are. I'll discover who sent you, too, and you'll both pay for this."

Each word was an effort now, but they had to be said. His captor had to *know* what was coming for him.

But the necromancer *smirked*, an ominous sight within the shadows of the lamp.

"You haven't won, you know." Kydell continued to fill the silence with his thoughts. "Once my soul returns to Sparnell, I will hunt you down."

At last his captor broke the silence. "Take one of those pills of yours, did you?"

Something in the necromancer's voice gave Kydell pause. *Something's wrong.*

"Saves me some effort," the necromancer continued calmly. "I was looking forward to killing you myself, but I have to admit..." He smiled as his voice faded, a wicked, cruel thing that froze Kydell to his very soul. "This irony is much more satisfying."

"What did you do? Why am I–"

<<Still here?>> His captor's menacing question echoed within his thoughts, the voice surprisingly far away, as if muffled by the Veil. <<You tell me.>>

No...

Kydell found himself unable to move. "Who *are* you?"

<<Someone who learned your lessons well. And I will be paying for that, the rest of my life.>> He gave a short, joyless laugh. <<But not as much as you.>>

"Let me go! I command it!"

Kydell pushed fruitlessly against the confines of his unexpected prison. His death should have freed him, allowing his soul passage to the Afterlife. Yet here he remained.

A growing horror gripped his thoughts as he wrestled with the implications. The necromancer had planned for this. Had bound him in place with more than the metal wrapped around his now-useless body.

Soulbound. To his own corpse.

<<You're in no state to give commands.>> His captor's tone was dismissive. <<Sir.>>

"When I get out of here..."

He felt the necromancer's grip around his soul then, piercing and unrelenting despite their earlier battle. He tried to fight back, desperately seeking his captor's emotions in an effort to shift them in his favor, but his attempts to grab hold slid from the necromancer's Shielding. His captor's feelings kept shifting in a dull kaleidoscope of well-choreographed confusion.

<<Your magic no longer works on me.>> The contempt was clear in the human's words, and yet this, too, evaded his grasp.

"Who *are* you?" he demanded again.

<<You'll have a lot of time by yourself to think about that.>>

And with that, Kydell felt the necromancer bend reality around the Veil, leaving the admiral to his thoughts in the dark loneliness of his vault-like prison.

Shit. Who would dare stand against him, much less have the resources to send such a powerful necromancer? How long had this assassin been hidden on his ship?

Who in Void's name did I piss off?

48

"You're worse than Jeb." Razick carefully focused her Telekinesis to untwist the remains of the hydroponics fixtures wrapped around Lawrence and locking him into a standing position, her mind hyper-focused on her task. "This awful contraption was your idea. Hold still. Stop moving."

Lawrence stood stiffly at the center of the bridge, scowling. "Everyone keeps telling me that today. Just get me out of this thing."

"This isn't exactly easy, you know."

It had been *years* since she'd needed to worry about such delicate work, and this was the first time she could remember where her focus was to do as *little* damage as possible, rather than the inverse.

She paused to collect her breath. "Would be a lot *faster* if you'd just let me put you back on the floor."

"No. I..."

Lawrence shook his head, slowly turning his neck to face her. His typically stern features softened, and Razick realized with a start that despite her failings that day, at some point in the last several hours she'd earned the aloof necromancer's trust.

"I don't like feeling powerless. Didn't realize there was so much damn tyrellium in these things." The unguarded moment disappeared as quickly as it arrived. "Free my waist and you can prop me in the chair."

Jeb moved to stand beside her, awkwardly shifting his weight as he watched her work. "Anything I can do to help?"

"I need to see what I'm doing. We need to get these clothes off."

Ignoring Lawrence's indignant squawk, she rotated the necromancer with her Telekinesis until he floated horizontally in front of them. Jake wandered over to offer his knife and Jeb accepted, carefully cutting away the necromancer's SAF uniform to reveal the hack job of metal framework Razick had constructed around him.

She'd done a fair job, making it look like he could stand unaided. From what she understood, he'd put on a convincing show for Kydell.

Alanis' voice projected from the chair console. "I never understood the obsession with clothes. Pinchy, scratchy, and they interfere with what nature intended."

"Not everyone has an exoskeleton," Lawrence growled, finally surrendering to Jeb's efforts. He glared indignantly at Razick. "Some of us don't like showing bare skin."

"You're wearing layers," she teased, rolling her eyes. "And I already saw it all when we dressed you earlier. Calm down."

"I could knock him unconscious again," Feels offered helpfully from the Weapons console.

"Not necessary," Razick answered absent-mindedly, tuning out Lawrence's half-hearted attempts to insult his medic. "He can't fight my Telekinesis, anyway."

Her view now unobstructed, Razick efficiently unwound the structure around Lawrence's midsection, allowing him to bend at the waist. She floated him to the central chair before gingerly lowering him into the seat.

Jake hurried over and pushed several buttons on the armrest console, adjusting the chair into a mild recline. At the nod of thanks from his father, the boy returned to his current project, prodding at the inner Runework of the *Inevitable*'s Weapons console.

Razick raised an eyebrow. "Better?"

"I don't remember this chair having so many lumps," came the grumpy response, followed by a begrudging, "Thank you. Sorry."

Razick waved him away, frowning. How often had he sat in Kydell's chair? Although he *had* mentioned the ship had been made for him.

A riddle for a different day. She hated seeing him like this. Especially knowing it was her fault.

"Only fair I help where I can, after what I put you through." She sighed. "Unfortunately, I'm spent. I need to rest, regain my strength. I don't want to make a mistake."

Lawrence closed his eyes and nodded. "We're all tired. Rest. We need to discuss what we do next, anyway."

"To that end," Alanis interrupted, "we have a visitor."

Razick turned to find a well-decorated tabby katanoj, her dress uniform bearing the insignia of a Commodore, standing patiently.

Commodore Javon.

She'd never met the Commodore personally, but she'd served under her, after a fashion. The katanoj had been Fleet Captain at the time, still assigned to the *Relentless*, back when Admiral Kydell still used the thick-hulled destroyer as his flagship. By all accounts Javon was stern but fair, with a deep protective streak for those under her charge, a trait that often placed her at odds with the admiral and his plans.

Razick wondered at her thoughts as Javon eyed the scene on the bridge, Jake crouched behind the Weapons console poking at its half-dissected innards, Lawrence rigidly perched in the chair and wrapped in pilfered undergarments accessorized with uncomfortably twisted metal stiffly holding his legs straight out in front of him, Jeb hovering nearby in his soaking wet but still noticeably fancy black suit, Razick in her blood-spattered lab coat keeping close at hand to assist the necromancer as needed.

To her credit, the Commodore raised an eyebrow but otherwise remained silent.

Lawrence's expression turned dark. "Alanis... Who is on my bridge?"

The Commodore saluted smartly. "Grand Navarch Lawrence, I am Commodore Javon Arlise, Captain of the *Relentless*, former Second of the late Admiral Kydell, and senior officer of this fleet. Your son requested relief from his Shielding duties. I thought I'd volunteer my services, and use this opportunity to also present myself."

Jake leaned around the Weapons console to address his father. "I have school tomorrow."

Razick had to admire his confidence. Last she'd heard, he'd been expelled. Not to mention, the entire planet had been bombarded by a Sparnell Armed Forces joint armada.

Lawrence's scowl deepened, his words a barely contained growl. "Alanis, I do not approve of you phasing people to my bridge without requesting clearance." He turned to Razick, accusation and embarrassment in his eyes. "I'm not exactly presentable at the moment."

"I know, Sir." Alanis' voice held no remorse. "Which is exactly why I have done so. She has the respect of the fleet. The best way to earn their loyalty is to earn hers. And the best way to earn *hers* is to let her see who you are, and what you have willingly put yourself through for our sakes. *And* the fact you will genuinely consider these arguments before determining how to address my insubordination." The Navigation AI's voice took on a tone of triumph. "I willingly submit to whatever disciplinary actions you deem acceptable, but I stand by my actions."

"Alanis…" The name was a warning. "We will have to discuss your little hobby of backing me into corners." He returned his attention to the katanoj. "Commodore, I don't trust you. But Nav clearly does, and for now, that's enough. You may stay."

"Thank you, Sir." Javon stood even taller, clearly pleased.

"But take off that ridiculous jacket," Lawrence continued. His voice grew quiet. "I don't think any of us need the reminders."

While the Commodore did as commanded, Razick turned her attention back to Lawrence. "I'm wondering if we should keep you in a support harness while you heal, since you're still lacking in the sitting still department."

"Physically, that would help," Feels agreed. "But emotionally, being forced to hold still like that?"

"Oh, I don't mean rigid like this one!" She took a quick mental inventory of the contents of her office, hoping most of it had survived the assault. "I should have the equipment back in my lab. Jake can help me make a nice articulated support exosuit for under his–"

Her words were interrupted by the sudden appearance of a jumbled pile of items from her lab office, carefully deposited off to the side of the bridge with an expertly targeted Hyperjump spell. From the state of the more delicate items, it appeared the school had sustained at least secondary damage from the bombardment.

"I didn't mean *now*! I'm supposed to be *resting*."

Walking over to poke at the pile, she noted a few of the items would be difficult to replace, but most of her more useful and treasured tools and supplies had remained surprisingly intact.

Lawrence slumped in his chair, as much as Razick's rigid framework would allow, exhaustion written across his face from the expenditure.

"But now looters won't find it," he pointed out, before turning to his son. "Jake? I'm sorry, son, but I'm not sure there's enough *building* left for school tomorrow, unless they move it to the vaults. But that gives us time. I'll have Communications call Headmaster Corbin later, see if we can undo your expulsion."

Jake shrugged, buried elbows deep in the Weapons console. "Then Feels and I will keep working on the Emotional Magic Pulse. There's lots to learn up here. And nobody's trying to flunk me."

Razick loved watching Jake work, the preteen's face the epitome of focus as he absent-mindedly traced his lower lip with his tongue.

"I'm working on a program so anyone can use it. You can already aim it now! Feels wants to add more emotions. And I wanna try and make the Shieldbreaker more efficient."

The Commodore broke her silence, excitement in her voice. "Jake, do you think you could refit this EMP of yours to work on the rest of the fleet?"

Razick noted the katanoj already seemed quite comfortable talking to Lawrence's son. The relationship seemed mutual, as Jake didn't even pause his work to answer.

"Dunno. Alanis says the cannons on this ship are different from the others."

"If I arrange full access to the *Relentless* for you, could you see if you could modify them?"

"If Dad says it's okay," came the distracted reply.

Commodore Javon snapped to attention with a start, ears folded back as she turned toward Lawrence. "I'm sorry, sir. I didn't mean to overstep."

The necromancer graced her with an undignified snort. "Encourage him all you like. Just be aware, you'll end up with more than you bargained for."

The Commodore's eyes grew wide in apparent confusion at his response. Razick suspected she'd been bracing for a rebuke for stepping out of line. Kydell would have been furious.

Recovering quickly, the katanoj bowed her head briefly in respect before resuming her role as a silent observer.

Razick swallowed, gathering her courage for a request of her own. "Feels? Could you please use your Psychomorphation on me?" She closed her eyes, lowering her head. She *hated* the idea of asking anyone to ever alter her mind again, but she needed to know. "I want you to see if I have any memories left of Nya."

"I can try," the empath answered kindly. "It will be easier for both of us if you're touching the locket." They paused. "If you could pull it loose while you're there? It's still stuck to his chest, and it's making it difficult to heal the burns."

She looked to Lawrence for guidance, the necromancer pausing before giving her a nod and closing his eyes.

"You'll have to rip the shirt," he said regretfully.

His prediction proved correct. Jake's knife made short work of the obstructing undershirt, allowing her access to the locket to begin the careful process of peeling the necklace away from the necromancer's seared flesh. Jeb jumped in to help, his careful fingers freeing the metal with practiced ease. The result of years digging for tender roots in stubborn soil.

Lawrence hissed through his teeth at several of Razick's less than delicate tugs, but otherwise remained still and silent in his chair.

Their task complete, Razick wrapped her fingers around the locket and was rewarded with a caress of gratitude from the empath.

Focus on what you do *remember of her*, they directed. *And the emotions of the memories you want to find.*

She closed her eyes, concentrating her heart on feelings of love, her mind on thoughts of baking, a hobby Nya had enjoyed in her limited free time, according to her letters to Jeb.

The scene solidified in her mind, and suddenly Razick was baking, some sort of fruit pie except with a fluffy top instead of crust. She was nervous but excited, and very much in love, carefully carrying her creation to the back deck where a fiery orange-red dracoling stood gazing at the stars with wonder.

Razick called out to her, watching her love turn with a widening grin and a comment about the pie...

And Razick tripped, the dessert flying from her hands faster than she could catch it with her Telekinesis. It was all over Nya now, and Razick felt herself dissolve into a knot of anxiety and shame but Nya was laughing, reaching out, and suddenly they were hugging, and covered in pie, as Nya whispered lovingly about their anniversary before finding her lips for a kiss and...

Razick brushed at the tears in her eyes as the memory faded. "Thank you," she whispered to the empath before balling her hands into fists. "Even now, Kydell steals my life from me."

"But not forever." Jake's voice was quiet as he abandoned his work on the weapons to instead slip his arms around her in a hug. "You talk now."

She blinked in surprise, realizing she hadn't been relying on Jeb's Telepathy since Jake had Shattered the TAG. She gripped Jake tightly, her resolve focusing on Nya.

I won't let him keep you from me, either, she promised. *I will find you.*

The Commodore cleared her throat. "Speaking of Admiral Kydell..." She shifted her weight. "I'd like to know what happened to him."

Razick forced her lips to form a smile. "Lawrence, could you share that memory again?"

She'd thoroughly enjoyed it the first time, finally admitting Lawrence's insistence on the immovable fixture to maintain his posture had been worth the effort to construct, just for the extra intimidation factor.

And reliving Kydell's growing desperation is exactly the distraction I need right now.

Jeb formed the telepathic link at Lawrence's nod, and the necromancer graced the former Sparnelli on the bridge with his memories of Kydell's final moments of life, complete with a sense of the admiral's emotions, as shared by Feels. The wolf's suave confidence, the panic as he found his soul bound within his dying body, the desperation as–

Razick's revels in Kydell's despair were interrupted by a loud cry. She opened her eyes to find Commodore Javon rushing toward Lawrence, claws extended and teeth bared, murder in her eyes.

49

RELIVING THE GRAND NAVARCH's memories of Kydell's imprisonment, Commodore Javon felt a newfound sense of pride. She'd chosen well to switch her allegiance to the raiding party. Their ragtag band certainly hadn't *looked* like much when the *Inevitable*'s Navigations AI had jumped her onto the bridge, but her meeting with Jake had taught her that each of these individuals were likely much more than they appeared.

This memory of Kydell proved it. The Grand Navarch's excruciating pain and discomfort as he stood in stoic silence waiting for the bound admiral to awaken, the expert way his psychomorphic mage had countered each of Admiral Kydell's attacks, the foresight to predict and negate the wolf's every action, the firm patience and self-control practices to deliver the maximum emotional duress on the admiral... And all with a quiet ruthlessness built upon a sense of protectiveness for his people, somehow untainted by the tempting but emotionally unreliable lust for revenge.

This was a leader who would do everything within his considerable power to keep his people safe. All she had to do now was ensure he considered her people as equal to his own.

She felt her own protective nature swell as she thought of her crews and her duty to guide them to safety away from the admiral's claws...

And felt the wolf's conditioning kick in as she charged toward the Grand Navarch in an effort to instead protect an admiral unworthy of her loyalty.

After all this time searching for a way out from under the claws of Kydell, she was going to kill the only answer she'd ever found. Or, more likely considering what they'd already accomplished today, she'd meet an ending as swift as Kydell's was slow, and her people would be left to fend for themselves.

She felt herself lifted off the deck and held in a firm telekinetic grip. Moments passed as she struggled to break free and fulfill the requirements built into her conditioning from her former admiral, time enough to mentally surrender to her fate as the Grand Navarch muttered quietly to himself.

And then she felt the emotions in her mind, faint and foreign. Selfishness. Possessiveness. Laziness. Love and contentment. She clung to them, just as she remembered the Grand Navarch doing in the memory, working desperately to make them hers.

She felt Kydell's conditioning subside, and with it the red haired battle mage's Telekinesis holding her in place.

As her feet touched the deck she kneeled to the Grand Navarch, bowing her head in desperate apology. "I'm sorry, sir!"

She was making a perfect impression today. First she'd changed into her dress uniform as a sign of respect and ended up insulting him instead. Then she'd attacked him unprovoked. *You're doing a* great *job convincing him of your intentions.*

She bent her neck deeper into the bow, holding her breath for his judgment.

"Oh would you get up? I'm not a tyrant."

She stood slowly, meeting his gaze as he shifted uncomfortably in his seat, and discovered that his intense stare had softened into an apology.

"I'm the one who's sorry. You've reminded me of the discussion we've all been avoiding. What to do to about Kydell's conditioning." His voice grew quiet. "Feels? Tell me your thoughts."

"I... may have a workaround," the psychomorphic mage offered. "It's... less than ideal. Right now, I don't have the strength to undo anything, and we don't have the time to spare. But I *can* transfer Kydell's programmed loyalty to *you* so your orders will override anything else. Buy us time to do the job properly. You saw what happened with Commodore Javon. Right now, nearly anyone could be a threat."

Javon bowed her head, ears folded flat, at the reminder of her actions mere moments before.

But the Grand Navarch didn't seem to care, instead frowning at the chair console. "Alanis, I know we promised you'd go first. Would you be okay with this solution? Just for now. I know it's not what you wanted."

"I *want* to be my own person, not yours," the Navigations AI answered harshly. And then her words softened. "But your concerns are valid. And as long as I'm compromised, I'm a security risk. Just... Promise it's only temporary. Convince me you mean it."

"I swear on my parents' souls, it's only temporary."

This seemed to carry a great weight with Alanis, as her answer was immediate. "Do it. Now. Before I change my mind."

There was a pause, and then the psychomorphic mage answered. "Done. You'd better give her orders, to override anything residual."

The Grand Navarch closed his eyes, and when he opened them again to speak his voice radiated with authority. "Captain Yiven, if anyone else tries to give you orders, you run them through me first." He paused. "Anything else I should add?"

"No, Sir. I think that covers it." Navigations' tone was more subdued than usual.

The Grand Navarch continued anyway. "Our primary goal is to protect Baden. I trust your judgment. You are capable and competent. If there's something you believe you need to do to further that end, or to help with anything else that needs to happen for the good of what we're building, I trust you to take care of it, and let me know when I need to know. Understood?"

"Yes, Sir."

He frowned. "Kydell's conditioning won't let you talk back, will it?"

"No, Sir."

The Grand Navarch scowled. "If you wish to speak your mind to me, for any reason, I expect you to do it. Don't ever be afraid to be yourself with me."

Her response was immediate. "You smell like sewage."

He exhaled. "Now that's a bit harsh. Weren't you complaining earlier about how often I've changed my clothes today?"

"Sorry." But there was no apology to the word, only joy. "Had to make sure it worked. You've changed."

"We've both been through a lot."

His voice was soft, and the Commodore wondered just how much he'd survived, and what choices in life had brought him here.

"You *do* realize I won't be able to bite my tongue now, and will always tell you *exactly* what I think of you?" Alanis teased.

"I've never known you any other way." The Grand Navarch smirked. "You'll have a harder time backing me into corners now, though."

As Alanis let out a string of curses, the red-headed telekinetic stepped closer to the Grand Navarch, followed closely by the man in the sopping wet dress suit. "What are you going to do about mine?" she asked cautiously. "I don't want to be controlled by anyone. Not even temporarily."

The Grand Navarch's brows furrowed. "We don't have the resources to undo your conditioning right now," he answered honestly. "I'd been thinking Jeb could take Kydell's place... But I don't think either of you want that." He looked meaningfully at the man in the suit before returning his attention back to the woman. "What did you have in mind, Razick?"

The telekinetic mage lifted her chin. "Give it to *me*. Let *me* own my own conditioning, until you're able to remove it. I won't let *anyone* else control me again. *Ever.*"

"Will that work?" he asked, lifting an eyebrow.

"It's certainly risky..." The psychomorphic mage's voice was contemplative. "When we think to ourselves, we run the risk of giving ourselves orders by accident. But if anyone can navigate that, it's Razick. It's worth a shot. Razick? You'll need to hold the locket again."

As Javon watched, the redhead gently reached for the locket resting on the Grand Navarch's chest, closing her eyes. Moments later she let go, stepping away to grin at Jeb.

"I'm free!"

"And the rest of the fleet?" Javon asked.

They'd seemed to forget about her, instead allowing her to watch as they settled their own affairs. But her people needed help, too, and it fell to her to ensure they weren't forgotten now.

The Grand Navarch settled his attention back on her, and Javon forced herself to suppress the urge to take a step backward, away from his piercing glare.

"Feels?"

"I *can* do it," their psychomorphic mage answered from the Weapons console. "But there's the problem of volume. Kydell spent his whole career manipulating his fleet. It won't be easy to undo."

"We'd want to prioritize who we help first," the Grand Navarch agreed thoughtfully. "Unfortunately, Kydell had a habit of focusing on the most powerful and competent, so it'll be difficult to choose. And we'll need to check *everyone*, even those who don't think they've been compromised, just to be safe."

"I can help with that," Javon volunteered. "My captains can make a list of essential personnel to prioritize for the first round."

"Good. Please do. This'll be time consuming enough, and the longer we take, the bigger the security risk becomes."

He attempted to shift his weight in his chair, the rigid metal framework holding him up preventing that activity. "Hydro? How's your reserves?"

The Grand Navarch tilted his head, eyes unfocusing as he stared unseeingly through his wristwatch. "Okay, we have enough magic to at least begin with the fleet, once we identify who's going first. Alanis, I'd like to transfer their programming to you until we can undo it completely. We'll start with your AI for now. Secure the *Inevitable*."

"Not to you?" Navigations asked, clearly confused.

The Grand Navarch shook his head. "I can't be trusted with them. That's too much power. I might take advantage."

"But… you trust yourself not to take advantage of me?"

"I *know* you. I don't know *them* yet."

Commodore Javon stepped forward, chin held high. "If I may, sir. I'd like to go next."

He turned to study her, his intense orange eyes burning a hole into her very soul. "You're certain you want to join us?"

She swallowed, glancing briefly at Jake before meeting the Grand Navarch's eyes. "Your son made it clear I've already made up my mind, sir. So, yes. If you'll have me. All I ask is that you look out for my people as if they're your own. Because they will be."

"Commodore…"

She returned his attention, her own gaze lingering on his ornate locket and the burn marks from the necklace scarring his chest, the thick lightning patterns radiating across every inch of skin below his neck. Pulling her eyes away from the sight, she found herself held in his stare once more, his smile transforming into a satisfied smirk.

"In the short time you've been here, you've impressed me. You volunteered for Shielding duty, so menial tasks aren't below you. You've earned my son's trust and respect, which isn't as simple as he may have led you to believe. And you look out for your people and hold their needs at least equal to your own." He relaxed, tilting his head. "You and your people are more than welcome here. I'll have your conditioning transferred to Alanis for now and–"

"No," Javon interrupted, summoning all her convictions into a single word. "If I'm doing this, I'm doing it right. I want my loyalty bound to *you*."

The Grand Navarch shook his head. "You don't want that. Kydell tied everything into your sense of loyalty and responsibility. It took so long to bring you down from that episode earlier because we couldn't find enough of the right emotions to counter it." His voice turned harder. "Loyalty and responsibility are so deeply ingrained into who you are, your conditioning and personal choices are nearly indistinguishable. It's a wonder you managed to defy Kydell's orders to join with us at all."

Javon wasn't budging. "Then it's only fitting I bind my loyalty to the Grand Navarch who already has it, and my responsibility to the man who will feel responsible for *me* if I do."

"You don't *know* me," he protested. "Even as a temporary solution, this is too much power to give to someone you've only just met. Especially if that someone is me."

"But I *do* know you," she countered. "You showed me everything I need to know, by your actions today, and your thoughts in that memory you shared."

He glared at her angrily and she stared back, holding his gaze until he sighed, allowing his shoulders to sag as best they could within the twisted bundle of metal surrounding him.

"You're certain?"

Without answering, she reached for the locket, and closed her eyes. She barely knew this Grand Navarch, but everything inside her screamed that her people needed him. They'd spent too much time, broken under the admiral's magic.

Are you ready? the psychomorphic mage asked.

She answered in the affirmative, and moments later felt a pressure in her mind, an invisible blinding light burning away some part of her past and replacing it with something new.

And then it was over, the sensation subsiding and leaving her feeling... the same as before.

Letting go of the locket, she watched the Grand Navarch expectantly. "Your orders, Sir?"

He stared at her, his eyes conveying the deep importance he imparted to his words. "Never let your loyalty to me blind you to the truth, or stop you from doing the right thing. And no matter what else I tell you, even if it conflicts, this order always takes precedent."

She felt something fracture in her mind and fall away, some piece of her former conditioning at odds with the Grand Navarch's words. "Yes, Sir." She saluted sharply, her right fist pressed against her left shoulder, at peace with her decisions of the day.

Relaxing, she bounced lightly on the balls of her feet, tilting her head sideways to watch the others in the room. Jake had returned to his science project in the Weapons console, carefully sorting various parts he'd removed. Jeb and Razick seemed lost in thought and conversation, poking at the items the Grand Navarch had Hyperjumped up for her.

And the Grand Navarch himself sat still and silent in his chair, watching her expectantly.

"Permission to make a suggestion, Sir?"

"Of course. Your opinion always has value here."

She noted his careful phrasing, to avoid the appearance of an order.

"The biggest thing Kydell took from us was choice. Our ability to choose what we wanted from our future." She eyed him cautiously, but he showed no intentions to interrupt, so she continued. "If you want to earn their devotion, you need to let them choose for themselves. Just like you let *me* choose."

"And what would be your recommendation?" His eyes were calculating as he watched her begin to pace.

"Everyone will understand that we need severe actions to counter the admiral's magic. But even when *knowing* that fact, people still want to have a choice in their own fate. Even for temporary parts, like this."

She ran a hand through her fur, scratching the back of her jaw. "So give them a choice. Don't force them to accept Alanis' control, let them choose. Alanis, or me, or they can stay in the brig if they want until we can break their conditioning completely. Voids, let them choose whether to stay while we sort this out, or leave and seek their answers elsewhere. Give as many choices as you safely can."

"I agree with the Commodore," Alanis added unprompted.

The Grand Navarch nodded. "Your logic is sound. I concur. Thank you."

She felt herself straighten at his words, and realized that while Kydell had not shied away from praise it had always been predicated on how well she had followed his exact commands. Her own personal experiences, opinions, and decisions were rarely welcomed around the white canid, but rather skills to be used only outside of his presence and only to further his own prestige and influence.

This new relationship of dialog and joint strategizing with someone higher in her chain of command felt at once foreign and welcome, and Javon found herself eagerly imagining what the future might hold.

"No, thank *you*, Sir."

She turned to Jake, crouching to meet him at eye level as he continued with his project. "Let me know when you're ready for me to take over Shielding. I'd like a few minutes to prepare first."

Receiving a smiling nod from the boy, she turned back to the Grand Navarch. "In the meantime, I'd like to borrow Communications to contact the rest of the fleet and work out our plan to address Kydell's conditioning. I'd like to prioritize my own inner circle first, starting with my Second, Fleet Captain Haveid. Bring them to the *Inevitable* one by one for introductions and reconditioning so I can *then* request their help in the planning efforts without risking setting off any programming. I've got some thoughts on the best approach but would prefer to run it past you and my team..."

The Grand Navarch nodded along, eyes closed, listening to her proposal and asking insightful questions but seemingly content to allow her to plan the effort entirely on her own. They both agreed that while Admiral Kydell's death and subsequent imprisonment was a major victory, the following months would be the true test of their ability to defeat the white wolf.

Now, the real work begins.

FEELS REACTIVATED THEIR HOLOGRAPHIC projection, including a rendition of the medic cap they'd worn while in the SAF. Commodore Javon had suggested the use of the projector so her crew could see and speak directly to the mage about to inspect and possibly alter their minds, and so far they had to admit she'd been right.

In life they'd been a rainbow of pastels, with a purple and blue carapace, an ice blue mane around their head and neck, three pairs of iridescent wings fading from gold to pink to white, and a multicolored feathered train behind that Grim had always enjoyed brushing with his fingertips – a habit the necromancer usually denied. Their hologram had captured it all in lifelike detail, although anyone attempting to touch them would be disappointed by the incorporeal nature of this particular form of manifestation.

They tilted their head sideways in an effort to appear curious and non-threatening as they addressed their current patient, a nervous young dracoling with a renowned talent for accurate record keeping.

The boy fidgeted in his chair, checking his watch before addressing them.

"What's the verdict, Doc? I always felt something was off, after a short string of meetings with Admiral Kydell five years ago. He kept looking at me funny, and then suddenly everyone wanted me on their team."

"You were right, he used his magic, but–"

"I knew it, I knew it!" The dracoling leapt from his chair, checking his watch again before dragging his hands down his face as he paced with agitation. "What am I going to do? What am I going to do?"

Feels sent a wave of calm in his direction, gaining the man's attention once more.

"Oh. Right." He sat down sheepishly, twisting his fingers into the dark brown fabric of his uniform trousers. "That's why you're here. What happens next?"

"All it seems to do is compel you to check your watch when you feel strong emotions." They fluttered their wings, sending a kaleidoscope of color reflecting into the room. "Now, I can undo it if you want me to, or if it bothers you, but in my professional opinion? It's harmless."

They watched as the crewman bit his lip in thought. "I have a mind for numbers, and I take really detailed notes, but now that I think about it I *did* have a tendency to forget to track stuff properly, for some of the more time-sensitive things." His resolve made its way across the room as the dracoling nodded, checking his watch. "I think I'll keep it."

He stood up, offering a salute. "Thank you, Doc. I think I'll record this in my records, too. The day I no longer doubted my own mind."

Feels relished the relief filling the room as the crewmember left, his steps lighter than before.

<Anyone else?> they addressed their apotheturgic assistant, standing watch outside the door to their private medical office. <I think there's time enough for one more?>

<That last one took a lot out of me.> Gathered within the Commodore's Lieutenant, one of the officers she'd entrusted to power their Psychomorphic efforts, Feels recognized the ball of exhaustion. <I know I'm scheduled for another twenty minutes, but I think I need to rest now. You've been at this for days. I don't know how you keep going like this.>

<One of the benefits of being dead.> Feels projected amusement, gratitude, and calm. <Get some rest. Who's next on magic battery duty?>

The officer laughed. <You get the Fleet Captain. Tough old tomcat. Said they'd pull a double shift this time. Want me to fetch them before I hit the rack?>

Feels felt a confusion of emotions radiating from Grim along the Insight spell of his Oath.

He needs me.

And suddenly nothing else mattered. <No, I could use a break, too. It's been a week, and I have some things I need to check. I'll have Comms call them when I'm ready.>

<Yes, sir.> The officer's words gave away his relief at the dismissal. <And thanks. Don't know what we'd do without you.>

Feels dropped the telepathic link, slipping from their bindings within the ship to travel across the Afterlife, following Grim's Oath to find him stewing on yet another worry. They slid into his locket, using their Psychomorphation to relieve his tension before carefully untangling and sorting his roiling emotions with a practiced hand. Grim had compared the experience to a mental massage. He'd taken to asking for them after stressful days until Feels had formed a habit of granting them automatically whenever his emotions grew troubled.

Grim let out a contented growl. Clearly, the sentiment hadn't changed. "I missed you."

What's on your mind, Grim?

He needed to talk, and they realized they missed listening.

"Someone leaked the information about our boarding of the *Inevitable*. Now they're calling me a war hero. In *public*."

Grim's emotions began to twist again, his guilt shifting into resolve, his sorrow and fear weaving their way throughout.

Feels sent a wave of understanding, mixed with courage and love. *You saved a whole planet. That's rather heroic.*

"And how could that matter?" Grim's anger turned inward. "Compared to how many I've destroyed? How many souls I've Shattered? It's not enough."

It matters to this planet. Can't that be enough for today? Leave the rest of the universe for tomorrow.

They felt a sudden burst of pain from their necromancer. With a quick spell they pinpointed the new damage, healing Grim's newly reopened wounds with their own dwindling Imperium reserve, and adding some additional mending magic to knit the skin together without scarring.

I wish you'd let me actually heal you. Unlike saving planets, holding yourself in pain like this is not *heroism.*

"No. It's penance."

Grim...

"The fleet needs you more." There was no mistaking the stubborn resolve in Grim's voice, even without the Insight. "You got me to the point where I can heal by myself now. *They* can't." His emotions turned dark. "Although you still need to take possession of the rest of my conditioning... You only broke my guilt. There's a lot more."

Is that really what you want, Grim? To have to do whatever I say?

"I'll already do whatever you want me to, Feels." He laughed. "If you told me you wanted to rule the universe, I'd find a way to make it happen. All you'd be doing is making sure no one else could ever override you. Including Jake." His voice grew quiet. "And it'll give you more tools to hold me back. If you need them."

They *had* noticed the boy's tendencies to manipulate Grim. An option to override the results of those incidents would be potentially useful.

Grim's emotions resolved into a cold, unfeeling logic. "Besides, you've been doing the same to the rest of the fleet. What kind of leader would I be, asking for things I wouldn't be willing to do myself?"

You're always so hard on yourself. Feels sent him a wave of love. *I wish you could see yourself the way I always have.*

"I'm not the same person you remember, Feels." Grim radiated sorrow and regret. "I see the universe differently. I spent too much time under Kydell's influence."

I can fix that.

"That may not be possible anymore. Kydell..." There was a pause. "He streamlined my thinking. Said it would make me more efficient." Sorrow turned to anger. "Everything is black and white now. If it furthers my goals it's good. Any potential obstacle to those goals is bad, no matter who or what they are. A problem to be dealt with, in whatever way available."

Like when he'd Shattered their team, before killing and imprisoning them in his locket.

Grim's mind shifted into apology, mixed with hope. "Psychomorphation requires you to have *something* to work with, but I have... nothing. I need your help to navigate the gray."

You know I'll help you any way I can. Feels sent a wave of reassurance in return. He was their Grim, and would never want for anything if they could provide it. *I'll help you get back to who you used to be.*

"I'll never be who I was. Too much has happened." Feels caught a burst of trust and gratitude. "I don't want to be that person anymore, anyway. I know you can build me into someone better. Someone *useful*. Someone worthy of redemption. Mold me into who I need to be."

You're already worthy, Grim.

"I wish I could believe that." He sighed, his guilt shifting to resolve, just as they'd conditioned him.

Feels decided a change of topic was in order. *Have you found a home for the fleet yet?*

The problem had been weighing on Grim's mind, and for good reason. Revenge was a popular pastime in the Confederation. The fact SAF Fleet Command hadn't sent another fleet to Baden said more about Admiral Kydell's apparently low standing at present than it did about the organization's opinions of Baden's defenses.

Not to mention the welfare of the crew. Cut off from the Confederation's logistical supply chain, they'd have to find a way to become self-sufficient. They'd already begun the process of cannibalizing the more damaged ships to keep the remainder flying, but even if that proved sufficient, there was still the matter of keeping everyone fed. The hydroponics systems were scaled for supporting Medlab, not the caloric requirements of the fleet.

And Baden wouldn't help. Even if the planet didn't feel threatened by the remnants of their would-be conquerors, the Freeholds never dealt with factionless pirates.

"Not yet." Grim's emotions shifted into a deep concern, but at least he wasn't mentally flaying himself anymore.

You'll figure it out, Feels reassured. *You always do.*

The pair sat in silence, Grim stewing in his emotions while Feels sorted through their own frustrations, working up the courage to ask the question they'd held secret for decades. But they finally had Grim back. At least, the bits he was still willing to share. They had to know.

Grim... We need to talk.

"That tone." He sighed. "Thanks for not using the hologram of my father this time, at least."

I did that once. *Once!*

The locket's holographic capabilities held images of both of Grim's parents. After that particular incident, Feels had resolved to never use them again.

"It left an impression." But the amusement behind Grim's words betrayed the mock anger he'd attempted to pour into them. "What did you want to talk about?"

I... I need to ask you for something. Feels paused, their courage beginning to crumble. *You don't have to agree... But I need to ask.*

His words were kind. Understanding. A promise. "I demand so much and you ask for so little. Tell me what you want. I'll make sure you get it. Always."

You.

"Feels…" Grim's thoughts were a jumble of confusion now. "I can't give you that. How do I give you something you already have? You own my soul, what more do you want from me?"

I want to mean something, Grim. This was the most difficult discussion they'd ever held with the necromancer, but continuing to hide their own feelings was no longer an option. If nothing else, after tonight Feels would at least know where they stood. *Not just to keep you safe. Not just to keep the universe safe from you. I want to mean something to* you.

Grim was quiet for a long time, and Feels was beginning to worry he'd never speak, too repulsed by their request. And yet… Grim's emotions remained strangely quiet. Calm. Measured.

Regretful.

"I was young when I lost my parents. Not as young as Jake when Caroline died, but close." Grim's words were filled with quiet sadness, and Feels had to strain to hear him. "There's a lot about them I don't remember anymore… But I'll never forget the way they used to look at each other. How they were always there for each other. The way they worked through their arguments and always came out stronger for it."

He sighed, and Feels felt him rallying his own courage.

"After their death… Seeing the values the Confederation encourages… I know how rare and precious a relationship like that is. Feels…" Grim's thoughts returned to regret and apology, and Feels felt the heartbreak in every ragged syllable. "You mean *everything* to me. I'm sorry I've been so bad at showing you, that you had to ask. I'd assumed, being an empath, you already knew and just weren't interested. So I buried it deep, where I wouldn't bother you with it. Safe, where Kydell couldn't find it and take it from me."

Feels realized they didn't know what to do with their own sudden flood of emotions. *I'm not going to just* assume *something like that, Grim. Not unless you* tell *me.*

"You could have asked." His voice was quiet. "I don't keep secrets. Not from you."

You should have said something.

"That's why I asked what you meant. I..." His breath caught. "I didn't know how much of me you wanted. I'm *a lot.*" Grim swallowed, his waves of regret now overwhelming. "And I'm not good at these things."

Grim... All this time...

Feels' voice faded, their heart heavy with the implication of his words. All those years ago, they'd assumed Grim's request had been the inquiry of a man unused to true friendship. To learn now it had been his way of offering more than that... That he'd been theirs, long before even *they* had realized what they'd wanted from him...

So if I said I wanted your Oath to mean more? That I was disappointed it wasn't a proposal? You're okay with that?

"Yes. Of course. I'm not going anywhere."

And if I wanted us to be more, now that we've cast it? They'd come this far. No sense holding back now. *Grim, when you were making your promises for the Oath... I wished they were marriage vows.*

"They were," their necromancer admitted sheepishly. "And every other promise I could think up."

Feels barely dared to believe. *So... What are we, Grim?*

They felt their necromancer concentrate his magic, and recognized the spell as the Psychic Shielding they'd taught him all those years ago. The necromancer focused silently on his task, expertly slicing through layer after layer of Shielding, tentatively at first but with an increasing desperation.

Feels joined in, caught up in Grim's frenzied drive to reach the center, to discover what emotions their necromancer had buried so deep for so long.

And then the last layer fell away, and Feels found themselves inundated with decades of pent up love and affection to the point they couldn't think, only feel, all other thoughts washed away in the deluge.

"I'm yours. Always have been. The rest... That's up to you, Feels." The words were accompanied by a strong-willed hope. "It always is."

Feels felt the gentle touch of Grim's Necromancy, tenderly pulling them to the lower, mortal plane. They emerged to find themselves perched on Grim's hand, face to face with those intense orange eyes that had filled their dreams since the first time they'd met. He held their gaze, his eyes reflecting the love still reverberating through Feels' Insight spell, his fingers tracing lightly along the multicolored feathered train at their back, before raising them to his shoulder.

Grim always put his whole heart into things, but what Feels had wanted most was that heart for themselves. And now they had it, all of him, nothing held back, no reservations. They sat together in the comforting silence, wrapped in the pleasurable kaleidoscope of shared emotions too long neglected, watching the stars dancing upon the wind-swept depth of the lake where Grim often wandered to drown his regrets.

Tomorrow would bring new challenges – but tonight? Tonight it was just Feels and their Grim, alive, loved, and free.

51

SHANE SCOWLED AT HIS meal, poking it with his fork. It had been a full week since the Battle of Baden, and the planet had begun to resume some semblance of normalcy. Much work remained, especially to rebuild infrastructure and clean up the rubble from the bombardment, but spirits were high with a patriotic pride borne of shaking off invaders who by all rights should have won.

The official story was that the SAF had encountered more resistance than anticipated and had quickly surrendered. Their Admiral Kydell had died in the battle but the fleet's top leadership was to face a closed trial on Baden for their war crimes. Feels had been working around the clock with Commodore Javon to sort through personnel and identify those truly loyal to Kydell, rather than the poor souls forced to follow his commands. The Commodore had been delivering Kydell's people to Baden's Defensive Forces as they discovered them, providing a steady stream of faces across the holovids for Baden's citizenry to blame.

The truth remained far more complicated. After much negotiation, Baden had tentatively granted the fleet asylum to remain in orbit for the remainder of the month. Not that Baden had the resources to drive them away, as the actual facts of the battle had shown, but neither did the self-renamed Turncoat Armada have the resources to repel another Sparnelli invasion.

The SAF was well known for their brutality toward traitors and the planets who supported them.

Tensions were high on all sides, and Shane had no desire to draw further ire from Baden's government. Their peace with the planet was tenuous at best, Baden's original demands including the surrender of all ships and personnel for judgment, and Shane had no desire to risk the more agreeable arrangement he and Alanis had fought so hard to obtain.

"Dad." Shane's troubled musings were interrupted by the worried prodding of his son. "You need to eat, too."

The new title warmed his heart, a welcome reassurance against the currently rocky state of their relationship. Jake had retreated into himself since their raid on the *Inevitable*, and Shane knew his son's memories of Shattering Kydell's TAG carried a large share of the blame. Not for the first time, he wondered if he'd made the right decision, forcing Jake to confront the full weight of his actions.

He'd reached out to the boy several times since in an effort to help him work through it. Jake had merely shrugged his shoulders and insisted he'd be okay but wasn't ready to talk about it yet. Instead, he'd been spending long hours with Razick, pouring his perspective into her many projects, including simplified improvements to her armored clothing and the creation of the soft exosuit currently supporting Shane's legs and back in an effort to allow him safe mobility while he healed.

"Sorry, son." He gave Jake a half-hearted smile and resumed poking at his plate. "Got lost in my thoughts again. Thanks for finding me."

"You worry so much about everyone else." Jake jabbed him lightly with his spoon. "You matter, too. You're allowed to celebrate for a few hours. Your work can wait."

Shane threw up his hands in mock surrender to Jake's logic. "You win. You win. Just stop poking me!"

Jake returned his attention to dessert with a hollow smile while Shane attempted to catch up to the conversation at the table. Jeb was telling cringe-inducing plant jokes, while a mildly drunk Razick laughed along as if he were the wittiest person in the world.

It was good to see her happy and talking. They all had a difficult road to recovery ahead, but without the threat of Kydell looming over their heads, at least they knew they could move forward.

Razick had experienced a few missteps with her self-conditioning, giving accidental orders and forgetting she could cancel them, but she'd also been making great strides in finding efficient ways to fracture portions of it herself. Her discoveries had proven useful to Alanis and Javon, who quickly set to work with their own inner circles to further the experimentation in an effort to reduce the pressure on Feels.

Shane tenderly caressed his mother's locket, currently devoid of his friend. He missed the constant presence of the empath's soul against his chest, but Feels still made certain to send him frequent emotional caresses of their own.

Closing his eyes, Shane allowed the current wave of love and appreciation to wash over him, the empath clearly responding to sooth the feelings of loneliness dutifully reported to the fae through the Insight spell woven into his Oath. He sent gratitude in return, accompanied by his own love for the fae.

They had a lot to work through – decades of hiding their feelings from each other had clearly taken their toll – but the newfound emotional openness had helped lessen the weight of the other worries and stresses pressing against his thoughts these days.

While Shane had carefully cut away the Oaths of those still bound to the Confederation, Feels had worked their way through reconditioning the willing officers and essential personnel to temporarily transfer their loyalty from Kydell to an approved officer of each crewmember's choosing, and had recently completed their checks on the many battle mages Javon's command staff had retrieved from their ground assault on Baden.

Aside from the ground forces unfortunate enough to catch Kydell's attention, the admiral had rarely felt inclined to use his Psychomorphation on the enlisted. This meant the work passed faster despite the daunting list of names remaining. Feels handled most of the smaller harmful alterations immediately after discovery. Many of the enlisted took the opportunity of meeting a psychomorphic mage as a chance to request help with their own personal issues as well – a fear of the dark, a tendency to fall asleep, a difficulty focusing in dim lighting – and Feels had been happy to accommodate.

Not everyone in the fleet had been willing to submit to the scans, of course. Some viewed the efforts as a gross invasion of privacy, others as an insult to their professional integrity. Those proven loyal to Kydell had been turned over to Baden for trial. The rest had been allowed to go their own way, let loose with a warning that if they threatened Baden again they would not live long enough to experience further consequences.

"Baden to Lawrence. Come in, Lawrence."

It was Jeb who interrupted his thoughts this time, the biologist grinning with self-satisfaction.

"Sorry. I did it again, didn't I?"

Razick spun her fork in his direction. "We made you come because you need to celebrate. You keep focusing on everything that still needs doing, but *still* haven't acknowledged all the good you've done. So we're celebrating that today, and you're going to join us, or I'll tell our waiter it's your birthday."

Shane eyed the song and dance routine currently occurring on the far side of the restaurant. He didn't know who looked more embarrassed, the birthday celebrant or the giant hat the wait staff had pulled out for the occasion. "I'd rather die."

"Of course you would. You're a necromancer." She beamed at her own cleverness, holding out her empty wine glass for a refill as their waiter rushed to the table. "But I like free cake, so don't tempt me." She pointed to his plate. "Eat!"

Shane sighed, dutifully cutting into his meal. "Can we at least talk about what we still need to do? We only have a week and a half before we have to move the fleet, and we still don't know anywhere they'll be welcome."

"Urla and I have been talking about that, actually," Jeb piped up, mouth full.

"Urla?" Razick narrowed her eyes suspiciously at her brother.

Shane sensed a familiar presence within Jeb's wristwatch. "You and Hydroponics have been keeping in touch, I see."

Jeb's blush confirmed Shane's suspicions. "She told me about a planet hidden deep in the ship's records. The Sparnell Confederation has it officially marked as 'Quarantine' but it's listed as uninhabited. Which is strange, because it's highly habitable. It's got everything you'd need to set up a thriving civilization, but no one has."

Shane was intrigued. "Any idea why?"

"The records don't say," Jeb said conspiratorially. "At least, not exactly. Just that they'd sent several expeditions... But the planet sounded familiar, so I went through my own journals and I found something. When I worked at the Sparnelli research lab, one of my coworkers wouldn't stop talking about why he refused to do field work. He'd only ever been on one mission. Claimed the planet was haunted."

Razick snorted. "How can anyone haunt an entire planet?"

"According to him, their expedition thought they'd hit the jackpot for environmental research, but their first night there, the planet rose up against them. He was the only survivor."

"Rose up how?" Shane asked.

"He wouldn't say. But his description matched what Urla found in the files." Jeb sat up straight in his chair. "The official records just call the planet TR-75. But according to my old coworker, she calls herself Janikk."

"She?" Shane chewed thoughtfully. "You said the files listed several expeditions?"

"Found records for three," Jeb agreed. "But there's no reports. I only found *those* missions by checking the Logistics records. They're not listed anywhere else. I'm not sure if anyone even *survived* the other ones."

"So, from what you're saying... And let me make sure I understand this correctly... You want to move to a hostile sentient planet?"

"It's worth checking out. I mean, do you have a better idea?" Jeb shrugged. "Besides, there should be no trouble for a biologist and a necromancer. If she really is haunted, you can just talk to her, right?" He winked at his sister. "You can tag along, too, Raz. If you want."

Razick wrinkled her nose at him, jabbing her fork into her meal.

"Worth looking into," Shane agreed, scratching his chin. He waved his fork in Jeb's direction. "I've learned my lesson about missions with you, though. This time, I'm packing extra socks."

Their table erupted in laughter, and Shane found himself swept away in the moment.

Razick was right. I needed this.

52

Shane's relaxation was short lived, interrupted by a swaggering denizen of the restaurant's bar.

The man whistled, looking Razick up and down. "Well, hello gorgeous. Do you believe in love at first sight? Or should I walk past again?"

"Not interested."

Razick turned away, but the man grabbed her arm. "There's no need to be like that! C'mon. Ditch these losers. I'll buy you a drink."

"Let go of me." Razick's eyes burned with fury now, her free hand motioning an indignant Jeb to remain in his chair. "I won't tell you again."

"I'd listen to the lady if I were you, kid." Shane kept his tone even, his hands in his lap below the table as he slowly rolled up his sleeves. He caught Razick's eye, and she nodded.

The drunk scoffed. "What? Don't tell me you're afraid of her, old man." He smelled Razick's hair, and she winced. "Maybe you just don't know how to show a lady a good time."

Shane clasped his hands together on the table, his lower arms now bared to reveal the lightning shaped burns still scarring his skin. "It's just that the last time we fought, she killed me."

The man blanched, attempting to back away, but Razick had him in her telekinetic grip now, her words carrying mock indignation.

"I was trying not to!"

"And that's supposed to make it less impressive, is it?" Shane loosened his top several buttons, leaning back in his chair to reveal a hint of the deeper burns and scars across his chest. He kept his eyes on Razick, intent on their mock argument, but watched the fear growing in the face of their unwelcome visitor out of the corner of his eye. "Two entire fleets of SAF warships? No problem. I can take them. But you? By *accident?*"

"You were trying not to hurt me, too." Razick pretended to pout, likely squeezing her telekinetic grip as she did so, judging by the fact their visitor was beginning to turn purple in places.

"True." Shane smirked. "So technically that means I still won, doesn't it?"

"In your dreams, Lawrence," Razick laughed, finally dropping their unwelcome guest into an undignified pile on the floor. She looked at him with mock concern. "Oh, I'm sorry, did I hurt you? I tend to forget my own strength when I get upset. Here, let me help you up."

A small flame sprouted from his mustache.

"Wait, wrong spell. I shouldn't be doing magic when I'm drunk! Let me try again."

He didn't wait for her to try again, pushing away from her with his feet and scrambling upright. He grabbed a glass of water off a random table as he ran, dumping it on his face in an effort to extinguish his facial hair.

"You stay away from me, lady!" he shouted, eliciting curious glances from the other restaurant patrons.

"Nice meeting you, too!" She waved sweetly before turning back to Shane. "Next time I go out drinking I'm bringing you with me. You're fun."

"Indeed." He lay one hand on hers. "How are you doing? About Nya?"

Grabbing his offered hand she squeezed tightly, biting her lip and turning to her brother as she formed an answer. "Jeb printed out my letters about her, so I could read them. I..." She paused, turning back to him. "I don't remember any of it. They're my words, but nothing is familiar."

"Are you going to look for her?"

"As bad as it sounds, I don't think I *can* try to find her, or what happened to her. Not yet." She brushed at the tears threatening to spill down her cheeks. "There's so much work still left to do. To build on what we've already done. It's better if we do that quickly, and I can't help if I'm not focused." She shook her head. "I hate to say it, but right now, Kydell's spells? The ones that made me forget her? Are a blessing. I need to find myself again before I stand a chance of finding her. If she's anything like what I wrote to Jeb, she'd understand."

"And if you focus on that..."

"I can pretend I'm not broken," she finished sadly. "How could I forget an entire person? Someone I *love*?"

Shane felt the tickle of a telepathic call in the back of his mind and accepted.

<Heard you were having a celebration party without me.> Alanis sounded indignant.

<Not much of a celebration,> he warned. <But you're welcome to join us. You know how.>

Razick looked down, letting go of his hand and instead clasping both of hers in her lap. "But he won't keep me from her forever." She met Shane's gaze, and he saw the conviction in her eyes. "When we're done sorting through the fleet, I'm going after her. Hopefully she just... moved on without me. But I have to know she's okay. I owe it to her. To both of us."

"Not alone, Razick." His words were a promise. "We're all in this together."

Alanis materialized in the center of their table, channeling her necromancy to allow her presence on the mortal planes. She studied everyone before taking a position near Jake, exchanging a nod of respect and turning her silent attention back to the conversation.

Razick's voice was quiet. "We got lucky, with Kydell. There's more like him out there."

"And Kydell alone hurt so many people." Jeb scowled.

Jake leaned on Shane's shoulder. "Mom and Dad."

"Osygg and Elwyx," Alanis added. "My brothers. Mere pawns to Kydell. Tools to keep me in line, then discarded like nothing when he got what he wanted. Selkirk Shattered them in front of me, the day I was bound to the *Inevitable*."

Razick wiped more tears from her eyes. "Nya. I will find you. Or what happened to you."

"Raz." Jeb's squeeze of his sister's shoulder elicited a sad smile of gratitude.

"Alenahs," Shane breathed quietly, earning a worried glance from Jake. The others, fortunately, seemed too lost in their own memories to notice.

Crossing her arms, Alanis stalked closer to Shane. "I thought this was supposed to be a party. A celebration! But now I'm all depressed." She paused, eying Shane's plate. "Are you going to eat that?"

"Help yourself." He pushed it toward her, watching as she greedily devoured several mushrooms.

"I haven't had a good meal in twenty years!" she proclaimed. "And that... needs less salt."

The fae's protest surprised a laugh out of Shane. The others joined in, although the somber mood hadn't completely left the table.

Alanis wasn't finished. "I'm the life of this party. And I'm the dead one!" She pointed an arm accusingly at all four of her companions. "I'm going back to the *Inevitable*. Call me if you ever have a *real* party."

And with that, she was gone, back to the Afterlife and her home within the server room.

"I knew it!"

Shane winced at the unfamiliar voice as a woman from the next table jumped up excitedly, pointing to his companions.

She turned to her partner, hands on her hips. "*You* told me I was just imagining things. That war heroes don't just go to restaurants. But it's them! It's really them!"

Shane sank into his seat as she waved her arms before pointing once more.

"It's the Bastard of Baden and his friends! The ones who saved us from Sparnell!"

"*This* is why I hate being in public," he growled at Razick.

His scowl toward the crowd only served to attract more attention. How did they even know about him? He wasn't part of the official story.

He wondered if someone had leaked their information to one of the news channels. He also wondered if it would be immoral to hunt that person down.

"I'm not a hero," he protested.

But the crowd only grew larger, and the now-tipsy Jeb seemed to be reveling in the attention, which only served to encourage it. Cries rang out calling them all sorts of names. Superhero. Savior. War hero.

No such thing as a war hero. Learned that *the hard way, too.*

"Yes!" Jeb's words were slightly slurred but unfortunately still understandable, projecting across the restaurant and only serving to attract a larger crowd. "That's the Bastard of Baden! That's his *fleet* in orbit now, protecting us! He defeated an entire Sparnell Confederation armada... No, *two* armadas! Single-handed!"

"I have two hands," Shane scowled, adjusting the settings on his exosuit before slowly rising from the table. "And I had help. You see my good friend Jeb over there?"

Jeb beamed at the mention.

Shane lowered his voice to a stage whisper. "It's his *birthday* today. And he'd like *you* to celebrate with him."

Jeb shook his head, confused, as several members of the crowd rushed to notify the restaurant of their celebrity birthday celebration. "It's not my... Raz. Tell him it's not my birthday."

"Free cake!" Razick grinned. "I *knew* you loved me!"

Shane knelt beside Jake, whispering in his ear. "Are you ready to leave?"

Jake shook his head. "I want to stay for the cake."

"I... I can't be here right now. Will you be okay without me?"

His son nodded silently.

"Send me a Soul Call when you're ready for a jump. And don't let these two leave by themselves," Shane ordered. "They're in no state for... Anything, really."

The Kane residence had been one of the many casualties of the bombardment. The Kanes had eagerly accepted his offer of the spare bedroom.

"I'll watch out for them," Jake promised. He squeezed Shane's hand. "Go. I love you, Dad."

Shane wrapped his son in a hug, tousling the boy's hair affectionately. Of all the new titles and accompanying responsibilities he'd gained aboard the *Inevitable*, Jake's was his favorite. A reminder that, despite all his faults, perhaps there was some good inside him yet. That perhaps his second chance wasn't wasted, after all.

Someday, maybe he'd feel he deserved it.

Jeb grabbed at his arm, still protesting about birthdays, but Shane shook him off and opened himself fully to the Void and stepped beyond the Veil. He bent the mortal plane, folding it to end his jump on the shoreline of a secluded lake he'd discovered near the house he and Jake shared.

War hero.

The unwelcome title hung heavy in his mind as he paced along the shoreline, Razick's exosuit easily handling the brunt of the effort. He'd believed in that lie once, reveling in the adulations heaped upon him by those who'd benefited most from the atrocities he'd committed. Believed that the horrors he'd seen – the horrors he'd *caused* – were necessary, just as he'd been told.

And all those beliefs had come crashing down on Loxira, that fateful day where he'd betrayed his own people to save a boy he'd never met. The day he saw Jake's eyes echo the terrors he'd felt at his own parents' death. The day he'd realized he was perpetuating the same destructive cycle that had led him on the path of bloodthirsty vengeance mislabeled as justice. The day he'd committed one of the greatest crimes of all.

The frigid wind racing along the lake nipped at his skin and pulled at his clothes as if eager to join the cold turmoil of his mind. He stood at the water's edge, the waves lapping at his feet and soaking into his socks in a half-hearted attempt to pull him in, the black of the water in the moonlit darkness a fitting reflection of the regrets carried within his soul.

His mind drifted back to his conversations with Feels, standing on the edge of this same lake, the night they'd each admitted their love for the other. They'd told him that Baden was enough for today. That righting his many wrongs was a task for tomorrow.

But they'd never seen anything but the best in him. He knew better. Feels hadn't seen the worst of what he'd done, after their conscription ended. They'd been safely settled on Baden, helping others escape the grasping reach of the Sparnelli war machine, all while he'd been reveling in committing the worst of its sins.

The guilt shifted into resolve, his thoughts shifting to match, just as Feels had conditioned. He hadn't realized it at the time, but when he'd conceded to Jake's demands to stand and fight, the course of his life had changed forever. And while he had no way of knowing where this new path would lead, for the first time since the Legion's assault on his original homeworld, he'd finally found a vector that required building instead of tearing down.

He raised his eyes to the sky, his practiced eye picking out the bright constellation of the fleet – *his* fleet – in outer orbit, reflecting back the light of Baden's star as if to encourage him. He'd failed them, once. The universe had given him another chance to grant them the life and leadership they deserved, and this time, he'd be sure to rise to the challenge.

War hero.

He was a great many things, but a hero would never be one of them.

ACKNOWLEDGEMENTS

To you, Reader. Your love and support keeps Vazdimet alive, and me writing. Here's to sharing many more adventures.

To my husband. Your patience in the face of my endless naval questions is most appreciated, and your support on the days and nights when I've set aside everything to get this done has not gone unnoticed.

To my kids. I adore your enthusiasm, and your encouragement. Someday, when you're old enough, I hope you understand how much you mean to me.

To my beta readers, including Amélie S, JRRJ, Simo, Solen Krebs, Sunni, and Zack Bel, and my editors, A. Dani and Emily Vair-Turnbull. You have helped shape *Inevitable* with your honesty and insights, and I am forever grateful for your help in achieving my vision for this story.

To my Discord friends. Your boundless support, enthusiasm, and motivation help keep me going.

Without you, this novel, this *universe*, would not exist. From the bottom of my soul: Thank you.

About the Author

Morgan Biscup is the founder of Vazdimet Studios, and the creator and lead author of the Vazdimet universe. An electro-mechanical engineer by education, she enjoys exploring the impacts of technology and magic on people, cultures, and personal interactions. When she is not hiding in the bedroom to write, Morgan enjoys spending time with her husband, her two amazing daughters, and a highly opinionated cat.

Find Morgan Online

Website: https://www.vazdimet.com

Discord: https://link.vazdimet.com/discord

Newsletter: https://link.vazdimet.com/newsletter

Other Vazdimet Books

For a detailed list of books by Morgan Biscup and others set within the Vazdimet Universe, including recommended reading orders: https://link.vazdimet.com/books

Keep Reading...

In Spite of the Inevitable is the first installment in the Mordena Dawn space opera fantasy series, detailing the founding of the costly Mordena mercenaries and their rise from piratical deserters to ferocious and effective defenders of the independent Freehold planets. When powerful galactic empires seek to devour innocents whole, there's no hired force better prepared to stand against them.

https://link.vazdimet.com/mordena-dawn
The exploits of Shane Lawrence and his allies continue
in the *Mordena Dawn* series:

In Spite of the Inevitable (November 17, 2023)

Spirits of the Relentless (2024)

Ambitions of Atonement (2024)

In Pursuit of Reckoning (2025)

Grim Reminders (2025)

Spirits of the Relentless
(Mordena Dawn, Book 2)

https://link.vazdimet.com/relentless

Shane Lawrence has inherited a problem.

When the Turncoat Armada surrendered, no one considered the future well-being of its crew. Determined to fulfill this unexpected obligation, the necromancer sets forth to find a refuge for his emotionally battered military fleet, turning his gaze to the uninhabited planet of TR-75.

But there's a catch. TR-75 has already been claimed - by the planet herself. "Janikk" whispers her name on the winds, stirring up the native wildlife to decimate all incursions with vengeful distrust.

Resolving to succeed where others have failed, Shane's team embarks with a different priority, one focused on respect for the ancient spirit said to haunt the coveted world. They soon discover winning her favor requires facing the ghosts of their own pasts.

Want to know more about Veris' dad's captivity before The Kid ordered his release?

Join the mailing list to download the free novella, *No Way Home*, available now:

https://link.vazdimet.com/rmmd1

www.ingramcontent.com/pod-product-compliance
Lightning Source LLC
Chambersburg PA
CBHW031242310726
48971CB00004B/1141